Love Across the Pacific

Love Across the Pacific

Robert K. Wen

Writer's Showcase presented by *Writer's Digest*
San Jose New York Lincoln Shanghai

Love Across the Pacific

All Rights Reserved © 2000 by Robert K. Wen

No part of this book may be reproduced or transmitted in any form or by any means, graphic, electronic, or mechanical, including photocopying, recording, taping, or by any information storage or retrieval system, without the permission in writing from the publisher.

Published by Writer's Showcase presented by *Writer's Digest*
an imprint of iUniverse.com, Inc.

The geographical, historical and
institutional references in the novel are largely factual.
A few exceptions are made for artistic reasons;
for example, the Technical University of California is fictitious.
The characters and their stories are all fictional.

For information address:
iUniverse.com, Inc.
620 North 48th Street
Suite 201
Lincoln, NE 68504-3467
www.iuniverse.com

ISBN: 0-595-09462-7

Printed in the United States of America

Acknowledgements

I thank Peter Kearly for his critique and editing of an early draft of the novel. It spurred me to learn more about the art of fiction writing. I am indebted to Jacquie Foss and Aloka Bagchi, who had copyedited a subsequent draft. I am grateful to the following persons, each of whom has read some version of the draft and given me helpful comments: Patricia Wen, Robert Ullmann, Marshall Chao, Theresa Shen, Paul Tai, Yunglung Dai, Judy Wen, Kwangyu Nieh, Wuyi So and Kwangwei So.

For the setting in Xi'an, I have drawn information from the book: The Ancient and Modern Xi'an, edited by Ma Zhenglin, and from talks with Professor Yang Erping. Arthur Wen has assisted me in gathering material for backgrounding the San Francisco Bay area; Connie and Cary Mak, for the Hong Kong scenes; and Marco Wen, for the medical case in the story.

I thank the many Chinese scholars and graduate students who had talked with me about some of their experiences in the 1980s.

~ 1 ~

Zhang Saiyue[1], class of 1981, Mechanical Engineering, Tongji University, was on a train from Shanghai to Xi'an to report to her assigned work unit. Through her brother's connections, she had one of the two middle berths in a six-berth compartment. Another woman had the other. Four men took the rest of the berths. The woman looked to be in her early forties. One of the men, whom she called "Lao[2] Diao", was about her age, bespectacled, and apparently her husband. Two other men were younger, probably early thirties. The fourth appeared older, fifties, perhaps. These people sounded like colleagues in some cotton mill in Xi'an, who were returning from a conference in Shanghai. They, the two younger men in particular, were sociable, almost solicitous, toward Saiyue, but found her polite yet distant, seemingly preoccupied with her reading. Eventually, the group pretty much let her alone during the journey.

From Shanghai, the train first went north-northwest some 400 miles to Xuzhou, where the locomotive was switched to one that would run westward

---

1. Pronounced sai—YÜE.
2. "Lao," meaning "old," used as an antecedent to a name, denotes familiarity with reference to an "older" person.

on the Longhai line. With the bottom bunk beds and traveling bags as chairs, and stacked suitcases as a table, the men played cards much of the time. When the woman of the cotton mill group got tired of watching, she would gaze outside the window, as Saiyue did at her breaks from reviewing her books. It was almost winter. The fields looked arid and forlorn, quite unlike the sparkling watery rice paddies in a village near Shanghai where she used to labor after high school.

The men, taking a break from their games, had some tea and peanuts; each was lying on his bunk bed. "Lao Diao," the middle-aged woman said, "These greenish fuzzy rows in the field outside, growing this time of the year, what are they?"

"I think they are winter wheat."

"They look awfully dry," she said.

"This is north country. The Yellow River should be just a few miles up. You can't compare this with the Jiang-nan[3] of harmonious wind and timely rain," Lao Diao said. In a moment, swaying his knees, he burst into a nasal chanting:

> Everybody says Jiang-nan is nice;
> Indeed it's the place to grow old.
> In spring the waters rise bluer than the sky,
> As we sleep in th' rain-pelted painted boat.[4]

One of the younger men, who occupied a top berth, said, "Lao Diao, that is a Tang poem, isn't it? Why don't you compose a poem of your own? We haven't read any new ones of yours lately in the Mill's Bulletin."

"You won't appreciate it," Diao said.

---

3. "Jiang" means river; "Nan," south. "Jiang-nan" denotes the region south of the Yangzi River, where in comparison with northern China, generally speaking, the climate is milder, land more fertile, rain more plentiful, and landscape more scenic.
4. The first stanza of a poem by the Tang poet Wei Zhuang (836-910 A.D.).

"Xiao[5] Mei," the woman said, "he won't do it for you. If Cao Rushi were here, he would scratch his head hard and come up with some 'oil fetching poem.'"[6]

"Only you would think my poems are doggerel.…Now, don't talk nonsense. It's our young colleagues who would wish Xiao Cao were here. Is that right?" Diao said teasingly, stretching his neck out to address his younger colleagues on the upper berths.

"I don't fantasy such," Xiao Mei said.

"Lao Diao, now *you* are talking nonsense," the woman said. "It could get him in trouble with that woman comrade of his."

"OK, not you, Xiao Mei.…Surely Xiao Liang, you.…" Lao Diao, addressing the other young man, chuckled.

"Don't drag me into this. It has been a most pleasant trip. I am quite relaxed right now," Xiao Liang replied.

"I suppose that's the point—to get you excited a little." Mei said.

"I'd admit that she is attractive," Xiao Liang said. "But she is so tall that some guys say that she intimidates them. Actually, she is a fine person, quite easy to talk to. Isn't she? Lao Diao."

"And a smart and good worker too—I don't mind telling you," Diao responded.

"Of course, don't we all know that," the woman said acidulously. "Too bad, I understand that she's got a boyfriend now."

"Yes, that basketball player," Mei said.

"And a darn good one," said Liang.

"I don't follow our basketball team. But I've met the guy a few times. Seems a rather pleasant fellow," Diao said.

"Not on the court," Liang said.

"A big fan like you ought to know," Mei said.

---

5. "Xiao," meaning "little," used as an antecedent to a name, denotes intimacy or familiarity with reference to a younger person.
6. A doggerel poem put together while doing some mundane chore.

"I heard that some big shot in the Electrical City, where her mother works, is also courting her."

"It won't be easy to get her away from our star basketball player," Liang said.

"Why?"

"The two are quite attached to each other," Liang said.

"How do you know?"

"Oh.…I don't really know.…Just gossip, I suppose."

The banter intrigued Saiyue a little, even as she kept her eyes outside the window.

At a stop in the dusk, a barefooted girl picked her way across the rails, ties and gravel. She went from window to window, holding a basin over her head, apparently trying to sell something, and was having little luck at it. Now she came under Saiyue's window. Even though the young teenager was in rags and stained with dust and dirt, her face could yet be seen to be quite delicate and finely featured. The shabby rusty basin contained several hard-boiled eggs. Saiyue thought that the girl, at this time of the day, should be at home, warm and ready for supper. She bought the eggs, all four of them, and told the girl to go home as the train jerked to resume its run.

The low-pitched whistle reverberated in the air. Beyond the fields and folds, dark little cottages huddled below blurring tree lines. A stream with sandbars slithered past. An occasional dome of brick kiln popped up and fast retreated. Long institutional walls heralded a village or town, and a crane truss rising behind told of a factory. The walls had on them white-wash slogans, such as, "Strive to Complete the Four Modernizations."[7] Amid the monotonous clickety-clack, utility poles endlessly slipping past one after another almost hypnotized her. However, it also dulled her anxiety about the journey.

---

7. "In agriculture, industry, national defense, and science and technology."

When in that early afternoon the train pulled in the Xi'an station, she had traveled some 850 miles in 24 hours. Struggling a little with her baggage, she managed to get out of the station and hire a two-seat three-wheeled motor cab. With her traveling bag in her lap, one hand on the bundle of the bedroll—packed with her enameled metal washbasin—beside her and a suitcase by her feet, she headed from the station on the city's north edge to the southern suburb.

In a while, the cab rounded a temple-like structure at the center of a wide traffic circle, with an arc of buses standing along the edge. She figured from the city map that it must be the Bell Tower in the heart of downtown; the driver confirmed it. They crossed a vaulted passage—the South Gate of the city. Further on, the road became a bona fide modern boulevard with islands of trees separating the main motorway from the parallel local side roads. It looked wide, neat, and rather grand, with traffic moving in orderly fashion, nothing like the congestion in Shanghai. It was Chang'an Road, the main north-south thoroughfare and pride of the Xi'an Bureau of Transportation.

The cab turned west. Shortly it pulled up to a gate under a deep plaque bearing the characters for the Xi'an Petroleum Institute in elegant sculptured calligraphy. A guard in a kiosk next to one of the pilasters supporting the plaque checked her identification and let her inside the compound. The gray buildings had the ponderous rectangular style of the Soviet Union institutional architecture. The one closest to the gate was the largest and also the main building.

The head of the Personnel Department, a somber, middle-aged man with big yellowish eyes and dressed in a Mao suit, drew himself up to receive her assignment document with tobacco stained fingers. He welcomed her officially, reciting a cant studded with such current slogans as "pulverizing the Gang of Four." (The radical Gang of Four had been sentenced and put away in prison earlier in the year.) The short speech with its quarrelsome Shandong accent sounded like a reprimand. She nodded lightly, letting it go in one ear and out the other. After filling out several forms and having her photograph taken, she was given a temporary work unit certificate—to be exchanged for a regular one later—along with an assortment of papers including her dormitory assignment slip and a map of the campus.

The compound appeared to be divided by concrete paths into rectangular blocks of buildings and open spaces bordered by plants. Late fall it was; the trees retained only sparse, discolored leaves. The shrubs wore pads of brown and yellowish green among clusters of spindly sticks. In the thin sunlight the air smelled cool and fresh. Only a few souls were making their way here and there. She thought that if it weren't for the cumbersome baggage, it would be a rather pleasant walk.

Building 8, a 4-story concrete structure, looking clean and new, sat near an edge of the campus marked by a brick wall. The building superintendent gave her a key for her room on the top floor. Like many public buildings she had been in before, the inside appeared inferior to the outside; there were stained patches on the walls, and even a couple of spots of exposed lath. She lugged her baggage upstairs, taking care not to swipe the stacked cylindrical holed briquettes off the windowsills at the landings. The smell of coal smoke and the crying of a child indicated families were also living in the building.

A light at the end of the hallway barely enabled her to locate the room and insert the door key. The room was bright enough. Through a wide window, she saw cultivated fields and a group of low, dingy, black tile-roofed tenements. There were two beds in the room. The one along the side wall behind the opened door was already made. A folded quilt with a gingham cover, having a motif of pink and blue flowers, sat at one end of the bed, and a pillow overlaid by a towel at the other. The other bed was placed against the opposite wall with only a tick on it. Associated with each bed there were also a small desk and a bureau. She hauled her baggage in, shut the door, stood her suitcase behind it, sat on the unmade bed and closed her eyes to rest.

"I am sorry that I am late, Chief," she apologizes to the man with a dark and severe countenance across the desk.

"You certainly are. Don't presume that you young people from big cities could expect special treatment." The bellicose tone of Shandong dialect makes the warning even more intimidating. He blows off a puff of cigarette smoke like that at the end of a fired cannon in the movies.

"I don't expect that at all. I'll do my best for my work unit....I wonder what my assignment will be," she asks softly.

"Well, we are sending you, like all new comers, to an exploration team. You are to go to the west of the Yumen oil fields."

"Gansu province?"

"Of course! Don't tell me now you new brainy college graduates don't know where Yumen Gate is!"

She understands that he is referring to the fact that she belongs to the first crop of post-Cultural Revolution college graduates who had matriculated on the basis of scholarship instead of ideology. "I do," she says, and seeing deserts, wilderness and desolation, she asks, "How long will the assignment last?"

"Five years." Under brush-like eyebrows, the yellowish eyes roll and bulge like a giant frog's.

"That's a long time," she blurts out.

"Not a day less! Five years!" He thumps his paw on the desk.

She started, opened her eyes and rose quickly. Standing between the door and her suitcase, now lying flat on the floor, was a young woman, medium height, with a moon face, a little on the dark side, and round black eyes. What a difference from those yellowish frog-eyes!

"I am sorry I inadvertently knocked your suitcase over. I must have frightened you. I hope nothing inside is damaged," the young woman said, moving over.

"It contains mostly clothes. Nothing brittle. I didn't expect to fall asleep. Had thought just to rest a while. I am Zhang Saiyue." They shook hands.

"I am Shi Renmei. I was told earlier this week to expect a roommate from out of town. I am glad it's you. Where are you from?"

"Shanghai."

"Shanghai! Good!" She gave her new roommate another quick survey. "You must be tired.…Let me help you make the bed and get settled a little first.…Later I'll take you to the mess hall."

The next morning Saiyue reported to Wang Tang'yi, Vice Chief of the Department of Machinery and Facilities.

After some polite exchanges, Wang said, "You have a very good record at Tongji University. I believe you'll be a big help to our Division." He had the gaunt and plain face of a peasant, probably in his fifties, like her father.

"I will do my best."

"What are your aspirations, Comrade Zhang?" he fixed his eyes on her.

"Right now, I just want to do a good job for my work unit," she answered.

"And later on?" The Vice Chief's seemingly careworn eyes now shone with some intensity.

"I haven't thought that far yet," she smiled, showing her white teeth.

"That's all right. You are young." The Vice Chief looked away, the intensity gone. He shuffled through some books and pamphlets on one side of his desk and handed her a small stack of literature consisting of introductions to the Institute and the Department, and a few engineering manuals. "Let me introduce you to Senior Engineer Zeng." He led her to a larger office, where a number of staffers were at work.

Senior Engineer Zeng, rising unhurriedly from her chair, warmly greeted her superior, "Good morning, Vice Chief Wang." She wore a dull gray Western style jacket, a tad too tight around the upper body. In her early forties and a little fleshy under the chin, she still had a handsome face. After introductions, he said to her, "Let Comrade Zhang first review some of our typical designs," and to Saiyue, "If you have any questions, speak to Senior Engineer Zeng."

After the Vice Chief left, the senior engineer chatted with Saiyue for a while; she appeared to be kind and solicitous. She showed the newcomer her desk, one of eight in the room, and introduced her around in the office. Saiyue began her career that day.

2

Saiyue was glad to realize that her first assignment—the "reviewing" of typical designs—amounted to an initiation and training for her job. It was essentially a learning process. After a slow beginning, she caught on fairly rapidly. However, she would have questions in spots. She went to her supervisor for help but found Zeng's responses affable in style but vague in content. When the questions required specific answers, the senior engineer would refer Saiyue to the engineer who had actually done the work.

Several weeks later, Zeng began to give her some simple components to design. Saiyue was glad to make the transition from academic exercises to engineering practice. Designing components was relatively straightforward. After a while, she began to look forward to more challenging assignments that would push her up the learning curve faster. However, she continued to receive simple, routine ones. Her hinting for more complex tasks did not draw the desired response. When she expressed her wish directly, it was gently deflected by the senior engineer. "What's the hurry, Xiao Zhang? You are young, just starting. Your work will get more involved later on."

One day Saiyue met Vice Chief Wang in the corridor; he inquired about her progress. She took the opportunity to express her desire for more challenging work. He looked at her for a couple of seconds, and repeated what Zeng had told her—to be patient.

Even with simple tasks, occasionally there still would be ambiguities. In one instance, for some apparent inconsistencies in the specification of design loads, she went to Zeng for clarification. The senior engineer's answer was again obscure. When Saiyue pursued her point, Zeng, as before, referred her to another engineer. Thus, gradually she came to realize that she would learn little from her supervisor.

Saiyue read on the Bulletin Board one morning that a new computer science course—Fortran 77—was to be offered. The class would meet during office hours, and to enroll, staff members would need written permission from their supervisors. Saiyue went to Zeng for her approval.

"Why would you want to spend your time on that? All we have heard about computers around the Institute are problems. If they are not what they call *hard* ones, then they are *soft* ones, or breakdowns due to line voltage fluctuations, when some other institute in our district drains too much electricity with their experiments. It seems to me much more efficient to do our work the sure way as we have been doing."

"Things may change soon in the future," Saiyue said.

"Then we should see what happens in the future," the supervisor said coolly, realizing that her graciousness seemed to have been wasted on this newcomer.

"It's only three hours a week. I can guarantee that my work for the unit won't be affected," Saiyue said.

"All of us have duties for our office hours. I cannot make any exceptions."

"Senior Engineer Zeng, I will make up the class hours by using my lunch break time," Saiyue said.

Zeng tucked in her lips to keep her composure with this persistent young woman. Finally, she said with a long face, "If you want it this badly, go ahead. I'll have the note for you after lunch."

One evening after the class had begun, having completed a homework, Saiyue was organizing her desk, singing lightly, "Girls in white dresses with blue satin sashes, snowflakes that stay on my nose and eyelashes,...These are a few of my favorite things...."

"I didn't know you could sing 'ocean[8] songs.'" Renmei had just returned to the room.

"You are back! I learned it from a radio program in Shanghai. It taught songs in English as well as the language," Saiyue said.

"You Shanghai mademoiselles are so modern! Some people around here are learning English all right. But until now I haven't heard anyone in the dorm who'd dare, or know how, to sing in English. You have a fine singing voice."

"I don't know about my voice. But I enjoy singing. You just wait. Before long, we'll have that kind of radio program in Xi'an too....Well, had a wonderful time tonight as usual?" Saiyue asked, throwing an impish glance at her roommate.

"You don't have to start! Shanghai mademoiselle! I used to hear that big city mademoiselles, unlike us small town girls, know how to have fun. Yet all I see of you is sprawling over the desk, hours on end, digging that Fortran 77 stuff. My mademoiselle! You are not living up to Shanghai's glamorous name, and are wasting your golden hours of youth!"

"I have enough R & R. Just last Sunday I spent the whole day on that outing to Emperor Qin's Tomb and Huaqin Pond. Where were you? Holed up with that basketball player of yours. You know you have the jock pretty much noosed. Don't be afraid that he would run away. Join the Institute's group activities sometimes."

"I am not afraid of any group activity except when a stylish Shanghai mademoiselle like you is in it."

---

8. Denoting "foreign, Western"—the Pacific Ocean was the main medium of more or less regular contact between China and the West since the late Ming dynasty.

"Don't use me to cover your shenanigans. Are you going to confess to me what you two did tonight?"

"What does a small town girl know about what to do? You'll just have to fancy." Renmei's big black eyes seemed to be losing focus, and the round face flushed a bit.

Saiyue noticed that her roommate's jacket was buttoned crookedly. She was about to comment on that, but her imagination stirred her to a rush. She simply said, "Is there really that much to fancy?"

Ignoring Saiyue's taunt, Renmei said, "Say, about group activities, our basketball team is going to have a match next Sunday at the gymnasium of the Textile Mills against one of their teams. Would you like to come with me to watch?"

"What time is the game?"

"It starts at three. If we leave after lunch, we'll have plenty of time. We'll catch the No. 3 Bus at the Bell Tower. It'll take us right out there."

Saiyue agreed to go with her.

Lo Yungchen, Renmei's boyfriend, a member of the Department of General Affairs of the Institute and its basketball team, got seats for the roommates almost at the middle of the sideline, three rows up from the floor. To their left were the benches of the Institute's team, suited in blue. On the other side of the court were the benches for the team of the Third National Textile Mill, suited in crimson.

The teams were in their pre-game warm-up. The players were loosening up, moving about and shooting the baskets easily. In a while they started drills, fast breaks, lay-ups, and such. Afterwards, they reverted to the earlier unstructured practice. Having watched enough of her Institute's team for a time, Saiyue turned to look at the crimson home team. By then only six or seven players were on the court. Her attention was drawn to one particular player. He was not only tall—almost all of them were—but, to her, well proportioned, if long limbs are considered that.

Someone had made an attempt at the basket and missed, the ball bouncing sharply off the rim. Like a big cat, he snatched it in the air, turned and dribbled it in a slightly stooped posture and moved quickly away from the basket. Suddenly, he ran a sharp circular arc, and, now facing the basket, straightened up and shot the ball, his hand and arms stretched up in a graceful follow-through. The ball swished through the basket. Bending at his waist, he gave his right fist a forceful upward swing. Tossing his head like a horse after clearing a jump in an equestrian competition, he jogged a few steps toward the sideline, and slowed down to a slight swagger.

"He is cute. Isn't he?"

Saiyue almost felt Renmei's lips touching her ear. "Who are you talking about? Your Lao Lo?" She felt hot under the ears.

"I mean that guy on the left. You couldn't take your eyes off him for the last half hour," Renmei whispered to her again.

"Who? That show-off?" Saiyue pretended indifference, knowing she was nabbed. A blast of the PA horn saved her. The referees were meeting the teams' captains, the graceful athlete on the other team being one of them.

The captain in crimson played right guard, just as Lo did for the blue team. As the game progressed, both teams seemed to depend more on the guards than the forwards. They were fairly evenly matched in the first half. At halftime the score was tied.

When the second half started, the crimson team had the ball. The handsome right guard slowly dribbled it down the court along the side where the two young women were seated. Saiyue now had a closer look at him. His skin smooth, eyes deep set, he had a high nose with a slight hook that appeared to point to his thin-lipped mouth over a somewhat jutting chin.

Raising his left hand with an extended thumb and forefinger, seemingly to signal some set play, he crossed the mid-court, pounding the ball slowly, limbs relaxed, the tip of the tongue curled over the upper lip and eyes piercingly alert. Saiyue could feel the floor vibrations excited by the bouncing ball. She saw the sleek well-tempered muscle of the bare thigh. As her sight shifted upward a bit to a vague protrusion over the trunks, her heart took a hop and knocked like a frightened fawn. She quickly flung her sight to the other side of the court, and then jerkily returned it to the ball.

In its first ball possession of the second half, the crimson team executed a perfect pick play. At its end, some 14 feet away from the basket, the right guard jumped up, holding the ball above his head, his body suspended in the air, and under the ceiling light, the tan muscles flexed. The rotating ball arched toward the basket. The gymnasium hushed. Then, a loud cheer erupted from the home team supporters. From that point on, the crimson team dominated the game. It won the match convincingly.

Saiyue followed Renmei to a post-game informal party for the players and their fans. The gathering took place in a large room adjacent to the courts. Bottled cold drinks, dumplings, baked corn on the cob and peanuts could be bought at a stall along a wall. The roommates bought orange drinks and two small bags of peanuts, and sat with two other supporters from the Institute at a table near the refreshment stall. The group chatted about the thin taste of the orange drink, the weather and the cheering decibels of the host team's fans. By and by, the players in twos and threes began to drift in. Lo Yungchen and the other guard of his team, after fetching their bottles of orange drink, joined Renmei's group. They made small talk while enjoying the refreshments.

"Lao Lo, you played very well this afternoon," one of the Institute's supporters said.

"We didn't do that badly in the first half," Lo said. "But, we were simply out-played in the second. Then, they are a pretty good team. Anyhow, leading in our division now. Actually they have the division championship locked up and are favored to win the league title too." As he spoke, the two guards of the crimson team sauntered into the room. "These two are the main reason for their team's successes," he nodded in their direction.

"Do you know them?"

"Oh yes, certainly. Pretty congenial fellows—off the court, that is. We played against them before."

While the conversation was going on around her table, Saiyue saw the two crimson guards huddled with a group of fans of both sexes. Among them was a young woman, whom it was hard not to notice since game time. At moments of the home team's brilliance or luck, rising with her fellow fans to applaud, she literally stood out with her height, the red full lips ovaling in the cheering. Her enthusiasm seemed to double whenever the handsome right guard scored. Now at the side of obviously her favorite player, she looked radiant, the large eyes smiling, like a competing figure skater who had just successfully completed her own program.

At intervals, the handsome basketball player would crane his head and cast his eyes about the surroundings, like a bird of prey atop a tree. Several times he had glanced Lo Yungchen's way. At a juncture, after saying something to the tall woman, he walked alone to the refreshment stall, got himself two packages of peanuts and sashayed toward the table of Lo and his friends.

"Lao Lo, Lao Sheng, good game!" he said as he reached them, smiling and rocking his shoulders slightly, the golden stripes gleaming along the pants and the sleeves, his limbs seemed even longer than they appeared on the court. Lao Sheng played the left guard for the Institute.

"Good for you and your team," Lo smiled.

"Really you fellows gave us a tough time in the first half. We knew we had to work harder if we wanted to keep our lead in the division."

"The perfect pick play you guys set up at the beginning of the second half really got your team going."

"Well, Lao Sheng wasn't giving me much space; I was lucky to get that shot off....Listen, why all this shoptalk. Let's not bore our women comrades here."

"Sorry, I should have introduced you first. I believe you've met Renmei before,"

Lo began to speak a little louder. "Everybody! This is Engineer Xu Haosheng of the Third Mill. I am sure that you all noticed—the captain and star of their team."

"What star? Don't kid, Lao Lo," Xu said modestly. "I am Xu Haosheng. How are you?" he nodded and greeted each around the table, as Lo presented them. Saiyue was the last.

"This is Engineer Zhang Saiyue of our Institute."

Nodding, she said, "How do you do!"

"Engineer Zhang! How are you!" Xu extended his hand. The handshake was brief. "I am glad you have come to watch us play. Do you like to watch basketball?" Smiling most genially, he looked softly at her.

"This afternoon was my first time in Xi'an," she said, smiling in return, the corners of her mouth turning upward.

"Is Engineer Zhang new in Xi'an?" he asked.

"How do you know?" she answered with a question.

"Just a guess—because you said that today's game was your first in Xi'an."

"She came from Shanghai just a few months ago," Renmei interposed.

"In that case, maybe we should play host and show Engineer Zhang the sights of Xi'an," he said cordially.

"By all means," Renmei said, smiling in an exaggerated knowing manner.

"Who says you can speak for me?" Saiyue said with mock seriousness.

"Maybe one of these days, we can all go together for some outing," Xu proposed.

"That's a good idea," Lo joined in. Saiyue said nothing but kept a demure smile.

That evening back in the dorm, "I think he likes you," Renmei said.

"Now you are speaking for him too. You are the spokeswoman for everybody.... Perhaps with the exception of that tall girl."

"What tall girl?... Oh, you mean the one who cheered for the Mill's team?"

"Yes. Notice how she stuck to him after the game as our team's Lao Sheng did during the game," Saiyue said.

"Yes, but he did manage to free himself to come over to talk to us. To you, actually. Consider this. Around our entire table, he shook hands with only you. He wanted you to know that you are special," Renmei observed.

"You know that too! That woman…she is rather striking. Isn't she? Must be his steady girlfriend. Perhaps even fiancée, or wife?"

"Not wife. Lao Lo had told me that he wasn't married. She is big, yes, not bad looking either. Girlfriend, maybe. Steady? I won't bet on that. Lao Lo said that this fellow had no lack of girlfriends, and supposed that he collected them as he did basketball trophies," Renmei chuckled.

A handsome man, surely, and such virility and grace on the basketball court, Saiyue thought. But I won't be anybody's trophy.

3

Saiyue was called downstairs in her dormitory to answer a phone call.

"Wey!"

"Wey, Engineer Zhang?"

"Yes, this is Zhang Saiyue." She recalled the athlete in the crimson warm-up suit.

After an exchange of pleasantries, Xu Haosheng said, "We talked about this the other day. Since you are kind of new in Xi'an, perhaps you'll let me play host and invite you to see a movie...." He added that he would extend the invitation to her roommate Renmei and Lao Lo also.

Saiyue hesitated a bit but accepted the invitation to see *Wu Zhetian* at the Chang'an Theater on Sunday. She also agreed, with some reluctance, to ask Renmei on his behalf.

That evening she brought this up with Renmei. "No, we wouldn't go with you," Renmei responded. "Are you kidding? We don't want to spend our time as chaperons. My goodness, you both are grown-ups. Now you go and have yourself a good time."

"I am not that sure," Saiyue said, looking vacantly outside the window. The tiny lights in the tenements beyond the compound walls glimmered in winter early darkness. In college she had socialized with male students before, though not often, at parties or in seeing a movie, but it was always with other female friends together. Then she was just too intent on her future career to go on any single date. Now she was still intent on that. However, those young men did not quite pack the same magnetism as this basketball player. And recently some nights she had come to wonder what gave her roommate that dreamy, contented look when she returned to the room. But then there was that tall woman.

Sunday came and she saw *Wu Zhetian*[9] with Xu. Coming out of the theater, Saiyue said, "Haven't you noticed that recent entertainment productions: movies, operas, etc., all seem to have to do with *bad strong* women."

"You are right," Xu said. "Come to think of it. *The Story of The White Snake* was on TV a few nights ago." He added, "Maybe the government wants us to be more aware of bad strong women."

Saiyue felt that she did not know him well enough to say openly that perhaps those productions were intended to reflect the jailed Jiang Qing, wife of the deceased Chairman Mao and the leader of the Gang of Four. Instead, she commented, "There really aren't that many *good* strong women recorded in Chinese history. Off-hand, I can only think of Mulan and Liang Hong'yu. *Good* women were not supposed to be *strong*."

"I have never given much thought to such questions." He seemed to be making an effort to keep up his attention on the subject, and managed to observe: "In modern times, we do have our Vice Chairman Song Qingling[10] and Comrade Deng Yingchao."[11]

They are not exactly Thatcher or Gandhi, Saiyue thought, but did not voice it. "Well, anyway, it's an interesting movie. Thank you for inviting me," she said.

"May I call on you again?" he asked.

She smiled at him and nodded lightly.

---

9. Wu Zhetian was a despotic and astute empress in the early Tang dynasty, condemned by some historians of later ages as being lustful and cruel.
10. Wife of Dr. Sun Yat-sen.
11. Wife of Premier Zhou En-lai.

On their second date, they were having noodle soup at a corner table in an eatery. The air laden with the steam from the huge wok of boiling water—in which the noodles tumbled riotously—felt even thicker with the beehive droning of a low ceiling restaurant. She asked, rather innocently, "How long have you known that tall woman who was with you after that ballgame?"

"What?" he leaned over.

She repeated the question.

"Tall woman!?...Oh, I know whom you are referring to. It was Xiao Cao. I have known her for about a year," he said expressionlessly and lowered his head to get to the chopsticks-held noodles.

"What's her name?"

"Cao Rushi."

"Rushi, nice name. Is she your girlfriend?"

"Yes. She is one of my girlfriends, a friend who happens to be a female."

"Don't you understand my question *really*?" she smiled.

"All right. I do.... Yes, my relationship with her was at one time beyond common friendship. But it's no longer that anymore."

"Why?"

"Don't you know?"

"Do you still see her?" She persisted.

"No, except when we run into each other at the Mill. It happens very rarely though. Our jobs are hardly related."

"She works at the Mill also?"

"Yes, she is in the Accounting Department."

"Lives at the Mill compound too?" She was told before that was where he lived.

"No. She lived with her mother in the Electrical Technology District in the west part of the city. Say, you know, you are quite an interrogator."

She was not amused by his smug smile during the exchange, but she was pleased that he seemed to be on the level with her. "I don't mean to pry—just want to know my own bearing. You wouldn't think my questions strange, do you?"

"Of course not." He nodded and had himself another chopsticksful of noodles.

Thereafter, when Xu didn't have a game on Sunday, he and Saiyue would visit the museums, walk around the department stores—seldom bought anything, except at times a small article such as a tube of toothpaste or a bar of soap—take in a movie, or sit in some teahouse and talk. Obviously he enjoyed small pleasures of life—a beer or a bowl of beef or chicken noodle. He seemed knowledgeable and nimble enough to carry on an intelligent conversation about anything she would bring up. Yet she would refrain from broaching subjects that she suspected would not interest him, such as computer science or graduate studies.

She often couldn't remember what they talked about; just to be with him was stimulation enough. She surprised herself at how much his handsomeness and his savoir-faire were in her thoughts. However, she tried to keep his smooth skin and sleek muscles off them, and had succeeded so far—with self-admonitions of possible threats to her professional advancement. And she rarely went to his games, as she needed the time to study.

When they were together, she would let him put his hand on her far shoulder. After a time she would let him hold her hand and squeeze it occasionally. Sometimes she would do the squeezing herself. Twice he tried to kiss her; each time she turned away and said gently, "Please don't." When he tried to put his hand over her breast, she would immediately remove it, saying the same.

Soon, it was Chinese New Year or the Spring Festival. It was one of the Institute's traditions to have a party on its Eve. Each member was expected to contribute something—whether in planning, decorating or arranging for food and drinks, etc. She chose an item that would take the least time; she would contribute a song to the after-dinner program.

She and Haosheng, who had come as her guest, were seated at a table of ten in the mess hall. The dinner started with four cold dishes, served with beer. He began to spice his with gaoliang, which he had brought over himself. "For this joyous occasion..." he said and tried to persuade her to add some of the spirits to her beer too. She said it was too strong. To prove her point, she poured some into a small cup and lit it with a match. The faint blue and white flames danced over the cup. Nevertheless, she agreed to add a smidgen.

After the dinner, the tables were cleared except for the drinks. Cigarettes were lit up all around. The chairman of the organization committee got up on a platform and made the usual kind of remarks for such an event—acknowledgments and thanks to the leadership and to each and all. The Director of the Institute was obligingly brief in thanking everyone for a productive year at their work unit, and wishing everyone a happy and prosperous "New Year." Then the entertainment program commenced.

It began with a dance of two lions, each acted out by two men shrouded in a large leonine headpiece and a mantle decorated as the body of the king of beasts. They pranced around to prerecorded music, the large heads shaking, big fluffy ears flapping, tiny bells, attached to the limbs, tinkling amid the rhythmic clashing of cymbals and beating of drums. It was a playful and humorous choreography, aptly setting the festive tone.

The dance was followed by a solo drum performance. By varying the impact of the strokes, the tempo and rhythm, and often a partial covering of the drum membrane with one hand, the performer created quite a stirring piece of music, with a single large drum, depicting a spring storm as annotated briefly by the program notes.

The next number, a comic skit, featuring a wife and her hen-pecked husband elicited much mirth and laughter. The husband ended the number with a story:

"Early this morning, my division chief assembled my colleagues in the meeting room. I thought we were going to get another lecture from him. But he simply intoned (the actor in exaggerated deep voice), 'There has been a lot of talk about henpecking in our division lately. Now I want the truth. Those who considered themselves henpecked go to the end of the room. Remember I want the truth!' After some initial hesitation, one by one, my colleagues slowly walked over to the end of the room. Then it was only the chief and I who stood put....My colleagues at the end of the room stared at us with admiration. Some with disbelief....Finally, the chief sheepishly walked over and joined them." Laughter filled the hall. "Then the chief said to me, 'So, you are the only one who is not henpecked.'" A pause. "'I don't know about that....But my wife has always told me not to go where there is a crowd.'"

Clapping and laughing with the rest of the audience, Xu turned to Saiyue and said, "There is the kind of husband for you!"

"I have no use for such weaklings," she said smilingly with a mock frown.

Saiyue was next. She walked up to the microphone on the platform. Buoyed up by the festivities and the spiced beer, in a pink dress she surveyed the audience. The attentive eyes augmented her confidence. Her flushing face shone with her black lustrous hair. After a few bars of introduction by an electronic piano, slowly she sang:

> The morning rain of Wei City settles the dust;
> Before the hostel the fresh green willow bends.
> Have another cup of wine we must;
> West out of th' Yang Pass,[12] you have no old friends.[13]

Her untrained voice was plain and clear. She sang slowly with a simplicity that invoked the poem's restrained emotion. It was a welcome change of pace from the hilarity of the preceding numbers. The strain was repeated. The audience applauded appreciatively. In response, she sang an encore,

---

12. Yang Pass was the main fort on the then northwest frontier.
13. The original lyrics were by the Tang poet Wang Wei.

At the Long River's head I live;
At the Long River's tail you live.
I see you not; of you everyday I think.
The Long River's water we both drink.
When will the flow be ceased?
When will the pain be released?
I only wish your heart were like mine—
That won't spurn the one who does pine.[14]

Amid the audience's clapping she walked briskly off the stage. More compliments came her way at her own table. Haosheng smiled at her proudly and sweetly: "You sang really well! Beautifully!" He held her hand underneath the table.

The next program was going to be a short play. The amateur stagehands weren't particularly proficient at handling the props; they appeared to be bungling. People puffed away at their cigarettes. A haze covered the room.

"The tobacco smoke is getting very bothersome," she rubbed her eyes.

"It is too stuffy here," he said, smothering his own cigarette in an ashtray. "Let's go out for some fresh air." They took their jackets, went out of the hall, past the building door onto the dim landing of the stone steps. Ice crystals drifted scintillatingly in the yellow light cones atop lampposts. He took a deep breath and blew out a white plume. "This feels better," he said and put his right arm around her. She had her hands under her armpits. He stretched his head forward and tried to steer her to face him.

"Don't. People will see us. It's embarrassing....And it's cold here."

"Yes, it is cold," he echoed. "Brrr....Too stuffy inside, too cold out here. Why don't we go to your room?" He knew from talking with Lao Lo about staying overnight at the Institute that Renmei had gone to her home in Kaifeng for the holidays.

---

14. The original lyrics were by Li Zhiyi of the Song Dynasty (960-1279 A.D.). The Long River is the Yangzi River.

Saiyue remained silent and motionless for a while. Then she began to walk down the steps. He followed.

The room felt warm, as heating in the dormitories was extended by two hours daily during the holidays. Silently they took off their jackets. She laid hers at the end of the bed, and he his on the chair. He held her and they kissed. His hands pressed her back hard toward him. She closed her eyes, blood rushing, breath shortened, and body levitating. His hand reached under her shirt and began its slow kneading. She mumbled huskily: "Haosheng, Haosheng!" With his chest, he lowered her down on the bed and lifted her dress. Like a lamb, she lay there with her eyes opened a slit. He began to pull down her underpants. She murmured, "What are you doing? Stop!" but was unable to offer any physical resistance. She felt a warm velvety object moving down her belly.

In a flash she saw two leaden eyes, like those of a dead fish, of a lolling head of a young woman, and bloodstains on white skin. Saiyue pushed the man on top of her aside and bolted up. "No! No! This isn't right! This isn't right!"

"What is the matter?" Xu was unprepared for the sudden turn.

"We shouldn't be doing this," she said.

"My love. Let me love you. I do love you." Sitting up, he looked at her soulfully, while she just stared straight ahead. He turned to massage her neck and shoulder.

"I know you like me. I like you too. But I am not ready for this just yet." She started to tidy up herself, shrugging his hands off her shoulder.

He got off the bed, backed away a step, and regarded her intently. Her mouth contorted a little, eyes wide open with cool lights, countenance forbidding.

"All right. What shall we do now?" He began to get his own pants back in order.

"We can go back to the party."

"I am afraid I am not in the mood for that anymore," he grumbled.

"Are you mad at me?"

"No," he said gallantly. "I think I owe you an apology. I thought our feelings had merged naturally. I have to work this out. One can't turn his passion on and off like a light switch you know....I think I'll go back to the Mill." He figured that the biking, if not the frigid air, would dissipate his passion.

"Haven't you arranged with Lao Lo to stay over here at the Institute tonight?"

"That's all right."

"Don't be mad," she touched and stroked his cheek with her fingers.

Xu was glad that her face had softened considerably. He had a notion of trying again, but thought better of it.

— 4 —

Saiyue sat alone in her room after Xu left. The celebratory firecrackers sounded sporadically, some close, some far, some with a single hefty boom and others with a burst of crisp fusillade. They all had the same effect of adding more loneliness. She thought that perhaps she ought to have gone to Shanghai for the holidays. Then the excitement just moments ago was recalled; and a sluggish warmth stole back. It was checked again by the reappearance of a recollection from her senior high school year. She had returned home, with the bag of the family's monthly grain ration fastened at the back of her parked bike. She ran to open the back door for her second floor neighbor, Mr. Song, who was carrying his daughter Ah Xi on his back. Her head was lying lifelessly on his shoulder, her light gray trousers and her bare ankle spotted with blood. Saiyue, connecting the sight with what she had overheard during a big row in the Song family a week earlier, gathered that the unmarried Ah Xi had an abortion.

Saiyue felt she did right to stop Haosheng. But she wouldn't blame him. In fact, she missed him already. She comforted herself by thinking, I'll see him tomorrow.

Next day she didn't even hear from him. The disappointment deepened as his absence and silence continued.

One evening shortly after the holidays, Renmei returned to the room later than usual. Saiyue flipped over her book so that the page she was reading rested against the desktop. "Had a hard time tearing away from him tonight, eh?" Having said this routinely, she was mortified for feeling a little envious.

"No, I haven't been with him at all. I was at a party for a friend, a colleague in my division. Actually, a relative—his wife is a cousin of mine. You don't know them."

"Some special occasion?" Saiyue asked.

"Yes, it is like that. He is going away to America as a visiting scholar, at last."

"How do you mean?" Visiting scholar! She was all ears.

"He received a visiting scholarship over a year ago."

"And he is going just now?"

"I understand he had a difficult time finding a reputable institution in America that would give him an invitation. Finally, he managed to get one from some university there," Renmei said.

"Yes, I have heard about such cases. When the program first started some years ago, a visiting scholar could have his pick for a host institution—name schools, Princeton University, Massachusetts Institute of Technology and the like. Now it's not that easy even to pull off one from one of the better known state universities.…By the way, how did he get chosen to be a visiting scholar in the first place?" Saiyue asked, leaning against the back of her chair in a casual pose.

"I don't know. Practically everybody would like to go. I suppose it boils down to the decision of the leadership. People say you can work hard to impress them, and yet there is no guarantee. The chances are so small that most don't bother anymore. My cousin mentioned that recently the leadership had made the qualifications even more stringent."

"How?"

"I have no idea."

"Oh yeah? What's the name of your cousin?" Saiyue asked.

"Lien Kekuan."

"It must have been a big party for your division."

"No. It's not a division affair at all. Just the five or six of us. I wouldn't have been invited but for my cousin."

"You mean the Institute, or at least your division, would not give him a send-off party?" Saiyue said.

"Are you kidding? You should know that. People go out of their way to hide this sort of thing—to minimize the reactions of envy-stung colleagues." Renmei sat at the edge of her bed, wagging her legs relaxedly. "By the way, what's going on between you and Xu Haosheng? He hasn't made an appearance around here recently."

"Nothing was going on between us in the first place. There are more important things in the world," Saiyue said.

"I bet."

A couple of days later, Senior Engineer Zeng told Saiyue that Vice Chief Wang would like to see her. She went.

"The Ministry has sent us a copy of a computer program, PAP-II, for 'Piping Analysis Program, Version II,'" the Vice Chief said.

"Yes?"

"I think we ought to try it out. I have discussed this with our Computer Laboratory. They want an engineer to work with them on it. Would you like to do it?"

"Do you know in what language was the program written?"

"I understand it was in FORTRAN 4 or 5."

She was daunted somewhat by the challenge. However, she said, with little hesitation, "I'll try my best."

"Good. The magnetic tape containing the program is in the Computer Laboratory. Here is the User's Manual." He handed a binder to her. "It also has some sample problems and solutions. After you are finished with your current assignment, get in touch with the Computer Laboratory about the program. I'll tell them of your role. Any problems?"

"No, I'll get started on it as soon as I can." She made to leave; then stopped. After a quick clearing of her throat, she said, "By the way, Vice Chief Wang, do you know a Lien Kekuan in the Institute?"

"Yes. He has been with the Institute for some years now. What about him?"

"My roommate told me he is going to America as a visiting scholar."

"Yes. He's going there for one year, officially," Wang said.

"What do you mean 'officially'?"

"Well, past experience has shown that most visiting scholars wouldn't return on time according to initial official understanding. He is not in our department, so his case doesn't really concern us. Anyway, I hope things would improve from now on."

"In what way?" she prompted. He fixed his eyes on her. For a moment she felt his eyes were younger than his face and were making her slightly self-conscious.

"I suppose it's no secret." He paused for a second. "It is like this. When the government began the program, practically all the scholars sent out had graduated from college before the Cultural Revolution. It turned out that many of them were technologically behind, and somehow not particularly motivated to learn new things. They did not acquire as much new knowledge and skills as the leadership had expected. I suppose that age may have something to do with it....Later on, younger graduates were sent, and a problem of a different kind came up. Few of them returned. By some means or other, they stayed on abroad, especially those who had gone to America. The leadership studied the situation and made some changes in the selection process."

"Yes?" she said softly.

"Are you interested in going abroad?"

She hesitated but for a second and looked into his intent eyes. "Yes. I hope that sometime in the future I can get that opportunity. Learn as many modern skills as I can to help in the Four Modernizations." Pausing momentarily as if to gather more courage, she pursued, "Could you tell me more about the criteria for selecting the candidates?"

He turned his eyes to the edge of the desk, and returned them to her, and said, "Well, I suppose it's all right for me to tell you. However, just to avoid gossip, you should not repeat what I tell you to anyone."

"Vice Chief, I am not a blabbermouth."

"And I must tell you that competitions for the scholarships are very strong. The Director is taking personal charge of the selection."

"I understand."

Wang pushed his chair back against the desk and opened its bottom drawer. He fumbled in it for a few seconds and withdrew a sheaf of paper. "Here they are," he began to read:

A tentative appointment may be awarded to a candidate who is:
1. In good standing in the Institute and a believer in socialism, although Party membership or proletariat family background is not required.
2. An outstanding worker for at least two years.
3. A graduate of a four year college, preferably one of the key colleges or universities, trained in a field that can effectively promote the Four Modernizations.
4. Preferably married, and a parent.

Final approval is contingent upon an invitation from a reputable university or research institute abroad.

"There you are! Any problems?" Wang shoved the papers back into the drawer, and pulled up his chair.

"Thank you, Vice Chief. I'd better go back to work."

He nodded and immediately lowered his head to return to his papers.

She walked back to her desk with a heavy heart. She wasn't sure what her commitment to the PAP-II program would entail. But she would try and work hard to get it done. What weighed on her more was the realization that she did not meet all the criteria for a visiting scholarship, let alone those for a "preferred" choice.

Two days later, after work she heard from Haosheng on the phone. "I thought you would never want to see or talk to me again," she said.

"Don't be cross with me. How are you?"

"What do you expect?...How about yourself?"

"I have been miserable," he said.

"Why?"

"Not seeing you," he said.

"I am here all the time."

"Saiyue, it's awkward to have the kind of talk I want with you through a wire. Do you mind if I come to see you now?"

"What a question! It's up to you."

"Wait for me?"

"It's up to you."

"Don't go for supper yet. Wait for me. I'll have it with you."

They ate at the Institute mess hall. He told her that some out-of-town relatives had come to visit him after he got back from the Institute that night.

"You had no time even to call?"

"True, I could have called you. But I didn't know what to say. It seemed that our relationship had come to a crucial stage. I wanted some time to think."

"Did you find the time?"

"Yes."

"What's the result?"

"I need you."

"Really?" She held back her smile, and changed the topic by telling him about the computer program challenge that she had to deal with. He followed her lead to talk about work and other ordinary things, thinking that a different place was needed for more intimacy.

"Can we go to your room?" he said to her lightly.

"My room?" She almost blushed. Chances are that Renmei wouldn't be there for a while, she thought. But what if…"We could take a stroll," she said.

They left the mess hall. Because of the chill the stroll soon changed to a walk and they reached a pavilion near the far edge of the campus. They went inside and kissed. But the air was simply too cold for romance. She led him to her office, where she let him put his hand over her bare breast under her shirt. When he tried to reach under her pants, she said, "Please don't."

He didn't want the episode of that night repeated. Suddenly, he said, "Saiyue, let's get married."

"Don't joke."

"I am not joking. I am serious. Let's get married," he repeated.

"Marriage is serious. I would have to think about that. Have you thought about it seriously yourself?"

"Didn't I tell you earlier that I had time to think?" he said.

"You are serious. Aren't you?"

"Yes."

"Now *I* need time to think," she said.

Later in the evening, she mulled over Xu's proposal. An engineer who would work in a "Department of General Affairs" probably isn't a very good one. Basically he is an athlete. When his basketball days are over, he could well prove to be just some sort of a hanger-on. I shouldn't rush into things.…The big cat-like movements on the court and the slick muscles appeared in her mind's eye. How many chances does a woman have in landing a man like that? And she remembered the pressure of the thighs and that warm thing strangely soft and hard at the same time! She felt ashamed of the thought and her face heated. Then she glanced at her computer science book. Is marrying him going to give me a better life? Would marriage tie me down and encumber me so much that I won't be able to go abroad for a graduate degree—and be the first in the Zhang family of Changshu to do so? Or…would it actually help—for a visiting scholarship.

She wrote to her family in Shanghai to ask for their permission to marry Xu.

Her father was a civil engineer, her mother a middle school teacher. During the years when Saiyue grew up, they were occupied much of the time by numerous political learning sessions and neighborhood meetings. Her grandmother had died before she was born. Her grandfather was her childhood nurturer. He had come from Changshu—some 45 miles northwest of Shanghai—attended and graduated from St. John's University, an American Episcopal missionary school in the metropolis, and taught senior high school English and history. After his retirement before the Cultural Revolution, he had devoted most of his energies to helping his only son and daughter-in-law to raise their three children: Saiyue, her younger brother and sister. He was particularly fond of Saiyue and had tutored her English and exposed her to elements of Western culture including Christianity. He told her that she had the stuff to excel and to shine among the Zhang clan of Changshu.

Saiyue's request for permission to marry was only nominal. The decision was hers to make. However, her elders all expressed their trust, support and blessing in whatever she would decide. Her grandfather's postscript drew a faint smile underneath her furrowed brows, as she read, "I also trust that you've taken into careful consideration your long cherished wish of graduate studies."

She answered Xu in the affirmative. In quick order permits were obtained from the "marriage desk" of their respective work units. The Institute could provide her with only one room like the one she was sharing now. In effect, she'd be sort of exchanging Renmei for Xu. The Mill, on the other hand, would allow the couple to share with another family a two-room apartment with a small kitchen and a toilet room. Since this would mean that she, rather than he, had to commute to work, Xu left the decision to her. She thought that while they could manage at the Institute dorm as a couple, it would be too inconvenient when a child arrived. She chose to share the apartment in the textile district.

They took out their marriage certificate at the neighborhood administrative office, and had a modest tea party in the conference room of the Institute. They decided to postpone the one-month matrimonial vacation, that the rules allowed, for a future trip to visit their parents. She also wanted to complete the PAP-II task as soon as possible.

On their wedding night, Haosheng, mindful of the experience of the Spring Festival Eve, was patient with her. He tried to prepare her by touching. In spite of all the curiosity, excitement and passion, the critical stage was a little painful for her. Then the sensation of flesh against flesh intensified. After his climax, she was surprised that the male passion could flag so abruptly. She could enjoy a little sweet talk, but he just went to sleep. She smoldered only for a while, feeling, all in all, it was a delicious new experience.

When they first moved into the apartment and met their apartment mates for the first time, Saiyue recognized the husband to be Xiao Mei, one of the young men in the train compartment. However, both acted as if they had never met before. The Xus settled down quickly in the new environment, aided considerably by their congenial apartment mates. Now to go to work, she would take the No. 3 Bus to the Bell Tower and change to No. 5 Tram, and after getting off that, it would only take a five minute walk to reach the Institute. When the weather was agreeable, she would bicycle to work. At a workday's end, it felt salutary to exercise the legs that had been confined under the desk for so many hours. She would first head north on Chang'an Road, east on Youyi Road and follow again a north-then-east right angle course. After passing the neat and tranquil zone of colleges and schools, and a stretch of about two kilometers of rural road, she would reach the "Textile City."

The district, encompassing several major textile mills, was indeed like a city into itself, having its own schools, hospitals, theaters, restaurants, etc. The shared apartment was at the southeast corner of the housing section, on the third floor of a six-story concrete building with two units of identical apartments per floor.

The early married life seemed a continuous bliss. They made love practically every night. For a while she behaved as though she wouldn't mind it if her life would never change as long as she got to return to her husband every evening. Each time sensing his climax, she would arch up her pelvis, her hand pressing his buttocks hard down toward her. He was pleasantly surprised by her proactiveness. She would ignore his joking about her "appetite" and his recalling that episode on the Spring Festival Eve—"I would never have thought that you'd enjoy this so much."

In two months, that appetite dropped precipitously. She ceased to be the initiator. But, as a rule, she would still respond to his "coaxing," for he was a male who was hard to resist.

— 5 —

It had been three months since Saiyue was told in the Institute clinic that she was pregnant. She had returned home last night after a weeklong out-of-town assignment. This morning she needed a pen to address an envelope for a letter to her Shanghai family. Having lost her own on the trip, she looked for Xu's. He was in the toilet. Not finding it in his black handbag, she reached into his jacket, felt the pen, but also the sharp corner of a folded paper. Curious, she retrieved and unfolded it. It had a letterhead: "Electricity for Modernization, Bulletin of Northwest Electrical Company." On it were lines of delicate, graceful calligraphy suggesting that of a female:

Oh, where, where? The cold, cold! Silence, silence!
Sad, sad! Woe, woe!
Hot and chill, it's so hard to quiet down.
How could a few flat drinks
Fend off the dusk winds that blow!
The wildgoose is gone! How sad—I've known him so long!

The yellow petals gathered aground, wan and sallow.
Who would have them now?

41

How am I to last till dark, alone by this window.
On the plane tree the raindrops fall with the black—
Drip, drip! Tap, tap!
How could all this be told in a single word—sad?

She restored the find. In the evening she said to Xu, "I lost my pen on the trip. This morning, I looked for yours in your jacket and found a sheet of paper with a poem on it. Who wrote that poem?"

He blinked. "Oh that? Let me see....Li...Qingzhao wrote it," he said casually.

"The name sounds familiar. A man or a woman?"

"She was a poetess in the Song dynasty," he said, as though it was a punch line.

"Em....Who copied it on that sheet of paper?" she pursued.

"Cao Rushi did."

He is telling the truth, she thought. "How come you have it?"

"Don't get too excited."

"I am not excited. Just curious."

"It's like this. The other day, Lao Diao, one of our senior accountants, asked me to join them in a farewell party for Xiao Cao. She is leaving the Mill for good to go to Tianjin."

"How come? Is she being transferred there?"

"Not exactly. Her husband has been transferred there."

"Her husband? You didn't tell me she's married."

"Just recently, several months ago."

"Oh. Her husband there at the party?"

"He was already in Tianjin."

"I see. Just you and she, the two of you?"

"How could that be?! Didn't I tell you Lao Diao organized the party? There were a number of us. But after some had left, let me see—five or six remained. We had some more refreshments. Yes, the topic of poetry got into the conversation—"

"I didn't know you are interested in poetry," Saiyue interrupted.

"Don't mock me. It's Lao Diao, who likes to dabble in that stuff. Every so often he pens an 'oil-fetching' poem for the Mill Bulletin. Xiao Cao said she liked Li Qingzhao's poems so much that she often copied them for amusement. She gave one to each present there. I happened to have that one."

"What happened next?" She recalled the bespectacled man and his nasal chanting on the train from Shanghai.

"We all left her apartment together."

"Really?"

"That's the absolute truth!" The uninflected voice seemed to vouch for the words' veracity.

"How come you didn't tell me about the party?"

"You only got back last night.... Come on! Don't fret. She won't even be around here anymore."

"Who's fretting! Just conversation. So she has got a new work unit in Tianjin in order to be with her husband?"

"Yes."

"That's not easy." Saiyue nodded her head. "They must know some big shots. Eh?"

"In fact, her husband is sort of a big shot himself. He used to manage one of the factories of the Northwest Electrical Company. According to Lao Diao, his father is a member of the State Council, and one of his uncles is on the Commission of Military Affairs. Both had been on the staff of Marshal Nieh in the North China Region during the Revolution."

"No wonder," Saiyue said.

"Lao Diao intimated that it's not all through family pull though. This guy is reputed to be a pretty able administrator."

"Have you ever met him?"

"Just once."

"What's his name?"

"Ju something, I forgot. But apparently he is better known as Ju Tiger. That's easy to remember."

"Quite a catch for your girlfriend," she said.

"But there is a catch." He widened his eyes at her.

"What's that?"

"He is a fucking arrogant son of a turtle! Maybe that's how he earned the moniker of tiger. Certainly not from his shitty appearance!"

"Watch your language. Why get so excited?"

"I'm not. He is a good head and a half shorter than his wife, and he hardly needs make-up to play a clown in a Beijing opera."

"Not everyone can be as handsome as you, you know," she said.

"Give me a break! Not everyone is as lucky as I am either."

She let the topic go.

One evening a few days later, as she was picking up in the kitchen, readying to leave it, Xiao Lin, Lao Mei's wife, standing by the door, said, "Take your time. I am in no hurry, just need to boil some water. Lao Mei isn't home yet."

"I noticed in the past several days you two had your supper late."

"Yeah, it'll be that tonight again. You'd think if people work overtime, they'd at least provide supper. So, not only the worker has to eat late, but the wife too. I don't mind this for a day or two. But it's been four days in a row now that he comes home late, hungry and all pooped out."

"That much work would tire out anybody," Saiyue said.

"Yeah, I know....He has not been of much use for me lately," said Saiyue's buxom apartment mate with narrow eyes and narrow hips.

Saiyue smiled at the last comment, but didn't want to follow the drift. "I am sure he will get his reward sooner or later," she said.

"Reward! What reward?" Xiao Lin sounded a bit agitated. "Those certificates of merits! A sheet of paper a year. He hasn't even bothered to hang up last year's. Could you exchange that for half a kilo of rice or half a bottle of cooking oil?"

Saiyue thought Xiao Lin was rather bold to disparage the certificates of merit. But times had changed. The ideologues had long gone from the seats of power. Deng Xiaoping, the pragmatic supreme leader, had visited America and, wearing a funny looking cowboy hat, he even hobnobbed with the capitalists. It was not surprising that the people too had become more openly pragmatic. "Not just that," Saiyue said. "I understand there are talks about bonuses or vacations in Beidaihe."

"Hum, vacations at resorts are for big officials. Bonus? I've to see it to believe it," Xiao Lin snorted.

"Anyhow, I think a hard worker like Lao Mei will be recognized. It is a matter of time." Saiyue meant to cheer up her friend.

"Now talking about hard worker, your Lao Xu is no slouch either."

"How would you know that?" Saiyue intoned.

"Well, I do. A few days ago before dawn I had the stomach cramps. I got up to have half a bowl of rice, and here he was—just returning home. Lao Xu told me he had to work through the night to meet a deadline on some report for his department. Talking about working hard! Oh yes, you were out-of-town," Xiao Lin added innocently.

Stammering an indistinct affirmative, Saiyue hurried back to her room, knitting her brow.

Later on near bedtime, the dormitory compound was quiet. The night news was being reported on TV in low volume. "Have you ever worked overnight at the office?" she asked casually, doing some maintenance work on a metal pot.

"No, not for my kind of job," Haosheng answered negligently, sewing back a button to his uniform.

"Really?" she put her hands down and fixed her eyes on him.

Reading her long face and screwed lips, he suddenly remembered. "Oh, oh yes. There was that night…I had to. Just a few days ago…not had to. But a colleague in the Shipping Department asked me to help, because, er…they had a deadline to meet and were shorthanded. I figured, what the heck, since you were out of town, I helped them. It never hurts to sow a few seeds of goodwill, you know." He nodded to himself to augment the good sense of his opinion.

The haltingness of her husband's response revived her earlier suspicion; and the different versions of the overnight work virtually confirmed it. "You think I..." she said with knotted brow, giving the last loose screw of the pot a vigorous turn. Her stomach, which had been simmering all evening, boiled like a cauldron, but her face was cold as ice. "...The International Monetary Fund and the World Bank...report from Washington..." The newscaster was looking right at her. She caught herself from saying, "I am a damn fool?" This is serious, she thought. If I press and he admits, then what? Divorce? I have carried the child in me for five months already.

"I see....I see," she said slowly to her husband to end the subject.

Later on in bed. "Let me smell you," he began his coaxing.

"I am tired," she said.

"Come on! Let me smell you!" He moved his head toward hers.

"I told you I am tired!" she jerked away.

The tone froze him from further efforts. His head back on his own pillow, a luscious Cao Rushi faded in.

After World War II ended, Nanjing reclaimed its status as China's capital. Xu Haosheng's father, a native of the city and an electrical technician at its power plant, was recruited into the Communist Party near the end of the Civil War. In 1952 he was sent to work in the party apparatus in the southern metropolis of Guangzhou, where he met and married a local party functionary, who used to be a physical education teacher. There Haosheng was born two years later, and grew up, inheriting his father's good looks and mother's athleticism. His father gradually rose to be a middle rank cadre in the early seventies and succeeded in bringing about a transfer back to his hometown. After high school, Haosheng worked in an electrical manufacturing factory for two years before he was selected—with the help of his father—to study in Central China Technical Institute. He completed a program in Industrial Engineering with a mediocre academic record, because he had no desire to do any better. His devotion was to basketball. The results showed—captain of the school varsity team and a first stringer of the city team. Like many of those endowed with natural talent, to whom success comes easily, and being an only child, he had developed a kind of bon vivant outlook. After college, he was assigned to the Third National Cotton Mill in Xi'an. He served as a staff member in its General Services Department, dealing with such matters as space utilization and travel. It was understood that he'd play a leading role on the Mill's basketball team while holding an engineer's title.

When Xu first met Cao Rushi, like most bachelors (and some married men too) in the Mill, he was enthralled. Unlike others, he was not intimidated. He pursued her with his considerable male assets and practiced skills. They became intimate within weeks. He was the more gratified to discover—in her bed in an afternoon when her mother was out of town—that Rushi had been a virgin until then. Since that time, she began to speak of marriage, a topic he would deflect. Subsequently, he found it wearisome that he had to make the effort to evade it at almost every date. Thus even before Zhang Saiyue arrived on the scene, he had already started weighing what he did enjoy with Rushi against what he didn't.

On the Friday following that post-ballgame party where he first met Saiyue, he told Rushi that he had to cancel their date on Sunday because he needed to take care of certain business with some relatives who would be coming from Nanjing.

The next Monday after lunch, as he was leaving the mess hall with some colleagues, he saw Rushi walking toward them and beckoning him with her eyes. He told his colleagues to go ahead and waited for her. She came and said, "Let's go outside." Under the eave near the end wall of the building where there were no others near, he began, "What's the matter? You look out of temper."

"You lied to me! I saw you yesterday with a companion." The tone was severe.

"What are you talking about? I didn't see you anywhere yesterday," he affected calmness.

"You were so attentive to your woman companion. How could you even cast a glance at a moving bus. You two were coming out of the Chang'an Theater. Weren't you? Who was she?"

Although surprised, Xu was glad that Rushi did not try to trap him. "My relatives didn't come as planned. Lao Lo invited me to watch the movie with his girlfriend. They did not show up. They had also invited a colleague of theirs. She is new in town, from Shanghai. It must be she that you saw," he said.

"O! From Shanghai! Should I be impressed? Only a fool would believe your lie!" Rushi huffed, turned around and walked quickly away. Although she did not have much of a lunch (or a decent supper the night before either), her anger propelled her quick pace. In a while she slowed down, hoping he would follow and catch up, and offer some more convincing explanations. None of that happened. She hid herself in the lavatory for a considerable time to shed her tears and then compose herself before she returned to work.

In the days following, she looked for him secretly in the mess hall, but didn't see him there or anywhere else. The disappointment and sadness were almost unbearable. She fought off—with the help of her mother—urges to contact him. The mother told the daughter that Xu was only a second rate athlete—first rate ones would have been called to Beijing and accommodated luxuriously by the central government. His good looks were but an embroidered pillow—filled with straw—and her beautiful and talented daughter deserved better.

That after-lunch confrontation served only to embarrass Xu briefly. In fact, he was relieved that the desired result was accomplished with practically no effort on his part. For now all he needed to do was to avoid Rushi and let the state of affairs consolidate. So he started to have lunch in a small eatery just outside the Mill. In the meantime, he felt emancipated and free to court the fair young woman from Shanghai. As previously told, things went rather smoothly for him until that Chinese New Year

Eve. After Zhang Saiyue checked his advances, he biked out of the Institute compound with a bruised ego.

The well-lighted Chang'an Road was virtually deserted. Along both sides of the street, some windows were still illuminated over dark facades in patterns like game boards. The pops and swishes of firecrackers propagated clearly in the cold night. He pedaled slowly northward with his head tucked down between raised shoulders.

What a way to start a New Year! he thought. Those warm lips, musky scent, drove me crazy. The firm breasts, like unwrapped *zongzi*, white, warm and firm—Dragon Boat Festival[15] came for me with Spring Festival this year? And the milky belly! What a body!...Then the next moment, those chilly eyes—like ice age is upon the earth!...Quite a woman, pretty, talented, studious, good voice, and what character! Tough character!...Never met anyone like that before. My judgment and moves never failed me before either, even with Rushi. With some others, I wasn't even the initiator....But this Zhang Saiyue is no common fish. But she is hooked. That's for sure. It's a matter of time when to take her in. Maybe she is getting the idea she is too hot for me. Let her cool off for a while and then she'll find out what she has missed. Yeah! We'll see!

A big pop from a firecracker hit his ears. He accelerated his legs.

The holidays were over and the Mill returned to normal operation. Xu decided to return to the mess hall for an early lunch. Afterwards he looked around and saw Rushi at a table with her colleagues of the Accounting Department. He sauntered over and saluted them cheerily with the season's greetings. She barely acknowledged him. He left and waited outside the mess hall. Later when she came out by herself, he went up to her and said, "How are you?"

"What do you care!" Rushi said.

"Your father home for the holidays?"

---

15. Dragon Boat Festival falls on the 5th day of the 5th lunar month. On that day *Zonzi* (glutinous rice wrapped in bamboo or reed leaves) is eaten, and boat races are held in many towns and cities.

"Of course." She kept walking.

"I haven't seen your parents for some time. I suppose I should go visit them and pay my respects for the Spring Festival."

"The holidays are over."

"The Old New Year season lasts until the 15th, you know."

"They are not expecting you. Save the time for your Shanghai girlfriend."

"Don't talk like that," Xu said pleadingly.

"What am I supposed to say! You disappeared for weeks. Now you want to offer season's greetings." Rushi wanted to reject his offer to visit, but she couldn't. "Suit yourself. I have work to do." She hurried off.

The next day Xu appeared at an olden style "four closure"[16] house in the Electrical Technology District in the west part of Xi'an. Rushi's mother had one of its rooms as her apartment. Xu crossed the courtyard and reached the door, carrying four apples in a flimsy red cardboard box. Hearing people talking inside, he knocked. Rushi's mother opened the door, seemed surprised, hesitated for a second and said over her shoulder, "Xiao Shi, it's Xu Haosheng." He heard vaguely a response from inside.

"Come in," Rushi's mother said.

As he crossed the threshold, "Aunt Cao, I have come to pay my Spring Festival respects," he said. "You are being too polite," she said. Rushi's mother, a writer for the Bulletin of the Northwest Electricity Company, possessing still considerable middle-aged female charm, spoke and moved her tallish person in a neat gray cotton jacket and pants with deliberation and a certain grace. He noticed that not only Rushi and her father were in the room, another man was there. Xu had a pretty good idea who the man was. There was something incongruous about him. He had a dark flat face, small eyes and the general physiognomy of low station. Yet there he sat, by the table, his shoulder squared, head raised, exuding a confident presence and authority. Xu greeted Rushi's father and Rushi. The former,

---

16. A house having four sides around a courtyard. Often the exterior wall with the main door constitutes one side, and rooms or apartments form the other three.

a graying man with weary eyes and a weary smile, introduced the stranger to him:

"This is Vice Director Ju....Vice Director, this is Xu Haosheng, a *colleague* of Xiao Shi at the Mill." Xu stepped forward to the official and extended his right hand halfway. Ju, remaining seated, merely nodded at him, a cigarette stayed between the fingers of his stationary right hand. Xu retracted his stiffly and turned to Rushi's father, saying, "I thought I should come and pay my Spring Festival respects to you and Aunt Cao."

"You don't have to do this. Very few of Rushi's *colleagues* do."

Turning to Rushi's mother, Xu offered the box of apples. "This is a little something for you and the family."

"You don't need to do this. Between *colleagues* there is no need to give presents." She accepted it politely.

Xu suddenly noticed that on the table lay a whole smoked ham wrapped in shiny waxy carmine paper, showing the characters, "Jin Hua," its famed place of origin. There were also a finely wrapped box, looking like the kind used by "friendship shops"[17] and two large cans of American instant coffee tied together by red strings. He surmised that the items were gifts from the Vice Director. It would have been less embarrassing, had he not brought over anything at all. But it was too late.

After a few uncomfortable minutes of small talk, during which Xu felt like an intruder, he was somewhat relieved when Ju seemed to be addressing Rushi's father alone, "Regarding that matter we were discussing earlier, I think it is quite possible. I'll look into it. Please be sure of that."

Rushi's father thanked him and began to speak in low voice to the Vice Director, ignoring everybody else in the room. Xu turned to Rushi, saying lightly, "You know I got a new bell and brand new tires for my bike. Would you like to see them?"

---

17. Shops for goods that only money exchanged from foreign currency could purchase.

"A bicycle bell and tires? Now?" She made no move to follow his hint. Although he liked to think that she was not the mocking type, he felt hurt.

Her mother addressed Xu, "Pardon me for interrupting," and then to her daughter, "Xiao Shi, would you go get the garlic? We ought to put it in the chicken now." Xu thought he had smelt of a fragrance of cooked meat, mixed with cigarette smoke in the room.

Rushi left the room. Embarrassment turning to rising anger, Xu quickly bid the others goodbye and went out. When Rushi came out of the neighbor's door with the borrowed garlic, she saw Xu crossing the gate of the house. She hesitated for a moment and hurried over to and out of the gate. The lane was empty. Well, he knows where to find me. Perhaps it's Heaven's will that I should put the happiness of Ma and Pa first.

— 6 —

A lazy September afternoon, denizens of the Xi'an Petroleum Institute leaving the mess hall sauntered on the paved path, most heading for the dormitories in the compound for a short nap before returning to work after a two-hour lunch break. It had rained last night. The sunlit emerald leaves of the elms, standing handsomely by the footpath, exhaled freshness and induced some who looked at them to take a deep breath, their chests out. The lunch had featured the biweekly mutton, costing 25 cents more, which most of them were happy to pay. Although one could buy meat from the market, it would be more expensive and often too fatty. They were still relishing the meat scent with ginger, garlic and anise taste in their mouths.

Vice Chief Wang Tang'yi was not in a mood to enjoy such ease. He had been in a meeting called by the Director. Now he was rushing to return to his office to prepare for yet another meeting this afternoon. However, he had a message to deliver first. He saw in front of him a young woman walking apace with small steps toward the main building, passing her co-workers inconspicuously. She paid no attention to the people around her or the row of pots of pink and red geraniums along each side of the entrance—still blooming brilliantly in the waning summer. When I was young, he thought, they never had engineers so delicate-looking and yet…

The woman's pace slowed after she got inside. As she was about to take the stairs, she glanced at an oversized poster, which had been there on an easel for almost two weeks. It announced in large characters: "LECTURES ON CONTINUUM MECHANICS, BY PROFESSOR LU PANZHE, THE TECHNICAL UNIVERSITY OF CALIFORNIA, U.S.A.," followed by smaller ones giving the dates, time and place.

Wang knew she was going directly back to the office to work. It had been three years now, and she had hardly ever taken advantage of a benefit available to every staff member not living in the Institute compound, i.e., to have a midday nap in an allocated berth in the dorm. Xiao Zhang deserves to be on the list, he thought. Zeng Lihong is a victim of flimsy technical training, too weak in fundamentals. She tries, and a nice person too. That wouldn't be reason enough to have her name on the list. Can't ignore Lao Zeng though—not that he is Vice Director, but we have been colleagues for so long. And he had behaved decently at my denunciation meeting, while others spat on me. It'd be embarrassing if I paid no heed to his urgings on behalf of his niece. Still, being a widow, she'll be considered single. That would put her at a disadvantage. Besides, I don't think either her uncle or her Worker-Peasant-Soldier University background will cut any ice with the Director. He seems to be adamant on considering only graduates of key universities....Now Li Zhongchi is a different case; he is just outstanding. Ambitious too. Two sides of the same coin. Xiao Zhang is like him in that way. But Li has a longer track record and his Qinghua University background should also help him.

One flight up the wide stairs, the hallway was illuminated only by the reflected natural light diffused from the staircase well. He entered Saiyue's shared office.

"Xiao Zhang, you are back," he said. As expected, she was alone.

"Yes, Vice Chief Wang," she stood up, giving her back a straightening. "You didn't go resting for a while? Any instructions?" she asked. Several years ago, the participation in installing PAP-II on the computer turned out to be not nearly as difficult a job as she had thought. The computer laboratory people had no problem in getting the program on the system. All she needed to do was to study the manual and run the sample problems, which were well documented. Since then, Vice Chief Wang had regularly asked her to work on special projects. For about a year now, she had been reporting to him.

As he apparently appreciated her work performance, she had developed a sort of admiration for him. She had learned that during the Cultural Revolution, he had stubbornly refused to cooperate with the then leadership to inflate the accomplishments of their work unit. Subsequently, he was accused of being a rightist and a capitalist fellow traveler and was sent to a "cowshed" for rectification. Saying that it was for the good of their children, his wife divorced him. Apart from sympathy for his past misfortune and esteem for his integrity, Saiyue also had much respect for Wang's technical knowledge. This she had not expected earlier, because, for most work units, the vice chief, generally the unit's Party Secretary, who controlled all personnel, financial and other administrative matters, usually would not be versed in the unit's technical functions.

"I have to prepare for a meeting later. I do want to tell you something I think you'd be glad to hear," he said, his weather-beaten and normally serious face breaking into a smile, showing his cigarette-stained teeth.

"What's that?"

"The Department has included your name in a list of three that have been submitted to the Institute leadership as candidates for Visiting Scholars."

"Visiting Scholars? Really?" A fever surged to her head, and she was stunned for an instant. "I don't know how to thank you," she said.

"I wouldn't be overly anxious just yet. I think that at best only one from our Department would be picked this year. The other candidates have seniority over you. But it'll help your case in the future to have your name brought up now. Be patient. I hope you get it someday. Any problems?" After his tag line, he left.

She wanted to resume her task at hand—to review for the Vice Chief, certain sections of the proposed new design criteria for storage tanks, sent by the Ministry of Petroleum for the Institute's comment. She was usually confident of her ability to concentrate. In her younger days, she could study even amid the drums and gongs of Red Guards entering the neighborhood. In college, gabbing roommates or even a loud radio wouldn't distract her. But this afternoon was different.

Early this week she had been trying to pick a time to talk to Professor Lu Panzhe, the short course lecturer from America, about her wishes for graduate studies there. Unexpectedly, Vice Chief Wang had asked her, on behalf of Chief Liu of the Department of External Affairs, to be the professor's tour guide after the completion of the lectures. She would be a substitute for Xiao Zhou, the regular guide, who had just had an appendectomy. She had helped him before, when two Americans from Houston, Texas, had come to discuss drilling bits and other machine parts, and she was asked to go with him to give them a tour of the area. So she decided to postpone approaching the professor until she would have established a closer rapport with him through the oncoming tour.

Past experience had taught her not to be too sanguine about such efforts. She had attended seminars presented by foreign experts before. However, her approaches to the speakers had been unfruitful so far. Once, after she had talked with an American professor and apologized for having been so bold as to bring up her aspirations, the burly redhead said airily, "Don't apologize. I have received these kinds of requests at every school I visited in China. Students approached me every which way. I wish I could help...." She did not doubt the truth of his statement; nevertheless, she felt a bit small and quite embarrassed. She resolved to be more circumspect.

The problem was that she needed *financial* assistance. If she had a visiting scholarship, all she needed would be an invitation from a reputable host institution to make her dream come true. Such a request should be quite proper, certainly more proper than a monetary one. Not this year, perhaps the next, even another year after that would be fine, she thought.

She opened a lower drawer in her desk and took out a letter, which she had received this morning and had read it only cursorily before going to

Professor Lu's lecture. It was from a former neighbor, classmate and good friend, Yan Yifeng. The Yan family used to live on the first floor of the three-story house, of which Saiyue's family occupied the third floor. Saiyue recalled how, in those days of want, her throat would sweeten when about once a month she smelled the redolence of a chicken being slow cooked on the Yans' stove. Neighbors gossiped that the Yans must have a well-to-do relative in Hong Kong, who sent them money regularly. But Yifeng hinted to Saiyue that the money actually came from her mother's sister in the "Beautiful Country,"[18] via an intermediary in Hong Kong. It was intended for the remitter's parents, Yifeng's maternal grandparents, who were living with the Yan family. Later on, the Yans moved out into a new apartment assigned to them. Yifeng's aunt and her husband were to come from the United States to visit, and the authorities didn't want them, and the country, to lose face on account of inferior, cramped housing. After Yifeng graduated from college, she went to the United States for graduate studies sponsored by the aunt. She had since taken a master's degree and now worked for an engineering consulting firm in Boston, Massachusetts. She and Saiyue had maintained correspondence, albeit with decreasing frequency.

Through the years, Saiyue had developed some ambivalence toward letters from this friend. Each one seemed to mark an advancement—small, perhaps, but distinct—of the writer's career in the United States: her first class, first paycheck (for two weeks' part-time work equaling about 10 times Saiyue's monthly salary), final grades of her first term, her master's degree defense, her H-1 visa to allow her to work full-time, her first day on the job, etc. Sure, Saiyue was happy for her friend's progress. But contrasting it with her own situation, she couldn't help feeling frustrated.

---

18. The Chinese characters for the United States, pronounced "Mei Guo," mean "Beautiful Country."

Now, she reread the latest letter, paying particular attention to the part, "…Although my means are limited, I do have some savings. If I can be of help, please let me know. Don't stand on ceremony with your old friend…."

The visiting scholarship candidacy distracted Saiyue all afternoon. On her way home, her bike almost sideswiped another near the South Gate, and it would have been her fault. For the rest of the way she had to admonish herself a few times to concentrate on the road and not to think about the looming Beautiful Country.

Inside the dormitory compound, she parked her bike and walked to pick up her son at the nursery. Xu Ming, two years old, was among the younger ones there. The little boy, moon-faced and bright eyed, ran unsteadily, with his body turned obliquely and arms flailing, up to meet his mother, while she and a supervisor called out "Be careful! Be careful of falling!" She caught him as he plunged into her open arms. Lifting him up from her crouched position, she felt the warmth of the toddler's buttocks exposed through his open-crotch pants.

They returned to their room in the shared apartment. The bed, under a mildew-stained ceiling, lay along the wall facing the door. A table stood flush against the opposite wall. On the table sat a small television and two thermos bottles and several pairs of chopsticks in a glass with renderings of two pandas and bamboo sprays. A wicker chair looked on the TV. The child's crib took the corner between the bed and a window. In the corner at the other side of the window was a straight-backed chair, under which was stored a rolled-up comforter, and on which squatted a wood box, opened at the front side, showing a few books and magazines. On a red and white plaid plastic sheet that lay across the box top, a dome-shaped wire screen covered several bowls.

"You like to stay in the crib and let Mama start supper?"

"No, no crib," the little boy shook his head, nonstop.

"All right then, if you promise not to get off the bed, Mama will let you play on it."

He nodded and was let loose on the bed, as his mother handed him some toys of geometric shapes from a small box underneath the crib. She bunched her hair behind her back and rolled a rubber band over it. She went to the window, retrieved the wash, that had been done the night before and hung in the morning on the outside clothes-poles (supported by a slender framework extended from the exterior wall), and dumped them at one end of the bed.

She slid out the dish that was under the wire screen, and sniffed at it to make sure that the pork strands cooked last night with the pickled mustard green had not spoiled. From under the bed, she took out a wok and a roll of dried noodles stored in a tin box. Usually it was her husband's job to start the stove; but today, he had basketball practice and would be late. She took the boy along with the cooking articles to the kitchen. In it each family had its own stove and a small cabinet to store such items as briquettes and bottles of soy sauce and cooking oil. The room was so small that when there were two people inside, only one should bend at a time, lest their behinds or some other parts of the bodies would bump. So generally the families took turns in its use.

She stuffed two crumpled sheets of old newspaper into the stove, placed some kindling over it and topped them with briquettes. Warning the kid to stand behind, she lighted the paper. The toddler, pointing to the flashing flames, squeaked: "Hot, hot," jiggling up and down on his bent knees.

"That is right! It'll hurt if you get too close," she warned. Although the window was wide open, the smoke still stung their eyes. She carried him in her arms and watched in the narrow hallway until the briquettes began to catch. She went back to the room, folded the wash, and returned to the kitchen. The briquettes had stopped smoking and a flame flickered in the middle. She boiled some water and put the dry noodles in it. The pickled mustard green with the pork strands was warmed in the wok and spread over the cooked noodles. She banked the fire with a moist mixture of crushed briquettes, cinders and clay, and placed over it a kettle filled with water. Realizing the Mei couple had already returned, she hurried to leave the kitchen.

She made a cup of tea, and sitting at the table, she chewed a chopsticks-hold of the food to a soft bolus before feeding it to Baobao (the boy's pet name, meaning "Precious"). In between the feedings, she also partook of the noodles herself with the tea. Afterwards, she turned on the TV and sat in the wicker chair holding the boy in her lap, cheek to cheek, rocking slowly from side to side. Within seconds, he squirmed free and started to knock about in the scanty space.

After the news had ended, she drew a well-worn enameled washbasin from under the bed and took him to the shared toilet room. With the boy standing over a wash area bordered by elevated cement edgings and a floor drain in the middle, she washed his face, hands, and buttocks, herself crouching next to a floor toilet.

"Now you are all cleaned up."

"Baobao clean," he said, letting his mother move his legs stiffly, one at a time, to put his pants back on. They returned to their room.

"Papa?" the boy asked.

"Papa is having basketball practice. He'll be back soon," she said. "You can go into the crib now."

"Sing song," he demanded.

"All right. Which one?"

"Grandma Bridge," the boy began to rock.

"All right. Here we go. 'Swing, swing, we swing to Grandma's Bridge,'" she sang while rocking the little boy in her arms. "'Grandma calls me a good Baobao; she gives me a piece of gaogao (cake) and sends me to bed.' All right, into the crib now."

"Gaogao, gaogao?" he turned to look at her with his eyes open wide.

"You little rascal! Never forget the gaogao part. All right, you'll have a piece and then into the crib you go."

"Gaogao!" he commanded forcefully.

She got a piece of biscuit from a bag in the wooden box and handed it to him. She sat down again in the wicker chair, holding the munching boy in her lap. On the TV a Chinese classical dance was being performed by a female troupe. "So slow!" she said disapprovingly. The little boy turned his head around and goggled at her, saying, "Baobao slow?"

"Yes, you eat slowly. You should. Mama was talking about the dance up there." After he finished the biscuit, she put a diaper—made from a worn-out shirt of his father's—on him, laid him in the crib and covered him with a frayed blanket, "You'll be Mama's good boy and go to sleep now." She kissed him on the cheek.

"Baobao sleep....Baobao sleep," he said. Shortly she heard him make light shrill sounds—bearing some resemblance to singing.

Today, like most days since Baobao was born, she had been laboring essentially nonstop after getting up at daybreak. Turning off the TV, she slumped into the wicker chair. The little boy was quiet now. She knew he had his thumb in his mouth and was falling asleep. Amid the evening cacophony in the dorm of TV, radio, squabbling, laughing and cater-wauling disguised as opera singing, she closed her eyes to rest, and to decide what to wear tomorrow....

"How come you are sitting in the dark?" Her husband had come in and turned on the 30-watt bare bulb, dangling from the ceiling.

"Just resting," she said.

He went to the crib. "Still sticking his thumb in his mouth while sleeping, he'll have buckteeth when he grows up," he said.

"He is so young. Don't worry....The noodles just need warming up."

"I know." He took the thermos bottles to the kitchen to have them filled with boiled water. After he ate the warmed over noodles and tidied up the kitchen and himself a bit, he plunked in the wicker chair to watch television.

His wife dragged out her suitcase from under the bed and took out a yellow taffeta polka-dot dress, her best one, which she had brought back from her last visit to Shanghai. She wiped her hands on the side of her pants, spread the dress out on the bed, and tried to smooth it with the hands. Then she hung it on a hanger, regarded it and frowned. "I better borrow Xiao Lin's iron," she said to herself.

Watching her busying herself about, he asked, "Some special occasion on tap?"

"Didn't I tell you I am going to be the tour guide for that Chinese American expert. Xiao Zhou is sick. Vice Chief Wang asked me to take his place."

"O yes. I forgot," he said. "So you'll have a couple of easy days and good food," he started to light a cigarette.

"I've asked you so many times. Don't smoke in the room. If you don't value your own or my health, think of Baobao. Won't you?" she complained.

"Just for relaxation....All right." he put the cigarette back in its box.

"You can relax without the cigarette, or go outside to smoke." After a pause, she continued, "You know, this afternoon Vice Chief Wang told me that they have included me in the list of candidates for a visiting scholarship."

"Candidate for a visiting scholarship! Hum, that's great! To where?"

"America."

"Did he tell you when you can go?"

"No. It just means that my name is in the pool. From what he said I gathered that I don't have much of a chance this year. Perhaps next year."

"There'll be competition, I am sure."

"Don't tell anybody," she told him.

"I know. People go about this sort of thing quietly. A couple of fellows in our Engineering Department studied on the sly. The silent mania of going abroad. Well, congratulations!"

"I haven't got it yet. In fact, there is no assurance I'll ever get it. But it is a step forward."

"As I see it, you are almost halfway there. Hum, that's nice. Your hard work seems to be paying off."

"All for a better life."

Is life in America, for a poor Chinese scholar, necessarily better? Xu thought. I heard that there are those who sleep on benches in railroad or bus station waiting rooms, wash dishes, waiting on people in restaurants, sneaking their own dollar bills as "decoys" on tables that customers had just left—as examples of tipping. How degrading! Here people wait on me. I am somebody....But then, those who return do not exactly come back with empty hands either.

"You can at least bring back the 'four big items.' What are they now? A refrigerator, color TV, washing machine and...O yes, a sewing machine," he said.

"That's not much, frankly speaking. As I told you, if I get there I'd like to get an advanced degree, find a job and earn some money....Perhaps even stay on for a while. I suppose I am getting way ahead of myself, dreaming perhaps."

After a moment, as she was finishing up with the ironing, he asked, "How old is this Professor Lu?"

"I think he is close to my father's age." She finished with the ironing, hung the dress at the back of the door and left to return the iron.

After she came back, he said, "Perhaps I should also try harder," fixing his eyes on the yellow dress, curling his tongue between the lips. "But then after my work at the office and basketball, I don't have much time." He wasn't sure in what direction he should try harder. He was vaguely aware of the possibility that a good American high school team could give his team a tough time. He just felt that he had to say something like that to his wife. Then he pictured her in that yellow polka-dot dress showing her curves.

A soccer game between a Pakistan team and a Chinese team came on the TV. "Soccer is the slowest, most boring game on earth. Let's go to bed." Grunting, he stood up, took a sip of the tea and stretched lazily. He knew the nodes of his arm muscles, creeping like the back of a stalking leopard, had that desired effect on women, the wife included.

"I understand it is also the most widely watched sport in the world. But I won't miss it either. I had thought I'd write a couple of letters tonight. They can wait."

After they got in bed, he rolled on top of her. "Give me a kiss," he said.

In the darkness she frowned. "Say, you have to haul in the briquettes soon. Haven't you noticed we are almost out?"

"Talking about this sort of thing now?"

"We can't feed ourselves without them."

"Okay, I'll do it tomorrow. Now give me that kiss," he said.

"I may have to walk a lot tomorrow."

"You are a strong woman."

She gave him a kiss. "All right. Now you get off."

"We'll see about that," he said and began to pull her pants.

"You did it day before yesterday."

"I am a vigorous young man. Some of my friends do it several times a night."

"You should keep better company." She yielded, like an anesthetized animal.

His spirit spent, he rolled down to sleep. He heard her getting up to wipe herself and saw her moving to the door to feel the ironed dress. He closed his eyes and thought of the succulent and responsive Rushi. He felt sore, realizing that that arrogant son of a turtle would be lying right beside or above her.

— 7 —

Wearing the yellow polka-dot dress, Saiyue attended Professor Lu's last lecture, sitting demurely, as usual, at the back of the room. After his concluding remarks, the applause, his answer to the last question, and another round of applause, the participants began to drift out of the door. Chief Liu and Saiyue came up to him. Liu, in his 40s, heavyset in a sharp Mao suit, introduced her in his courtly manner as the professor's tour guide, substituting for his assistant Zhou, who was still recovering from an appendectomy.

"Yes, of course Engineer Zhang and I had met and talked before. She had made me more careful in my delivery," Lu said.

"Professor Lu is making fun of me. Sometimes I was too slow in catching his point," Saiyue said to Liu, and to the professor, "I hope you didn't mind my asking questions. But I have learned a great deal, indeed."

"You are very kind," Lu said.

Liu cocked his head toward her, smiling, "Well, in any case, the professor has done his work. It's your turn now." Then to Lu, "You will be in good hands. Don't forget dinner at 6:30 tonight," he said, tapping the air with his hand for emphasis, and left.

Saiyue found herself alone with the professor for the first time. She had of course regarded him before. Medium height, about 5 feet 8 or 9. Below a deep forehead and dark thick eyebrows, the eyeglasses with black rims obscured the crow's-feet at the corners of the eyes and the small patches of flabbiness below them. The eyes themselves were clear and somewhat large, and looked with a simple directness—as Vice Chief Wang would often do. But with the professor, the directness seemed constant. They were so different from the shifty, or obscuring, or wary ones that she had come to meet regularly in her life thus far.

His easy, confident and open manners during the lectures made her wonder to what kind of family he was born, and in what kind of environment did he grow up. When introducing him at the first lecture, Vice Director Zeng had mentioned that the professor had graduated from college in 1958. He should be around 50. He still had a full head of hair, hardly any gray, and his skin still smooth.

The navy blue suit always appeared to be just pressed; the blue tie with slant scarlet stripes accentuated the white shirt with buttoned-down collars, wrinkle free and spotless. She had a liking for the looks of men's dress shirts from America. Somehow, the collars of Chinese brand western styled shirts did not quite have the same flair.

"Professor Lu, there is much to see in and around Xi'an. And we have a day and a half. Are there any places in particular that you would like to visit?"

"I am totally at your disposal. But I hope we'll have a chance to view the terra-cotta warriors of Emperor Qin's Tomb, and the Stelae Forest."

"Yes. Those two, of course. I believe we have time to cover most of the more famous sights. Suppose today we visit some sites in the city and tomorrow go to Lintong, where the Qin Tomb is. What do you think?"

"That sounds excellent."

"All right. Then, suppose I meet you in the lobby of the Guest House at, say, 1:30."

Lu Panzhe had lunch in a small dining room reserved for *foreign experts* in the Guest House of the Institute and returned to his room. Taking off his suit and dress shoes, he lay on the bed to rest.

When he was a Chinese literature major at National Taiwan University, understandably he had an ardent wish to visit the major cultural centers of China. That wish had not diminished in spite of the fact that, in deference to future job opportunities, he had changed his major, first in Taiwan, to physics, and then, at the University of Illinois, to Theoretical and Applied Mechanics. Later on, even though his academic career at the Technical University of California demanded practically all his energies, that wish had only lain dormant. What overshadowed it were mainly the political realities of those years—the *bamboo curtain* and the adversary relationship between the United States and the People's Republic of China.

However, one evening in 1972, as he, now an American citizen, watched President Nixon step off the ladder of Air Force One onto the tarmac of Beijing Airport, he felt then like a married woman watching her father-in-law entering her own parents' house for the first time. In subsequent TV coverage, the ancient Great Wall and the graceful West Lake beckoned him.

He had learned, since junior high school, that Xi'an was the cradle of Chinese civilization and the political center of the Chinese people till the end of the Tang dynasty (907 A.D.). He was particularly impressed by the fact that the two most famous Chinese poets, Li Bai and Du Fu, along with a number of other major poets, such as Wang Wei, had taken residence there. The thought that his ancestors had come from Xi'an—a fact he had no proof but his father's word—had given him a measure of secret pride. Then, of course, there was the recently discovered Emperor Qin's Tomb with the amazing terra-cotta warriors.

Now, he found himself, lying abed inside this perhaps the most Chinese of the major cities of China, obligations to his host discharged, with nothing more to do but to enjoy the forthcoming tour. In this state of anticipation, the image of a young woman would flash across his mind. At first, she had reminded him of Chong Kimoon, whose memory had begun to blur some lately.

It was at an "International Night" program at the Union of the University of Illinois that he first saw Kimoon, playing the piano. At the following party, he found out that she was from Seoul, Korea, daughter of a librarian and a master's degree candidate in library science. Her high cheekbone, delicate feature and demure demeanor represented to him the quintessential oriental beauty that he had fancied in his reading of Chinese novels and listening of Chinese classical music. A vigorous courting ensued. With some help from his prosaic but earnest poems composed in Chinese, in which the Confucian librarian's daughter had a fairly good grounding, he succeeded. They were married the following year, living frugally on his assistantship.

That was over two decades ago in the corn-rich land of Lincoln. Now on the good earth of Emperor Qin, he came upon this young woman. The first time he noticed her, she was sitting there in the back of the lecture room. It was a serene and inviolable presence. It inspired in him a feeling almost like that when he first heard Schubert's *Ave Maria*. Then, on several occasions later into the short course, she had come to him to ask questions. Intelligent ones too, with respectful smile. Now she was about to be his guide.

He thought that now he understood what some poet had written, "delicate skin with a healthy glow, eyes clear as the lakes in Jiang-nan's spring, eyebrows graceful like a hill line over the waters." Perhaps it was the romanticism he had associated with this old capital of poetry that had stimulated his attention to this person. He admonished himself that she was not only a stranger, but obviously, of his daughter's age, and he could do better than indulge himself in an *old man's fantasy*. He got up, put on a pair of slacks and tennis shoes, took the travel bag and came downstairs to the lobby.

Zhang Saiyue was already waiting in one of the chairs along the wall. She rose to meet him, saying, "I hope Professor had a chance to rest after lunch?"

"I did. I am sorry to have kept you waiting."

"Actually I was a few minutes early. If you are ready, shall we get started?" She led him to a car parked in front of the building. She made to open the back door for the professor. Instead he got to it first, opened it, stood aside, saying, "Please."

"I'll sit in the front," she said, stepping backward, a bit awkwardly.

"Please sit in the back, that is, if you don't mind," he said. She went in and squeezed herself in the far corner.

After Lu got in, "This is Professor Lu.... This is Lai Shi-fu,"[19] she did the introduction for the guest and the driver of the car, who had been sitting mutely at the wheel.

"How are you?" the driver said blandly, barely turning around to give Lu half a look.

"How are you, Lai Shi-fu? Thank you for the trouble of taking us," Lu said.

"That's all right," Lai answered hollowly. He looked like a discharged or straggling soldier, wearing an unbuttoned brownish frayed and stained military overcoat, which seemed much too warm for the day. His shirt was rumpled and yellowish—which might be the color of the fabric, but more likely, the result of soiling from use. Hair disheveled, and a cigarette hanging from a corner of his mouth, he clearly didn't think much of his assignment this afternoon.

"We'll rely on your service now for these two days," the professor tried again. There was no response. To improve the atmosphere, he turned to his guide, "Engineer Zhang, are you a native of Xi'an?"

"No. I came from Shanghai."

"Shanghai! Interesting! I heard that, as a relatively new city, Shanghai had very few real natives. Most Shanghainese actually had come from other places," he said.

---

19. "Shi-fu" literally means "master," but it is also used as a generic polite appellation for a skilled worker, service person, etc.

"That is true. But I was born there. My grandparents had moved there from Changshu."

"Changshu, I had read of it. It was referred to as a place of 'green hills and graceful waters,'" he said.

"I have been back there with my grandfather a number of times. I would think that the area probably deserves that phrase," she said.

He thought that the place was also known for its beautiful women nurtured by the serene natural environment. But he didn't say it. She in turn asked about his birthplace, and the polite conversation continued.

"Madame Lu has not come with Professor on this trip?" She felt slightly self-conscious after saying this.

"My wife died four years ago—in an automobile accident."

"That was most unfortunate. I am sorry."

"Thank you." A pause. "Engineer Zhang, where did you go to college?"

"Tongji University in Shanghai."

"Good school. What was your major?"

"Mechanical Engineering. I am with the Department of Machinery and Facilities. Thus, as I told you before, your lectures interested me very much."

"Thanks. What are you working on these days?"

"Mainly having to do with storage tanks, piping and the like."

"Very interesting. Your family still in Shanghai?"

"Yes....My parents still live there....Well, you see the Bell Tower is right in front of us." The slight stumbling in her speech passed unnoticed.

The Bell Tower with its pyramidal roof and flying eaves at three levels was over 100 feet tall, not including its massive 30 feet high base. From the height, they viewed on this partly sunny day the dense dark roofs of the city's older low lying houses resembling sea waves, penetrated hither and thither by modern high-rise buildings like oil-drilling rigs. Leaving the Tower, Lai Shi-fu drove them through the downtown area featuring the large department stores on the Big East and Big West Streets. As the professor started to wonder when he would get to see some really significant sights of Xi'an, his guide said, "We are now going to visit the Museum of Stelae."

At the museum, they walked through the "Stone Classics," (the classics literally carved in stone) which included some 650,000 characters on 114 stelae. The next group of tablets contained the calligraphy of the masters of the "regular script (Kai Shu)." Lu stopped in front of a stela, and gazed at it for a while, first with a serious and awed expression, and then a faint amused smile. "When I was young in Taiwan," he said, "I used to copy these lines during my summer vacation nearly every morning before the air heated up. The dignified strokes seem even more powerful here in stone." It was the calligraphy of Yan Zhenqing.

"I like his forceful strokes too," she said. "I prefer it to, say, the delicate form of Liu Gongquan. I believe the stela bearing Liu's art is just a few paces down."

Later after looking at the "Nestorian Tablet," they came to the group of stelae showing the five main types of Chinese scripts, from the ancient "seal characters" to the "cursive hand." Viewing the artistry of Wang Xizhi and the Monk Huai Su, masters of the cursive style, the professor said, "Imagine, most of these masters lived in the Tang Dynasty—Wang even preceded them by several centuries—and their artistry, like the Tang poems, has not been surpassed."

"I can hardly decipher Wang Xizhe's writing, let alone imitate his style," she said.

"Neither can I. I suppose you don't want to either; it's just against the instincts of an engineer, who would desire a clear, stable form, and clean, regular lines. These calligraphic styles remind me of some Western modern paintings."

"You mean that an engineer shouldn't try to be artistic?" she asked.

"No. As an engineer, one should get the specified task done in the most practical manner. If it turned out to be artistic—for some eyes—fine. If not, fine. He need not be concerned with the idea of art."

"I see what you mean. I am glad to hear that. I would be at a loss if I had to defend my design, say, of a derrick, on an artistic basis."

"Of course you don't have to. On the other hand, you never know. Art is not always created consciously as such," he smiled. "I suspect that anything worked at with deep enough thought and dedication could turn out to be 'artistic.' For example, some ancient structures, even the Great Wall, the great bridges of the world, and the modern jet plane—created mainly for utility purposes—are all pleasing to the eye and could stir the heart strings. For me, anyway."

It makes sense, she thought and told him so.

Leaving the museum, they rode on Chang-an Road for a few kilometers and stopped at the Da Yan Pagoda (The Big Wildgoose Pagoda). The structure was on the grounds of a Buddhist monastery. The driver, as throughout the tour, stayed outside as they went in with tickets that Saiyue purchased.

The air smelled sweet and a bit thick. Far off over the horizon, cloudbanks hung with scattered luminescence. The pagoda had seven levels with square cross-sections. Each level featured an arched opening in every face. Crossing a paved path, bordered by locust trees with begonias and geraniums underneath, they entered the monument from the south side.

A spiraling timber staircase led them up in gentle rises. At every level, the doors and transoms were adorned with fine sculptures and carvings of Buddha figures in faded red and blue, some backgrounded with lotus and nimbuses. When they reached the fourth level, she suggested they have a look around before going on to the top, presuming a break would be good for the older professor since the exertion had even warmed herself.

He followed her toward the opening on the east side. A knot of young soldiers, apparently off duty, were loitering about. One of them saw the two approaching, said something to his companions, and the group started to leave.

"Please don't hurry. We can wait," she said to them.

"We are done," said the one who first noticed them. She thanked them as they ambled past.

"Courteous people, aren't they," Lu remarked.

"Yes, soldiers of the People's Liberation Army usually are," she said. At the opening, they both took a deep breath in the breeze. "You see this expanse of greenery. It used to be a scenic area through which a river meandered before it emptied into a lake," she commented, her hand sweeping an arc over the verdure underneath. Below the yellow polka dot sleeve, the white wrist recalled for him the lines of Wei Zhuang:

Like th' moon she stands by the wine urn;
The white wrists are like frost and snow.
Unless old don't you north return.
Your heart'll be broken if you go.

"In olden times," she continued, "royalties and high officials built villas there amidst the flora and streams that were fed by underground springs. In fine weather, ladies decked with flowers and scholar-officials supplied with wine would all come out to enjoy the day. It was told that Du Fu wrote his 'Song of the Beauties' about them."

"I remember that poem," he said, almost eagerly. "It begins: 'On the third of the third month, fresh is the day./ By the waterfront Chang-an beauties walk gay./ Alluring, aloof, mild-mannered and true,/ Smooth skin on fine figures, bone, and muscle tone./...'"

Smiling, she looked at him with her right eyebrow raised a little.

He saw her in an ancient Tang flowing-style costume, but stopped short of blurting out, "Du Fu could be writing about you." Instead, he said, "As you know, most of Du Fu's poetry is on the somber side, but that poem is one of his more light-hearted compositions. By the way, I don't see any lake," he said.

"It's long gone. In the Song dynasty, a canal that fed the lake was cut off, and this place pretty much dried out except for the small streams flowing from underground springs. Now a number of orchards still flourish down there.…I heard recently that the city has been studying plans to restore this area into a major tourist center. A canal would be rebuilt to draw water to make a lake. In fact, it was reported that some investors from Hong Kong and Australia are interested."

"Hong Kong and Australia? Umm.…" he sounded impressed.

"Professor, have you ever been in Hong Kong?"

"Yes."

"What's it like?"

"Well, it depends on your perspective. It's quite modern. But if you are a Chinese, particularly a non-Cantonese, the place has the most exasperating street names.…I believe that Emperor Qin's Tomb is in that direction. Right?"

"Yes.…Why are the Hong Kong street names exasperating?"

"They represent English names transliterated into Chinese characters to be pronounced with the Cantonese accent.…"

"Umm.…Have you ever been in Australia?" she asked.

"No. I was close. Went to New Zealand once.…So on the horizon must be the Li Mountain range. Right?"

"Yes, we'll be visiting that area tomorrow."

They resumed walking up the stairs. The room at the top level was considerably smaller. Wind whistled around the structure. "Engineer Zhang, do you hear a tinkling sound?"

"Yes, it comes from the bells hung at the corners of each level. They ring in the wind."

There were a few visitors standing by the openings. The southern one soon became vacant and they went over. Pointing to the far horizon, she said, "Beyond are the Qinling Mountains—in this region they are also known as the Zhongnan Mountains. The mountain folds are now half shrouded in that blue haze."

He did not respond right away but squinted into the distance, nodded slightly and muttered, "Yes…indeed."

"What is it, Professor Lu?"

"Do you know that, Cen Shen, a contemporary of Du Fu, had written of the view from here?"

"I don't. You mean the view from this very pagoda?"

"Yes," he wiped his hand over his face and said, "He wrote: 'Mountain chains are like heaving waves/ Of the river rush eastward to the sea./.../Autumn color creeps from the west,/ As the midland still waxes green./...' Now I understand what he was talking about."

"I presume Professor Lu likes poetry," she said.

"Yes, I do—in a rather superficial way."

"You are being modest," she said. "Professor Lu, do you write poems?"

"No. Not any more. I tried a little some time ago. But I embarrassed even myself, and I stopped."

"I can't imagine you having the time."

"I'd like to think that's one of the reasons. But not really. If I had the talent, I might be tempted to emulate Cen Shen as he concluded that very verse: 'I vow to hang up my hat of office/ And follow the Way to Infinity.'" He raised and spread his hands toward the infinite space outside, and then retracted them behind his back.

Saiyue watched his arched thick eyebrows and thought of "Mountain chains are like heaving waves." For an instant she imagined the professor in a loose rippling gown of the classical Chinese scholar.

"But we all have to make a living....Sorry, Engineer Zhang, I am boring you." He smiled thinly.

She blinked and said, "No, not at all. This is very interesting...and educational for me." Her fingers—which he noticed were long and white—were trying to rein in some loose hair trailing in the wind. Their eyes met squarely for the briefest moment.

He followed her to the north opening. "Here you can see most of the city," she said. "Of course, the broad boulevard is Chang-an Road, running north-south. In the middle there is the Bell Tower—where we were. Beyond the city, you can see the Wei River flowing from the west to east."

Lu stood still, viewing the landscape. In front of him had been the site of so many kingdoms. Beyond the spread of the city and the dark green stretches of farmland with brushings of tree lines and huddles of dwellings here and there, the Wei River glimmered faintly like a belt of smooth lead. Indeed, Xianyang, once the ancient capital of the Qin Empire, was right across the river. It had flowed for millenniums, irrigating the valley and nourishing the people that were his ancestors.

After they exited from the north side of the structure. She suggested that they take a break at an eatery. The place was small, but styled with sculptured columns and carved beams and paintings on the wall, ostentatious in red and gold. They sat at a small table by a window, which framed a clump of pines afar and a flowerbed near.

She ordered green tea and a dish of thinly sliced cake with powdered sweet osmanthus flower.

"Professor Lu, are you tired?"

She is treating me like an old man, he thought. "No, I am not. By the way, why is it called 'Da Yan Pagoda'?"

"I am not sure. I was told that Yan (wildgoose) probably had something to do with the legend that Buddha turned into a dove. In the times of Tang, the wildgoose was the people's favorite bird. So probably the dove was changed to a wildgoose."

"I wouldn't have guessed that."

The refreshments came. He insisted on pouring the tea for her. "But I am supposed to be the hostess here," she said.

"I am not used to having a young lady pouring tea for me," he said matter-of-factly. "I thought that traditionally, in Chinese literature, wildgoose symbolizes a longing of someone far away."

"I believe that's true. Professor, are you missing someone far away in America?" She surprised herself with the question and tried to cover it up with a bold smile.

"No, that is not the case." He also smiled, to hide his surprise.

His even tone told her that he was not offended or annoyed. For all his seeming nostalgia for China—those poems and all—she thought, he is not Chinese. A Chinese professor would have been disturbed, at least outwardly by my question.

The professor continued, "But after I return to America, I might be thinking of a wildgoose."

She had not expected this. Disquieted, she almost blushed. She fumbled to say something. "How long has Professor lived in America?"

"Let me see....24 years."

"That's a long time."

"Before you were born, I suppose," he said quietly, gazing at the pines outside the window.

For a moment she was tongue-tied. Finally she said, "We better be getting back so that you can rest a while before the dinner."

At the banquet, toasts were offered and responded to. Some of the more junior members of the Institute, taking advantage of the free food and drinks, made among themselves a boisterous occasion of it. Lu was contented with polite chats with Vice Director Zeng and Chief Liu. Saiyue sat at right angle to Lu at the round table for twelve; at times their eyes would meet and a faint smile flit past each other's face.

Next morning, awakened by his wristwatch alarm, he shambled over to the window. He made out in the sunless dawn that the bicyclists outside the compound were wearing ponchos. He thought unhappily, of all days, it has to rain today!

By the time he finished breakfast, the rain had subsided to a light drizzle. He waited in the lobby. Around 8:30, Saiyue walked briskly in, wearing a blue cloth jacket with the collar of a crimson shirt laid over it, smartly pressed light gray pants, and sneakers.

"Good morning, Professor Lu. Are you ready to go?"

"Good morning, do you think the weather will cooperate with us?"

"It's just a very light drizzle now, more like a mist. I think it'll be all right. The forecast says that it'll turn fair later on. The car is ready."

She didn't even carry an umbrella. It had indeed brightened considerably. So had his mood.

"Good morning, Lai Shi-fu," he greeted the driver, who replied with a guttural grunt, barely moving his lips and the toothpick in between. Lu wondered, What's the matter with this guy? What did I do to him? He had a notion to ask his guide about it, but when he turned to look at her, she was expressionless. He held back. The car started to roll out of the compound.

"By the way, we will visit the City Wall before leaving for Lintong," she said.

"That'll be nice."

"As you probably know," she continued, "Xi'an is one of the four famous old capitals of the world. It has the most complete city walls among the ancient cities, including such capitals as Beijing and Nanjing, which are considerably younger."

"What are the other three famous old capitals of the world?"

"I believe, they are Cairo, Athens and Rome."

"Hmm....One learns something new every day, even though old," he said light-heartedly.

She took his "old" as referring to the cities. "I think you knew those cities and were only trying to make fun of me."

"No. I wouldn't do that. I know those cities, of course, but not in that connection," he chuckled.

"Not knowing that! A scholar like you?" She demurred, but resumed her guide duty. "The city walls were first built in the Tang dynasty. Through the ages, maintenance work had been done on them sporadically. About a year and half ago, the city started to refurbish it. We are going to have a look at the East Gate area."

The "Gate" was an imposing building some six stories tall with curving eaves at two levels. Covered with dark blue brick facing, the wall itself seemed to be some 40 feet high. The drizzle had virtually stopped.

Although it was still overcast, bright silvery splinters poked out of the slate-gray clouds on the west. Only a few buses stood on the wide parking lot. The tourist season was on the wane, and the weather had not been enticing either.

On top of the wall, Saiyue pointed out that beyond the stretches of mist-covered fields was the Li Mountain. Close by, sloping from the top of the wall was an extensive glacis, covered with stone slabs at some sections, and sodded at others. A moat girdled the foot of the glacis. Several boats, each with two or three people, moved leisurely about. A few more were tied to docks. Between the wall and the moat, trees had been newly planted—as betrayed by their sparse foliage.

The wall seemed wider than it was high, and battlements jutted from it a distance about the wall width. "I wonder how they determined the spacing of these things?" he asked.

"You mean these 'horse faces,' or battlements?"

"Yes."

"I understand that basically, they were so arranged that the defenders could counterattack the invaders from three sides. That being the criterion, then the range of the arrows and such could determine the spacing. That's what I think. But, I am not sure." Smiling, she shrugged and cast him a playful glance.

"That sounds reasonable," he intoned contentedly.

They walked into a room over a battlement in which were exhibited weapons of ancient warfare: spears, swords of various lengths and designs, battle axes, maces, chains and barbed balls, hammers, halberds, and, of course, an assortment of bows and arrows—all designed to kill or maim, or at least to inflict pain. He gazed at them, and heard battle cries, and screams and groans, and then, the words of a poet: "If you fight, you'll be killed by your enemy. If you run, you'll be beheaded by your commander!"

Leaving the City Wall, the car headed east. After crossing a river—the Chan River, she told him—in about ten minutes, they traversed another bridge. "This is the Ba River. The bridge, well-known through the ages, is called the 'Soul-melting Bridge.' In olden times, it was where the traveler would say goodbye to those who had accompanied him from the city to see him off on his journey."

"That's a little depressing, but the name is apt and poetic," he said.

"Of course, if one likes Chinese poetry, this is the place."

"I know."

In less than an hour, shops and mongers' stalls began to appear by the roadside. "We are entering the town of Lintong. We will pass it now and go first to visit the museum of the terra-cotta warriors of Emperor Qin's Tomb. After that, we'll return here to visit the Huaqing Palace."

8

Coming out of the large arched structure that covered the excavated terracotta warriors, Lu said to his guide, "They are truly a wonder. Imagine these full-sized figures were created over two thousand years ago."

"I am impressed by the fact that they have those different attitudes and countenances: some determined, some belligerent, some thoughtful, and some even serene," Saiyue said, using the descriptions for the second time since she had prepared them for the two visitors from Houston, Texas.

It had brightened considerably. The tour buses glared in the sun's lances through cloud holes. The trees and vegetation luxuriated in deep late summer green. At the car, they noticed Lai was munching on an ear of corn.

"You must be hungry," she said after getting in.

"You eat when you are hungry," he grumbled.

"Perhaps we can have lunch next," Lu suggested.

They returned to Lintong and stopped at a restaurant close to the entrance to the Huaqing Palace grounds. The driver joined them. A waiter poured tea and stood by.

"Let's have some beer," Lai said expansively, lighting a cigarette with a bit of ceremony, "and some cold dishes to go with it." A shadow swept past Saiyue's face with a contraction of the eyebrows.

"How many bottles?" the waiter asked.

"I could have a glass or a small bottle," Lu said.

"Professor, this restaurant is noted for a special item, called the Guifei chicken. It takes a little more time than usual. Would you like to have that?" she asked.

"Since Guifei is also the name of the restaurant, it ought to be their specialty. If we are not in any particular hurry, why not try it?" he said pleasantly.

"Good," she said, and turning to the waiter, completed the order of drinks and food.

Shortly the waiter brought the beer and four cold plates, including a dish of threaded processed jellyfish. Lai put his cigarette in an ash tray, poured the beer into a glass, elbow tilting high and wide, and quaffed. He wiped off the traces of foams on the stubble above his upper lip with the back of his hand, shoved a piece of the jellyfish into the mouth, stuck the cigarette back between his lips and began to chew noisily, his right eye half closed to fend off the smoldering smoke.

She now regretted having proposed the time-consuming Guifei chicken. Before she could think of something to say, Lai, after blowing out a whirl of white smoke, addressed the guest,

"Professor Lu, we all know that America is a very rich country. Life there is easy and luxurious. Professors get lots of money and lots of respect. You must have a wonderful life out there. Is that right?"

Lu gave him a quizzical look, paused for a moment and said, "Life in America is not *that* easy, certainly not for professors of engineering. But like most of my fellow citizens, I make a decent living from my work."

"Ah, professor, you are being too modest! Decent living? Your standards are not like ours here, particularly us drivers'. We lead a tough life. We watch other people have fun, ourselves just waiting around, hours upon hours. When we do our work, driving, we have nothing but responsibilities—for the safety and comfort of our passengers, honored guests like you. And you wouldn't believe how poorly we are paid," Lai said.

Lu now figured that Lai was fishing for a gratuity, which was officially forbidden. He uttered a few words of appreciation for the efforts of Lai, and all the drivers in the world.

Saiyue blinked her eyes to calm her resentment against her colleague's crassness. She steered the conversation to the weather and the cold plates, and eagerly looked for the waiter to appear with the main dishes. Finally, they did come.

Lu and Saiyue finished their meal while Lai was taking his time over the food. They left him to enjoy it leisurely.

"I suppose you have read much about the Huaqing Palace?"

"Not much. Practically all I know about it is from Bai Ju'yi's poem, *A Song of Everlasting Sorrow*," he said.

"But there is more to this place than the romance between the Tang emperor Xuanzong and Yang Guifei."[20]

"On that point, don't you think it regrettable that a businessman would use 'Guifei' to name a restaurant and its special chicken dish. It vulgarizes the tragic romance so beautifully told in Bai's poem," Lu said.

"Well, that way they make more money....Don't you have the same sort of thing in America?" Saiyue said.

"I am afraid we do," he chuckled.

"Professor, just a quick word about this place. The features of this whole scenic area are based on the lay of the Li Mountain range. It is a spur of the Qinling Mountains that we saw yesterday. The area covers some 30 square miles. Its variable topology largely resulted from several geological faults, which also gave rise to the numerous hot springs that feed many of the ponds in this region," she recited.

They crossed the entrance marquee. A pond spread in front of them, set off by the greenery and colorful structures around and across the water.

---

20. "Guifei" means royal concubine. Yang Guifei, whose name was Yang Yuhuan, was Emperor Xuanzong's favorite concubine. Involved in a rebellion, she was forced to commit suicide by the Emperor's army. Her story (including her mythical afterlife) was told in Bai's poem.

"This is the Huaqing Pond. The whole complex with the halls and villas in this area were first built in Xuanzong's reign," she said.

They walked over a terrace to the edge of the pond, trimmed by a stone ledge that had statues of mystic animals squatting at the corners. Near the water's edge, pink water lilies with curled petals ensconced themselves on jade plate-like foliage.

"Beautiful!...Those whitish vapor patches hovering over there, do they indicate hot springs underneath?" Lu asked.

"I think so."

Across the pond, gargoyle-like animals rode on the concave roof ridges of a pavilion. Below it and along the bank, bushy green willows drooped narcissistically to touch themselves in the water. Further away from the pond, the land rose to join the hills. With some focusing, Lu could see among the verdant tapestry half-hidden gray and golden rooflines, curving eaves and crimson columns.

They crossed the pond through a zigzag covered bridge having overhead beams embellished with paintings and carvings. Passing an arched gate, a small distance to the right, they entered an old-styled courtyard. "This is the 'Five-room Pavilion,'" she said, pointing to the house on the left. "Here was the temporary residence of Chiang Kai-shek before the celebrated 'Xi'an Incident.'"[21]

They followed two fellow sightseers up a few stone steps to peek into the front rooms of the house. "Chiang was sleeping here when Marshal Zhang's soldiers came to apprehend him. He escaped, initially. See these bullet holes? They were made during the operation," she told him, pointing to the window frame damaged decades ago.

"Yes," he nodded. "This must be his bedroom—just a stark bed, a small plain wooden desk, and a modest wardrobe. How austere!" He then

---

21. In 1936, Marshal Zhang Xueliang seized the then Generalissimo Chiang Kai-shek, leader of the Nationalists, in Xi'an and forced him to agree to desist from attacking the Communists in order to form a "united front" against the encroaching Japanese.

thought of Mao Zedong's bedroom that he had seen in Beijing. It, too, was similarly simple. Mao's bed, however, seemed larger, but string-stitched books of Chinese classics took up almost half of it. Thus the two arch adversaries had a common trait. It's not unusual for men who could command luxury to live modestly. Still, such austerity is particular. But their appetite would lie elsewhere—great feats, power....

Coming out of the Five-room Pavilion, she said, "A little distance ahead is a public bath house featuring flow from the hot springs. The bath reputedly has therapeutic value for a number of maladies, including arthritis and rheumatism."

"Is that so?"

"O yes....Would you like to take a bath there?" She gave him an impish look.

"I may be getting on in years, but I am not suffering from arthritis or rheumatism. Not yet. You are joking, Engineer Zhang."

"Yes, I was. I am sorry. But I didn't mean to imply anything about your health—you know bathers go to hot springs not always for health reasons." She looked down a couple of steps and then straight ahead, at nothing, walking a bit stiffly, swinging her handbag.

"There is no need to apologize. On such a pleasurable occasion, formality is not called for. I am all for fun too."

"Professor Lu, you have a way with words."

"Anyhow, about the bath, I'll take a rain check. Mind you, next time, I wouldn't mind having one here."

"Then, like Yang Quifei, 'Bathing in the Huaqing Pond chill of spring. The warm spring shower'd the slippery skin,'" she blurted out the couplet from Bai's poem.

"That's very nice," he said, smiling wryly and appreciatively. "By the way, speaking of Yang Quifei, where is the 'Longevity Hall'?"

"There is no such structure standing around here anymore. But the site is marked. If you don't mind some climbing, we can go up there."

"Of course not. That's what we, at least I, came here for."

They trekked up the winding path, laid with crudely worked stone slabs, in the mottled shade of overarching branches. They came upon yet another pavilion. On the plaque below the eave were carved the characters: "Zhuo Jiang Pavilion."[22] She commented, "This was built to commemorate the spot where Marshal Zhang's soldiers apprehended Chiang Kai-shek, who was then hiding behind a large boulder after he had escaped from the bedroom we saw earlier."

"This is properly a landmark of historical interest. But the pavilion's name sounds somewhat short on elegance, if not decorum," he remarked.

"It expresses the people's feeling," she said blankly.

"Of course," he played along. Freedom had indeed grown in China lately, but on matters having a political connotation it was still prudent to adhere to the official line.

On one side of the walk was a stall for cold drinks. Along the other, several women—shabbily dressed, with sunburned, wrinkled faces—squatted on the ground, trying to sell the small batches of scrawny pears and pomegranates set in front of them. When Lu remarked about a little child strapped at the back of an oldish woman as an amenable grandson, Saiyue told him that she was pretty sure it was the woman's son. The women were actually much younger in age than they looked because of the tough lives for some peasants. He wondered how much could each of them make in a day from selling those stunted fruits.

He bought a can of soda for each. The climb had warmed them. They took off their jackets, even though the air was cooler and the breeze more noticeable. After finishing the soda, they resumed their climb up the West Embroidery Ridge—one of the two ridges of the Li Mountain. From that point on, the path became steeper and poorly maintained. When it was awkward to proceed with two abreast, she would lead the way, a step or two ahead of him. On one occasion when she looked back to check on her

---

22. "Zhuo Jiang Pavilion" (Catch Chiang Pavilion) was later changed to "Bing Jian Pavilion" (Pavilion of Martial Plea), a more magnanimous and literary appellation.

charge, her right foot tripped against a tilted stone slab heaved up by woody roots, and she stumbled. He hurried and caught her.

"Are you all right?" he asked.

"I am fine," she said quickly. "I am sorry I hadn't noticed the slab was raised." She turned her head toward him and smiled. He could see her pinkish, somewhat fleshy upper lip stretching, thinning and curling upward at the corners, like a pink Chinese caltrop,[23] revealing the caltrop meat-like white teeth. Since she was flushed by the exertion, her blush wasn't noticed.

"We'll go slower," he said solicitously, and released her arms, which felt surprisingly firm.

"That's all right. I'll just have to be more careful myself. Actually I was trying to watch you. It's embarrassing that I should stumble."

"Why?"

"You are our guest and a 'senior,'" she said.

"Guest, yes. 'Senior?' Well, that too. I suppose I am getting on with age," he conceded light-heartedly.

A moment later, she said: "I heard that in America people don't like to talk about their age."

"That's pretty much true everywhere, I'd think, unless the person is at either end of the spectrum. In America, it is perhaps pathologically so. But this age thing is one that nothing can be done about, in China, America or anywhere else. It is the one item that nature is impartial to all," he pontificated.

"Professor, you may be senior, but you are not old. I mean you look youthful enough."

"Well! Thank you. As we say in America, 'You've just made my day.'"

---

23. Caltrop, or water caltrop (called *ling* in Chinese), is the fruit of a water plant, common in Jiang-nan. It resembles an elongated nut with a reddish shell having two (sometimes three or four) corners turning upward. Its meat is white and edible. The term "caltrop mouth" is sometimes used to describe a mouth with up-turned corners—implying a fine, engaging shape.

"Truly, besides, you take the slopes just as easily as anybody," she turned to look at him, nodding.

"Engineer Zhang, you've just made my day again," he tried not to look too obviously pleased.

They picked their way carefully in the flecks of sunlight through the leafage of the trees. They would sometimes sidestep a boulder that had fallen from the slope and sometimes hop over a tiny streamlet that shimmered like a snake's back.

At the first peak of the West Embroidery Ridge, a stone slab marked the site of a "warning smoke station" (to signal the approaching of invading nomads) of the Zhou dynasty (ca. 1027-256 B.C.). Crossing a col, at the second peak, they came to the "Old Mother Hall," a temple honoring the legendary Nu Washi.

"Of course, you know who she was," she said.

"Yes. She was the younger sister of the god-king Fu Xi, who was supposed to have taught our ancestors how to domesticate the animals. She had herself carried out a number of tasks of the 'move-earth-and-heaven' category, like tempering stones to mend a hole in the sky," he said.

"I am impressed you know all this. I came to hear of such only during my previous visit to this place," she said.

"But I have never, until now, seen a temple for her, and wouldn't have expected one here. I would guess that in modern times more people come to know about her from *The Red Chamber Dream* than from the mythology."

"I suppose that's true. But to me Jia Baoyu was nothing like a tempered stone that could help to fill a hole in the sky. He and the major female characters, such as Lin Daiyu, were so effete that I doubt they could survive in a modern competitive world."

"But to be fair, one has to consider the environment they were raised in. The portrayal of that feudalistic society is supposed to be a major contribution of the novel," Lu said. This young lady may look like Lin

Daiyu or Xue Baochai, he thought, but her mind is probably more like that of Wang Xifeng.[24]

They continued their trek onto the third peak, which was the lowest. There they found the "Grand Man Hall," honoring the philosopher, Lao Tse, who was deified in Taoism.

"Over there was the site of the Longevity Hall," Saiyue pointed to the right. There was no man-made structure but a grove of tall pines, the tops gently swaying against the sky, like sea plants in the blue waters of a lagoon.

"So this was where Emperor Xuanzong, ignoring the multitude of his concubines, ensconced himself with Yang Quifei." He gazed at the pines for a while, and recited under his breath the lines from *A Song of Everlasting Sorrow:*

Short was th' spring night and soon the sun rose high.
Th' Emperor wouldn't morning councils preside.
...
Three thousand beauties did in here reside;
Three thousand favors focused on but one.
...
The Longevity Hall, day sev'n, month sev'n,
In the still was whispered a midnight vow:
Up like two birds touching wings in heaven,
Or down, we'll be two sprays of the same bough.

He proceeded to walk toward the pines. She stood there watching him, like one watching a painter before his canvass. The silence was suddenly broken by a burst of cawing; two magpies darted from a treetop. Startled a little, the two souls followed the flight of the birds. Their black-and-white plumage glistened in the sun, and with almost touching wings, they

---

24. The shrewd and astute mistress who managed the large Jia household of the novel.

soared skyward, and then wheeling, banking to the west, shrinking gradually, finally disappeared.

He stayed motionless, as though his senses had joined the birds in flight. In a moment, turning around, he slowly walked back. "Perhaps we should go now. Lai Shi-fu may be getting anxious."

"Yes."

"Excuse me. Please let me take a couple of snap shots first." He crouched and snapped a frame of the pines, and another of the path whence they had come. Ready to return the camera to its case, he noted her standing there—serene, straight back, pleasingly curvilinear at other places, the goose-egg shaped face glowing in the sun and surrounded by black tresses laced with a hazy nimbus of golden threads.

"Could I take a picture of you?"

"Of course," she flashed her caltrop smile.

Halfway down on their descent, "By the way, I'd like to apologize for Lai's impertinence. Visitors have no idea how spoiled drivers are these days," she said. "His brazenness embarrassed me."

"That was all right," he said. "Certainly it was not your responsibility. I was told of the situation. The system is such that practically no worker can be fired. Although drivers don't control the use of the cars, they do operate them. And they could make things sticky for their passengers. It is human nature to take advantage of one's position."

"I am glad that you understand."

"All the waiting around *is* boring. I suppose he expects a gratuity."

"I don't know that. If so, he would not like me to witness it; neither would I," she said discreetly.

"I think he deserves one," he said, but held back the remark "in spite of his boorishness."

He found that coming downhill was harder on his body than going up. "I did not realize my knees would hurt coming down," he said.

"Are you all right, Professor?"

"I am fine. Just a little sore at the knees. Don't worry. But you seem to be all right," he said and added quickly, "Of course, you are much younger than I." He remembered that a number of times in his student days in Taiwan, and indeed, not that many years ago in Yosemite National Park, he had negotiated his way downhill like this. He couldn't recall he had felt any soreness in the knees then.

After exiting from the Huaqing Palace grounds, noting the car parked some distance away, she said, "Professor, why don't you get in the car first, I'll be back presently." She walked off toward the stalls, some already starting to close. He understood that she didn't want to witness what he was about to do.

Approaching the car and not seeing Lai inside, he stood there and waited. Wreaths of smoke rose slowly in the distance—the villagers started supper early in order to utilize the daylight. He turned to have another look at the mountain. In the slanting golden rays, the mountainside was a chiaroscuro of yellowish greens and cavernous shades, toward which a V flock of slowly flapping wildgeese were homing.

The emperors, the palaces and banquets…he thought. The scholar-officials, poets, and their ladies, all the splendor, the elegance, all the love, all the lust, all the longing and lonesome nights of the palace beauties; and then, the glory and treacheries of the generals, all the strife, all the blood and pain of the loyal warriors, that had come to and passed here in these hills and valleys. Where are they now? Any one of the thousands of faces of the Chinese men he had seen lately—including his own while shaving—could be on any of the terra-cotta warriors in Emperor Qin's Tomb, and no museum visitor would ever register anything unusual. What would his own face be like in 700 or 2000 years, or the next year?

The last stanza of Browning's *Love Among the Ruins* came to mind:

In one year they sent a million fighters forth
   South and North,
And they built their gods a brazen pillar high

  As the sky,
Yet reserved a thousand chariots in full force—
  Gold, of course.
Oh heart! Oh blood that freezes, blood that burns!
  Earth returns
For whole centuries of folly, noise and sin!
  Shut them in,
With their triumphs and their glories and the rest!
  Love is best.

"Where is love?" he let out a sigh.

"You are back. Isn't the scenery beautiful? I am sorry that I didn't see you coming out," Lai was behind him. "Hope you haven't waited long."

"It certainly is. I should apologize for having kept you waiting so long."

"It's all right. I am used to that. After all, it's my job," Lai said.

Lu thought he was kind of out of character, now a chap of veritable geniality. "Still, by the time we return to the Institute, it will be way past your regular working hours. But Engineer Zhang should be back very soon," Lu said.

They got inside the car. He took out Exchange RMB$30[25] and held the notes over the empty front seat. "This is for your cigarettes—a trifle to show my appreciation for your help in the past two days."

"Come on, Professor. This is hardly necessary," Lai turned his head to have a look at the money between Lu's fingers, but avoided his face.

"Please accept it, just a token of my appreciation for taking me around," Lu deposited the money on the seat beside the driver who had another quick glance at it.

---

25. RMB denotes "renminbi," currency of the People's Republic of China. Exchange RMB is a type of RMB bought with foreign exchange.

"Truly this is not necessary." His declination softened. As Saiyue was approaching, he picked up the notes and put them in the upper pocket of his military style shirt.

"Ready to go back now?" Lai asked as she came in.

"Yes, it's time to go back."

He lit a cigarette before he started the engine; and the passengers opened the windows. When they returned to the Institute, it was twilight. He left with the car almost immediately, leaving Saiyue and the professor by the stone steps of the Guest House.

"I am indebted to you for your hospitality," Lu said. "I'll send you some of the pictures taken during the past two days."

"It was my job. I very much enjoyed the last two days myself. Indeed, I'd appreciate having a print of those pictures with me in them, if it's not too much trouble." After a slight hesitation, "Do you have a few minutes before dinner? I would like to talk with you about some matter, if I may."

"Of course, perhaps we can have dinner together."

"No, thank you. I don't want to bother you that much. It would be inconvenient."

"There is no inconvenience for me. But if you prefer, we can talk in the lobby. I am in no hurry," he said. They went in the lobby and sat across a small table by the wall.

"Ever since I graduated from college, I have been hoping to go to graduate school. My work experience here at the Institute has further convinced me that, to keep up with modern developments in technology, and to deal with future ones, graduate studies are almost necessary. It's not just for the title of an advanced degree. Though we have graduate schools here, we know that those in America have more up-to-date programs and facilities. I am wondering whether Professor could lend me some help in this regard."

The question was not unexpected. He had encountered similar initiatives many times before. They had come from relatives, friends, their relatives and friends, acquaintances and even strangers. It had been his policy to respond purely on merit basis—help only for the academically worthy. He reminded himself to act fairly.

"I'll do what I can for you. So far as my own school is concerned, financial aid, such as fellowship, research or teaching assistantship is almost never awarded to new foreign students. Even for students who are already enrolled, competition is very keen."

"Financial aid would be wonderful indeed. I realize that it is difficult. However, I hope before long I would receive a visiting scholarship from my government. When that materializes, an invitation—even without a stipend—from Professor's school, as the host institution, would be very helpful to me."

"Oh, that should be easier," he sounded relieved. "How are your grades in college?"

"They average about A-minus," she took out from her handbag a document. "Perhaps Professor would like to take a look at my transcript." She handed it to him, and he eyeballed it.

"Your school has a very good reputation. I think that with these grades and your practical experience, chances are good that my department would agree to host your visiting scholarship. But I am just a faculty member. I can recommend; it's up to the administrators to act officially."

"I will be very grateful if Professor would give it a try."

"All right. You know my U.S. mailing address at the University. Write me a letter, stating your academic background, work experience, your objectives and the length of time you would like to stay. I'll take the case from there." He returned the document to her. They said good-bye, she adding her left hand to the farewell handshake to emphasize her earnestness.

He stood in the lobby and watched the svelte figure pass the door and melt into the dusk. After washing up a little, he went to the dining room. There was no other guest around. In the feeble yellow light, used dishes and cups lay about disorderly on the soiled tables. He located a clean one and plumped into a chair, the knees still aching some and legs feeling like stone.

A service person brought his dinner—three small dishes, a bowl of soup and another of rice and a cup of tea. Scenes of the past two days replayed past his mind's eye. Against a blue sky a lissome female, with a fair face bathed in gold light, tarried for a while. She seems as young as Sharon; why should I think this much about her? he mused. After his wife died, not that he had not thought of finding a new mate, but his job seemed to be an energy sink. Still, his relatives and close friends had tried to help. They introduced him to possibilities. In four years, he had met them across dinner tables. For one reason or another the opportunities had not panned out. (He had found one divorcee almost antagonistic toward the male race, a widow too inquisitive about his finance, a spinster too self-conscious. Then, there was that sharp and shapely broker of Merrill Lynch, who seemed to be bent on being his financial consultant and having him invest in the ML Capital Fund.) Now, the vacation is ending, the party is over, he thought. I am not sure I'll ever see this Zhang Saiyue again. He drank some tea and, taking up the chopsticks, began to think about packing to return to the real world.

— 9 —

After the usual hustle and flurry of domestic activities, Saiyue sat down at the table to write the letter that Professor Lu had suggested. Her husband, sprawling in the wicker chair, was watching a TV serial story on the life of a notorious gangster by the name of Du Yuesheng in the pre-Revolution Shanghai.

"By the way, how did the tour go?" Haosheng asked without taking his eyes off the screen.

"It went fine."

"Did the professor like it?"

"I think so."

"What do you think of the person, now having spent much time with him?"

"He is nice—no self-important airs, rather polite, actually."

"The old guy didn't get tired out or something?"

"No. Except when coming downhill, he complained of sore knees. Otherwise he seemed all right. It was—" She unconsciously gave her own left arm a squeeze to recall the faint pressure or pleasure she felt when the "old guy" grasped it as she tripped. "...Strange, you know, throughout the tour, not a word about science or technology or mathematics. Yet a real bookworm, quoting literature and poems right and left," she said.

"Maybe he wanted to show off, impress you."

"Why would he want to do that?"

"You'd never know."

"Seriously, this bookworm could give me some real practical help, like getting me an invitation to a good graduate school in America when I need it."

"I don't know about graduate school in America. It'll be interesting just to visit there. But then it seems that nowadays you can get practically anything here if you have the money. Before, power was the only means," he said.

"As of now, we have neither," she said coolly.

The night's segment on the Tu Yuesheng story was over. "You know, this rascal led such a luxurious life. And it seems that he could have any woman he wanted," he commented.

"Those days are long gone. Xu Haosheng, forget it! The country is socialist now. The days of easy women and decadence are history."

"Well," he said, "I am not so sure. It seems that what power or office can no longer coerce, money can buy. By the way, this is quite true: some of my old schoolmates who are now in Shenzhen and Shanghai are making out splendidly in business. A couple of them are rich even by Hong Kong standards. I heard that the lives they lead are a far cry from the puritanical kind that you implied for a socialist country."

"You envy them?"

"If I had their connections, I wouldn't mind giving business a try."

Next morning Saiyue mailed Professor Lu the letter and was in a pretty good mood all morning. In mid-afternoon, walking out to check the mailbox, she almost literally bumped into Senior Engineer Zeng at the office door. "Oh, sorry! Senior Engineer Zeng!" she stood aside. Zeng leered at her and grunted "Humph!" with a sneer and stalked off.

Isn't that perverse!? Saiyue thought. The witch was all right this morning, seemingly speaking congenially to everyone. It's a good thing she isn't my supervisor any more.

At the workday's end, Vice Chief Wang asked her to come to his office. "Xiao Zhang, I just want to tell you that the Director has selected Li Zhongchi of the Machinery Division for the visiting scholarship....Don't be too disappointed."

A hot wave passed through her body. She collected herself. "This is no surprise. He deserves it. I have heard of his outstanding performance. Besides, he's been here longer than I have. I do appreciate your support though." She tried to be gracious.

"We'll put your name in again next year," he said.

"Oh....Maybe I'll get lucky next year."

"Xiao Zhang, it's not all a matter of luck," the Vice Chief said.

"I understand. I am sorry. None of this would affect my sense of responsibility to my work unit."

"I know that."

At night, her husband asked, "Why the long face all evening? Did that Zeng witch give you a hard time?"

Saiyue was now pretty sure about the reason for Zeng's rudeness of the afternoon—the news about the visiting scholarship. "I don't give a damn about her!" Saiyue went on to tell him of her own failure to get the visiting scholarship.

"As I recall it, you didn't really expect to get it this year. Anyhow, that's all right. This is just like a ballgame. There can just be one winner. Wait until next game....I mean next year."

She understood that he meant to console her, but she didn't appreciate his analogy.

Next week a letter from Professor Lu perked her up some—his department had agreed to host her when she had her visiting scholarship. She also sent out her application for admission to the graduate school of TUC (Technological University of California).

Two months passed. In an early December afternoon, before her colleagues would be returning after lunch break, Vice Chief Wang had no sooner crossed her office door than he began to address her, "Xiao Zhang!" There was a slight quavering in his voice.

Standing up to meet him, she said, "Yes, Vice Chief?"

"Xiao Zhang, Director Kang wants to see you."

Did I do anything wrong? Her nerve tightened up a little. "Do you know what it may be about?" she asked.

"Don't worry. You should go as soon as possible. I have to go. Someone is coming to see me. Any problems?" Before he left, he gave her a soft look and a smile like that which a high school principal wears when he hands a diploma to one of his favorite students.

At the Director's suite, his aide went in first to check, returned and told her to go in. Director Kang was at his desk, the left hand supporting the forehead bending over a document, the right forearm rising from the desk top with a cigarette sticking out from the hand, as if it were in a tobacco advertisement. Middle-aged, trained in petroleum engineering in Moscow, he was one of the younger technocrats promoted to leadership roles in recent years. She had met him a few times before, but only briefly each time. The experiences certainly corroborated his reputation of gravitas, even standoffishness.

There would be none of that on this occasion. He sensed her presence, lifted his head, quickly opened his chiseled face up into an amicable smile, and motioned her toward a table encircled by several chairs, adjacent to a row of bookcases and file cabinets. As she thanked him, he rose and joined her across the table that was barren but for a couple of ashtrays.

She looked at him with seeming calmness, "Does Director Kang have any instructions for me?"

"Umm, not exactly. How is your family?" the Director asked. She answered him politely and thought it strange since he was not known for idle chat.

The Director put his hand over his mouth, coughed lightly, and set it down in his lap. "Umm, Xiao Zhang," for the first time he used the more familiar term to address her, "As you know, from time to time, the Institute is allocated visiting scholarships. We award them to workers of special merit in our unit. Your name had been brought to my attention for some time. I am aware of the good work you have been doing and your aspirations to advance your technical capabilities. The leadership of the Institute has decided to offer you a visiting scholarship to America now at our disposal. Would you accept it?"

She blinked to make sure she had heard correctly. She checked an impulse to say that she understood the scholarship had been already awarded to someone else. But he is the Director; his word counts. "Accept it? Director, I have been hoping for this for some time. I don't know what to say. I am truly grateful to you," she said.

"I take it that you accept."

"Of course. Thank you, Director."

"Don't thank me. Vice Chief Wang has made a strong case for you from the very beginning of our review. I'd agree that he has good judgment."

"Thank you."

"Vice Chief Wang will discuss with you the effect of your absence on the work of your Department and his expectations. The Department of External Affairs will give you the appropriate forms. You need to find a first-class host institution in America, where you can learn advanced skills that will help to achieve the objectives of the Four Modernizations." The tone was more official now.

"Of course, I'll follow the rules precisely. Thank you, Director Kang," she said. He queried her perfunctorily a little about what she'd plan to do with the opportunity. She was expectedly noncommittal. He gladly let her go as it was not really among his direct concerns.

After she left the Director's office, her head buzzing and feet walking on clouds, she went, like an automaton, straight to the Vice Chief's office. Before she opened her mouth, he asked:

"Have you gone to see Director Kang yet?"

"I just left his office. Thank you so much. This is a wonderful opportunity for me....But what happened?"

"Well, Li Zhongchi had received some kind of grant, assistantship, fellowship or something, from his school in America. They say it would support him through his doctoral degree studies. In any case, he has surrendered the visiting scholarship. That's what happened," Wang said. "You are a diligent and capable worker and a fine person," he slowed down a little and continued with averted eyes, "I wish you a bright future."

She thought he was speaking as though she was leaving the Institute at that very moment, and for good. But then he was no dumbbell. She changed the subject, "I'll have to discuss with you about my work between now and—"

"Don't worry about that. We'll work it out. I think your unfinished items can be handled between Xiao Dao, Xiao Chen and, of course, myself." The former two were younger graduates who had joined the Institute in the past two years. "Any problems?" he said.

"I better go back to work."

She returned to her desk, her lips clamped with a meditative twist, staring at the blurring technical journals and reports that were spread over it. At last, the first real break of my life, she thought. (She used to consider that to be the village party secretary's permission to let her take the college entrance examination.) She clenched her fist under the desk and gave it a full-blooded shake. Before she left her work place that evening, she wrote to Professor Lu regarding the visiting scholarship award and requested a formal invitation letter be sent to her as early as was convenient.

That evening, after she had put Baobao to bed, she told Haosheng about the unexpected happening of the afternoon. He goggled at her. "Well! Congratulations! Isn't that something!" he exclaimed. "How come you didn't say anything about it earlier? You surely can keep things to yourself."

"I am telling you now. You know that coming back right after work, we all have so much to do to keep the family going. I just didn't want to disrupt the routine."

"So you are going to America."

"Not yet, I need a host institution first. I'll have to wait for an invitation from the Technological University of California."

"So when do you expect to leave?"

"As soon as I can manage it."

After a moment, he said, "How about Baobao?"

"We talked over the possibilities before. During the scholarship period the Institute will continue to pay me regular salary. You can use part of that to hire help. Otherwise, my family would be glad to take care of him. I am sure Grandpa would be quite willing. Will you be all right?"

"Don't worry about me. I am talking about the child. There is no need to trouble the grandparents. With some help I can take care of him. At least I can give it a try," he said. "Just that this seems to come up so suddenly."

"The way it happened this afternoon was a surprise. But a visiting scholarship we had talked about off and on a number of times. Perhaps you hadn't paid that much attention."

"It will be only for one year, right?" He ignored her last comment.

"Yes, the scholarship is for one year.... But I'd like to stay there longer. We had talked about that too. I'll keep my eyes open.... If it could be worked out, perhaps Baobao and you can come later."

"A visit to America. That'll be interesting," he said.

A couple of days later she found in the department mail box a letter for her from the Admissions Office of TUC, advising her that the Department of Mechanical Engineering had rated her an acceptable candidate for the MS degree. However, they could not offer her any financial aid. The University would send her an official certificate of admission, along with a Form I-20 for student visa purposes, only upon receipt of proof that she had the financial means to support herself. The amount needed was US$8500.

She had considered this contingency before. She wrote to her friend Yan Yifeng in Boston, Massachusetts, requesting a *nominal* loan for that amount with the promise of paying it back soon after she arrived in the United States. She did not reveal in this letter, or in the earlier one to Professor Lu, that the main reason that she would like to enter the United States as a student was for immigration purposes. It would be less difficult to extend her duration of stay—should that time come—if she held a student visa than a visitor visa. The point, she felt, was of no consequence to either Yan or Professor Lu.

The host's letter for the visiting scholar soon arrived. It was signed by the Chairperson of the Applied Mechanics Department of TUC, extending an invitation to her to spend a year in the department to work with Professor Lu with privileges of auditing classes, access to libraries and computing facilities, and, if available, some limited office space, but no stipend. An official certificate of the invitation—a Form IT-66, for visa purposes—was also enclosed.

With the TUC letter and the Institute's visiting scholar appointment notice, she applied for a passport at the Xi'an Bureau of Public Safety, which acted for the Ministry of Foreign Affairs on such matters. Shortly after that, she received from her friend Yan a statement from the South Street Bank of Boston certifying a credit for the sum she asked for.

She received her passport in early February. In two weeks, which seemed like two years to her, the official admission as a graduate student at TUC arrived. It was only then that she told Vice Chief Wang that she would be leaving for Beijing in two days, and she would need only one more day to have ready the report on a storage tank design project which she had been working on in the past two months. The Vice Chief had already reviewed and approved a preliminary draft of it.

He complained mildly that she had not given the department time to arrange a proper send-off party, and expressed the hope that, after she had her visa, she'd return to Xi'an before leaving for the United States. She said she'd try.

Later on that day, after her office mates had left, the Vice Chief came in. "Xiao Zhang, here is a small gift for you," he handed her a marble paperweight.

"Vice Chief, why do you do this? It's embarrassing. For all your guidance and kindness of these years, it should be I to present you a gift. Now you are giving me one!"

"Not much of a gift. Just a small token—" Then he pulled out an envelope from inside his jacket. "This is a letter of introduction addressed to Chief Zhu of the Department of External Affairs in the Ministry. He is an old friend of mine. You may not need this. But I think it could be helpful. Take it."

She did, nodding her appreciation. "Thank you. Vice Chief Wang."

"By the way, there is no need to call me Vice Chief Wang; we have known each other for several years now. You may just call me Lao Wang or—" he couldn't say his own name, Tang'yi, as he had intended. When she looked up at him, his eyes turned away from her face.

"That will never do. You'll still be my leader when I return."

"Really?"

She wasn't sure whether the query was referring to his being her leader or her return. "Of course," she answered—whatever the reference, it didn't matter.

"I—we'll miss you around here....Good luck," the middle-aged man extended his right hand kind of abruptly as though with resolution. She took it with both of hers and gave it a good squeeze, saying,

"You take care of yourself too. Thank you again for everything. I should have the report on your desk tomorrow."

"That will be fine," Wang smiled wanly, nodded, turned and quickly walked out. Watching the slightly stooped figure, her mentor in Xi'an, disappearing from the door, she felt a little tightness in her chest.

In the evening before her departure for Beijing, Saiyue was busy packing while her husband sat in the wicker chair, thumbing through a magazine.

"I suppose you'll be back after you are done with the papers?" he said.

"I would if I could," she replied in a sort of slur.

"How long will it take?" he asked.

"It's hard to predict. It may vary anywhere from two weeks to a month or two, or even longer. Some applications were even denied. But it usually happens to those who have close relatives over there....I have none, close or distant." Her voice began to sound fretful, as she stuck two pairs of socks hard into a corner of the suitcase. "If it gives me too much of a headache, I can always go as a visiting scholar. As far as I know, there has not been a single case of a visiting scholar's visa being rejected."

"You ought not to give up so easily, having spent so much energy already to get to this point," he said evenly. She was now smoothing her folded yellow dress just laid in the suitcase; she paused and cast an appreciative glance at him.

"Yes, I know." She sounded calmer.

"You'll be staying in—"

"As usual, the Ministry's dormitory. By the way, did you give the advance to Xiao Lo?" The latter, a neighbor's cousin, who was visiting from Anhwei, had agreed to assist the Xu family for at least two months in Saiyue's absence.

"Yes."

"Will *you* be all right?" She looked at him.

He shrugged his shoulders; "I told you I'll be all right. How about yourself?" he asked.

"I don't expect to live on easy street. But I'll manage. In due time I'll look into the *green card* thing," she said slowly.

"Green card?...Oh, *permanent residency*. That'll be interesting....You are a headstrong lass."

"We do the best we can. For a better life, right?"

"Of course...yet, honestly, we have been getting on rather well here in Xi'an. But I suppose you are right. In fact, recently, sometimes I wonder what my situation will be like five years from now. Often think of those former schoolmates of mine. Now businessmen. Making a lot of money, even by overseas standards, they say.... Oh, I suppose I had told you this before." He clamped his mouth and then slid his tongue out and curled its tip over the upper lip. "But again," he resumed, "it sounds like general knowledge. If you want to get ahead, you have to go through some backdoors, get to know some high officials, or their children. Middle rank cadres like my parents simply don't have the clout. What a hassle!" he shook his head. Silent, she kept on her packing. In a moment, raising the pitch of his voice a little, he said, "You know what? The game next week will be for the league championship. I hope Lao Yang's ankle is 100 percent before then. Lao Lei has not been shooting well. We need Lao Yang...."

She responded with a guttural sound while putting the book, *The Finite Element Method,* in her handbag.

Later on in bed, she turned her face to him, "I won't be seeing you for a while." She thrust her head below his chin and moved a thigh on top of his. This was a rare occasion since after she became pregnant with Baobao that he was called upon to respond.

Respond he did, and vigorously. Afterwards, staring at the dim ceiling, she said with a suspiration, "You take care of yourself now," and squeezed him several times in her embrace before letting him go.

"You too," he mumbled, turned and went to sleep.

In the darkness, she could hear the gentle breathing of Baobao, just a few feet away, and soon joined by the light blowing of Haosheng's exhaling. She moved her thigh to feel his—slick, firm and warm—now totally still, and wondered when this moment would happen again.

Early next morning, Xiao Lo came to help take Baobao to the nursery. Saiyue was to leave later in the afternoon. "Can't you just skip this one practice and take Baobao to the train station?".

Pausing for a second with pursed lips, he said, "As I told you, the coach had emphasized that this one is especially important. Our next match is for the league championship. I'll see you when you return from

Beijing.... Besides, I am the captain. If you had told me earlier, I could have tried to make some arrangement beforehand. But—"

"That's not necessary. Forget it," she said petulantly. "Let's go. Baobao!" She carried her son in her arms, thinking that she might as well avoid the parting scene at the train station. When they were out of the building, feeling the weight, she stopped to set the boy down. Turning her head to have a look at the apartment, she saw the back of Haosheng on his bike gliding away in the opposite direction.

At the nursery, she introduced Xiao Lo to the attendants. Saiyue crouched to look at her son. He stared at his mother, puzzled by this morning's deviations from routine. She embraced and squeezed him, swallowed and said, "Mama is going away for a while. Baobao be a good boy, all right?"

"Mama go choo-choo train? Bring cake?" She was surprised that he remembered what she had told him the evening before.

"Yes, on choo-choo train." Her voice broke. The image of a lone airplane up in the vast space over the Pacific flickered past her mind; she squeezed him again.

The confused little boy leaned back his upper body to have another look at his mother. Noting her teary eyes, he said, "Mama not cry. Mama not cry. Baobao good boy!"

"That's my Baobao. You listen to your Papa and Auntie Lo here while I am away. All right?"

"Baobao good boy!"

"Now you go and join your little friends," she stood up, signaling the attendants to take charge of the kid. To Xiao Lo, she said, "We have to rely on your help now," and quickly walked out of the nursery, as its workers looked at each other with surmises.

In the dormitory of the Ministry of Petroleum Industries in Beijing, she shared a room with two out-of-town women from the Daqing Oil Fields in Heilongjiang. She paid her respects to Chief Zhu and delivered Vice

Chief Wang's letter of introduction. Chief Zhu offered the Ministry's help for her visitor visa application. She told him frankly that she would rather manage on her own to apply for a student visa and hoped that it would meet with his approval. The Chief, a gray-haired man in a rather natty Mao suit, glanced with hooded eyes at the ceiling, at the floor, and then at his old friend's letter on the desk, and said that he had no objection.

Between filling out forms and patiently presenting her case to self-important Chinese employees at the U.S. Embassy, she waited—usually studying in the Ministry's library. She got her visa on a mid-March morning. Before noon, she went to see Chief Zhu, reporting to him that she had all her papers ready and hoped to proceed with the trip as soon as possible. Zhu told her to come back in the afternoon. When she did, he advised her that she could get on a China International Airline plane leaving in three days. Her heart jumped on hearing a definite date. She accepted the offer. The Chief also helped her to obtain for her journey a loan of US$400 in cash from the Ministry. Furthermore, he told her that someone would meet her at San Francisco Airport.

She placed a telephone call to Haosheng.

"How are you and Baobao?"

"We are fine. As I told you in the letter, Xiao Lo has worked out very well."

"That is good. Let me tell you—I got everything done here," she said.

"Really! When are you coming back? I mean before you go abroad."

"Well, I don't think I have time. My plane leaves on the 15th."

"That's just…three days away."

"I'd like to get there as soon as possible. Perhaps I can still catch the spring term."

"Are you in that much of a hurry. Er…" he paused for a second, "It appears I won't be able to come to see you off either."

"Don't bother. It's not worth it," she said. "Haosheng!"

"Yes."

"I want to tell you again that I'll work hard to take advantage of this opportunity. I have striven so long for it."

"That's certainly true. Take care of yourself."

"I will."

"Well, may the winds be behind you."

"You take care of Baobao and yourself too." she felt her nose souring, "I'll write you as soon as I find a toehold there."

"Do that. Well, long distance calls are expensive. Goodbye!" he said.

"Goodbye!" she hung up and sighed.

She also called her family in Shanghai at their lane phone—one shared by the neighborhood—and said goodbye to her parents and grandfather. They were excited but not surprised, as she had intimated in her letters earlier that she might not have a chance to go to Shanghai before leaving the country. For many months afterwards she remembered her grandfather's shaking voice over the phone, "You are to be the first Zhang of Changshu to cross the ocean. The Heavens protect you!"

She had never been on a plane before, and had never imagined that it could be so big inside with seemingly endless rows of seats. Hers was a window seat—which, as Chief Zhu had pointedly told her, he had requested on her behalf. After a battery of announcements from the intercom, attendants walked slowly down the aisles, heads lowered, looking sharply right and left, to check the passengers' seat belts. The plane jerked. Ponderously it got on a runway, paused, revved up the engine, started to go, accelerated with increasing noise, and in a thunderous roar, her seat began to raise her up and up while the engine gradually grew quieter. On the ground, the parked planes and land vehicles of various kinds and the airport buildings all became smaller and smaller while she could see more and more.

The dun hilly terrain was marred with yellow bald patches. Around a hill, concentric terraces, which she presumed were for grain producing, curved like sculptured eddies. The bands, ocher and still fallow at this time of the year, struggled up the hillsides, became narrower and shorter, and ended at where the slope became so steep that apparently working it wouldn't yield enough food to justify the labor.

Now the land seemed flatter and more hospitable. Moving backwards were huts with dark thatched roofs nestled in clumps of leafless trees as well as buildings with roofs in brighter and cleaner lines, probably tiled and new—as suggested by the surrounding barrenness. Highway lanes, power lines and dark ditches with sporadic light-reflecting pools lay parallel to the railroad that ran south to her hometown, Shanghai, and beyond. Away from the transportation strips, in streaks of green patination on the rolling stretches, winter wheat, after a season's rooting, waited for vigorous growth in the warmth of the coming months.

After she couldn't see much for the altitude, she turned and rested her head against the back of the seat. The bright-eyed boy says, "Baobao good boy!" Her mouth contorted, she opened her warming eyes and stared out the window at the stripes of red and white clouds and a blue horizon.

10

The PA announced the plane was about to land. She saw only jagged mountains along the ocean coast. Shortly, the captain was chatting about bridges. She caught the name Golden Gate and saw the slender cables flowing atop from orange towers thrusting from blue waters. Then white sail boats and wafting sea birds. Ahead, a multi-pier bridge lined across a bay. The descent was felt at an accelerated rate. Crisscross waterways, circular patterns of docks, rows of boats and white-walled houses were becoming larger and larger. Then, a jolt. Amid an angry rumble and loud whining of the engines, a whitish strip streaked backward blindingly. A female voice lilted that they had landed; and the cabin was suddenly flooded with bright light and lively music.

It felt considerably warmer than Beijing. At the Immigration booth she noticed with interest that an Asian-looking officer manned it. She retrieved her suitcase from a carousel's moving plates, like the scales on some gargantuan, slow crawling, growling subterranean animal. A dog briefly sniffed at her belongings and sashayed away, its snout pointing this way and that, leading the man who held the leash. She figured they must be hunting for illegal drugs.

At the Customs station, an African-American woman officer asked her, "Is this your first visit to the United States?"

"Yes." Following those who had preceded her, Saiyue had unlocked her suitcase and opened the two bags she carried with her.

"Student?"

"Yes."

"Okay." She squiggled something on the suitcase and bags with a piece of chalk and waved her on, never even touching the contents of her baggage. Such trusting people, she thought, and was pleased to become a legal, albeit not permanent, resident of the United States.

With the other cleared passengers, some wearing a semi-lost look as they nudged their baggage carts uncertainly, she exited from a partition into a large hall. Across a low railing, a small crowd viewed them intently. Soon her name written in Chinese on a cardboard sign struck her eye. It was held by a woman leaning against the railing. She hastened as fast as her hand-carried baggage would allow. The eyes having made contact, they met behind the waiting crowd.

"I am Zhang Saiyue," she introduced herself to the woman wearing a brown short sleeve sweater over her blouse. Thin, almost gaunt with hollow cheeks, which made her eyes to appear large, she had a smallish frame even for a Chinese. With an abbreviated smile, she let Saiyue shake her hand briefly.

"How are you? I am Qin Liang'yu. The consulate had advised our Students and Visiting Scholars Association of your coming. I have come to assist you." Her Mandarin had a native Beijing accent of a rolled tongue.

"Thank you. Sorry to trouble you so much."

"It isn't much trouble. Outside our own country, all the more we should help each other. When I first came, someone met me here too. It's my turn....Have you made arrangements for a place to stay?"

"No. My unit told me that I would be put up for a few days," Saiyue said slowly.

"You can stay with us for a while. We can go now."

Saiyue thanked and followed her on a crimson carpet, passing potted slender palms on pedestals along both sides. The huge public place felt strangely quiet and orderly to her. She remarked about it to her hostess.

"In any public place in China, such as an airport or railroad station, people need to talk louder in order to be heard over the din of the multitude because of the density. The population density is much less here. One doesn't need to speak as loud to be heard," Qin said.

They took an escalator down to the parking level. The sight of acres of parked automobiles impressed Saiyue. Later on, riding inside Qin's car and watching the endless streams of vehicles in both directions on the multi-lane highway, she said, "I have never seen so many cars moving at such high speeds before. Where are they all coming from or going to?"

"At this time of the day, I suppose most of them are going home from work," Qin said.

"Teacher Qin," she said, thinking this would be a safe way to address her—indeed, she did remind her of a grade school teacher of hers—"how long have you been here?"

"About a year and half. I worked for Beijing Chemical Corporation. Came here as a visiting scholar.... I understand you are with the Ministry of Petroleum Industries." Her hostess sounded more cordial now as they chatted on.

They came out of the freeway at the San Mateo exit. After traversing short distances over some narrower streets, they got on a wider road. "This is El Camino Real. It goes all the way to Los Angeles," Qin said.

"Teacher Qin, I am so impressed that in a short year and half you are driving with such ease, like a fish in water, on the complicated road systems here," Saiyue said.

"It's not that hard. You'll learn in time just as quickly, probably more so."

Saiyue thought she even sounded like that grade school teacher of hers. "El Camino Real, what a euphonic name!"

"Yes, Latin languages are lyrical. Spanish names are common in California. There are lots of people with Mexican background here. Of course, this area also has the greatest concentration of ethnic Chinese in America, and probably other Asians too."

"I've heard about that.... There! 'Golden Pagoda'... It looks like a Chinese restaurant." Saiyue read the receding gold letters on a bright sign board over a black door with gold traceries.

"It is. There are quite a few around here. Some more recently arrived Chinese found work in them."

"Do they pay well?"

"Minimum wage... at best. For waitresses the tips could be good, particularly if you don't have to share them with others. In the kitchen, the boss would try to pile a lot of work on you. People tend to exploit others, you know, even their own compatriots. Ironically, sometimes Caucasian Americans seem more generous, fair-minded.... We are approaching the campus," Qin said.

On the right, two massive columns marked the main entrance to the university. Cars passed both ways freely—there was neither gate nor policeman to be seen, while in China the entrance of any major institution would be gated and manned. Behind a line of palm trees and a tract of green lawn ranged a group of institutional type of buildings.

Further on, multi-storied buildings of offices and apartments rose on both sides of the road, followed by low-rise structures of small businesses: laundromats, small groceries and the like. They turned after a mile or so, crossed a pair of railroad tracks and drove onto a narrow street.

The surroundings now had an untidy look. Peeled paint curled over lintels. Pots of houseplants and flowers stood in jumbles on window ledges. Fragments of waste paper were trapped in weeds growing tall in pale sunlight along the gray walls of flat-roof houses.

Qin steered into an alley, then into a yard and parked the car under a shed. "Our apartment is on the first floor of the first building there," she pointed to a pile of tawny three-story buildings. She opened a wire fence gate with a key and led her guest into a compound. Two rows of apartments stood separated by a concrete walkway bordered by clusters of bushes and ground cover. After a few doors, Qin stopped, saying, "Here we are!"

Saiyue followed her into a foyer of sorts. To the left was a kitchen. Separated from it by a waist-high counter were a round table and a few chairs. A little ways in, a sofa squatted along the left-hand wall.

"Please have a seat." The hostess brought out two bottles of soft drink and a saucer with a small heap of wafers and sat down with Saiyue at the table. "There are two bedrooms in here. Liu Rong, my apartment mate, has the one in the front. Mine is in the back. As the saying goes: Although the sparrow is small, it has all the five organs."

"In that case, you would understand that my living quarters in China is not even a vertebrate," Saiyue said.

"The standards are different—we all know that," Qin said dismissively. "For the time being, if you don't mind, you could sleep on the sofa. It can be pulled out to make a full bed. And I have an extra set of bedclothes that you can use. I inherited them from a former visiting scholar."

"Thanks. The sofa is fine for me as it is. I don't need it pulled out. However, I should like to chip in on the rent. What is the rent for this apartment?"

"You need not concern yourself with that. I believe Liu Rong would feel the same way."

"It's only fair that I pay my share," Saiyue said.

"Don't worry about it now. I'll talk to Xiao Liu later if it's needed." Qin said. "The rent is relatively cheap because of the location. This is what is called a *low income area*. You might have noticed the railroad tracks as we came in. The neighborhood is not as neat, relatively speaking. And there is no view to speak of."

"I can understand the point about the neighborhood and railroad tracks. Inside a city would there be much difference in 'view'?"

"Oh, yes. Some apartments or houses command much higher prices mainly because of the view they afford; for example by the oceanside, or even nearby here, at higher elevations, one can have a good view of the Bay. I was once in my department chairman's house. Actually quite close to the campus. On a hillside, the view was very impressive, particularly at night."

"I saw a bay before the plane landed."

"That must be it, San Francisco Bay."

"It was quite grand."

"You should see it at night," Qin said. "One of these evenings I could drive you up on the slopes to have a look at the night scene of the bay.... By the way, we have made some space for you in the closet for your baggage."

"Thank you. Teacher Qin..." Saiyue hesitated, "I am not sure how to call you."

Qin quickly answered, "Just call me Liang'yu or Lao Qin. Not long ago people used to call me Xiao Qin. And I'll call you Xiao Zhang, all right?"

"Fine. Perhaps I should call you Da Jie (Big Sister), the way you have been taking care of me."

"No need for that."

"May I ask you another question—here how do people get around? Of course, you have your automobile."

"It is a major problem all right. Most newcomers use the bicycle. That is good on campus. On the street, it could be hazardous. You must learn the traffic rules here and take them seriously. Even so, you are basically at the mercy of the automobile steel carapace. That is why I got that old buggy as soon as I could, and had an American colleague in the laboratory teach me to drive."

"Are there many Chinese students or visiting scholars using automobiles?"

"Quite a few," Liang'yu said. "Many men do. But, one needs to be cautious there also. I have heard of a case when a woman student asked a man to give her rides, he demanded favors in return."

"What favors?"

"What favors would a man want from a woman?" she sneered.

"That's outrageous!" Saiyue shook her head.

"They say it's not that rare either. In any case, to start out, you can use the local bus. They are fairly convenient. I'll show you later....Oh, it's close to suppertime. Would you like to rest a while first? I have to go back to the laboratory to check on an ongoing experiment. It'll take only a few minutes. Then I'll pick up a few items at the grocery. I can go now while you rest."

"I am not hungry or tired. I had napped on the plane. You can understand that I am excited and curious. Do you mind if I come along with you?"

She rode with Liang'yu again. It was almost dark. In less than half an hour, they entered the campus. Under cordial yellow road-lights, the car rolled smoothly on the blacktop; Qin pulled up to a two-story building and went in. Saiyue waited in the car. She noticed many windows were lighted inside; her heart lifted with the thought that soon she would be joining those unseen scholars in spirit.

Shortly Qin returned. Saiyue said, "I hope that meeting me at the airport hadn't hindered your work."

"Not the least, the experiment is going just fine," Qin seemed to be in high spirit. After they got back on El Camino Real, she asked, "Hungry?" "No." "Well, perhaps I can take you to have a quick view of the night scene at the Bay." They got on California State Highway 92, heading west for some two miles, exited at West Hillsdale Boulevard, drove upgrade a little and turned into an open area that looked like a plaza.

The place was brightly lit by lamps on poles projected from square beds of ground cover. Qin said it was the parking lot for the office building complex on their right. The place was largely empty except for a few cars at the far edge. They drove over and got out. To the left, high on a tall skeletal frame was a neon sign: "Charlie Brown." It was the name of the restaurant just behind it, Qin told her.

She led her to a hedge that marked the beginning of a declivity. "We are looking east. Down there, the main road is the Bayshore Freeway we were on earlier; beyond, is San Francisco Bay. The other side of the bay is the City of Hayward....There, you see the string of lights across the Bay.

It is the San Mateo Bridge. To the north, that string of lights is the San Francisco-Oakland Bridge. To the south, that line of lights, a little faint, is the Dumbarton Bridge."

Although Saiyue, standing on the lookout, followed everything being said, her mind saw more. Above and in front of her the firmament spreads like a vast cape of velvet. From the blackness afar to the sapphire hue close, innumerable spots of light twinkle and pulsate on the coat of darkness. On land, blink the streetlights, lights of the numerous tiny windows of the numerous homes and buildings, low and high, lights from commercial neon signs, of radio towers, and atop antennas. Along the Bayshore Freeway, like endless strings of luminescent pearls, bright white vehicle headlights pull themselves in one direction, and faint red taillights in the opposite. Traversing east and west are lights of vehicles crossing the long bridges, with draping cables glistening like necklaces. There! Right in the middle of the Bay, above the darkly glimmering surface, appears a single bright diamond gliding along slowly. An aircraft!

A thin golden glow hovers in the space below. She recalled the Chinese name of San Francisco: the *Old Gold Mountain*. Although it refers to the abundance of the precious metal diffused underground, northeast of this place in years past, the name still fits.

She thought of all the human energy released from an essentially Western culture that led to the accomplishments that these lights represented. How different this world—built in less than a century and a half—is from the charm of antiquity of Xi'an. She could feel the radiation of freedom and opportunities, and sense the challenges ahead in order to grasp them. A breeze blew to her face. She took a deep breath of the cool fresh air. *But I am here now. In a New World, so energetic, so energizing, so various and so beautiful....Among all the thousands of the lighted rooms down there, when could I find one of my own?*

Saiyue had been in a small supermarket before, inside the Shanghai Jin Jiang Hotel compound. But this A&P store was much larger. Under bright lights everything was spick-and-span. Customers quietly pushing their shopping carts, picking up items here and there—none of the hustle and bustle of the noisy, odorous market in her Xi'an neighborhood. She thought of the clause in the Communistic ideal: "Each takes what one needs." But, of course, when checking out here, one would have to pay the cashier from what she had earned elsewhere, in most cases, by her own labor and skill.

Liang'yu took a head of lettuce, and later a pack of chicken legs, saying, "When I first came here, I used to buy bags of chicken wings because they were inexpensive. I would make chicken wing soup, chicken wing stew with potato, onion and soy sauce. Had them everyday until I got sick of them."

"I understand meat is relatively inexpensive here," Saiyue said.

"Not only meat. Relatively speaking, in terms of percentage of income, food is much cheaper here than in China. I used to think that the United States was mainly proficient in producing goods of technology—cars, airplanes and the like—and was later surprised to learn of their efficiency in agriculture, which should be China's specialty, because we have done so much of it through the ages."

They each selected small boxes of pre-cooked noodles (made in Korea), a pack of Kellogg dry cereal, a carton of half-gallon milk and a dozen eggs. Converted by the exchange rate, the milk price was lower than in China. At $0.30 a dozen, the eggs could be cheaper also. She opened the cardboard box—formed to fit the individual eggs—to inspect them. For a second, the image appeared of the twilight barefooted egg girl by the tracks of the Longhai Railroad to Xi'an.

Back in the apartment, Liang'yu started to prepare supper, saying her roommate Liu Rong would have hers outside tonight. She marinated the chicken legs in soy sauce for a few minutes and baked them in the oven. She cooked rice in an electric rice cooker—made in Taiwan and bought at K-Mart—and made tossed salad with the lettuce. Saiyue said it was her first time ingesting raw vegetable without washing it. They also had Coca-Cola to drink.

After they finished, Liang'yu said, "Sorry, not much of a dinner. You know in this country you have to be efficient."

Saiyue helped to clear the table and offered to wash the dishes. Her hostess would only let her watch, because it was her first night. Saiyue was most impressed with the kitchen sink garbage disposal, grinding and flushing away everything down the drain, even the chicken bones. Compared with what she'd have to do in Xi'an, it was so simple and neat. After they cleaned up, they sat down and had tea.

"You must be tired. Why don't you prepare yourself for bed?"

"I am fine....By the way, Qin Da Jie, would you give me some further guidance?"

"What about? Sure, if I know how."

"About finding a part-time job."

"I'll tell you all I know." She paused to give the question some thought. "As far as I know, generally, it's best to work for some professor who has a research grant. In particular, try to get, say, a half-time research assistantship. I understand that these days some professors offer quarter time assistantship only. Even that is pretty good because it pays wages regularly, certainly ample for living expenses; and it also exempts you from tuition. Besides, it also entitles you to a parking permit on campus, which is no small benefit.

"If your English is good, you may be able to get a teaching assistantship. However, nowadays university administration is hesitant to use foreign students as teaching assistants. Some undergraduate students have complained that foreign teaching assistants are hard to understand. All the same, there are still quite a few in our department as well as the physics and mathematics departments. For the many basic service courses that must be offered in these disciplines, not enough Americans are available to fill the need. I don't know about the situation in your department. I suppose in a professional program the need is less."

"I wonder why there aren't enough Americans available as graduate assistants?"

"Basically these days a lot of academically qualified American graduates with BS degrees see no need, or aren't willing, to postpone enjoying the good life their jobs with industry could support. And competition forces the schools not to lower their standards in order to use American students. Thus qualified foreign students are given the chance," Qin said.

"Hum....Is it difficult to get a research assistantship?"

"It's not easy, particularly for a newcomer—without an established record here....But there are also work opportunities that pay hourly. They include work on research projects, in a library or cafeteria, or janitor crew. People outside the university sometimes advertise at school for help. You can find such advertisements on the bulletin boards in the Student Services Office....And finally, one may find a job by word of mouth as you enlarge your circle of acquaintances; that is, through a sort of networking....Well, I may not have covered everything. But that's about all I can think of at the moment."

"You have given me a lot of information. Thank you." As Saiyue finished the sentence, they heard a click at the door.

"Liu Rong is here," Liang'yu said. The door opened. "Xiao Liu, I'd like you to meet Zhang Saiyue from Xi'an, or is it Shanghai?"

Saiyue was impressed by Liu's youthful appearance—light blue denim jacket and hip-hugger jeans, a red shirt showing under the chin. They shook hands. "I am sorry for having imposed myself on you two," Saiyue said.

"Liang'yu had talked with me about your coming. I am glad that we can be of help," Liu said amiably. She had long black hair and a richly made-up face—dark trimmed eyebrows and red thin lips. On closer look, the texture of the skin would betray that she was probably appreciably older than her clothing suggested. But her relatively tall—around 5 feet 6 or 7 inches —and slender figure, moving in a kind of languid air, lent her a certain feminine charm. She joined them in light conversation, brief but long enough for Saiyue to learn that she was an associate professor of English at Chengdo University in Sichuan, and now a visiting scholar in the English Department of the university. Shortly they disbanded for the night.

11

Next morning, wearing her yellow polka dot dress, Saiyue rode with Liang'yu to the University and got off near the Administration Building. The morning cool air invigorated her. The grass looked neat and flat like carpeting; the flowerbeds were trim. In the bright glass-walled lobby, the lights were on, adding unneeded luminance on a black framed directory that sent her to the office of the Advisor of Foreign Students and Visiting Scholars.

The Adviser wasn't in. She reported her presence as a visiting scholar to an administrative assistant, a woman about her age. By the time the business was finished, the assistant had discarded her condescending manner, as the new arrival's competency in English became apparent. She said pleasantly to Saiyue, "Welcome to America and TUC!"

Using a campus map, she found her way to the Aeronautical Engineering Building, which housed the Department of Applied Mechanics in addition to the department whose name the building bore. She located on the third floor Professor Lu's office that had his nameplate on the door below a frosted glass panel. She paused and knocked lightly. No answer. She stood by the corridor to wait.

Presently two husky figures strutted in her direction, and a slenderer one could be intermittently seen walking behind. After two students passed, she recognized that coming toward her was Lu Panzhe in an easy gait, carrying a brief case. She was a little surprised at his casual dress, a sports shirt and sweater rather than a business suit such as that he wore while lecturing in Xi'an.

"Professor Lu! Do you remember me?" she said in Chinese, stepping forward half a step.

"Oh, Engineer Zhang....It's you. I am glad to see you here. Welcome! When did you arrive?"

"Just yesterday. How have you been?"

"Fine. Thanks. Please come to the office." He took out his keys, opened the door and turned on the ceiling light. Wasteful, she thought, recalling the overabundant lighting in the Administration Building lobby and last night's parking lot. Apparently the office was his only. She could not recall that any of her former professors in China had a private office.

"Please have a seat," he pointed to the chairs around a table in the middle of the room. The right wall was lined with book shelves. A green chalkboard on the left wall faced the table. Further in, several file cabinets stood on the left, and a microcomputer system was set up on a two-tier work station on the other side. Below the window a desk butted against the wall.

"Miss Zhang," he said—it sounded as though he had always addressed her that way. "You did get admitted to the graduate program of the Mechanical Engineering Department. Didn't you?"

"Yes."

"Have you reported to the ME Department yet?" She did not quite appreciate the line of questions—so business-like so soon. He could have begun by asking me about the trip, she thought, or where am I staying. But who am I to complain? He is the big professor here.

"No," she said. "I thought I would first come to thank Professor Lu for the help you have given me."

"You are quite welcome. I am glad it has worked out so far."

"I have already reported to the Office of Advisor for Foreign Students and Visiting Scholars."

"Oh yes, you needed to do that."

"I think I should also go and pay my respects to the chairperson of my host department," she said.

"Yes, but you don't have to do it right away. Later I can introduce you to the Department secretary so that you can get an Identification Card. The spring term has already begun. But you may still be able to sign up for some courses. You will have to pay a late registration fee though. Talk to your graduate degree advisor about it."

She was aware of this. It was all in the bulletin. "Yes, I know." After a pause, she asked, "I wonder, what are you teaching this term?"

"I am teaching Theory of Elasticity. This term I have just this one course."

"I have enjoyed and learned a great deal from your lectures on Continuum Mechanics. Would you allow me to come to your class here and just listen?"

"You mean auditing?"

"Yes."

"Er....Strictly speaking, you need to enroll even to audit. The administration has not enforced that rule though. A note from the chairperson should waive the fees for you as a visiting scholar. In any case, it makes no difference to me personally. The class is not that big. There are plenty of seats in the classroom. You can just come, and take a seat there. I have no problem with that....Do you know where and when the class meets?"

"If there is no change from the schedule book, I can look them up there."

"There is no change."

She studied the edge of the table for a moment, blinked a couple of times and turned to him, "Professor Lu, what kind of research are you doing nowadays?"

"Well, I am involved in several projects. Let me see....The main one has to do with 'wave propagation in anisotropic media.'...I believe I talked about it briefly in my last lecture at your Institute."

She recalled that subject and his mentioning that it was supported by some government agency. "Oh, yes. I remember that. You mentioned that you had been using some high-power computer for the research."

"Yes, several graduate students and I have been struggling with that for some time. I am also involved in a few smaller exploratory projects."

Another pause between them. "Professor Lu, that wave propagation study sounds very interesting to me. If possible, I would like to do some work in that area. I wouldn't dare say that I could help your project. But I am sure I will learn much from the experience," she said, looking earnestly at him.

"Well. Let me see. You are a visiting scholar...." He turned his head and fixed his eyes for a moment on the lines of symbols and equations splattered on the chalkboard. "Do you know Fortran 77?"

"Yes," she answered.

"Of course, now I recall that from your records. You also had numerical analysis."

"Yes, I had a basic course in my senior year and an advanced course at the Institute."

"Umm....I think we probably can work something out," he said slowly.

"That will be very helpful to me, Professor Lu."

He proceeded to explain the work that involved the numerical integration of a set of differential equations by a variant of the Runge-Kutta method. Initially she could only recall some vague notions of the method; but as he went on it became clearer. After he finished, she said enthusiastically, "This is very interesting. I think I can give it a try."

"We'll do this in several steps. You see our starting point had been the mathematical equations. Before you dive into the nitty-gritty of programming for the numerical solution of them, I would like you to spend some time reading up some on the practical background of the work. Secondly, get some general idea as to how the physical realities have been idealized and modeled mathematically, and how the equations have been derived. Don't try to understand every detail because you probably don't yet have the background for it. But try to get an overview of the research. This way the later programming work should be more meaningful to you."

"Where can I find the reading materials, Professor?"

"I need a little time to gather them for you. Perhaps you can stop by...." He paused and looked at the chalkboard blankly. "How about tomorrow? In the morning...say, around 10." He took off his eyeglasses, wiped his face with his hand as though to clean it, and sucked in his lips.

"All right. Thank you...." She stood up, ready to leave.

He unclamped his lips and said, "By the way, since the work properly falls in the domain of the project, I am afraid I have to pay you."

"Oh.... That's not important; I only wish to learn new things," she said.

Leaving his office a few minutes later, she had accepted an offer of a part-time job at $6.00 an hour for 20 hours a week. He led her to the Department office, introduced her to the secretary and left. Saiyue had the administrative details taken care of, including a TUC ID card, processing for part-time employment and directions to get a Social Security number.

After leaving the Department office, Saiyue had a notion to go back to Professor Lu's office. But for what? She returned to the Administration Building in which the Office of Student Services was located. Therein the bulletin board for employment opportunities carried a bewildering assemblage of notices, letters, and cards in different colors—like a montage of modern art. Opportunities were available for baby-sitting, house sitting, laundromat attendance, warehouse work, bottle washer in laboratory, janitor job, etc. But one caught her eye; it had to do with the University cafeteria. The map indicated that it was right in the next building, the Union.

She went over there and got to talk to the supervisor, a big tall blond woman. At the end she told Saiyue: "Oh, Visiting scholar. Sorry. For hourly, we like to hire our own *students* first. Most places on campus have that policy."

Saiyue, a little dejected, walked out of the cafeteria and found herself standing alone on the terrace in front of the Union Building, glancing aimlessly at the students passing by in all directions. The number of non-Caucasian students surprised her, a good many of them were Asians, certainly out of proportion of the general population makeup that she was aware of.

She moved to an empty bench by the side of the building and read the map again. She went inside, located a telephone booth, read the instructions, looked up the directory and dialed. "Pagoda Restaurant! May I help you?" "Pagoda Restaurant?" she said gingerly. "Yes, Pagoda Restaurant. May I help you?" "Yes, I am calling to inquire whether you are hiring new waitresses." "You looking for a waitress job?" "Yes." "Just a minute."

She waited, the familiar tune of *Night of Spring River, Flower and Moon*, played by a combo of Chinese flute, fiddle, and lute, coming over the line.

The subsequent phone conversation told her there was no vacancy for a waitress job; but she agreed to go over there at 2 o'clock for an interview about work in the kitchen.

She was hungry. On a chalkboard at the cafeteria entrance, the cheapest entree was macaroni at $2.50. It would be over RMB$10—almost over 20 times she would spend at the Institute. There was a "coffee corner" by the cafeteria door, offering cookies, cold drinks, milk as well as coffee and tea. She bought a large oatmeal cookie and a cup of tea at $1.20, thinking that was still a hefty RMB$5 but much better than RMB$10.

She ate the cookie and drank the tea half hidden in a corner of a large television room. Still had an hour and half to kill. She walked around the building. It had a lot to offer—book store, electronic games room, table tennis and billiards, a small automated post office, etc.

She returned to the TV room and followed a show in progress in which a man, one hand holding a microphone and the other gesturing flamboyantly, was questioning a panel of four persons, two men and two women. It didn't take her long to make out that the subject was about extramarital affairs, each sex being represented by one who had such an affair, and another whose spouse had one. The subject momentarily piqued her curiosity. She kept at it for a while before walking out of the room and the building. She thought she would prepare a little for the interview. But what was there to prepare for an interview for a kitchen job.

It was between classes. A stream of students—young men and women—some walked alone, briskly and purposefully, some strolled in twos and threes, talking and laughing. Suddenly she felt adrift, like a patch of duckweed. The scene around her—the buildings, the people—all appeared underwaterish—insubstantial and weaving. The tolling from the school belfry disquieted her some more. She quickly walked onto a tree-lined side path, told herself to settle down and blinked back her tears in the dappled shadows.

At the Pagoda Restaurant she was interviewed by a Mrs. Joyce Wang who, together with her husband, owned the business. She was also the chief cook. The title did not jibe with her fair, matronly face and bespectacled, schoolmarm appearance. She told her that she and her husband were college graduates from Taiwan and were glad to help students to pursue their studies. And a visiting scholar was practically a student.

After some rehashing of their prior telephone conversation, she offered Saiyue a kitchen job—to cut vegetables, meat, and to operate the dishwasher, and if there was time left, to help make egg rolls. She would work three hours a day, from 11 to 2, five days a week, everyday except Sunday and Monday. (On Sundays the owners' children would work there, and on Mondays the restaurant would be closed.) The pay would be $3.35 an hour, the prevailing minimum wage.

Before returning to the apartment, Saiyue bought a dozen eggs, five pounds of rice, a small bag of onions, a bottle of soy sauce and a package of eight pieces of pork chops, which happened to be on sale. She felt pretty good about her first full day in the United States. Before she started preparing supper for her apartment mates, she changed into her Chinese white shirt, gray pants—both rather wrinkled —and black cloth shoes.

Later on at the round table, Saiyue and her hostesses had pork chops. Saiyue gave them an account of her day.

"You are a born American—what they call—go-getter. Mrs. Xu or Ms. Zhang?" Liu Rong asked.

"Ms. Zhang, please," Saiyue smiled.

"OK, Ms. Zhang, you'll do well here."

"In America, you only need youth to do well. Things get harder when you get older," Liang'yu said. Her unsmiling face halted the conversation for a moment. "Did you see your academic adviser to-day?" she restarted it.

"No. I didn't go to the Mechanical Engineering Department at all.... I'll go next week," Saiyue said.

"By then you'd be late even for late registration."

"I don't quite have the money for tuition." Until she had additional income to her scholarship (US$400 a month), she had to watch her expenses very carefully. Her situation wasn't that unusual to her new friends. The topic was dropped.

After they cleaned up the kitchen, looking at Saiyue, Liu Rong said, "These clothes of yours will not do. Let me help you to get some more appropriate ones." She took her to the Evergreen Shopping Mall, while Liang'yu returned to her laboratory to check on her experiment. At the mall, Saiyue and Liu Rong did mostly window-shopping, with the unavoidable comments on the great varieties of goods on display.

"I feel like Granny Liu visiting the Grand View Garden,"[26] Saiyue told her companion. A brown alligator skin handbag attracted her attention. Taking a look at the price tag and making a quick conversion to RMB$, she realized that it was more than her annual salary at the Institute. She thought, I probably would never own one like this my whole life.

Then they went to K-Mart. In consultation with her new friend, she bought a couple of inexpensive casual wears in line with the campus milieu.

---

26. An episode in the novel *The Red Chamber Dream* about Granny Liu, an old and crude countrywoman, who was bedazzled by the grandeur of the garden of her rich distant relatives.

12

"Good morning!" Saiyue greeted the professor.

Surprised by her altered attire—blue denim jacket, matte white denim jeans and tennis shoes—Lu was a trifle slow in responding. "Good morning, Ms. Zhang.…Please have a seat." She had hardly settled in the chair when he continued, rather rapidly, as it were, to compensate for the earlier tardiness, "Here are some reference materials for you. As I told you yesterday, you need not try to understand every detail. I'll be glad to try to answer any questions that you may have." He handed her two spiral-bound reports and a folder containing several reprints. "Take your time. See me next Monday. I don't mean you should finish reading all these by then. But if by then, you have a good enough idea about the project work, we could resume our discussion on the numerical solution of the equations."

"Monday…same time as today?"

"That is fine.…Did the Department secretary assign you a desk somewhere?"

"No. But I can work in the Library."

"It is more convenient to have a desk at school, to have a base of operation, so to speak.…Let me find out." He called the Department secretary. After hanging up, he said, "Apparently space *is* very tight. But, she expects a desk to be available in about two weeks. A graduate assistant, who had just completed his thesis defense, should have moved out by then. In the meantime, you can work in the Library or in the Department computer room. You can get from the Department a building key. Then you'd have access to the computer room, even on weekends."

Leaving his office, she thought that he was again all business—rat-a-tat, rat-a-tat. Well, that's the way it should be. The Xi'an experience has no relevance. At the Department office, she received the building key after handing over a deposit of $5.

She had thought that before going to work in the Pagoda Restaurant she would, as yesterday, have a large oatmeal cookie; but there wasn't enough time. Not wanting to be late first day on the job, she got there ten minutes before the starting time.

Wearing a loose white coat and a hair net, she cut chicken, pork, beef, pickled cabbages, carrots, onion, chives, black fungus, re-hydrated black mushrooms, celery, etc. into slices or dice. She cleaned prawns, snapped off the end bits of snow peas and string beans, and opened cans of water chestnuts and bamboo shoots. The work was simple enough. For her the hardest seemed to be the scaling and dressing of a defrosted "yellow fish."[27]

Next, she would turn to the rack of soiled dishes and tableware. She was taught to steam rinse them down and load them in a dishwasher. The tasks were easy enough but she had to move fast—so fast that today she forgot her own hunger in a place permeated with the smell of food. Before she left the restaurant, Mrs. Wang offered her a couple of egg rolls as a snack. They felt too greasy for her empty stomach.

She wanted to go to the Library to study the literature that Professor Lu had given her in the morning. But hunger prompted her to return to the apartment and have a bowl of the Korean noodle. Sitting down at the dining table, she couldn't give her mind to studying. She wrote two letters: one for Shanghai, the other for Xi'an, reporting her status, leaving out the restaurant job—thinking it not particularly honorific.

---

27. A fish bred along the coast of East China Sea.

She was now able to focus on the literature until Liang'yu came back from school. They had supper. Liu Rong came in around eight, already having had hers. They sat around and talked. From many a session like this, she would pick up additional information about her new environment: life in the United States, that of Chinese Americans in particular, the culture of the American academe and the subculture of mainland Chinese students and visiting scholars, immigration laws as well as such items of interest as the women's liberation movement.

Over the weekend she continued to study the literature on Lu's project. It was not hard to comprehend the introductory descriptive parts, including possible applications of the research to such fields as seismology and radio astronomy. But it soon became difficult because of the mathematics and the physical interpretations. She was frustrated even though she remembered Lu's repeated advice that, for her short-range goal, she didn't need to understand the material fully. Unconsciously and out of habit, she took that as a challenge. She labored in the Library, first reviewing the sections on wave propagation in physics textbooks, and then trying to cull helping information from monographs on the subject.

As she told Liang'yu later, her repeated efforts were like digging into a hardpan using her fingers only. Although they did not bridge the gap between the project reports and her knowledge, they narrowed it some. She now recognized that the equations were basically statements of Newton's laws of motion and of the constitution of the medium material. The variables now appeared less strange and alien to her. On Monday morning, she returned to her supervisor's office.

"I tried to study these reports and papers. They were quite hard to follow."

"As I had told you, you probably don't have the background to follow through the analysis. All I expect is that, after going over these papers and reports, you will have a better idea of what we are trying to do overall," he said.

"That I think I more or less have. I believe I am ready to start working on the programming. If it's all right with you, I'd like to keep these reports for a while so that I may continue to study and refer to them."

He agreed and then methodically went over certain technical points of the work, including the choice of dimensionless variables, which she found rather enlightening. Next, he told her to prepare, for him to review, an outline of the procedure, i.e., a "flow chart" for the computations, leaving the input and output parts to be considered later. Before she left, he gave her a copy of a flow chart for a similar work.

For the next week, her activities revolved around her two part-time jobs and attending the Theory of Elasticity class. On the following Monday afternoon, the first after the closing of late registration, she presented herself at the office of the Mechanical Engineering Department as a new foreign graduate student, and requested to see the department chairman, Dr. Andrew Duan. The secretary first located her folder and, casting a glance at the telephone buttons—none lit—handed her the folder and motioned her to go in toward an inner room. A few cautious steps took her to the door of the chairman's office. At the desk in the middle of the room a man, who had his back turned away from the door, seemed to be finishing a drink from a bluish bottle, and then proceeded to put it in a drawer. As she was about to knock, she heard a buzz, and he picked up the phone:

"Andy Duan...Jack! Yes....Umm...umm....You received it....But we couldn't have anticipated that. Before we made our offers for the two new positions, we had a verbal commitment from the grants monitor in Washington....I know it doesn't count....Our entire travel and supplies budgets can't cover this....Umm...umm....What can I do?... Umm...umm....But we have to depend on soft money[28] for the Department to grow....As of now, practically all our teaching assistants are covered by soft money. Provost?...Umm...umm....That may get me out

---

28. Revenue of a relatively uncertain nature, such as that from external grants or contracts.

of this jam.... Will you do that?" The head nodded in synchronism with successive bowing of the back. "Thank you.... Thank you."

After he hung up the phone, he sat stiffly, looking outside the window, and let out a burp as he pressed his hand over the stomach. Saiyue knocked lightly on the door; it didn't get his attention. She tried harder; succeeding, she said, "Professor Duan?" and was invited in by a gesture and a flashing smile. She sat down across the desk and faced the chairman, a rather handsome man in his forties, even with the brow deeply furrowed. She noticed a bit of whitish smudge around his upper lip. She had read from the Department bulletin that the chairman had graduated from the National Cheng Kung University in Taiwan, received his doctoral degree from MIT and had taught at Purdue University. He glanced at the first couple of sheets of the folder that she had handed him and remarked, "Tongji University...very good," he looked up and flipped a smile at her.

"Zhang. Yes, Ms. Zhang, you haven't registered for this term. It's too bad the deadline for late registration has passed....And your advisor is—" he turned the sheets, "Yes, Professor Williams." He took a look at his watch.

"Professor Duan, I was wondering whether I can apply for an assistantship in the Department—" Saiyue said softly and was going to build a case for herself.

"Ms. Zhang, your advisor, Professor Williams, should be able to answer all your questions of this kind." He grinned briefly and lowered his head to have another look at his watch.

A regular watch-watcher, she thought. It would be futile, if not counterproductive, to stay on. She quickly took her leave, quite disappointed at her prior hope that common heritage might lead to a more fruitful meeting with this decision-maker. She recalled a remark she had heard that some Chinese American faculty members often went out of their way to shun students of Chinese origin in order to show that they were not influenced by their ethnic background.

Professor Williams' office appeared smaller than Professor Lu's. That could be because it was so cluttered—with books, folders, binders, journals, students' homework, etc., lying disorderedly everywhere: on bookshelves, atop bookcases, file cabinets, the desk, and even over parts of the floor.

Two-foot high stacks of potpourris of papers stood like a parapet on a "rampart" in the form of a narrow rectangular utility table, separating the professor from his visitor. They sat and face each other across an opening of the parapet, like a crenel in a battlement. Behind the table and perpendicular to it, his desk was so cramped with books and magazines that she wondered how he could ever do work at it.

He must be in his sixties, but still had a full head of hair, though gray. His face had a slight bluish tinge that betrayed perhaps a heart condition. Yet his eyes twinkled as he shook her hand, and welcomed her rather warmly. In the ensuing conversation, they agreed that she, using the information in the catalogue, should prepare a tentative master's degree program, which would serve as a basis for them to jointly formulate her official program at a later date. That having been decided, she asked:

"Professor Williams, are you doing any research?"

"Yes, I do some research. Probably not the kind that would interest you. It is not funded," he said with a gleam in his eyes. She thought of a witticism attributed to a graduate student from China, as retold by Liang'yu in one of the evening chitchat sessions in the apartment. Young assistant professors are eager and enthusiastic in encouraging students to do research, particularly with themselves, but they generally have no money to support the students. Older or near middle-aged associate professors have grant money to help, but they are enterprising and pushy, driving their assistants mercilessly. Still some older full professors are nice and kind, even fatherly; however, they are usually sans money to help the students. In any case, so far as financial aid was concerned, she learned nothing new from her advisor. She left his office, feeling like last night when she had just done her laundry.

Today was one of her off days at the restaurant. She did not quite enjoy the work there—it was monotonous at best. It also broke up the day, making it difficult for her to use her time efficiently. She went to the Student

Placement Office to have another look at the bulletin board. New items were few and unattractive until she got to one that read: "Female Help Wanted: To cook dinner and provide part-time companionship for elderly lady. Call...." She copied down the number and went to a pay phone.

The phone call set up an appointment with a Mrs. McNamara at 2:30 that afternoon in her home at 55 Oak Street, which, Saiyue was told, could be reached from the university via the No. 9 City Bus.

She got there almost 15 minutes before the appointed time. It was a two-story white wood framed house with windows trimmed in black. A knee-high blue picket fence ran across the front of the house and stopped at a few feet short of the driveway. Screens of tall cypresses bordered the neighbors. A small yard was divided by a dark red brick walkway leading to the wooden steps of the porch.

With time to kill, she walked around the neighborhood. It was a quiet one, in spite of the fact that it was recessed just a block from the bus route. The dappled sycamores that lined the street reminded her of the scholar trees in Shanghai. Most of the other houses seemed larger than No. 55, and the yards more elaborate with at least one or two rows of planted flowers, some in elevated beds, while at No. 55 only a band of dwarf evergreens couched below the porch.

Few cars were parked on the street or on the driveways. Occasionally one rolled by. An elderly man, walking a funny looking brown dog with a sausage-like body and very short legs, passed her with a "Good afternoon," which surprised her. In China, people wouldn't normally greet strangers. She quickly reciprocated the friendly gesture. The exchange relaxed her. The place is practically empty as compared with Shanghai, or even Xi'an, she thought.

She rang the doorbell at precisely 2:30 on her watch. An elderly woman opened the door. She was almost half a foot taller than Saibing, in a blue chintz dress, silver hair combed smooth back in a bun. "Ms. Zhang?" she said lightly and genially—quite unlike the sour-visage of a single old woman Saiyue had imagined and prepared to meet.

"Yes, ma'am."

"I am Ann McNamara, please come in." They shook hands. The elder lady led the younger to a living room, and motioned the latter to have a seat on a sofa along the inner wall. She smoothed the lower back of her dress and sat herself down in a chair by the end of a coffee table in front of the sofa. Her movement showed no sign of infirmities of age.

"Would you like a cup of tea or coffee? The instant kind, I am afraid."

"No, thank you, ma'am," Saiyue sat only halfway into the sofa.

"Zhang.... The name is Chinese, I presume. Or is it Korean?"

"Chinese."

"Oh. You said you are a graduate student."

"Yes, in the Mechanical Engineering Department."

"How long have you been here in the United States?"

"Two weeks. I came from Shanghai."

"Umm, interesting. My late husband, Dr. McNamara, had always been fascinated with Chinese culture. He passed away five years ago. My children have all grown up. It's been three years now since I moved into this house. What I would like now, as I told you over the phone, is to have someone cook my dinner, do the dishes, clean up the kitchen, and then sort of keep me company for two hours or so every night. Would you be able and willing to do that?"

"Yes, I would."

"Good. The pay would be $250 a month plus room and board. We would each take care of our own breakfast and lunch from the groceries I'd buy. Of course, you are free to use the appliances including the washer and drier."

"Yes," she nodded, keeping her countenance amiable while trying to do some quick calculations.

"Would you take the job if offered to you?"

Saiyue figured that the pay was about the same as she was earning at the restaurant, but adding on the room and board part would make this job a lot more attractive than that one. Besides the work should be appreciably lighter, considering the fact that the lady was apparently in good health. And I won't have to hand wash my clothes. (Although Liang'yu had shown her the coin-operated washing machine in the apartment laundry room, to save coins, Saiyue still hand washed her clothes and had come to miss her washboard in Xi'an.)

"I think I would, ma'am."

"Good.... Tell me a little more about yourself, if you don't mind," Mrs. McNamara said gently.

"I was born in Shanghai. After I graduated from college there, I went to Xi'an—it's a city in the northwest part of China—"

"I have heard of Xi'an. It was an ancient capital where an army of terracotta warriors buried before the time of Christ were uncovered fairly recently. Correct?" Mrs. McNamara interjected.

"Yes....I worked there in the Xi'an Petroleum Institute as an engineer. I realized that with the rapid development in modern technology, I had much to learn and decided to pursue graduate studies. So here I am," she concluded with a demure smile, hoping that would be the end of the subject.

"Are you married?"

Even on the plane, she had considered how to answer this question in America. She decided she'd tell the truth when asked, but would not volunteer the information. "Yes," she said.

"Any children?"

"A boy two years old." She felt a twinge in the chest.

At the end of the interview, Mrs. McNamara said, "I marvel at how well you can speak our language, being here just two weeks." Saiyue thanked her. The white-haired lady continued, "I think we would get along very well. However, there is yet another young lady coming. I'd like to make my decision after I've talked with everyone. If you would leave your phone number with me, I will call you about my decision in a day or two. Is that all right?"

"Of course. Thank you." On a pad that Mrs. McNamara handed her, she wrote down the names and affiliations of Professors Williams and Lu as her references. They shook hands and parted company at the porch.

13

Two days later Saiyue accepted the job offered by Mrs. McNamara. Unwilling to give up the income from the restaurant work, she decided to keep that too. She moved into 55 Oak Street on the Saturday afternoon with Liang'yu supplying the transportation.

Mrs. McNamara showed her the kitchen—the appliances, cupboards, a modest pantry between the hallway entrance to the kitchen and a kitchen desk. "My tastes are quite simple—casseroles, spaghetti, roast chicken, baked fish fillet and the like, and only occasionally beef steak. I am trying to avoid red meat, as are most of my friends these days," she told her.

From a shelf above the desk she picked up a small box. "This is my recipe collection." Noting Saiyue's puzzled expression, she opened it, took out a card, and began to read: "Spaghetti with mushroom: half a pound of ground beef—lean…"

Saiyue smiled and said, "I get the idea." She quickly read the card her employer handed her and nodded: "I believe I can do this."

"Perhaps you could try it tomorrow or the next evening. Tonight I'll do an easy one. Have you had tuna fish casserole before?"

"I don't think so."

"Then I'll show you that tonight." Mrs. McNamara started by picking a can of tuna fish out from the pantry. "Normally, I'd just have a dish of meat, fish or poultry, salad, and sometimes a hot vegetable—green beans, corn, broccoli or cauliflower. Of course, bread and coffee. Generally, I like a piece of pie, pudding or fresh fruit for dessert. It all depends on what I bring back from my weekly trip to the grocery."

Saiyue diced the onions and helped to prepare the casserole and salad. Later, sitting at the table ready to start eating, Mrs. McNamara said, "You had told me you are not a Christian. But I hope you wouldn't mind if I say a grace before we begin."

She bowed her head. "Dear God. Thank you for the food tonight. Thank you especially for having Saiyue here to share our first meal together. Help us to make this night a pleasant and mutually beneficial experience and many more to come. In Jesus' name I pray."

Saiyue thought it quaint, but was also touched and a little awed by its simplicity and sincerity.

Over the supper, Mrs. McNamara told her that she had graduated from Claremont College nearby, and taught high school English for a number of years. She had married her late husband some 40 years ago. They had two daughters, both married, one living in San Diego and the younger one in Portland, Oregon. She also had four grandchildren. Her daughters and their families visited her occasionally. Each had asked her to move closer to her family, but she was reluctant to leave the Bay area where she had spent practically all her life.

"You see I still have most of my friends here. I used to do volunteer work at St. Luke Hospital. I have my church activities. It'll be hard to pull up my roots and move away. Maybe one of these days I'll have to. I know in time it'll be harder to get around. But as long as I can manage…Particularly now with your help—"

"I hope I can meet your expectations."

"I am sure you will, dear," the old lady said softly with a natural and open kindness. A Caucasian could indeed be this "civilized" also, Saiyue thought. "By the way, do you believe in any religion?" her hostess asked.

"No. Religion has rarely been as great a force in my country as in the West. This is even truer now under our socialist government than before. In recent years, however, there has been a revival of religious activities. Buddhists and Taoists practice their rites in the open. In fact, Christians also have been holding services publicly for several years now. But I myself have not joined any religion."

"Do you know much about Christianity?"

"Not a great deal, but some. You may be interested to know that my grandfather went to an American missionary college. He had told me some of the basic tenets of Christianity."

"How interesting!...Can you tell me something about them? Just as you can recall them....Now, my dear, I don't mean to test you or anything. I am just wondering. If you don't want to, I surely understand. It's perfectly all right."

"I don't mind to try. But I am afraid I'd sound ignorant. Let me see," Saiyue paused for a moment. "A Christian believes in the existence of a supreme God, who created the world and everything in it, including mankind. As they became corrupted and would be destroyed, God sent his son Jesus into the world to save them by teaching them how to live properly, by the rule: 'Do to others as you would have others do to you.'...Mrs. McNamara, please don't laugh at me if I am way off," she smiled shyly.

"Laugh at you? No, my dear, I don't know I could do better in those few words."

"You are being too kind to me. Thank you....Have you heard of a similar behavioral rule taught by Confucius?" Saiyue asked.

"No, dear."

"It says: What you yourself don't like, don't do it to others."

"Very interesting! The two rules sound similar, don't they?"

"My grandfather said that if we consider 'not to act' as an action also, then the two rules are the same."

"It sounds reasonable....I suppose we'd be all right if we follow either. Wouldn't we? I wonder, what is the basic difference between Christianity and Confucianism?"

"I don't know much about either. But I understand that Confucianism is not really a religion. Confucius never discussed death or the supernatural. He had said, 'I don't know enough about life, how can I know about death.' My grandfather had told me that the main difference between Christianity and Confucianism lies in the concept of an afterlife. Christianity holds that there is life after death—as after death a virtuous person goes to heaven. In Confucianism, afterlife is a non-subject."

"That being the case, I can see why it may not be considered a religion. I suppose every religion accepts the idea of an afterlife."

"I don't know about *every* religion," Saiyue said. "But I know some Buddhists do. An old neighbor of mine, a devout Buddhist, used to talk about that. Apparently she believes not only an afterlife, but cycles of afterlife. The lot of one's next life depends on one's behavior in this life—in cycles. The next life sort of holds this life hostage."

"Hum....It should encourage good behavior. Shouldn't it, dear?" Mrs. McNamara said. "Interesting...by the way, would you like to go to church with me tomorrow?" As if she suddenly realized that she might be imposing on her young helper, she quickly added, "Of course, I'd understand if you don't wish to, or you have school work or other things to do."

"I do have much to do, Mrs. McNamara. But to visit your church is a tempting idea...."

"The service starts at 11. I usually leave about 20 or 25 minutes before. It lasts about an hour. Afterwards, people are invited to stay on to socialize a while, 10 to 20 minutes or so. But that is entirely up to the individual. Anyway, you can decide tomorrow morning."

After the supper and cleanup, Mrs. McNamara led Saiyue to her cozily furnished family room. She took her seat on a sofa and Saiyue on an easy chair.

"Would you like to watch the television, or we could listen to some music," the older lady said.

"Whatever you like. I'd enjoy either."

"I seldom watch the television, except for certain special programs that usually appear on Public Television....Do you like classical, I mean Western classical music?"

"Yes, I do. My grandfather used to play records of them. But I have no real training for their appreciation."

"One doesn't need *training* to enjoy music, dear!" Mrs. McNamara said in a tone of mock reproof and went over to the stack of several black cases of electronic apparatus on a stand against the back wall. "My daughters gave me this system three years ago. I have enjoyed it a great deal." She inserted a cassette into one of the black cases. As a tiny bit of a sharp green light hopped seemingly randomly along a slit in the top unit, Mozart's *Eine Kleine Nacht Music* began to dance in the room. After it ended, she played Mendelson's violin concerto.

Both works Saiyue had heard before on her grandfather's phonograph. The quality of the sound then—a blurred melody—of course, couldn't be compared with tonight's hi-fi.

The next piece—Bach's double violin concerto—was new to her. Nevertheless, she enjoyed it deeply; the largo movement especially entranced her. It instilled a special feeling of peace, contentment as well as optimism. It had much to do with her own frame of mind. Before this time, she often felt the weight of uncertainty about the chances for a better life. Now, she sensed that she had got on the right track. Although surely there would be much hard work ahead, she could afford to steal a moment to relax, and open up herself to enjoy the beautiful music in the tranquil surrounding.

After it ended, Mrs. McNamara asked, "Are you tired?"

"No. Not at all. I enjoy such music. I hope you'll introduce more to me later." She had a notion that her landlady might have chosen the more popular pieces for her initiation.

"I'll be happy to. But for your first night here, you need to get settled…in your new room. I'll read a little before I call it a day. Why don't you go on and do whatever you like for the rest of the evening."

Saiyue's room was a small one upstairs—about the same size as the "pavilion room"[29] she had shared with her grandfather and brother in Shanghai. The fully opened door pointed to an armoire standing along an interior wall. A single bed with a bedspread of white and blue stripes lay along one windowless wall—on it two pictures of humming birds hung. The headboard butted against the exterior wall with a good-sized window. A desk was set almost flush with the windowsill.

She sat down at the desk and pulled the beaded chain of a banker's lamp to turn it on. Now a room of my own, she reflected, or is it? She gazed outside the window. A sycamore stood between it and a street light. The glowing and shades reminded her of the Lantern Festival[30] in the dormitory compound in Xi'an. Diagonally across the street, drawn window curtains, lighted canary, told of domestic warmth inside.

A lone car hummed past. It was quiet again. She looked at her watch: 8:15. In Shanghai or Xi'an it would be 11:15 of "the next morning" already. Pretty soon, Baobao would be having his lunch at the nursery. The compound of the Petroleum Institute should be buzzing at this time. What am I doing here? She plunked her head down on her arms folded over the desk, the black hair spraying and glinting in the lamplight.

After a while, she straightened up, unpacked her things. Then she was at the desk again, studying a set of notes that Lu Panzhe had given her on

---
29. For a typical lane house in Shanghai constructed prior to the Revolution, a "pavilion room" is a room situated at a level between two successive main floors. It is much smaller than the main room of a floor.
30. The Lantern Festival is on the 15th day of the first lunar month.

the use of the Control Data CDC 205 supercomputer. Though the subject matter was of great interest to her, she found the writing—CDC CYBER 200 series Computer System, VSOS Reference Manual—even more raw and arcane than the usual computer literature. She felt drowsy. Then she recalled her earlier student days, or rather nights, of gloomy dimness and wintry damp chill, in which she, clothed in lumpy cotton, did her homework. Now she blamed herself for being unable to make progress in tonight's comfortable setting. She opened the drawer, which she had arranged earlier, and took out a pair of scissors that lay beside a paperweight. Slowly she pressed the point of a blade into her thigh until droplets of blood appeared. She felt the pain, blinked her eyes, sharpened their focus and continued her studies late into the night.

Later on, lying in bed, she considered whether or not to go to church with Mrs. McNamara next morning. Considering what a great force Christianity is in Western culture, she thought it would be a worthwhile experience. Besides, since they wouldn't leave until late morning, she should still be able to get some work done before then.

On their way to church, Mrs. McNamara told her that this particular Sunday for Christianity is called "Palm Sunday." It commemorates, she explained, the day Jesus entered Jerusalem, people cheered him and laid palm leaves in his path. Later in the week, he would be arrested and accused by the worldly powers—who saw him, inspirational among the common people, as a threat—and afterwards crucified.

Mrs. McNamara parked her car in the lot beside the Hillsdale United Church building. She led Saiyue along the sidewalk, nodding, smiling and sometimes briefly greeting her younger fellow churchgoers, who would apologize for overtaking them. The church, fronted by a terrace paved with gray square flagstones, was a brown brick structure with clinging ivies encircling past the rose window in the gable.

An elegantly dressed couple together with a well-groomed girl, apparently their daughter, welcomed the stream of attendees and shook their hands. As

Saiyue took the white-gloved hand of the girl in a blue chiffon dress with matching hair band, she couldn't help again think of the "egg girl" in the dusk by the Longhai Railroad tracks. Mrs. McNamara told Saiyue that member families of the church took turns to serve as "greeters."

At the entrance to the sanctuary, an usher handed each a booklet and seated them. By now the sanctuary was almost full. Organ music droned with growling saturnine chords supporting sprightly high notes like little birds flitting over ponderous clouds. At the far end, silvery organ pipes arrayed high up against a reddish background with multi-colored stained glass windows and lancet arches. Underneath, a cross stood on an altar. Closer in, perpendicular to the assembly, on both sides of the hall, sat several rows of worshippers in their special habiliments of blue and white. They were the choir, Mrs. McNamara told her. A crimson carpet ran down from the altar passing the choir, dropping two steps and ended before the first pew.

Saiyue took a look at the first page of the booklet; after the name and address of the church, it read: "Passion/Palm Sunday, Order for Worship." Mrs. McNamara whispered to her: "Just follow it," and reaching downward, she retrieved a book from a shelf under the bench in front of them and handed the hymnal to Saiyue.

A tall silver-haired man in a maroon robe came out from the side door, followed by a younger woman in a black robe, each wearing a short smock and a glossy embroidered white stole. Saiyue surmised they must be the minister and his assistant. The man stood erect facing the assembly and said:

"The grace of our Lord Jesus Christ, the love of God and fellowship in the Holy Spirit be with you all."

The assembly responded: "And also with you." A covey of young men and women slowly walked in from behind, and laid palm leaves on the center aisle. The minister intoned:

"O God, who in Jesus Christ triumphantly entered Jerusalem, heralding a week of pain and sorrow, be with us...."

Then the assembly followed with, precisely as printed in the order for worship:

"We thank You for these branches that promise to become for us symbols of martyrdom...." In a while, every one was saying the Lord's prayer that Saiyue could identify from the words—"Give us this day our daily bread." Her grandfather had once gone over the prayer with her as part of an English lesson. At the time, that plea in the whole prayer made the most sense to her.

Then, the choir sang: *All We Like Sheep*, by Handel. As she listened, she felt the chorus exulting; in particular the variations were exquisite—they sounded so convoluted, elegant and yet so precise, balanced and pleasing.

The service went on. A plate was passed. Almost every one was putting either a small envelope or some cash in it. Mrs. McNamara whispered: "You don't have to." Saiyue wasn't sure what to do and let it pass. Following two readings of the Bible, the minister delivered the sermon. The topic was "Martyrdom and Majesty."

He pointed out how Jesus in his love of men went through great humiliation and suffering, but eventually ended in glory. Humankind can learn from Him. Life is often suffering or appears to be suffering. We may not understand why, but it is God's will. And if one holds fast to one's just beliefs, in spite of humiliations and sufferings, one would prevail like Jesus Christ. In upholding one's beliefs, one should be unwavering and act on them—learn from Jesus—with gentleness and love, without rancor and hate.

The just beliefs and steadfastness of purposes, in spite of suffering, being spoken of reminded her of the martyrs that had laid down their lives for the cause of the Chinese Revolution. But she could not find a match for the part of gentleness-and-love-without-rancor-and-hate.

A hymn with an easy, flowing melody was sung; one stanza had:

"Fair is the sunshine; fairer still the moonlight and all the twinkling starry host. Jesus shines brighter. Jesus shines purer than all the angels heaven can boast."

She thought of a song that she used to sing while marching with her high school classmates on dusty roads from village to village:

"The sun is the reddest; Chairman Mao is the dearest. Your brilliant thought always stays in my heart. The sun is the reddest; Chairman Mao is the dearest. Your brilliant thought directs the voyage."

They'd march 10 to 15 miles a day for two weeks, in emulation of the People's Liberation Army.

After the service, Mrs. McNamara led her to meet the minister, the Reverend Norton. On their way out they came upon a bearded man, who looked familiar to her. "How are you, Ann?" he addressed Mrs. McNamara.

"I am just fine. Mike, I'd like you to meet my friend, Zhang Saiyue, from China....This is Mike Bellini. Mike is our choir conductor." Now Saiyue recalled him performing his role dressed in the ceremonial robe and smock.

"I am pleased to meet you," Bellini said to her. They shook hands.

Saiyue nodded and said earnestly, "I am most impressed with the music of the service, especially the choir."

"Thank you. I am glad you like it. Have you sung in a choir before?"

"No."

"Do you sing?"

"A little."

"May be you would consider joining us some day."

"I don't think I am qualified."

"We won't know that until we get together and find out. Right?...I have an appointment. Got to be going. Nice seeing you, Ann. Nice to have met you, Ms. Zhang."

Mrs. McNamara took her to a restaurant for lunch. "What do you think of the service, dear?" she asked her.

"Well, I don't understand everything that went on. The pamphlet, order for worship, helped a lot....I enjoyed it. It's all new to me....The choir was wonderful. Their singing had varying tempo and volume—and sounded so disciplined and sophisticated. Not loud all the time."

"Loud all the time," the old lady echoed and chuckled, "That would be like the rock music my grandchildren enjoy.... What do you think of the Reverend Norton's sermon?"

"It's thought-provoking. I remember a Chinese motto my grandfather taught me: 'Only if one who could eat the bitter of the bitter, can he be a man above men.' But I've always taken it as an encouragement of worldly accomplishments. How many would apply it to spiritual advancement?"

"Jesus certainly set an example, dear. There were numerous martyrs and ascetics in the past. Even in the present.... Have you heard of Mother Teresa?"

"Yes."

"And there are more like her—but toiling quietly and anonymously in the thickets of Africa and jungles of South America, trying to relieve the sufferings of other human beings, help the helpless," the old lady said.

"I guess I am not cut out to be a Christian."

"You don't have to do all that to be one, I hope. By their standards, I'll never make it either. We have to rely on the grace of God to give us peace and comfort, even when we are undeserving."

"Grace of God...even when we are undeserving," Saiyue mused. Before their chat turned away from the service, she agreed that she would go again with her landlady next Sunday.

She was a little surprised when Mrs. McNamara told her that, in Christianity, Easter is the most important day of the year. She had thought Christmas was—from what she had heard about the festivities surrounding that occasion in Western culture. She recalled that her grandfather had told her about the quaint practice of caroling on Christmas Eve—roaming over the college campus and singing in front of the faculty residences thereon, and the parties afterwards.

"Why is Easter more important than Jesus' birthday?" she asked her hostess.

"Easter is the day we celebrate the resurrection of Jesus, his rise from death. It symbolizes good over evil, life over death. And, in addition, in tune with the spring season, it proclaims the possibility of renewal of a spent or failed or unfulfilled life. In short, rebirth. It is the consummation of our faith, our proclamation of victory over all that seems bad about life, including death," Mrs. McNamara said.

Saiyue was quite impressed with the cadence of the speech, and she thought she comprehended the assertions, but she could not quite apprehend how they would come about—like some statements in a computer software reference manual. Nevertheless, she respected the old lady's sincerity enough not to discard her words lightly. She would keep them in the back of her mind, like some venerated professor's passing comment in classroom. Although she had not understood it when first heard, its meaning would sometimes come to her like an epiphany at a later time after she had gained a deeper insight into the subject.

A bright day it was. Birds chirped in the trees that were bursting with young tender leaves hung over patches of varicolored tulips. A little girl wearing a gay bonnet skipped intermittently in patent leather shoes, handbag swinging from her small shoulder, and a little boy in a shirt with cuff-linked sleeves and a little bow tie shuffled along stiffly, holding onto his mother's hand. Only a few years older than Baobao, Saiyue thought.

The service began with a rousing hymn. She was particularly struck by the rhymed stanza: "Lives again our glorious king. Alleluia!/ Where, O death, is now thy sting? Alleluia!/ Dying once, He all doth save. Alleluia!/ Where thy victory, O Grave? Alleluia!" Following an invocation by the Reverend Norton, the choir performed from Haydn's "Creation": "The heavens are telling the glory of God. The firmament itself shows his handiwork....Neither speech nor language, yet their voice is heard...Ever, ever, Yet their voice is ever heard...." Hearing the solos, the duets and the chorus, she felt transported to a new world—of beauty and sanctity—away from the one of hustle and bustle she was used to.

The scripture reading also made an impression on her: "Peter opened his mouth and said: 'Truly I perceive that God shows no partiality, but in every nation any one who is God-fearing and does what is right is acceptable to

Him...."' Another part stated that a woman by the name Mary Magdalene actually met the resurrected Jesus.

That afternoon sitting at the desk in her room, she thought about her experience of the morning. Really? Jesus, a man, was killed, dead, and resurrected. Is that supernatural, or superstitious? Then why so many highly educated and apparently very intelligent people—certainly more intelligent than I—would believe that? But, Jesus is not an ordinary man; he is supposed to be God, or son of God? It's confusing.

If God so loved the world and He is so all powerful, why would He not just make everybody good and happy, and be done with it—bypassing the sin, repentance and redemption process?...But considering the stirring music, the martyrs and the Mother Teresas that the faith has apparently inspired through the centuries, there must be something to it....

What does all of this have to do with my situation right now? With that thought, she turned to her notes on supercomputers.

14

The Monday after Saiyue had moved into the Oak Street house, she was assigned a desk at school. It was an old gray steel one, soiled and rather beat-up, but complete with a hutch and a florescent light. Two desks in three days, I am making progress, she thought. One of nine in a large bright airy room on the 4th floor of the Aeronautical Engineering Building, as expected for a newcomer, hers had the worst location—only a few feet from the door. When it was open, as between classes, she felt like she was sitting in the corridor, people brushing by, coming in and going out, adding to the draft when the window was raised. So she'd avoid being there at those times. Since then, however, her life fell into a pattern of sorts—among studies and work, the latter including that for Professor Lu, for the restaurant and for Mrs. McNamara.

On Sundays, as a rule she would accompany Mrs. McNamara to Hillsdale United Church. After that, she would often go to the apartment of Liu Rong and Liang'yu. At least one of them would be there to meet her. They would go out for lunch to either a Chinese restaurant (not the Pagoda) or an American buffet restaurant. At the latter, they felt in one meal they could make up all the possibly missed nourishment during the week. Liu Rong would tease Saiyue that it was similar to a Christian's or her weekly church attendance, which would garner enough devotional credit to offset all the sins of the week, and the devotee could be ready to sin again for the following week.

When Saiyue was alone with one of her former apartment mates, every so often she would hear things about the absent one. She came to learn from Liang'yu that Liu Rong had been going out with a professor in the Communications Department. While she was divorcing her spouse in Sichuan, the professor was trying to gain his freedom from his German American wife, whom he had married in Europe when he was in the Army some 30 years ago. Saiyue thought that the professor must be a lot older than Rong. Liang'yu had also mentioned that on occasion Rong had taken up waitressing. Rong told Saiyue that she had been assisting the professor on a research project studying violence on TV, and that she had a daughter back in Sichuan whom she devoutly wished to bring over to the United States.

The story about Liang'yu was that before her visiting scholarship ended, she found her present job as a full time research assistant. She had repeatedly urged her husband in Beijing to come with their son to the United States. He, who had received advanced training in some institute in Moscow but knew little or no English, balked at the proposal. He didn't like the possibility of facing the same fate as that of one of his Chinese classmates in Moscow, who had been washing dishes in New York City's Chinatown. Resigning herself to his will, Liang'yu had decided to go back to China. Since then, she had also become more patriotic as well as moralistic, Rong remarked. Saiyue thought of the Chinese saying that "In every family there is a volume of scriptures that is hard to recite."[31]

After lunch, the friends would enjoy a bull session, or watch the television together for a while. One day on TV they chanced to tune in an interview with the Australian writer, Germaine Greer, on her latest book: "Sex and Destiny." At first they found her views on birth control and family planning rather unusual. But as they listened on, they realized that she

---

31. The saying means that every family has its own complex situation or conflicts that are hard to resolve.

was trying to redefine the frame of reference from that of the "haves" of this world to that of the "have-nots." She seemed to be advocating a more humanistic, vis-a-vis materialistic, viewpoint and placing greater emphasis on distribution and use of resources for all peoples of the world than on keeping the population down in order to better ensure the advantages of the "haves."

She also made the point that children need to have their lives integrated with those of the adults. On this point, the three women couldn't help to be chagrined, thinking of their own children, thousands of miles away, living their lives without their mothers around.

Liu Rong told her friends that Greer was a leading feminist, and per se often controversial. She had read her first book, *The Female Eunuch*, in which the author advocated for women an essentially masculine psyche, except for the sexuality part, which should be "equal responsibility," thus, in a sense, making society "unisex." The author also contended that such a society could be achieved via a sort of nonviolent sexual-cultural revolution.

"It will not work. Women can never be the same as men," Liang'yu said.

"Of course they are not the same. Neither are any two men. But that does not prevent society from treating them as equals," Rong said.

"Well, men are stronger, not only physically but also mentally. I think there is a lot to the saying: 'If you are married to a chicken, you follow the chicken; if married to a dog, follow the dog,'" Liang'yu said.

Saiyue couldn't believe that Liang'yu was so old-fashioned. But she wasn't sure whether the latter's pronouncements were the chicken or the egg of her decision to go back to her husband in Beijing.

Rong said, "All those old sayings and all the cultural traditions essentially had their roots in the *means of production*."

"You are talking like a regular instructor in Communism," Liang'yu smiled.

"No, the basis lies in Capitalism—economics. Society makes rules to protect itself for its stability and well being. On the whole, the fundamental of well being rests first in material sustenance needed for physical survival. Having secured that, one can then talk about such ideas as spirituality. Looking from the historical perspective, those who control material resources and production define *values*, or 'make the rules of the game,'" Rong said.

"What do you mean by that?" Liang'yu looked at her friend as if in wonderment.

"Well, since the cave dwelling days of mankind, human power for material production had been largely physical, brawn power. Men dominated in that, and it was they who made the rules; saints and wise men wrote their books accordingly. Remember what Confucius said: 'Only women and low characters are hard to deal with. If too close, they forget respect; too distant, they sulk.'

"Similarly in an English classic I studied in college, the supposedly first woman, Eve, said to the first man, Adam, 'What thou biddist /Unargu'd I obey; so God ordains, /God is thy Law, *thou mine*; to know no more/ Is woman's happiest knowledge and her praise,'" Rong said.

"Good Heavens! Those attitudes have been changed for a long time!" Saiyue said.

"You know why it changed? Not voluntarily on the part of the powerful. But because of the invention of the steam engine, raw physical strength became less important. It followed naturally women's position would rise, relatively."

"Well, the Industrial Revolution took place—when? 17 hundreds? It's a long time ago," Saiyue said.

"Yes, generally speaking women gained suffrage not until the 1920's. So there was a considerable time lag, a period of development and evolvement, during which the underlying cause unrelentingly ground out the effect. The waning of brawn power has accelerated with every advance in technology, such as the harnessing of electrical power, including telecommunications. Partly related to the latter, there has been a universal rising of sentiments for human rights and democracy, and against racism and totalitarianism. Such sentiments of course also favor equality between the sexes. But the cultural roots of male dominance run deep. It takes time for the new tendencies to work their effects.

"The development of the computer gives another major push to the relative decline of brawn power, and we can look to more changes in righting the unbalances between men and women," Rong said.

"What kind of unbalances are you talking about? Job opportunities, leadership roles?" Liang'yu asked.

"Those kinds too. But I would emphasize the moral or ethical kind. We are all aware of the unbalance between the sexes in China. However, it is essentially universal. As I had read, the stories in such famous novels as *Tess of d'Urberville* and *The Return of The Native*, by England's Hardy, *Anna Karenina* by Russia's Tolstoy, all took place well after the Industrial Revolution. Yet they revealed that, for a woman, the 'deviation of a single thought,' leading to one 'mistake,' would be her ruin; or, as for the good-natured Mercedes in *The Count of Monte Cristo*, 'One first fault ruins all the future.'"

"It's a matter of morality," Liang'yu said.

"If so, why doesn't man also suffer ruin for a similar 'offense'? Often, even in modern times, after almost any number of similar 'mistakes,' he gets only a slap on the wrist, if that. Why? I tell you why. First, because men are financially independent. In olden times, women didn't have independent status financially; often they had no means to make a living by themselves. Thus they couldn't physically exist by themselves. This cause is relatively easy to correct, and it is being corrected now. Today, women in general are being brought up to be able to make a living themselves.

"What's harder to correct is the second cause, the entrenched cultural idea that a woman is intrinsically insufficient by herself. While a man is viewed complete by himself, body and soul, a woman somehow exists sort of like a disembodied spirit. She needs a man to be complete, in order to gain recognition as a full member of society. This view and the cultural environment and tradition sustain each other. The cause is harder to correct. Thus nowadays, as many women have the means of financial independence, some are still willing to be subservient to men. But change will come. It is a matter of time, because the underlying machine of the change—that in the means of production of wealth—is in existence," Rong said.

"What you have said is totally based on materialism," Liang'yu protested. "I don't think man is really all that complete by himself alone."

"I am talking about the relationship *socially*. If you mean *individually* or *emotionally*, that, of course, is a different matter. It can't be that unfair," Rong said.

"Whatever, I think we should always put our family first, over our personal desire," Liang'yu said. "Family is the basic unit of society. Your idea of independence would only do injury to family harmony."

"On the contrary, I think true harmony can result only from fairness and justice. The latter can be guaranteed only by the ability to be independent," Rong said.

"I generally agree with Rong, whether we like it or not, we are heading in that direction of a more equal relationship. As you said, there would be a time lag. Let's hope it won't be too long," Saiyue said. "This is all very interesting. But we all have work to do. Rong, do you think you have time to give me another driving lesson this afternoon? If not, I'll go back to work."

Rong gave her that lesson.

By mid-May, Saiyue got her driver's license. With her first paycheck from the University, she had opened an account with Wells Fargo Bank and its balance had been steadily rising. (Within two months after her arrival in the United States, she had returned the $8500 loan—which she had hardly touched—to her friend Yan in Boston.) Now, with $1800 of her own money she bought a 1979 Buick Century.

15

Saiyue's work for Professor Lu had been progressing well. She had coded a number of subroutines, had them checked one at a time, and was now in a position to assemble the appropriate ones to execute the numerical integration procedure. Meanwhile, the professor had received a supplemental grant from the National Technological Council to use a supercomputer for the research project funded by the Council. After studying the reference material that he had brought back from a seminar, in addition to what she had read before on the subject, she together with the professor managed to hook up with the Purdue Supercomputer Laboratory, and use its CDC205 machine via a modem and the Telnet.

After her arrival on campus, initially she had hoped that the professor would sometimes show his "softer side"—that she had seen in Xi'an—and be less businesslike with her. She was disappointed. But in time the disappointment was replaced by a respect for his consistent proper conduct. Especially now in his private office, he was business-like but courteous, seldom looked at her squarely. When he did, it was always in obvious innocence, such as when he was making a point in the scholarly discussion at the time. Never an unbecoming word. He had hardly made any physical contact with her. In fact, they didn't even shake hands the first time they met in the United States or since.

However, by mere propinquity their relation became less formal. She sensed a gradual easing of his strictly correct and polite manners, which at times she'd taken to be a guise for standoffishness. They usually met in his office in late afternoons. Now sometimes at the end of a technical session, when pleased with the progress of their work, he'd offhandedly broach matters outside their official business. His relaxed and casual manner made her feel comfortable enough to stay on visiting.

Topics of their conversation usually concerned news items having to do with their commonality (outside their profession): China or Chinese. They talked about the push toward privatization and a market economy in China, for example, the selling of government military transport planes for the development of provincial or semi-private airlines. For such major changes and complex undertakings in a vast country—with little experience in modern finance, operations and management—opportunities for unusual achievements abounded along with temptations of corruption camouflaged as easy money. Thus stories of business successes in the new enterprise zones, such as those in Shenzhen, and of scandals, such as the egregious fraud of the Hainan Island officials, provided juicy material for conversation.

Topics of those kinds were rather removed from their personal experiences. But there were others, more familiar to them, like the report that graduate schools in China were having difficulties in attracting students. Considering the substantial differentials in income, many bright young graduates would choose business over graduate studies. In practice, however, many of them would be little more than peddlers, taking advantage of a poor distribution system at the time.

The occasional after-work chitchats brought them in degrees closer as equal human beings. However, both had kept, so far, their behavior within the bounds of a *student-teacher* and *employee-employer* relationship, and as if by mutual agreement, their talk seldom touched upon personal matters.

As a rule, she was busy almost all the time. Still she was not immune to occasional attacks of loneliness and emptiness, feeling languid and longing for companionship and stimulation of the opposite sex. Her recent contacts with men, other than Lu, had been casual and brief, as in a couple of social gatherings of the Association of Chinese Students and Visiting Scholars. As a first impression, the men appeared no match either for Haosheng physically, or for Lu intellectually and in social grace. And she had no time for forming a second impression.

She would not compare the professor's physical asset with Haosheng's. But the professor, for his age, seemed still to possess substantial attraction as a male—the deep voiced chuckle, the confident and decisive gesture of the hands, steady dark eyes, a stippled jowl in the late afternoon. She had even taken notice of the moderate strips of flexing muscle in his forearms when, excited about the work, he would roll up his sleeves, as prior to reviewing a computer printout.

Thus, recently she had grown to look forward to coming to meet Lu, not only to advance their joint research, but also for a session of companionship, however short it might be. Upon leaving the office after such a meeting, she would have a mixed feeling of fulfillment and vague yearning for more, like a high school girl after a chaperoned dancing party.

For Lu Panzhe, he had been quite mindful of the temptation he could be facing if he did not regard her as merely one of his students, and conduct himself accordingly. The first time she sat across the table from him in his office, she was wearing the same yellow polka dot dress she had worn on the first day as his tour guide in Xi'an; the light from the window and the ceiling shone on her smooth oval face, the clear eyes looking at him placidly. He was struck anew by the freshness of her presence. It came alive again—the snapshot he had taken of the lithe young woman in the setting sun at the site of the "Longevity Hall" on the Li Mountain. Since he returned to the United States, he wondered why that image would reappear every now and then. Each time he would admonish himself that it was the occasion and the place that had predisposed him to romantic notions. Now back to the real world of competition and survival, he could ill afford such diversions. So, he thought, here she is, a visiting scholar, basically a student. Treat her like any other student.

Being her supervisor, however, he was committed to giving her enough technical guidance to be fair to her scholarship, and thus he couldn't avoid a certain amount of contact with her. He did try to minimize the social ones. For example, he had thought it would be appropriate to buy her a lunch, at least as a token reciprocation of the hospitalities he received in Xi'an. He didn't do it because, as he rationalized, there she had been acting on behalf of the Institute, and here she was essentially a student, and virtually an employee of his to boot. And on the latter point, he had wondered whether he had been too rash in offering her a job, albeit only on an hourly basis. Later, however, her performance for the project convinced him of the correctness of his judgment, technically at least.

Thus, their conduct had never been anything other than proper. At each appointment, as she entered the office, he would turn around from his desk and gesture her to take a seat across the round worktable. With no more than one or two exchanges of small talk such as a comment on the weather—which for those months of that year in the Bay Area had been monotonously fair and could hardly elicit a zestful conversation—they would get right to work. After they finished, she would put her notes back in her large handbag and quickly leave, routinely apologizing for having taken up too much of his time.

To his treating her just like another student, he did allow one exception. As a rule, he preferred to work in his office with the door closed. However, for any woman student—usually an undergraduate—he would tell her to leave the door open. He had been told of cases of a woman student calumniously accusing a male faculty member of molestation in his office. Having the door open would be a good practice, like that of a male physician having a female nurse present when examining a female patient.

Around the appointed time, Lu would hear Saiyue knock on the door, and after he said "Come in," she would open the door, walk in and close it almost in one continuous motion. He felt that it would be not only awkward but inappropriate to ask her to open the door again. The possibility did occur to him of having the door already in an open position shortly before her appointment time, but he dropped the idea, thinking that to go to that extent for the *open door* practice in her case would be farfetched and ludicrous.

One warm Thursday afternoon in early June, he had just made out the final examination for the Theory of Elasticity class. It would be another 10 minutes before her appointment. He reviewed the notes of their last meeting, and looked forward to the new computer results she was to bring in this afternoon. At the appointed time, she did not show. He wondered, because she had never been late before. It was not until 20 minutes later that she came in, carrying a thick pile of printouts, her face flushed.

"Sorry I am late. The Purdue supercomputer was down almost all day. I sent in the test problem yesterday before I went home. I had wanted to come before, but the results were already in the output queue. So I waited."

"That's all right."

"I rushed here as soon as I had the output file downloaded and printed. I haven't had time to look it over yet." She held out the sheaf of computer paper. "Would you like me to go back to study them first and come back?"

"That's all right. We can look at them together, right here."

"OK.... It's so warm today." She wiped her moist nose, took off her jean jacket, set it on the chair between them, and sat down, as usual, facing her supervisor. As they started, she felt that it was awkward for them from opposite sides of the table to read together the printouts on connected sheets. She exchanged chairs with her jacket. The computer results did not appear strange at first. But as they viewed on, apparently something had gone awry. The computing was incomplete and had an abnormal termination. Further examination of the diagnostic exit output indicated that the calculations apparently had been looping, repeating themselves like a stuck record.

Skipping the following sheets, he turned to the very last one that contained the log of the computer use. The latter indicated that the computing had stopped because it had exceeded the set time limit. Furthermore, to their surprise, the log also indicated that the central processor had been used for 4000 seconds! That was a huge amount of computing.

She hurriedly flipped through a notebook among the pile she was carrying, murmuring: "I had checked it before sending it out." She ran over her notes with her forefinger, stopped and said, "It's right, 40. How could I have missed by two digits!"

Apparently in her data input the central processor time limit was mistakenly entered as 4000 seconds instead of the intended 40 seconds. Thus, more than one hour of supercomputer time was wasted.

Her brows knitted tight, her lips contorted, she sat there stiffly, utterly mortified. Tears began to come out of her eyes. "I did check it. Even though I was in a hurry to leave to pick up my landlady's medicine, I should have checked it more carefully. There is no excuse." She laid the notebook on the table, folded her arms over it, and dropped her head in them.

Her shoulder jerked slightly; he did not know what to do. Then he said, "This sort of thing happens. It is all right.…You probably concentrated your checking on the parameters of the physical system. The time limit had never controlled before—when you were checking the subroutines individually. Perhaps I should have alerted you more emphatically about it when you started to assemble the subroutines."

Her head was still in her arms, her hair glistening over it. He patted her shoulder: "Come on. It's all right. It's no big deal. Who doesn't make a mistake? Particularly for you, consider how much work you have to do each day."

"It costs you over 500 dollars!" her muffled voice sounded from the hollow between her head and the notebook on the table.

"That is all right. There is no need to be so upset," he patted her shoulder some more. She turned her head; against the whiteness of her blouse and the black coils around the ears, her face blushed delicate and vulnerable. She looked at him through beads of tears, slid over, stopped and continued toward him. He bent down and kissed her. She lifted her head and responded. Still sitting, they embraced.

Panzhe let go of his hold, "I am sorry about this. I shouldn't have done it. I will not do it again." He turned around and reached to pull two pieces of Kleenex from a box on the side of his desk and handed them to her. She pressed them around her eyes and arranged herself.

"It was not all your doing. Don't worry. It won't affect the work....I'll go over this, try to find the mistake. You can deduct the computer charge for this run from my pay."

"Don't be silly," he chuckled, but liked her gumption.

She gathered the papers. "Let me look over this first. All right?"

"OK. Take your time," he said.

She gave him a faint smile, turned around and walked to the door. He was still sitting in his chair, thinking that he ought to do or say something more—like apologizing again—but he couldn't manage either. He watched her open the door and the next moment there was just the door.

His feelings were a mixture of exhilaration and uncertain apprehension. For years now he had not been this physically close to a woman. And this is not just any woman but the one who for months he had been simultaneously idealizing and willing himself to stay emotionally uninvolved with. On the other hand, he imagined that his indiscretion might make himself vulnerable to university sanctions. This sort of thing is the only item not protected by the tenure system, he told himself. Yet no female had ever put her tongue between his lips before, even for a brief moment. He couldn't get it out of his mind.

He did not see her in class the next day. She showed up at the following Monday's class, after which she told him she had found the error and would have some new results for him to review.

He heard the knock and said, "Come in." After she closed the door behind her, both were a little tense and assumed an ostensibly businesslike air. He reviewed the results, which she had already summarized on a separate sheet of paper, showing a rapid convergence of the iterations, and a normal termination of the computations. He agreed with her that the results looked correct. The atmosphere warmed. They discussed the next step: to considering the effect of the size of time increment used in the numerical integration. The work seemed on track again.

"Good job," he said, moving away a little from the table and leaning his head back in the cradle of his laced fingers.

"Thanks," she smiled glowingly. "I'll let you know when I have the results. Sorry to have taken your time." She picked up her notes and jacket, made to the door, hand on the knob.

"Saiyue!" she heard. She turned around and saw his open arms, resembling those of the Reverend Norton at his benediction. Dumping the notes and jacket on the table she thrust herself into his embrace. The world was silent as in deep space but for the other's heart beat. She lifted her head. After a long kiss, during which he had felt a sting on his tongue, she put her head on his shoulder.

"Saiyue," he said.

"Umm," she croaked lightly.

"We have to meet some place else."

"Where?" She let go of him.

"How about dinner together?"

"I need to cook for my landlady every night."

"Oh, yes. Can we meet after you are free from your obligations?"

"It'll be kind of late."

"How late?"

"Around nine."

They agreed to meet at the Red Lion Restaurant on El Camino Real at nine that night.

He hadn't waited long by the door of the restaurant when she drove into the well-lit parking lot. He walked up to meet her. They held hands and squeezed them a couple of times. Sitting in a booth, they ordered cheesecake and decaffeinated coffee.

"How are you tonight, Saiyue?" He liked the sound of her name. So did she, when it came out from his mouth—much better than Ms. Zhang.

"Fine, and you?"

"I feel good."

"Not getting much work done tonight, umm?" she said.

"Neither are you!"

"That's all right....Do you live far from here?" she asked.

"No, not too far. West of here. It usually takes me around 15 or 20 minutes to get to school, depending on the traffic."

"You live alone?"

"Yes," he said.

"Do you have any relatives in town?"

"No, not even in the Bay Area," he said.

"I remember you told me your wife died in a car accident four years—no, now it may be five years—ago."

"Yes."

"I am sorry," she said.

"Thanks. It's been a long time now."

"I recall in Xi'an you told me you have a daughter. Where is she?" Saiyue asked.

"She works in New York City."

"What does she do?"

"She works for a stockbrokerage firm."

"Is she married?"

"No." He proceeded to tell her that his parents were still living in Taiwan. He had two brothers and no sister. One brother was a chemist in Los Angeles and another a businessman in Taiwan.

"So much about me," he said. "I remember you told me your family was in Shanghai. Right?"

"Yes. My parents are in Shanghai. My grandfather lives with them. He's retired. I also have a younger brother and a younger sister."

"Your parents still working?" he asked.

"Yes, my mother teaches in a middle school; my father is an engineer."

"So you are following your father's footsteps," he commented.

"You may say so. But actually I quite like the work of a teacher, like you." They exchanged a smile. "I used to do a little teaching in a village school—for little kids. It is satisfying to help develop the intellect of the young."

"Interesting. I am sure there will be opportunities in the future for you to go that direction—at a higher level of course....Do you write to your family often?"

"I write to my parents and grandfather. But I won't say often. Maybe every other week or so." After a short pause, she continued, "Every other week I mail two letters to China."

"Two?"

"One to Shanghai; one to Xi'an."

"Xi'an? Reporting to your Institute?"

"I did write the Institute once. But more regularly I write to my husband."

"What!" He started in his seat.

"I write to my husband mainly to ask how my son is doing," she answered.

"You never told me you were married."

"You never asked."

True, he never did ask her explicitly. Now he realized that, considering her bachelor's degree and her looks, it was perhaps naive of him to assume that she was not married, even allowing the fact that she did appear younger than her age. Perhaps he had not wanted to know. But he remembered that in Xi'an he did ask her about her family.

"Didn't you tell me in Xi'an that your family was in Shanghai."

"Yes, that was true and still is."

He felt now that they were playing games, and he wanted a timeout. He fell silent.

She took a sip of the coffee. "You don't care about me anymore?" she asked.

"Of course I do." Again a moment of silence. He asked, "Does he, your husband, work for the Institute too?"

"No. He works for a national cotton mill."

"What does he do there?"

"He works in the Department of General Affairs. He has a degree in industrial engineering, but he is a sort of semi-professional basketball player."

"Oh, a national athlete."

"He is an athlete all right. I am not sure he is quite up to the appellation *national*."

"How old is your son? You just have one child?"

"Just one. He is almost three years old."

"Who is looking after him now?"

"He is being cared for by his paternal grandparents in Nanjing....After I left, his father used to take care of him with the help of a nanny."

They were mute again.

"I have never been in this position before, Saiyue," he resumed. "I am confused...." He tried to think and find some focus. Involved with what's essentially a graduate student! A married woman, with a child! A visiting scholar, husband and child half a world away. Strictly speaking, she is no graduate student of mine. What difference does that make? I ought to know better? He took a clear look at her across the table. Her pearly skin, pellucid eyes, pink lips—those pink, fleshy lips.

"Do you love him?"

"I don't know. Back in China, we were just husband and wife with a son, living together."

"Does he love you?" he asked.

"I don't know that either."

"What do you mean?" he asked.

"Well, once he..." frowning deeply, she said, "That has nothing to do with us. I have nothing more to say about that."

The waitress came over to ask whether they'd like to have their coffee refilled. He told her to get rid of the cold remainder first. She did that and left them with two fresh hot cups. He took a drink and moistened his lips. "Do you care about me?"

"What kind of question is that?" Saiyue sounded piqued. Then she stretched her hand over to hold his and squeezed it lightly. "Would I let what had happened happen?"

"What are you going to do?"

"I don't know," she said. "What are *you* going to do?"

"I don't know either," he said.

She withdrew her hand to her chin, her lips twisted pensively. He swept his hand over his face. The silence was getting oppressive.

"I think I better go back," she said.

He left a generous tip, paid the bill and accompanied her to her car. She opened the door, turned around and gave his lips a little peck, got in and drove away.

He couldn't sleep. To end it or not to end it. He leaned one way, and then the other. What a new life it would be to have such a bright, beautiful—and sensual—woman as a lover. But she was encumbered. What pitfalls lay ahead! Finally, it all became very clear to him: her being a student/employee would be enough to cast aspersions on his character; now the fact that she was married and had a child would make it much worse.

Besides, he was twenty years her senior; he should know better even if she didn't. Conventional wisdom would foretell that, if he did not end the romantic relation, the age difference alone would eventually lead to nothing but headache and heartache. One couldn't fight biology. So he reached the decision that he had to end it, and went to sleep.

She showed up in class the next afternoon. However, by the time he had satisfied an inquisitive student after the class had ended, she had disappeared. That night he again pondered on the "to end or not to end it" question, which had actually resurfaced in the early morning. The answer was the same. He had to end it.

End it! How did it begin? First in Xi'an, she had reminded him of Chong Kimoon, with that brooding look while listening to his lectures. That look Kimoon seemed to carry much of the time after the Caesarian birth of Sharon—a small frame and too many milkshakes and sweets. Later the look would sometimes deepen to a morose cast. Saiyue had that brooding look last night before they left the restaurant. But apart from that and the times when she was concentrating for studies or work, generally her disposition was bright and lively, particularly during the tour in Xi'an. Physically, she was more filled out—those firm-flesh arms—and her kisses did carry a lot of charge.

Shutting off the sweet thought of her embraces, he considered that perhaps they could continue their relationship in an intellectual space after the short detour in a romantic one. In any case, for the next 24 hours he hoped that she would call him, if only for an appointment to discuss the research. No such or any other kind of call came from her the next day. She must call for an appointment sometime, he reflected.

There was no call the next morning either. It was Thursday, when they would normally meet. He thought about how to tell her that they should end their short romance. He told himself that after this meeting he would be rid of all the anxieties and uncertainties and regain his usual concentration on work.

At 4 p.m. there was still no call. He figured that it was going to be another long night. Then two gentle taps on the door. Doing away with the customary "Come in," he hurried to the door and opened it. There she was. The door was closed behind her. She looked worn. There were dark circles around her eyes and her lips had that curling of emotion. He felt hurt and opened his arms and she plunged into them. Silent for a time, he noticed a pleasant lightly piney smell of her hair, and he said, "Your hair smells fresh."

"I miss you so much!" ignoring his comment, she sounded like a high school girl in love for the first time. Then she added, "I couldn't sleep—shampooed it last night."

Indistinct talking was heard in the corridor. He lifted his head to listen; it receded. "Can we meet tonight?" he asked.

"At the Red Lion?"

"Uh....Do you mind coming to my house?"

She hesitated for a second. "You'll be alone?"

"Until you come."

"All right."

He sketched for her a convenient route to his house from Oak Street. Then they sat down to do project work. It was not easy to focus. Nevertheless, at the end of the session they felt that they had accomplished enough.

Lu Panzhe's house was in a subdivision on a hillside. But for the sketch it would not be easy to find, especially at night. Once she got on the right street, she had no difficulty in locating it with all the lights turned on in the front: the porch light and the flood light over the garage illuminating the entire length of the sloping driveway. She parked, got out, paused to look around for a few seconds, and walked over the curved path bordered by beds of ground cover and serrate slanted brick edgings, all lighted by low mushroom-shaped lamps. As she stepped onto the porch, he opened the door.

"How did you know I am here?"

"I have been watching from the living room window." They embraced and kissed in the foyer. He turned on a light and said, "Should we sit in the living room?" It was carpeted, well furnished, a large picture window, giving on the lighted walk in the front yard. "Or, perhaps, we should go to the family room, or my study?"

"It is up to you. Is this what is called a ranch house?"

"I think it is called a bi-level. From the street it appears as a single story. Actually there is another story below because the house is on a slope."

"Oh. Is that so?"

"The family room and my study are downstairs." He led her slowly down the hallway. To her left, a room with a large oblong table and a chandelier over it suggested a dining room. Behind it was a passage along which she could see shaded closed doors. They entered the alcove by the kitchen. Past a dinette table they came to a glazed sliding door. He flipped a switch and a patio was lighted outside. Against a dark background, a table and several chairs were grouped near a wood railing.

"This house is on one side of a ravine," he said. "There are only a few houses on the other side." Now she could catch a few glimmering lights in the distance. He led her down the staircase beside the alcove.

Saiyue had seen some fine American homes before, but they were in the movies, magazines or on TV. Some were truly luxurious. But this house—probably nothing special by American standards—was actually the best home she had ever been in, considering the spaciousness, the cleanliness, the carpeting, the fine furniture and modern conveniences. It seemed even larger and newer than the Oak Street house, which was considerably more commodious than the apartment of Liang'yu and Liu Rong. It would be pointless to compare this with the two rooms of the third floor of the Shanghai house in which she grew up, or with the shared apartment in Xi'an. She looked and tried to see everything, but outwardly she kept her nonchalant demeanor.

Stepping off the stairs, she figured she was in the so-called family room—a couch, several chairs and a TV under the ceiling recessed light. To the right, near the wall, a darkly glimmering piano lent elegance to the space. They walked over and noted a couple of framed pictures on it. He turned on a floor lamp.

"This is your daughter?"

"Yes," he said. "And this is Kimoon, Chong Kimoon."

"Is she Chinese?"

"No. Korean."

"She was beautiful," Saiyue said.

"She was," he said.

"This was taken at—"

"In front of the Main Library of the University of Illinois. She majored in library science."

"Oh....I wish I could play the piano. I have not seen such a fine piano before," she said, stroking the smooth surface of the baby grand.

"I am sure you can if you want to learn," he said.

"Well, that'll have to wait," turning to face him, she smiled. "Would you like a cup of coffee, decaf?"

"No, I don't need it. It's too troublesome to have to go to the kitchen upstairs."

"No, we can make it right here—in the kitchenette just behind the stairs."

They made and tasted the coffee, and set the cups on an end table. Sitting down on the couch, they turned to face each other. Speechless for a moment, he said, "What have I done to deserve this moment? You are so beautiful."

"As beautiful as Chong Kimoon?...No, don't answer. That is not a fair question."

"You know the answer," he extemporized. She didn't respond but gazed at him, her eyes intense and serene, inquiring and comforting, her mouth contorted a little, and her hand stroking his cheek slowly.

"Do you want me?" she asked.

"Yes."

"To be your wife?"

"Yes. But you are already…"

"I want you to be my husband too." They embraced. "I'll marry you when I am free," she said, her head on his shoulder, and her eyes on the hyperbola thrown on the wall by the cylindrical shade of the floor lamp. "Would you like that?"

"Yes," he said.

"Sure?"

"Yes."

He took off his glasses and put them on the end table. She let him unbutton her blouse and bra and sink his head into her bosom with her arms around his shoulders. That was the limit of intimacy they allowed themselves at the time.

16

After supper and cleaning up, Mrs. McNamara and Saiyue had coffee and chatted. In a while, claiming an exigency, Saiyue asked to be excused.

She went to see Liang'yu and Rong. She had told them before of Professor Lu's fine qualities and the assistance that he had been giving her. They would kid her about her "professor boyfriend." But the tease had been restrained, as Liang'yu, her return date approaching, often seemed preoccupied, and Rong was herself vulnerable on the same "professor boyfriend" score. All along Saiyue had denied any romantic element in her relation with the professor. Tonight, however, she disclosed the recent development and that she was contemplating marrying him. They listened attentively. After she had finished, Liang'yu said,

"Well, I am not surprised. In fact, the first time I met you at the airport, the thought did cross my mind—such an attractive young woman is not going to have a simple life here!...I am sure you've thought this over carefully—about the family, your son in particular. It's a pretty drastic move."

"I believe my son will benefit from this," Saiyue said.

"Well then, it seems that it's a matter of time that you'll be settling down here," Liang'yu said.

"I am not sure about that. There are hurdles ahead," Saiyue said.

"As I see it, just one. Will the man in Xi'an let you go?"

"That I'll have to find out. But I need to know the procedure for divorce in China," Saiyue said.

"I don't need to tell you—-Rong here can show you the ropes," Liang'yu cracked a smile.

Liu Rong, who had been quiet until now, said, "Xiao Zhang, of course I'll tell you everything I know."

"Before long, both of you will be members of the *Faculty Folks*, drinking coffee or tea with other faculty wives. Too bad, I'll be in Beijing then, unable to get some of the luster rubbing off on me," Liang'yu said.

Saiyue took it as a joke; ignoring that, she turned to ask Rong to give her the lowdown.

Although she had written Haosheng routinely just a week ago, on this Sunday night, she placed, with considerable trepidation but greater determination, a long-distance telephone call to his department at the Third National Cotton Mill in Xi'an. With some persistence, she got through.

"Haosheng! Is it you?"

"Yes, is there anything the matter that you are calling long distance? Are you all right?"

"I am fine. How are you? Have you heard from Nanjing lately?"

"I am all right. Received a letter from my father last week. The boy has been doing quite well. Why are you calling?"

She thought the ugly daughter-in-law has to meet her mother-in-law anyhow. "Yes, I do have something to discuss with you....You may recall...er...we used to talk about...how to better our lives. Er...we all knew that one way was to come to America. Of course, you remember...I had told you, before I left Xi'an...that I'd try to get a green card, you know, the certificate of permanent resident—"

"Well, yes. We talked about it. Umpteen times. And it's a long shot. Yes. What's up?"

"It's indeed very difficult. Now I see that there is only one way."

"Yes?"

She took a breath and braced herself, "First we need to get a divorce."
"What?" He wasn't sure of what he had heard.
"A divorce, an official divorce," she said slowly.
"You joking?" he chuckled, "Are you drunk?"
"No. I am serious. I am calling to ask for a divorce."
"What's the matter? You..." he said, then silence.
She thought the phone line had gone dead.
"You have found a new man? Eh?" he came on again.
"That's not the point." Now that the cat was out of the bag, she felt strangely calm.
"What *is* the point? What is this! You left home for a few months and now you are ready to dump me and your family here?" His voice was getting louder, and then suddenly it lowered. The words sounded as though they were uttered with his teeth as much as tongue, distinctly, almost in staccato.
"Don't get excited. Listen! I need to get a permanent resident status here. Right? To accomplish that we need to be divorced."
"Are you going to marry someone over there?"
"It would seem necessary," she said evenly.
"For good?" he asked and then answered himself, "What difference does it make!"
"I didn't say 'for good.' Just for a green card...for a better life," she said.
Another moment of silence. "This is *absurd*! You are *mad*! Certainly mad about America. It's ridiculous. I won't have anything to do with this. It's shameful."
"Don't get so worked up. Think of Baobao's future....I'll send you one hundred American dollars a month."
"I don't want your stinking money."
"It's for Baobao...."
"Money! Who cares!...You have found the man?"
"Possibly."
"Who is he? Some big nose and blue eyes?"
"No."

"Who?"

"That doesn't really concern you."

"Who?"

"A Chinese-American."

"Chinese-American!...Ah hah! Could he be that Lu guy you went out with as a tour guide?"

"Yes," she answered lightly.

"You stinking whore! You said yourself he was old enough to be your father!"

"Don't talk like a bully! I'll tell you again. It's all for a better life."

"A better life! What a fine thing! You went abroad, and before I know it you put a 'green cap'[32] on me. My life here is quite all right. I have no desire to be a turtle."[33]

On that general subject, she thought—in connection with his "working all night" after Cao Rushi's farewell party three years ago—what kind of animal have I been? A she-cuckold or she-turtle? But she held back. Instead, she said, "If we are divorced, you won't be one," and she sounded perfectly serious.

"What kind of logic is that! Maybe I am one already!" It was all teeth.

"Don't be ridiculous! You see. This is a chance of a lifetime—to take a major leap forward. Think of Baobao, if you won't do it for me."

"Anyway, I can't go along with this *crazy* idea of yours."

"Perhaps you need time to think it over. I can tell you one thing. I did not come to this decision quickly or lightly. Think it over. I'll call you again in a couple of days."

"You do that! I tell you again right now. It's a crazy idea—crazy, cra-zy, CRA-ZY!" he hung up. In a daze, he saw Saiyue's face floating in front of him with those cool eyes and contorted mouth.

---

32. "Green cap" is a symbol of a cuckold.
33. "Turtle" denotes a cuckold.

After a moment, recovering his composure, he quickly sneaked a look around from the rickety phone table in a corner of the office, which he shared with half a dozen colleagues. Nobody was paying attention to him. He lit a cigarette and rushed out of the room and the building. At mid-morning everyone seemed busy. He sat himself down on a stone step in front of an emergency exit door, puffing hard at the cigarette. "Quiet down! Quiet down! Her mother's!"[34] he swore. "Green cap for a green card? What a laugh! What green card? But greed card! Her mother's!...Damned professor, taking advantage of me. What kind of scholar is that! Such a hypocrite deserves to die! His mother's!" He threw the cigarette on the ground and slammed it hard with his heel and twisted it for good measure.

That evening he had a game. He played like a mad man. Called for charging thrice. After grabbing a rebound, he swung his elbows like a weathervane in a blast of gust and bloodied the nose of the other team's center. A brawl nearly broke out before the referee sent him to the shower.

At night, he lay abed thinking. I am wasting my time. Of course the answer is no....What's she going to do?...What would I do then? Over there—ten thousand miles away. Maybe I am wearing a green cap already. Has she no shame?...Then again, to be frank, such cases are not unheard of these days. Not for me, Xu Haosheng! His mothers!...All for going abroad. For a better life? How far would one go?...There has to be a limit!"

He didn't fall asleep until almost dawn. He had a late breakfast. Having moped away the morning, he went by himself to the mess hall for a late lunch before the line closed. He was startled to see a familiar face among the scores of heads and faces. He took another look. In the window light, the full lips like a ripened red persimmon. No doubt about it. He hurried to the lavatory, groomed himself a little, came out and approached the table by the window.

---

34. "Her mother's!" is a vulgar interjection (similar to "Damn!" or "Fuck!")

"How are you, Lao Diao, and everybody?" He nodded quickly at the bean counters, and before they responded, he turned to the visitor, "How are you, Xiao Cao? What brought you here from the metropolis?"

"I am fine. Came to see my mother. She has had an operation."

"Oh, I hope everything went well."

"She is recovering nicely."

"We have finished. Just talking," Lao Diao said. "Have you had yours yet? Why don't you sit down and join us."

Haosheng felt a deja vu. A similar invitation from Lao Diao three years ago flashed across his mind. He readily accepted this one and sat down with them on the untruth that he had eaten also. He thought she looked different from before. Is it more beautiful, or dignified, or sophisticated, or successful? Or all of the above. Black hair in a bun above a creamy neck accentuated further by the two emerald earrings. Big eyes, and long fleshy arms out of a short sleeve white blouse. A swan. His mother's! The toad has the swan!

In the ensuing conversation, he understood that she would be at the First People's Hospital of Xi'an during the visiting hours from 2 to 4 p.m.

Back to his office, he thought about his past with Rushi. A distinct feeling of regret came over him. He had underestimated her; perhaps she had underestimated herself. She had been so good to him, even after they were separately married. That night after her farewell party was still vivid in his mind.

About that party, what he told Saiyue was true that he did leave Rushi's apartment together with the other guests. But he did not reveal what followed.

As they came down the dimly lit stairway, Rushi pressed a small paper packet into his hand. At the edge of the Northwest Electric Company dormitories, sitting on his bike, shoulder leaning on a street lamppost, he unfolded the packet and read those sad lines.

He pedaled on. Although unable to recall the exact lines of the poem, he retained a semblance of its emotion and rhythm, and dressed his own feelings with it. Cold, cold, alone in such a cold night. The swan is gone! How sad! We've known each other so long! When would we ever meet again? He turned back.

When Rushi opened the door, he told her that the poem haunted him so. She invited him to take a seat at the table where noodles were served a few hours ago within a cone of yellow lamplight.

"That poem you wrote....I am sorry you felt that way," he said.

"Do you care?" she asked, looking down at the tabletop.

"Do you need to ask that? I am here."

She lifted her head, her eyes shining with moisture. Her lips moved but no word came out. Then she said, "I know you have come because of the poem."

"I have come to see you! Xiao Shi, you!" After a pause, "I don't know much about poetry. But this one I understand," he said with a faint tremor. She did not respond. "How are you doing? Is he treating you right?" he resumed.

"I am all right. He treats me fine. As he promised, Pa is being transferred to Xi'an." Her face brightened some.

"You mean his work unit in Taiyuan is letting him go?"

"Yes, Ju Jun has also arranged a position for him at the Switching Units Factory of the Company," she said.

Haosheng understood what a difference this would make to her family. Taiyuan in Shanxi province is north-east of Xi'an, about 350 miles by rail. He recalled Rushi had told him that her father usually came to Xi'an biannually to be with his family, and she and her mother would travel to Taiyuan to see him once or twice a year. In fact, it was owing to one such trip, when on some pretext Rushi didn't go with her mother, that he slept with Rushi for the first time.

"That's some help he has given your family. Quite a son-in-law," he said.

"The offer of the help was made before he was that. Anyway, he has his good points. For one, he is certainly a diligent worker, and I think his work will be, actually is, paying off. I should have a good future if I adopt his life philosophy as mine also."

"Oh," he could guess what that was.

"How are you doing?" she asked.

"Well, Zhang Saiyue is almost like that fellow, hard driving. But, of course, she doesn't have the kind of powerful relatives he has. She virtually has no capital but herself. I don't mean to underestimate Ju Tiger's own capability. Yes, the combination of his assets is overpowering."

"Yet in some respects, he is a rather poor person, a poor man," she said, eyeing Haosheng warmly. He noticed her face begin to flush in the yellow lamplight.

"In what aspect?"

"No need to talk about that.... Well, what's she up to?"

"I have the feeling that she has set her mind to go to America."

"That's not so special. These days everybody under fifty wants to go to America. I won't be surprised if someday I end up there myself. But it's not that easy. Perhaps Hong Kong is more realistic. In fact, I could have accompanied him to Hong Kong once. Just as a visitor, of course.... Again, how are *you* doing?"

"The usual. As you know, I have my basketball. About that, we are doing quite well. But I sense that she isn't much impressed. And sometimes I feel the pressure."

"Pressure, really?"

"Maybe not exactly pressure....I don't feel that comfortable with her. Not like I'm with you."

"Hmm...."

They paused, each eyeing the crackle of the tabletop. The soft yellow light seemed to be wrapping them in a cocoon and heating them up.

"Wonder when we'll meet again," he said.

She fixed her eyes on him and stretched her hand across the table. He held it. So soft. Then each added the other hand. They went to bed and reignited their passion. When he left in the small hours of the morning, they agreed that the night was the last leg of their shared journey in their stars, and they wouldn't try to contact each other again, ever. Before he left, the last thing she told him was that the poem wasn't hers; the poetess Li Qingzhao wrote it.

That was three years ago. Now this afternoon, when Rushi came out of the arched gate of the First People's Hospital of Xi'an, she appeared to be surprised to see Haosheng walking up to her. He offered to buy her a refreshment at a nearby eatery. She hesitated and then declined, saying that she had to go back to her parents' apartment to see her father. But she added that she *might* call him at his office later in the evening. "You need not wait though." Later, before he went to his office to wait, he had reserved a room in the guesthouse of the Mill (with the assistance of its youngish manager, named Liang, a basketball buff, who was proud to be a buddy of the Mill's star player).

The phone did ring. That night, under cover of darkness, the stars of Haosheng and Rushi shared another excursion in the guesthouse, where they had done a number of times before either was married.

The very clandestineness imparted extra excitement to their passion. For Rushi, the night's encounter meant more. To many, her voluptuous body would suggest a corresponding appetite. However, Haosheng had once heard in the locker room—it was the captain of a visiting team from Shanghai talking—beware of the dried look with narrow hips you can grab both cheeks in one hand; they won't quit until they squeeze you dry. When Haosheng and Rushi were intimate before he met Saiyue, he at times felt that Rushi's case was a sort of corollary on the converse of the captain's theory, i.e., that a voluptuous body may actually have a thin appetite.

She was neither; she was what might be termed normal, except that after her marriage, her bedroom experience (or lack of it) with her husband had forced her to channel her libido to a business career in order to have a calm psychic life. But this chance meeting with her old flame was an exceptional opportunity to enjoy a rare revisit to that basic dimension of life's pleasure, from which she had all but shut herself off. And enjoy she did. As he started to help her undress, she began to feel like the parched African plains being hit by the heraldic liquid globules with the thunder blaring overhead. After the clouds and rain, with Rushi nestling in his sweaty arms, Xu said tenderly, "I have never known such pleasure."

"Me either."

"I would die for another experience like this."

"You probably would too, if Ju Jun found out," she said.

"How is Tiger doing?"

"He has been really busy and doing well. His activities have much to do with his now governor father and lieutenant general uncle. He is involved in all kinds of business for his family."

"What business?"

"Textile, shoes, minerals, appliances, electronics, etc."

"That is a lot."

"There are more, other kinds he won't even tell me."

"Really? Like what?"

"I told you he won't tell me.…Some seemed to involve negotiations with Mid-easterners, Pakistanis or Iranians. Arms? Maybe…I shouldn't say that, because I don't really know." She caught herself in time. Her experiences in Tianjin had raised her consciousness of, and skills in, matters having political and business connotations. It had been the particular mood of the moment that had made her talk this much, like a British agent in bed with a Russian blonde on a Vienna bed.

"Humm.…What's in all of this for you?" he asked with a rising inflection.

"Good question. Of course I asked myself that. I told him that I don't like him doing business in such secretive ways. He said it's for his family. I told him I am not getting any younger, I don't want to be just his soft doll to come home to a few days a month. I'd like to have a reliable, solid career myself. He listened.…We are making headway in setting up a business of our own without all that secrecy.…After tonight, I don't know if I'll ever see you again. That's why I risked my life to meet you here for the last time."

"I understand. I will always remember tonight—your sharing of my feelings toward our past. Much has been added tonight. Needless to say, you can trust me," Haosheng said.

"Would I be here if I didn't?…So much about me. How about you? Is you wife coming back?"

"I don't enjoy talking about it.…She is trying hard to extend her stay over there." Heavens! "trying hard" hardly does justice to her efforts, he thought.

"That's to be expected."

"What do you mean?"

"I have heard stories—no, I know of cases—a man, or a woman, had even divorced the spouse for that purpose. It's not that uncommon. Haven't you heard about such cases?"

"Yes, I have," he admitted dejectedly.

"She is educated, an engineer going for a graduate degree. I understand it's a lot easier for a technical person to stay on in America. She should have a good chance."

He was tempted to tell her about the phone call the night before, but he didn't. "I wish she was as nice and open to me as you are," he said.

"Well, you see, I am nice to you because, in my previous life, you probably had saved my life or something. It seems that I have been paying you back in this life. Open?…After tonight what do I have to hide from you? My life is in your hands."

"So is mine in yours."

17

On the day following his tryst with Rushi, Haosheng received the second long distance call from Saiyue regarding a divorce. He told her to *suit herself*. Though the tone was gruff enough, it was devoid of bite, and it encouraged her to say, "I would like to get Baobao over here as soon as I can."

"Aren't you being overly selfish?"

"How do you mean?"

"He is now perfectly happy in Nanjing, cared for by his grandparents. He also gets to see his father every now and then. Why would you want to stick him in a strange place where you are the only person he knows?" Haosheng said.

She knew that he had a point; besides, her own immigration status at the time provided her no solid ground on the issue. Taking a fallback position, she said, "In any case, officially I must at least have joint custody of him."

He was silent for a moment, and said, "I am not experienced in this sort of thing. Of course, I won't deny that you are his mother. But as far as I am concerned, his name is forever Xu, and he is staying here."

"I'll send him US$100 a month. That is, to you, for *his* support."

"It does not matter to me," he said.

"I must have joint custody."

Silence. "Of course, he's our joint responsibility. Quite likely he will need your assistance at some point in the future."

She thought he was at bottom a pragmatic person. In spite of his wish to deny her satisfaction, he wouldn't want to close the door on getting her help in the future, as he hadn't refused getting her salary at the Institute or the offer of US$100 a month.

Subsequently, with the assistance of Liu Rong's lawyer in Chengdo, Saiyue retained another in Xi'an to handle her divorce case. Although she did not tell Panzhe about her conversations with Haosheng, before mailing out the power of attorney and the marriage certificate, she did ask Panzhe whether it was all right for her to do so. His reply was to the point—reaffirming that he would marry her when she was free. She sent the papers. The lawyer filed on her behalf a divorce plea in the District Court of Xi'an on grounds of character incompatibility.

She told Panzhe of the lawyer's optimistic view that in China at the time, precedents indicated that the chances of a divorce being sanctioned were much greater if the wife initiated it than if the husband did. There was nothing more they could do but wait. They carried on their dual relations reasonably smoothly. She continued to assist him in his research. Then generally twice a week—usually on Tuesdays, Thursdays or Saturdays—she would visit him at his house at night. They would spend an hour or two together—to relax, have coffee or tea, talk, or listen to music. But the piece de resistance was a moment of tenderness.

Not infrequently, desire would stick out its livid tongue of fire, flickering, threatening to turn tenderness into a conflagration of passion. She would tell him that, as a matter of principle, she could not let him quench his fire until they were married. For this reason she felt it would be easier on their nerves if they did not live together before they were married.

"Your name 'Sai Yue' becomes you," he said to her one night. (In Chinese, the name means "Emulating Moon.")

"How so?" she asked.

"Haven't you heard the term 'ice wheel'?"

"Oh, so I am cold! You would just pick that association of the moon for me!"

"No, no," he chuckled. "Your beauty, er…romanticism and mysteriousness are understood." The Song poet Su Shi's line also occurred to him: "The moon can be shady or clear, full or cuspate; we mortals…" but he didn't follow the thought.

"You are really imaginative tonight. Well, it takes a philosopher to understand me," she said in like jest. (In Chinese, 'Pan Zhe' means "Gazing Philosophically.)

When Saiyue returned from school one afternoon in late August, Mrs. McNamara handed her a registered letter, which she had signed for. It was from her attorney in Xi'an. She sat down at the kitchen desk and opened it. She found a copy of a "marriage record," issued by the police substation having jurisdiction over her former residence in Xi'an, certifying that the marriage between her and Xu Haosheng had been declared annulled by the District Court, and that they should have joint custody of their son. The letter simply stated that her attorney had done his job, and she was to remit the balance of his fee of RMB$2000. In silence she stared at the document, her face tightened, trying to control and conceal her emotions. As her landlady watched in surprise, she rushed upstairs to her room. Sitting at the desk, she looked out the window at the sky, hearing her own heart throbbing.

She knew that this paper was key to her tie to America; a green card, even citizenship, would follow in due course. She felt as though she were divorced from China, the "new old-China," that was still largely poor, undereducated, narrow-minded, constraining—in a word, not that different from the "old old-China." Although she herself hadn't particularly suffered, it was only because of luck and her tireless mind exertions to navigate through the system's inconstant channels. She would now feel liberated, being relieved from the need for that constant exertion—for matters of no real substance—or from so much dependence on luck. From now on, it will be different. It'll be the new, modern American rules, open and transparent.

I am still Chinese, she thought, and China is still most dear to me—I couldn't change that any more than I could change the color of my eyes. And my feelings toward…well, everybody will not change because of this piece of paper. Of course, it has to do mainly with Xu Haosheng. Well, just legally. With or without this piece of paper, he is still the same person, with his good qualities and defects, as am I.

The paper made her feel that her autonomy was essentially complete, as though she had been held in bondage before, and that the divorce had cut her free of a leash across the Pacific. She was joyous that soon her life would be raised onto a higher plane.

After moments of such exhilaration, she realized that Baobao was now a child of a broken family, and visualized an image of the little boy withdrawing from her, and her chest tightened. I'll get him here with me, I will, she said to herself.

A knock on the door was heard. "Are you all right, Saiyue?" Mrs. McNamara was asking.

"Yes.…I'll be right out."

"That's fine. I just want to make sure you are all right."

Over supper, she told Mrs. McNamara that she had fallen in love with Lu Panzhe, her professor and "boss," and had just obtained a divorce from her now ex-husband in Xi'an. Mrs. McNamara responded with a series of "Dear, O Dear!…Dear, O Dear!" and concluded with, "I wish you lots of luck. Things sure happen fast with you in the United States. Don't they? And, by the way, I'll be losing you as my part-time companion. Won't I?"

After finishing the dishes, Saiyue, with her landlady's understanding, excused herself early. She called Panzhe's home; no one answered. She reached him at his office. "Still working?" she asked.

"Yes, I just need to look up something in the files to prepare for a meeting tomorrow morning."

"Can I see you tonight?"

"I am almost done....Why don't we meet at the house...."

After he let her in, they began with the usual hug. "I have something to tell you." Over his shoulder she said, "I am free." He did not say anything but responded with a tightening of the embrace. Holding each other thus for a while, they kissed and went to the family room. She sat on the couch and he took a chair close by to face her. She told him in more detail that the petition had been granted and she was no longer married.

When he wanted her to consider becoming a full-time housewife, she rejected that outright. She wanted to pursue her master's degree as planned. That being the case, he suggested that she should pursue it full time, to wit, quit all her part-time work, and he would pay her tuition. She said she couldn't accept the latter either, but the pronouncement didn't sound as resolute as the preceding one.

She realized that, if she went full time, she should quit her jobs at the restaurant and with Mrs. McNamara since she wanted to do well in school. She could still work on his project. He said that it depended on when they would "go public" with their relationship. He felt that once they did that, it would seem inappropriate to have her on the project payroll, even though experience indicated that their romance had not affected her good performance for the project. She said she understood that, but fretted about the fact that without those jobs, she would have no income, since now she would have to resign her position with the Petroleum Institute and give up the visiting scholarship.

"Don't worry about it. I'll give you an allowance to replace the scholarship," he said.

"I don't like the idea of getting an allowance even before we are married," she said. "In the meantime, I'll help you on the research, pay or no pay."

"I appreciate that, Saiyue. I tell you what. As long as you are doing the work, you should accept the pay, be it from the University or me. All right?"

She hesitated for a moment. "Well, we can leave that open for now."

He took it as a tacit acceptance of his proposal. "Saiyue, under the present circumstances, why don't you move in here?"

"Now?"

"Not necessarily tonight," he chuckled. "But, say, next week?"

"I need to give Mrs. Wang at the restaurant just one week's notice. But I don't want to leave Mrs. McNamara until she's found a replacement," she said.

He did not pursue the topic of her moving in. They turned to the question of a wedding plan. Although they didn't intend to have a big wedding, there were still legal procedures to be followed. It was agreed that since the fall term was to begin soon, the earliest appropriate time for the wedding would be between terms, say, sometime near the end of December.

After they finished talking, she stood up, moved to sit in his lap and hugged him. "Would you like to come to my bedroom?" he asked. She thought for a while and said, "You bad boy! I thought you were just a bookworm! But let's wait. We have waited this long. I like to do things the right way."

For him tonight, the answer sounded almost a relief. The gravity of marriage, now suddenly looming imminent, began to weigh on him, and dampen his amorousness. After she left, he thought about how to have the romance "go public," and how to tell his daughter, parents, and brothers. He mused for a while, brought his brief case to the study. He sat at his desk, mused some more and decided to sit tight and do nothing about going public. That night, he put in the usual nightly hours on his research, but without the usual accomplishment—a situation that had existed for some time, since the beginning of the romance, to be precise, and he was just becoming aware of.

Returning to her Oak Street room, Saiyue surveyed it like a bride-to-be looking upon the room where she had grown up. She would like to postpone, on some kind of principle, moving in with Panzhe until after they were married. But it simply wasn't commonsensical. Moving in before the wedding wouldn't be so bad now; even the inevitable wouldn't mean a green cap for Xu Haosheng. She thought momentarily what's the color of the cap I have been wearing since that night of Cao Rushi's farewell party, and why should I care?

A few days before the fall term classes began, Saiyue moved into the Pleasant Drive house (after Mrs. McNamara had found a replacement). Saiyue wanted the guest bedroom downstairs, saying that she'd move upstairs after the wedding.

That night she cooked spare ribs for dinner, made coffee and they had ice cream for dessert. She did the dishes also. After Panzhe had helped with the drying, she told him to go listen to music or watch TV, while she tidied up the kitchen.

He went down to the family room, sipped coffee and listened to Arrau play Mozart piano sonatas on the classic music radio station. After a while, she came down, carrying a cup. "This is for you," she said.

"I have my coffee here."

"This isn't coffee. Take it. You'll like it."

He took over the cup. The slightly yellowish drink was quite warm. Five or six whitish slices like cuttings from ginger or bamboo shoot lay at the bottom. He sniffed at it. "Hey! This is ginseng! Isn't it?"

"Yes. Drink up. You'll like it," she said.

"I remember my father used this in his wine. Sometimes in winter time, my mother would put some in chicken soup."

"So you know it won't kill you," she said with a smile.

He took a bit of umbrage at first. But quickly it was replaced by the humor he saw in it. He chuckled, "Thanks for the vote of confidence....Just so to ease *your* mind." He drank about half of it. "It does have a pleasant, light fragrance."

"I told you you'd like it."

He drank some more. She came over and sat beside him on the couch, putting her head on his shoulder. They listened to some more music.

"Are you going to work tonight?" he asked.

"No. Not tonight. Are you?"

"No."

"That's good." She said, and moved to sit on his lap. They kissed. He began to unbutton her blouse, then stopped and asked, "Would you like to come to my bedroom?"

"Just tonight, Bookworm," she said. "You go up first. I'll come soon." She went on to wash up a bit and changed into her pajamas.

As they were getting into his bed, he suggested that she take off her pajamas. She insisted that he turn off the lights. "It's too bright."

"Won't you let me appreciate your beauty?"

"Don't talk like that….As they say, in the dark, there is no difference."

"That's true only for beasts. Even if true, that would be reason enough to have the lights on. Tell you what. How about just the reading light?" He turned off the ceiling light and turned on the lamp on the nightstand. She didn't protest.

Before his eyes could be satisfied, she had the sheet and bedcover over her. Undressed he got under them also. They lay down facing each other. He slid one hand behind her head and the other over her waist, which felt slippery. Her upper lip contorting a little, she gazed at him. He saw the irises darken, giving off an aura of a saint or a tiger. They nearly hypnotized him, but only momentarily. He moved himself and her body closer. They embraced and kissed.

Alternately he caressed one breast and suckled the other, like a baby. Afterwards, to her surprise, he moved downward and began to kiss her body. "What are you…" she said no more but instinctively clamped her legs. He did not answer her unfinished question and pressed on. She put up only token resistance, a little twisting and heaving, and the mattress crackling low. Shortly she opened the legs, wide and wider and synchronized. She heard herself making soft cries like an evening bird in the woods.

Then stillness—the motion, the mattress, the bird, all ceased—but the hard breathing.…She said, "Come. Let me hold you." He reemerged and saw her face flushed pink surrounded by her glistening hair, fluffy beside the abused pillow. He was surprised to see her eyes wet. She turned off the light. He turned it on. She turned it off again. "Nobody loved me this sweetly," she said. They embraced tightly and kissed. He felt a sharp pain on his tongue. In a while, she said, "I can tell—you are craving...." He got above her.

Afterwards, they lay still, the breathing decelerating beside each other's ears. She said, "Finally, I have you. Bookworm!" patting him lightly on his back and changing it to slow stroking.

He hardly heard her. "How do you feel?" he asked, hoarsely, responsibly, though he could hardly move even his lips.

"I feel good. No more ginseng for you!" She thought of what Xiao Lin, her erstwhile apartment mate in Xi'an, had commented on once, "The inside is for men, and the outside for woman." She asked, "How about you?"

"Like in heaven, my angel!" he croaked.

18

Lu Panzhe woke up early. Cries of blue jays were heard and gone from the patio. He thought of the magpies at the Longevity Hall site on the Li Mountain and the lovely young woman steeped in the golden light of the setting sun, like an angel descended from heaven. The angel had shared with him the ultimate. He suddenly recalled her first utterance after the climax last night: "Finally, I have you, Bookworm!" He was in such an ineffable state then, as he lay like an animal just molted, or in nirvana, that only the word *Bookworm* registered as an endearment. Now it dawned on him that he too was an object of desire. The thought doubled his bliss, if infinity could be doubled.

He turned to look at her, sleeping beside him, the black hair spraying out on the white pillow. Her eyebrows flowed with Liu Gongquan's grace and Yan Zhenqing's[35] force on the alabaster brow. The full lips with the slightly upturned corners had a pinkish hue. Her wrist, white as frost and snow, rose and fell softly above the cleavage of her breasts incompletely covered by her aquamarine pajama trimmed in red—which she had bought just for the occasion—the upper red frogs untied. The blanket was

---

35. Both Liu Gongquan and Yan Zhenqing were noted Chinese calligraphers in the Tang Dynasty, as alluded to in Chapter 7.

201

almost down to her waist. How delicate she looked, he thought. And the hard work she had done thus far in her life, and would still yet have to do—the labor and toil ahead of her, to work for a master's degree to begin with. And who could tell, beyond that what would be asked of her by circumstances, other people or herself.

He desired to kiss her but feared it would awaken her. He wished he could compose a poem that would do her justice. To use the camera to catch her fascinations, he should have her permission first, he thought.

He stretched, and like a newly oiled old machine, got out of bed, briskly and quietly. He pulled the blanket slowly up to her shoulder, and went to the kitchen to make breakfast, all the while humming lightly the haunting melody of the adagio movement of Rachmaninoff's Second Symphony, and the body feeling all loose.

He had everything set up including the batter for pancakes when she appeared in a white terry cloth bathrobe over the aquamarine pajama. Like the dawn her face flushed from the night's sleep.

They embraced for a while. "You are cooking breakfast. For me too?"

"Yes, of course," he said.

"I have never had a professor cook breakfast for me before. Let me help."

"No, everything is set. I'll only need to make the pancakes over the hot plate. You just sit down. This is your first morning here."

"You mean you won't do this again later?"

"Well, that depends on how good a wife, or...lover, you are. If you are good, maybe I'll do this once a year on your birthday."

"That rare, huh? I better enjoy this." She tiptoed quickly to sit down while he poured a glass of orange juice for her. She drew almost a third of it in one drink. Standing behind her, he handed her over the shoulder a small velvet box.

"This is for you."

"What is it?" she opened it. A ring with a small colorless stone glinted blue, gold and silver in the morning light.

"This is a diamond. Isn't it?"

"Yes."

"This is too expensive, must be...too expensive."

"No, not that much. I can't afford expensive ones. It is small, but real. It is yours. Consider it an engagement ring."

"I have never seen a real diamond close before. Put it on for me." He put it on her ring finger. She looked at her bejeweled hand, rotating it slightly in alternating directions, her eyes twinkling with the jewel. She turned her head and lifted her face to him; her pink lips parted slightly, her eyes, clear, soft, full of love. He bent down and his teeth clasped the tip of her tongue.

It was the first of three days for registration. She rode with him to school. At the school year's beginning, there is excitement on campus, an almost festive air. The students are back; the faculty are back. The breeze carries the marching music of the football band at practice. It also carries the rock music loud from the open windows of the fraternity houses, in front of which bare-chested young men run after a giant vulcanized olive sailing through the air, turning on its major axis.

There is yet no homework. The students are free to spend all their time exchanging stories about their summer experiences and exploits. They indulge themselves in their youthful exuberance—like panty raids, gunning the engine, burning the rubber, and of course, pizza and beer shindigs and every manner of hormonal shenanigans.

The faculty, after the seasonal hiatus from regular campus life, are anxious to get back to the classroom again. They are like actors or actresses, who have been absent from the stage for some time, itching to try out for their art and craft some new ideas which they had not the time to seriously consider during the day-to-day show-must-go-on pressure in the preceding season.

They look forward to beginning their journeys with new classes of students through the fields of knowledge, where they will cultivate and reap together. In time the students will leave the grounds, use the crops to feed themselves and seed the next generation. They, in turn, will arrive here and keep these grounds flowering, fertile, and on it goes. Indeed, a university is like a city of eternal youth, suffused with physical and mental energy, radiating at daily as well as longer cycles. The main cycle, however, is defined by the beginning and ending of the academic year.

Caught up in the spirit of a new cycle's beginning, on this first registration day, Saiyue wore her new straw color denim jeans and a pink cambric blouse. She had her hair permed anew a month ago—first time in the United States. She had already had her master's degree program approved in June. For this term she would enroll for four courses: ME841, Control System Design; ME861, Computer Aided Design; CE872 Finite Element Analysis and MTH481, Boundary Value Problems-I.

She signed up for the courses, paid the fees, and returned to her desk in the Aeronautical Engineering Building. Her adviser, Professor Williams, had told her, and Panzhe had also confirmed, that the courses would be heavy and time consuming. However, they deserved the effort. She admonished herself that she was getting into the sinews and the meat of her MS program, a real challenge and opportunity to raise her level of professional competence, which would be the true foundation for a better life.

But first she had a letter to write. She wrote to Vice Chief Wang in Xi'an to explain her situation and request the Institute to release her so that she could stay in the United States after marrying the professor; and, for her part, she would refund the visiting scholarship monies she had received.

During the term she and Panzhe would leave the house early in the morning and return late afternoon. After supper they would each do their own work. Panzhe stayed in his study; Saiyue preferred to use the dinette table in the kitchen alcove. When she pondered on a problem, or a point, she'd gaze into the darkness outside. Not infrequently, as her mind caught a hint, a thread, her eye would fasten on some bit of faint glimmering light across the ravine, and at some moment, it would flash forth as she saw a bigger picture. She would then put her head down and set to work out the specifics.

She went after knowledge as some people after money. Every new concept grasped, every new method comprehended or applied in solving a problem was to her tantamount to a deposit in her personal account with some unbreakable bank. It was all the more gratifying to her to do this in such a tranquil environment. It was sometimes enhanced by the music emanating from Panzhe's study through the intercom. She would know then that he was grading students' homework or test papers. He had told her that he would not listen to music when studying or doing research because it'd be distracting for the level of concentration needed.

Oftentimes at night during the workweek, or on a Saturday or Sunday, she would need to return to the computer laboratory, and he would offer to drive her there. While waiting in his office, he'd do such *odd jobs* as writing recommendation letters for job-seeking students, committee work, serving as referee to review papers for technical societies or proposals for funding agencies.

In their normally busy lives, she relished most an occasional leisurely breakfast on the patio on a Saturday or Sunday. On such mornings they would sit at the wrought iron table having pancakes or toast, hard-boiled eggs, fruit and coffee. When it is early enough, they'd notice first a bright yellow sliver appearing on the brow of the hill across the ravine. The sliver grows and seeps downward, ever so slowly, urged on intermittently by the crispy calls of the cardinals, to present in shining gold the scrub oaks on the slopes. Below the enlarging triangle of brilliance, the dark frustum quivers in the air, nocturnal animals slinking to their burrows. The contrast of the composition, the balance and mystery are to gradually vanish, as the whole hillside bares itself in the sun. All would remain still though, except on occasion along the bank, two or three horses in gleaming bay could be seen carrying teenage riders, slowly swaying their way through the meager vegetation of the brown hill.

Initially, Saiyue would at times think of those mornings in Xi'an, when she drudged on her bicycle to work and noted how the sun similarly peeled the darkness off the roofs with the curving eaves. But reminiscences of this kind were pushed deeper and deeper into the background.

Two days before Qin Liang'yu left for Beijing, Saiyue and Panzhe gave a party in her honor. Liu Rong came with her boyfriend, Seymour Smith, who, she told her friends, was really not as old as his wrinkled face and white eyebrows would suggest. Late 50s she said. He had grayish blue eyes and thin lips. Usually reticent, when he did speak, he hardly opened his mouth—seemingly only the lips twisted. However, he could be talkative on certain topics, such as the faults of the trickle-down economics of the Reagan administration.

Present were also the Wus and the Chis. John Wu, a 6-foot professor of mathematics, had a B.S. degree in civil engineering from Taiwan, but in graduate school in the United States he shifted his major to mathematics. A few years older than Lu, easygoing, worldly—certainly for a mathematician—and unflappable, he would be vexed only at the remark of his friend Larry Chi, even made in jest at parties, that he was *only* an *applied* mathematician rather than a *pure* one. Ann Wu, his wife, a researcher in the State Health Department, was smallish, neat, still pretty—for her middle age—with a slightly curling mouth and chin. Sometimes an acquaintance or friend would comment that she looked like Sally Field; and Ann would argue against the suggestion in order to prolong it.

Larry Chi, a professor of linguistics, was about the same age as John Wu. Urbane and an amateur musicologist, Larry always had in hand a pipe, though seldom lit nowadays. John Wu, to reward Larry's elaboration on his academic background, enjoyed telling their common friends how the undergraduates got a kick out of watching and imitating Professor Chi—in his tweed jacket with leather elbow patches and a bright red ascot—chant Tang poems in his high-pitched voice. Karen Chi, his bright-eyed, thin-lipped, and absent-minded-looking wife, was an ABC (American Born Chinese) and a dietitian at St. Luke Hospital. Her eyes would dim when conversation at a party of Chinese Americans, often conducted in mixed English and Chinese, would drift into one in Mandarin only. On the present occasion, however, that would be unlikely to happen because of the conspicuousness of Seymour Smith.

At the party, Saiyue, in spite of her unconventional hostess status, carried herself quite naturally. It was Ann and Karen who appeared somewhat self-conscious, unsure how to behave towards her and Liu Rong as well. Liang'yu stayed with Saiyue practically all the time, that is, in the kitchen half the time. Thanks to the men, the atmosphere was pleasant enough and the party a fair success.

Saiyue significantly made the same dish—pork chops with onion—as she had done the first time she cooked in the United States and shared it with Liang'yu. The latter also gave her an A for the tossed salad that she had *taught* her. Two days later, at the airport, Saiyue again thanked Liang'yu for her assistance. They vowed to keep in touch.

Thus life went on. The daylight hours became shorter and the fall term was approaching its end. The lives of research professors—other than the teaching part—do not entirely follow the rhythm of campus life at large. Often it is during the days when classes are out that their work is the most intense—time to push on or catch up. If lately on Panzhe's love life, luck had been smiling sweetly, on his research work, all it showed him was mostly a fractious frown. Although the numerical integration that Saiyue had been working on was proceeding nicely, the other tasks were not. The Fast Fourier Transform method was giving unreasonable results; the boundary element approach for an infinite half-space was going nowhere. His grant had less than a year to run, and he had to be thinking about submitting a proposal either for a new grant or for a renewal of the present one.

The success of a proposal depends on not only its technical content, but also the proposer's reputation. At times it even seems that the latter is the more important because it affects, often unconsciously, the referee's judgment, particularly when there is a moot point. It is not that rare to come upon a referee, short on confidence, or competence and integrity, who would base his or her judgment almost entirely on that reputation.

The most direct route to build, maintain or improve that reputation is through publications. But to publish in major journals is no easy task either. Professors have teaching duties of course. Panzhe had two courses this term, an undergraduate and a graduate. While at times he would wonder whether his research, largely theoretical, would bring any real tangible benefit to society, he never doubted the value of his teaching. He'd never *borrow* time from teaching for research, and would not subscribe to the argument of some research faculty that only they could do the *creative* research in which they were engaged, while practically any degree holder in the discipline could do the *routine* teaching.

Recently, however, his research faltering, and time to catch up limited—as if to balance his many moments of bliss in romance—a dark shadow would fall upon him when he thought of the prospects of his *scholarly production*. That thought came on more frequently as the termination date of his current grant drew nearer. Besides, the thrust on research that he could normally count on making during a term break couldn't be realized this time. He was getting married.

Lu Panzhe had ended this afternoon a not too upbeat session on Discrete Fourier Transform with a graduate assistant. He pondered what he and his student could do, if the new approach just discussed wouldn't pan out. The phone rang. John Wu would like to visit him.

Wu came in and showed Panzhe the transcript of a graduate student of mechanics from Tianjin, China. The young man, a distant relative of Ann Wu, aspired after graduate studies in the U.S. with some form of financial support from the school. Panzhe was asked for his opinion as to his chances with TUC. The discussion, which lasted but a few minutes, ended with his telling John that an admission was likely, but not financial help—an evaluation that John seemed to have expected. The visitor stayed on. "How are you doing?"

"With respect to what?" Panzhe replied.

"In general."

"Well, in general, OK, but my research isn't going that great. All kinds of problems, you know, like the 'songs of Chu from all directions.'"[36]

"That bad, huh?" Wu said.

"Not all. The numerical integration work has been progressing well. In fact, the programming should be done soon."

"Is it the program being worked on by Ms. Zhang?"

"Yes."

"Lao Lu, you must know that the troubles in research you are facing are a balance for your 'Peach Flower Luck,'"[37] John said teasingly. Then his tone changed, "Seriously, the other night I happened to mention your marriage plan to Ann. She gave me a load and told me I ought to talk to you. I thought, as your old friend, perhaps I should, although I think you probably have already heard of those kinds of stories."

"What are you talking about?"

"It concerns *Mainland women*," Wu said.

"What about?"

"Well, she mentioned several so-called 'horror stories'—you know how the ladies like to exaggerate. She had heard at some of the social gatherings of the Chinese American groups, when, after dinner, you know, men and women would segregate themselves. Men gossip about politics and 'big issues,' like the economy; and women, well, they just gossip. A story went this way. A Mainland woman, after marrying an older Chinese American man, got her green card as spouse of a citizen, and shortly afterwards, demanded a divorce. She retained a Caucasian lawyer, and fought tooth and nail for the husband's property. She succeeded in getting a good chunk of it, including his house, and turned around and married the Caucasian lawyer."

---

36. An allusion—The King of Chu on expedition (circa 200 BC) found himself under siege by the Han army. On hearing the singing of Chu tunes all around his encampment, he suspected that his own kingdom might have already fallen to the Han force, and that the singing came from his countrymen in captivity. The expression denotes "bad news heard in every direction."
37. Luck in love.

"Then, it is that big-nose lawyer's turn to lose his house," Panzhe said with jocosity.

Ignoring him, John went on, "There are a number of stories like that. Now this is supposed to be absolutely reliable, and it happened in our own city. A Mainland woman, who had run into debt due to some business failure, married a retired Chinese American businessman. She recently told a creditor of hers to be patient, saying, 'The old oaf has all kinds of physical problems. His days are numbered. Just wait.' How do you like that, huh?"

"What have all those to do with me?" Panzhe said with apparent irony.

"I know you. But Ann felt that as an old friend, I should at least mention these stories to you," Wu said sincerely.

Panzhe had been aware of such talk for some time. In most communities, there were self-appointed protectors of morality. In the Chinese American community around him, Mainland women were spoken of as aggressive, predatory or even ruthless, although most of the members of the morality guild had themselves come from the same segment of the earth.

"John, I appreciate your thoughtfulness and Ann's. Of course, I know what you are talking about and mean well," Panzhe said softly. "In fact, I noticed at the party in my place the other day that Madame Wu and Madame Chi weren't exactly at ease. I figured that there would be talk. Besides Saiyue, I suppose Liu Rong wouldn't be immune either—"

"Then you won't be surprised that she has been credited with 'luring the old muddle-headed Professor Smith away from his German American wife of 30 years.'"

"That…well, I wouldn't exactly put it that way. Smith is neither green nor senile. To live with his hardheartedness, or heartlessness, in abandoning his wife of 30 years should be a burden for him to carry. It seems unfair to load it on the other woman," Panzhe said.

"From the outside we can see only so much. Right? Huh?"

"Whatever.…Regarding your concern about me, frankly, Saiyue is not that kind of woman you are worried about for me."

"I know you have sound judgment. But still, I hope you wouldn't fault me for bringing it up. It will not be repeated."

"I appreciate it."

After his friend left, Panzhe thought to himself, with all the things on my mind, he had to lay this too.

Saiyue had at one time a notion of a church wedding but soon discarded it. It wouldn't be appropriate since neither she nor Panzhe had been baptized, and trying to have the sacrament in a rush before the wedding wouldn't be right either. Besides, this would be the second time for both, and they were busy. So they decided on a small civil wedding, inviting only a few friends and close relatives. Saiyue didn't have any relatives in the United States. "I wonder whether we should invite my department chairperson, Dr. Duan and my advisor, Dr. Williams."

Panzhe didn't answer for a moment, and then, wiping his hand across his face, said, "Andrew Duan and I were fairly close when he first came here. Apparently he enjoys administrative work. He had told me—in an unguarded moment, I suppose—that he would like to be Dean of Engineering some day, not necessarily here. He entertained his colleagues a lot. Still does, I understand. He seems to be on that track though. He and I are of different feathers. After he became chairman—on the promise that he'd try to build the department to twice its size, doubling research grants, graduate enrollment and faculty count—we have sort of drifted apart. I heard that he has been having some physical problems lately, stomach ulcer or something."

Saiyue remarked, "Ah, I recall seeing him taking something that seemed to leave a white smudge above his lip."

"Oh, probably some antacid like Mylanta. In any case, I don't know how much our invitation would mean to him," he said.

"Well, then—"

"I have no problem if you would like to have him at the wedding," he said.

She thought for a while and said, "No, I don't think so. Neither need we invite Dr. Williams."

During the term they had done the blood tests and registered at the courthouse. The ceremony was held in mid-morning the first Monday after the fall term ended. In attendance were Mrs. McNamara, Liu Rong and Smith on her side, and his daughter, Sharon, who had come from New York City, brother Lu Panbao and sister-in-law Lucy from Los Angeles, the Wus and the Chis. Lu Panbao, a biochemist with a pharmaceutical company, a little taller and stouter than his brother, had the same dark eyebrows and clear eyes as Panzhe. He seemed to wear a smile constantly. On the other hand, Lucy, his angular and prim wife, appeared to be ill at ease, almost unhappy, throughout the whole affair.

A judge officiated at the ceremony. John Wu, bending his tall body and revealing a sizable barren plateau on his pate, also signed the marriage certificate as witness of the union. Saiyue wore an ensemble that she had her mother make for her in Shanghai—a light pink Chinese satin gown, embroidered with a multi-colored phoenix in the front, that hugged her body.

Sharon, a tall, slim 5 feet 7 or 8 inches, with slanted narrow eyes, high cheek bones and long legs, in a brown tweed suit and matching leather boots, looked like a New York model of haute couture. Since college she had lived away from home—on the U.C. Berkeley campus during the school year and in either Los Angeles or New York on account of summer jobs. Although she did not see her father that often, they remained close, not that their shared memory of Kimoon was the only bond. But as Sharon now saw Panzhe so spirited and intimate with this stranger, she couldn't help recalling the evening after her mother's funeral. The relatives had left; alone in the house, father and daughter first looked at then held each other and had a hearty cry, almost a wail.

"Sharon, this is Saiyue," her father said.

"I am glad to meet you, Saiyue." The daughter tried to smile but the command couldn't reach the facial muscle.

Saiyue was stunned for a second, for the Chinese in her had expected the introduction to be along some such line as "your step-mother" or, at least, "aunt." However, she quickly recovered and said, "Your dad talked a lot about you, Sharon. Finally, it is so nice meeting you." In fact, the father's American styled introduction bothered her less than his daughter's coolness. Saiyue wished that she could say, "Don't worry about your inheritance." The tension was quickly broken though, by other guests.

Mrs. McNamara said to Saiyue, "You look absolutely gorgeous." And Liu Rong told her that "Seymour confessed to me that he felt so envious of Professor Lu." Even the greetings and good wishes of Ann Wu and Karen Chi sounded warm and sincere, certainly more so than the perfunctory handshake of Lucy.

Later on, sitting at a round table, the wedding party had dinner in the inner dining room of BCD Seafood Restaurant—a Chinese restaurant in Foster City and considerably more elegant than the Pagoda. After the dinner, the newly-weds said good-bye to the guests and flew to Cancun, Mexico for their honeymoon.

19

When Saiyue and Panzhe checked in the Sherry Hotel in Cancun, it was already dark. In the lobby a young swarthy winsome woman placed a lei around the neck of each and offered them a fruit drink pungent with spicy liqueur.

A porter drove them in an automotive cart, with their baggage at the rear, along a lighted path gently winding through a garden, passing sculptured bushes and red flowers with protruding yellow pistils proud in foot lights. Beyond the dark vegetation of the garden, rock music and waves of laughter emanated from under a screen of tall trees, over which quivering luminescence danced—the main swimming pool, the driver told them.

Their room was on the fifth floor of one of the buildings in the hotel compound. The porter set their baggage on a rack, showed them the frontal view of the ocean—as Panzhe had requested when making the reservation—and the canned and bottled drinks in the refrigerator, tarried, but disappeared in a wink after the tip.

After washing up, they walked around the grounds close by the building, did a little scouting and chose a beachfront restaurant. It was not at all crowded, as Christmas was still more than a week away. They had a table by the corner of a terrace edged by a low parapet wall with red and purple flowers planted on top. Beyond the wall, the sandy beach extended into pale darkness. Belts of surf gleamed dimly, twisting with light hisses and sighs. Silverware on the white damask tablecloth glistened in the candlelight from a pink glass chimney. In soft sea breeze they had wine and red snapper.

They went to bed early. The fragrant night air and rhythmic surf added spice to their romancing.

The next morning they had continental breakfast at the same restaurant. Afterwards, they took a taxi downtown. Saiyue got herself sandals and shorts. Panzhe had brought his. They had lunch at a "San Francisco Cafe." The hamburgers were greasy, but the pungent Mexican salad helped to neutralize the oily taste.

In the afternoon they went to the beach. They took the sandals off to feel the warm white sand. After watching the waves for a while, they started to walk along an imaginary line where they estimated the incoming waves would wet them no higher than the lower calves. The estimation held for a time. Then came a big one that rolled in like a team of wild horses with flying white manes. By the time they realized its potential, it was too late—the wash pounded against their thighs, staggered them, and knocked the sandals off their hands. Panzhe quickly recovered and helped his young bride to steady herself. They chased the wallowing sandals in the foaming, whirling, retreating water, with Saiyue laughing and shouting, "Grab it! Grab it! Hurry! Bookworm!" Eventually, they retrieved them all. Panzhe pulled her close and helped her to brush back her disheveled hair while she giggled.

The waves were mounting even taller. They set the sandals on higher ground. Panzhe showed her body surfing, and assured her of its safety thanks to the beach's gentle gradient. It took her a few tries to get it right. After she learned to time her leap-and-dive with the arrival of the wave, and to relax her body afterwards, she soon got the hang of the sport. First a jolt propelled her. As she lay flat, almost limp in the water, rising and falling with it, she floated forward. A sound like a muffled bell: "doong-doong…doong-doong," patted at her ears. The warm water together with the gradual brightening of the sandy bottom to a milky color as it became shallower gave her an elemental feeling of security—like being in a womb. Though it lasted only seconds, she felt the primal bliss of a child.

That evening while dining at Captain's Cove, a restaurant outside the compound, they enjoyed the view of a docked ship, glittering smartly in the luminosity of strings of lamps along the shore and trailing on its deck and hull. Further on, dispersed harbor lights twinkled alluringly.

"This is beautiful," Saiyue said, suddenly thinking of the cooking she used to do, crouching in front of the pavilion room in Shanghai to fan the coal briquettes, trying to coax them to produce more heat than smoke.

"You like it, I presume," Panzhe said.

"Of course, how do *you* feel?" she asked.

"How do I feel?...I...feel like Fan-li."

"Who?"

"Have you heard of Xi-shi?"[38]

"Yes."

"Fan-li was the scholar-official who discovered Xi-shi. Later on he took her travelling and boating and they enjoyed themselves on the lakes of Jiang-nan."

"Oh...I am no Xi-shi. Neither do I wish to be a canary in some scholar-official's golden cage." Although she said it with a smile, and the tone was mild, it had a sort of sobering effect on him.

The next morning they decided to try tennis before breakfast when the courts weren't yet hot from the sun. Saiyue had learned previously that tennis was his favorite sport and had wanted him to teach her. But they never quite had the time to do it before. A stiff breeze was blowing, but on the courts the windscreens that were lashed to the high fence around them blunted it.

She was a fair table tennis player and had thought she could pick up the tennis game rather readily. To her surprise it wasn't the case. But after Panzhe

---

38. A paragon of beauty in the "Spring and Autumn" period (722-481 B.C.).

told her to turn her body one way first and then the hip and shoulder the other way and keep her wrist firm for the stroke, she began to be able to hit the ball with some pace and accuracy. She wanted to learn to serve too, but after a few frustrating minutes, she agreed that they should try it at a later session. So they practiced ground strokes. A little native boy worked hard at retrieving errant balls for them and was generously tipped afterwards.

After shower, they set off to a Denny's Restaurant at an arcade entrance a few minutes from the Compound. Before crossing the road to get to the arcade, they were hailed from the other side by a Mexican man in a bright green shirt carrying a brief case. With a couple of young cohorts smiling along with him, "O-hi-o go-zie-i-mus," he shouted.

"Don't pay any attention to them. They'd try to get you into some real estate deal. The travel agency had warned me not even to talk to them," Panzhe said under his breath. "They must have mistaken us for Japanese."

"O-hi-o!" the green shirt said loudly, as they stepped on the curb.

"No. Not *Ohio*. We are from *California*!" Panzhe couldn't help the jest. Nodding and smiling politely but without breaking stride, they walked on. Like a good sport the green shirt smiled an arc of golden teeth and let them pass.

In the afternoon, they went to watch a show presented by the Mexican Folklore Ballet in a theater near the arcade. She liked the cheery spirit of the brassy music played by the musicians in their bejeweled uniforms and wide band sombreros. The women dancers in their throbbing rhythm exuded much energy—to Saiyue, certainly more than the usual classical Chinese women dancers seemed to.

At sunset, they climbed up a promontory. Beneath a somber, hoary vault, the sea was restless, whitecaps popping everywhere over the wimpled leaden surface extending onto the horizon. Rolling waves dashed the shore endlessly. Clumps of tall thin grass, shivering and kept bent by a whistling wind, clung to the darkened sandy slopes. Two lone pelicans took turns to hurl themselves headlong down into the surging waters, reappear a while later, rise from the water sharply up high in the sky, and dive again toward the rollers.

Standing there watching, mesmerized, they put their hands around each other's waist, through a cloud hole the declining sun shedding its last rays on their back. She took out a stalk of beach grass that she had been holding between her lips, "What an evocative scene!"

"Yes," he said, "but look at them. What a way to make a living!"

"The pelicans?"

"Yes."

"How about the fish?" she asked. "As Mrs. McNamara quoted, 'All creatures great and small…the Lord God made them all.'"

"In the beak pouch?"

"Yes," she said.

"Well, I see what you mean. But one has to limit his frame of reference. In any case, one must do what's necessary to survive first."

"All right, I agree. Let's not get philosophical and just enjoy this moment," she leaned her head on his shoulder and turned her body a little to encircle him with both arms. The newlyweds stood there, silhouetted in the gloaming.

For the next day they bought tickets for a tour to Chichen Itza to visit the ruins of the ancient Mayan civilization. The bus took off around 8 a.m. and arrived at the destination four hours later including a rest period of about 45 minutes at a roadside market-cafe, where each had a can of the familiar Coca-Cola and bought a hat to protect themselves from the raging sun.

A guide led the group of tourists through the better known sites such as the "ball court." The visitors came to the observatory building and were greatly impressed by the architectural skills and sophistication of the ancient Mayans. "I can almost imagine how beautiful and imposing it must have looked when it was first completed," Saiyue said.

"Now the crumpled cylindrical shape only invokes, for me, an image of a post-accident nuclear power plant," Panzhe said.

"I used to think that China was the only ancient civilization of the world. Then I learned about how far back the histories of Egypt and India went, and now this," Saiyue said.

They came to the pyramid. Saiyue scaled its 100 feet or so with Panzhe following. They also climbed up the inner pyramid. At the top where visitors could view the stone "red jaguar," she noticed he had held his forehead and leaned against the metal fence that protected the exhibit.

"Are you all right?" she asked.

"I am OK," he said.

Out back on the ground, the guide led the tour group to lunch at a cafeteria. "You OK?" she asked again.

"I am perfectly fine now. I think it was the muggy and stuffy air in that passage of stairs that made me a little light-headed."

On their way back to the hotel, they stopped at a small Mayan village. The guide showed the tourists a couple of palm-thatched huts, with chickens picking, and dogs nosing about. Little kids goggled at them with big innocent eyes above their brief but stout necks. The guide solicited questions from the tourists. Panzhe asked him that, knowing what the conquistadors had done to them, how did he feel about the Spaniards. Pursing his lips, the guide thought for a couple of seconds. Seemingly amused, he shrugged his shoulders, "I don't know. I don't think about them. That's history."

"Do you hate them?" Saiyue asked.

"No, not particularly. Besides, what's the use?"

The answer surprised her a little. She thought some people were able to derive great energy from hate. "These people are so forgiving," she said to Panzhe.

"They are blessed," he said.

Night had fallen when the bus dropped them off at the hotel compound. Fatigued, they went to bed a little earlier than usual.

When she woke up in the morning, the drawn curtain was already soaked in sunlight. Panzhe was sitting at the table, his head over a heap of paper.

"What time is it?"

"It is almost nine," he glanced at his watch.

"You are really a bookworm. How long have you been up?"

"Since about five."

"What have you been doing?"

"I've been putting down some ideas for a proposal."

She checked herself from complaining that he should not have brought work with him on their honeymoon. She knew he had much to do, and they were going back in a couple of days anyway.

They did not do much that was new in the remaining time of the honeymoon, except a visit to a nightclub. On the last day, they were supposed to check out of the hotel and leave for the airport before noon. After brunch, they walked around the compound once more. They bought a few small souvenirs, sauntered into the main building lobby and sat down in one of the leather divans.

A patter was heard in the high ceiling hall; a small child had run in from an entrance followed by a young woman, then a young man—apparently the child's parents. The child in a white T-shirt and short pants was giggling, advancing himself unsteadily by fits and starts, the head leading the body. "Stevie, Stevie, be careful," the woman walked rapidly, bending from the waist as though she could catch him if he started to fall. The young man had a satchel and a milk bottle in his hand. In turn, he was followed by an older couple smiling in the direction of the romping kid. The man had a camera in his hand. Panzhe reckoned that they were the grandparents. No sooner had the young woman caught the kid than he twisted free and was off running again in his little blue canvas shoes. This time the young man did the chase.

As the older couple were passing nearby, Panzhe greeted them. The man replied, "Good morning! That little fellow tired out all four of us."

"A boy, eh? Fine looking boy!" Panzhe smiled congenially, his eyes following the kid and the rest of the family heading toward the front door.

Saiyue also had been watching the boy silently, thinking of another, ten thousand miles away, particularly with that manner of unsteady running.

Panzhe, eyes still following the child, said, "Look at that little boy!" and then turning to her, lowered his voice, "Say, Mrs. Lu, what do you think if we also—" Noticing her shadowy eyes and slightly contorted mouth, he stopped.

"What did you say?" she asked.

"Oh, I think we ought to start checking out now."

20

The night they returned from Cancun, in the kitchen alcove over a cup of coffee, Saiyue said to Panzhe, "I suppose now I should apply for a change of my immigration status."

"Of course. But there is no need to rush," he said.

"We might as well get it done and not let it hang," she said.

"We can write to the INS[39] any time. The paper work ought to be straightforward enough."

"Liu Rong said that she had heard via the grapevine that major rule changes are in the works. I think we better do it soon," she said.

"What changes?"

"I don't know the specifics. Whatever they are, the purpose, I heard, would be to make the status change more difficult."

"We could write them tomorrow," Panzhe said.

"I also understand that it'd be much faster if we retain a lawyer to do this," she said.

"Our case is perfectly normal and regular. Why need a lawyer?"

---

39. Immigration and Naturalization Service.

"A lawyer will get it done sooner before the rules change. I don't like things hanging. Anyway, I'll pay the lawyer's fee," she sounded impatient.

Smiling, he said, "I am not worried about that, but if you feel that way, we'll get a lawyer."

So they retained a lawyer—recommended by Liu Rong—by the name of Oliver French, who had actually worked for the INS before, to handle their petition.

For the winter term she again took four courses. (She received three A's and one B for the four she had in the preceding term.) He continued to teach one undergraduate and one graduate course. Although busy as ever, both felt more settled. Panzhe bought her a new Toyota Corolla after trading in her Buick. However, usually she'd still ride with him in his 1981 Cutlass.

She was appreciative that in the house there was practically no conspicuous item that would remind her of its previous mistress, except one. It was the framed picture on the piano of a decorous Chong Kimoon —with her books cradled between the right arm and chest. Panzhe had asked his new wife whether she would like it put elsewhere. "It's up to you; either way is all right with me." Her answer not clear-cut, the picture stayed on the piano. Afterwards, she seldom turned on the floor lamp near it.

He had noticed that she liked the intimacy of hugging. In the morning, before they went to the garage to leave the house, they would hug for a few seconds. They would do the same after they came in the house from school. When she told him, more than once, that she hadn't done this with her first husband, he had thought it might be something that she had picked up recently as an American practice. Nevertheless, secretly he was quite pleased.

In mid-February they were notified to appear at the INS Regional Service Center for an interview. On the appointed day, they brought along proofs of marriage and cohabitation: passports, marriage license, driver's licenses, bank statements of joint account etc. (After their marriage, they had opened a joint account while each still kept their own. To Saiyue's,

Panzhe had been depositing $500 a month, after she had ceased submitting her university time sheets for his signature.) Mr. French accompanied and presented them to the officer in charge of their case and left the room. After the officer reviewed the various documents with the couple together, he briefly interviewed each of them separately. He asked a few questions about their personal habits of a nature that a married person ought to know, such as whether the spouse would put on a bathrobe when getting up in the morning, and if so, what color. The petitioners had no difficulty in satisfying the officer. Afterwards, he told them jointly, "You should be hearing from us before long."

Soon the winter term rolled by. After a short break, and a week into the spring term, Saiyue came to Panzhe's office one late afternoon to return home together. He greeted her with a faint smile, saying in an undertone, "Hi." She answered likewise, and asked, "Are you ready to go?"

"Yep." Ordinarily he would go on to select his notebooks and files to take home for the night's work. This afternoon he simply stuffed a couple of binders into his briefcase mechanically. His eyes looked dull, shoulders drooped, and face elongated. She couldn't remember ever seeing him so drawn before—work and pressure, no doubt. On the way, she told him about her day—the classes, the homework, and the assignments. She added enthusiastically, "I can handle these. Just imagine by the end of this term, I'll have only six credits of Special Project to do in the summer before I get my degree."

"That's great," he turned to her, forced a quick smile and returned to the road. At the house driveway, he let her off to go to the mailbox, while he steered the car into the garage. Inside the house, he headed to the refrigerator for a beer. She followed him momentarily into the kitchen, casting a glance at the damp wrapping over the chicken breasts—that she had gotten out from the freezer in the morning to defrost. She laid down her handbag and books, and began to look through the stack of mail. Soon she stopped and fixed her eyes on an official looking envelope. It was from the INS. She carefully poked her index finger under an unglued corner and opened it.

There it was—her "green card," together with a form letter. She called Panzhe and opened her arms. He came over for the embrace.

"I got it!" she said with her head on his shoulder.

"What?"

"My green card."

"Oh, congratulations. Now we have that behind us."

"Let's go and celebrate. I'll buy tonight. Where would you like to go?" she bubbled over.

"Any place," he said lukewarmly.

"You name one."

"Charlie Brown?"

"Come on! Let's go some place different—Belle Vista?"

"We may need a reservation," still sounding less than eager.

"Okay. Charlie Brown it is. Anyway, I don't want to cook tonight." While putting the chicken breasts in the refrigerator, she thought Charlie Brown would be a fitting place too, as it was only a little past the anniversary that she first saw the restaurant on her first night on United States soil.

On the way, in spite of the occasion, the conversation was desultory and insipid, and it was not her choosing. After they got out of the car at the parking lot, she asked him to accompany her to have a look at the Bay. They walked to the bushes at the edge. The scene had hardly changed at all—the dark silken waters, the bejeweled bridges, and the spread of uneven steps and blocks of buildings by the water's edge, thinning, far-flung over the rolling land, populated by glinting studs under the night's high dome. Taking a deep breath, she rejoiced silently, I am no longer a guest in this place.

The restaurant was crowded, no table overlooking the Bay was available; they had a booth by the wall. The waitress laid the menu on the table and left. As he was reading it, she said: "Let's have some wine."

"All right…some wine," he responded listlessly.

She knew he could be pleasant and charming, as during such times as the tour in Xi'an and their honeymoon. Nevertheless, oftentimes he would appear preoccupied, even somber at times. Such a temperament was not out of the ordinary for a scholar; his was probably just a more serious variant of the proverbial "absent-minded professor." However, today's sluggishness was unusual even at the end of a long day at the office. Perhaps it's the nature of his work, which drained his energy day after day. Living like that, most people would eventually burn out. Nevertheless, it was a very special day for her and she would like to find out why he couldn't share her feelings and spirit of the occasion. "What's the matter, Panzhe. You seem especially absent-minded today. Is there anything wrong?"

He did not answer right away, his eyes averting her gaze. Slowly he said, "I am sorry if I am spoiling your happy mood. I know this is a special occasion for you. I am glad too. Your immigration status concerns me also, even though I had never thought there would be any problem. It was essentially a procedural matter. We were not competing for anything...." He hesitated, "Unlike my case...I've heard from the National Technological Council...that they will not support my proposal."

She understood immediately. She knew how important it was for a faculty member like him to get external financial funding. Yet she thought also that, while she could empathize with him, he did not quite appreciate the depth of her feeling toward the green card, the crystallization of her years' mental energy. Still, she asked softly,

"Why? Did they give you any reason? Did they say the proposal wasn't good enough?"

"Not exactly. They said that they liked it, or rather the referees did. They say it's sound, well thought out and all that. But there is no money to support it."

"Then it is not your fault...from the standpoint of scholarship or technical merit."

"Yes and no. You see, they have money to support other proposals —in their words, those that they call—more 'in tune with societal needs.' So, my proposal was good but not good enough in the competition for funding. And that is the bottom line—funding. If the rub were a technical point, I may be able to offer a rebuttal or amendment, but the present case leaves me no chance to salvage it.".

The waitress came. "Two glasses of Chablis, please," he told her.

"It's not necessary," Saiyue's spirit flagged.

"But I like to," he insisted. "Two glasses of Chablis," he confirmed the order.

"What are you going to do?" Saiyue asked.

"I don't know....Saiyue, I don't mean to blow my own horn. This is just the first time I have been turned down outright. I have been successful, or lucky, in all my previous proposals, although for some I had to present a rebuttal to a reviewer's criticism or query. But in the end, I got the funding....Now I suppose I'll have to try again. Try, and try harder," he continued.

"We students have heard of the 'publish or perish' dictum. You know I had often wondered why in the College Newsletter the dollar amounts of research proposals by the faculty members, approved or even just submitted, are always so conspicuously printed. And the names of those professors whose grants have totaled a million dollars or more are listed and lauded in the University Daily News. It's like that local real estate company's listing their million dollar sales people, and glorifying them as members of the million-dollar club. So now, it sounds like, along with *publish or perish*, you have *cash or perish* or *cash and flourish?*"

"It is intended to be recognition and encouragement for the efforts made," he said.

"But I don't know how much more effort you can or should put in. You even brought your work on our honeymoon. After all, you are not anymore a young scholar struggling to find a place in the sun. After so many years of mental labor, you are an accomplished scholar and professional. You are entitled, after putting in the normal hours of work, to leading a normal life with a reasonable amount of time for leisure and recreation," she said.

"That's an innocent, almost naive, way of looking at it. It's not the way it works in academic engineering in America these days, Saiyue. Sometimes I wish I were a professor of Tang poetry or a Shakespearean scholar."

"I know you like literature," she said.

"I do. But I also enjoy science. What I meant is that a literature professor doesn't have to face so many new challenges—to learn new things and then teach them—at such close intervals; Tang poetry and Shakespearean plays do not change, although their interpretations might, certainly not that much nor that fast. In engineering research, much of the new knowledge or scholarship acquired has a progressively shorter half-life relative to the typical career life span. I remember my old Dean of Engineering once admonished us to recognize that survival in modern engineering research demands adaptability and versatility. 'Today solid state physics must be grasped, tomorrow microbiology may take over,' he pronounced—".

"He sounded as if getting into a new scientific discipline is like going to the store to pick up a new fashion dress," she interposed.

"Well, he was just trying to tell it like it is.... Fortunately, so far I have not had to face that kind of drastic shift. However, one shouldn't rest on his laurels. At my performance review, when the administrator asks me, 'What have you done for me *lately*?' I should be able to answer, 'Mr. or Dr. John Doe, my fearless leader, this is what I have done for you lately,' in dollars, plus graduate degrees produced as well as student credit hours. Competition is the way of life. Competition! Yes, I can work harder; there is more I can do." Nodding for emphasis, he looked at Saiyue with a wry smile, wiped it off with his hand and stared woodenly at the silverware in front of him.

With contorted lips she had been listening attentively. Now looking at him as if she had discovered something new, she said, "You sound as if research is more about money than knowledge and scholarship—a sort of macho thing, and getting grants having to do with manhood."

He seemed surprised by the remark. In a short moment, he said, "I am afraid that is the culture of my work world. You have to have that attitude in order to compete and survive. That's about the size of it." He forced a smile.

"Maybe so. But I also understand that, generally, a research professor in engineering gets paid quite a bit more than a professor of literature," she said.

"That is a fact. But the implication—that money is the only issue—is not necessarily true. Many of us in engineering could make more money in industry, but the university attracts us with what it symbolizes—that aura of purity. Well, if it's not as pure as the cloth, it is seen to be halfway between the church and the chamber of commerce. But it withholds part of it from us and pays us in money instead."

"Are you implying that that money you'll have to pay back in the form of grants, and that the liberal arts professors, though paid less, don't have to pay back anything besides scholarship?" she commented.

"Not quite. According to Larry Chi, the professional life of a liberal arts faculty may not be all that pure either. They need to worry about enrollments, student credit hours and put their energy into what's fashionable rather than where their intellectuality points," he said.

"Industry does not have a tenure system. Don't you tenured professors have protection for your academic freedom?"

"Only for those who are willing to bear the insolence of the 'management.'"

"Are you talking about *personal pride*?"

"Hum.... You are probably right. I thought it was *honor*....You know I was first hired with the understanding to do both teaching and research."

"Research supported by outside funds?"

"Not explicitly."

"You have a contract?"

"No. No self-respecting university would be brazen enough to put it in writing. There was a sort of understanding."

"In perpetuity? Remember you have been doing this for over twenty years now. Don't you think you are imposing this responsibility on yourself by yourself?"

He was silent for a while, and said, "Maybe....Like attributing that aura of purity to academic institutions."

"Anyhow, as you see it, the engineering research professors have to pay back in grants."

"That's what it generally boils down to....But once you get rid of your illusions about others, and about your own self, it is easier to handle. And this is a free country, you know. Nobody puts a gun against my head to stay in this business." Again he wiped his face with his hand.

The waitress brought the wine, apologizing for the time it had taken her. After the food was ordered, Panzhe lifted the glass, and said, "Let's forget about my problems, and drink to the green card!"

"Thank you. I couldn't have gotten it without your help." She sounded as if the green card was her individual business and quite external to her husband. They touched glasses and swigged.

21

With her permanent resident status, Saiyue signed up at the University Placement Office for interviews with representatives of potential employers. She also began sending out letters with her resume. Due to such activities and the heavy load of her course work, in particular that of ME 886, mechanical systems design, she spent less and less time on household chores. Bed sheets remained unchanged for weeks, and wash piled up. Panzhe would often run out of clean underwear or socks, which never happened when Kimoon lived with him. At dinnertime, leftovers became the rule rather than the exception. He did not mind having leftovers every now and then, but they tasted too flat after being served three times in a row. Furthermore, he felt that somehow—maybe it was because of the passing of the honeymoon period or of her workload—she was not as caring and affectionate as before.

Once in an unguarded moment of displeasure, he mentioned that he was never used to having leftovers of leftovers. She responded by saying that she knew she wasn't as good a wife as Chong Kimoon. He wanted to say something to mollify her pique but was tongue-tied. By the time it occurred to him to say that he recognized her heavy school load, it seemed too late. Yet, it's true, he thought, rarely did Kimoon serve leftovers, and she resumed taking care of the house the next day she returned from the hospital with their newborn daughter. Her efforts had helped him to finish his doctoral thesis in one year. Even after she took a full-time job at the University library when Sharon was old enough to care for herself, she wouldn't let him help with housework either.

Now with Saiyue, in fact, shortly after they were married, he had offered to help with house chores, but she firmly declined, saying that since he had been paying all the bills, housework should be her responsibility. Now he thought he wouldn't mind offering again to help, had she been nicer to him. He kept quiet.

She seethed silently. Every time she cooked a fresh dinner, she would feel as if it were a capitulation to his big-man-ism.[40] Neither would she ask him to help as she would unhesitatingly have asked her ex-husband back in Xi'an.

In the days following, it seemed that the pressures of their work made the coordination of their schedules difficult. When she was ready to go home, he would prefer to stay on to finish something, and vice versa. The spirit of cooperation and compromise waned. Now they drove separately to school. The daily hugs and kisses became mechanical, and after a time were dispensed with altogether. Tension set in at bedtime. Their style of lovemaking had been built more on affection and empathy than on carnality. Now as she would become impatient, he would grow anxious, nervous and clumsy. Lubricants, which had never been needed before, would now be used; the act degenerated, and love wasted away. One night, as he was struggling above her to manage his manhood, she told him, in her plainspoken manner, "I can feel you are getting soft." That cut him. Afterwards, he had problems even with getting it up. Surreptitiously, he tried ginseng, but it didn't help, and he came to dread the bed.

To enhance the chances of having his research funded, he decided to go into more practical, application-oriented studies. He began exploring the

---

40. Male chauvinism.

application of his specialty, the theory of wave propagation in heterogeneous media, to the generation of computer simulated earthquakes so that engineers could use them for the design of important facilities, such as nuclear power plants, for which seismic hazards must be considered. Going into, for him, an essentially new area, he needed to do a comprehensive literature survey involving much search, studying and critical evaluation.

Once, in the library, he saw Saiyue sitting across a table from two young men, who seemed no older than his daughter. Their heads would come close over something on the table, perhaps an engineering drawing. Apparently someone had said something humorous; each recoiled back into the chair and, with a hand covering the mouth, tried to smother laughter. Her black hair gleamed and bobbed in the ceiling light.

That evening at the end of supper, he said to her, "Saw you in the library today."

"In the afternoon?"

"Yes.... It seemed you were having a good time," he said.

She cocked her head for a second and said, "Oh yes, you probably saw my two partners too. We were working on our system design project."

"I have not seen you so happy or laughing so heartily in recent days," he said.

She ignored the edge and replied, "Oh, Greg was making fun of the mannerism of our young instructor."

"What's so funny?"

"What's this—an inquisition?"

"No, no. I just wonder whether I still have a sense of humor."

"Come on! Panzhe..." She gave him a skeptical look, and continued, "Well, it is like this. The young instructor was kind of nervous and had sweaty hands. Every time he wanted to emphasize a point, he would slap his hand on the blackboard, and leave a dark damp imprint of the hand on it.... We all thought it was so funny." She chortled.

"Hum-hum," he responded with a sort of talking doll-like, closed-mouth chuckle. "Glad you can be happy sometimes, and with someone else."

"What do you mean?"
"Apparently you are not happy with me these days."
"How is that?"
"I don't know....I am too old, perhaps?"
"Don't be ridiculous! I knew your age when I married you."
"I know that. And that may be the point. It seems that my age didn't matter *then*," he said.
"What do you mean by that?" she bristled.
"Now that I am not that much use to you....There is no need to elaborate. We both know in our hearts."

A cloud of silence descended in the room. Her brows knitted, lips contorted, she squinted into the darkness outside the window. In a while, she said,

"Panzhe, you have hurt me. I would never have expected this from you."

He swept his hands over his forehead inside out and down his cheeks as though to wipe off some imaginary cobwebs. "I am sorry. I don't mean it the way you seem to interpret it."

"What *do* you mean?" she asked.

"I just mean that perhaps you have grown bored with me—and don't enjoy our time together anymore."

"Enjoying our time together is a two-way street. How can I have fun with you while you are morose all the time—preoccupied, like a brooding hen, with your research!"

"I am not doing research; I am just trying to write a proposal to do research. Anyway, I am not morose. I think you are cool and distant —all of a sudden since that day."

"Which day?"

"I don't need to say it."

"Here you go again! If you think that I am such a low character, why don't you stay away from me?"

Panzhe did not answer. From that night on, he slept in the bedroom downstairs. And he found life, at least at night, a great deal less tense. So she lived upstairs and he downstairs. They were like two unrelated tenants sharing the house; one engrossed in her degree work and job-hunting, and the other with his proposal preparation—both for their own careers.

For the dozens of resumes she had sent out, all she had gotten back were a few polite letters of rejection. The fact that she would not have her degree until the end of August was a significant factor, because there was a good supply of candidates with degrees in June.

After the finals of the spring term, she went to see her advisor to confirm the state of her degree program. "After you sign up for the six credits of special problems, the department will send forward your degree certification for August graduation," Professor Williams said. "Have you got a job lined up after graduation?"

"No. I think it's hard for me to compete with those who are graduating this month."

"With your husband's position, I suppose, you don't feel the same pressure as some others do," the aging advisor said with some familiarity. Saiyue and Panzhe had realized that although they were in different departments in the College of Engineering, still their relation could put themselves and his colleagues, who were aware of it, in a delicate position. She had avoided in every situation to mention the fact that her husband was a faculty member. Also they had not appeared together at any social occasion of the college or their departments. They figured that this abstention needed to last only until she had completed her studies. In reality, however, such circumspection was hardly necessary, since her academic performance was of a high quality.

"Professor Williams, I don't know how much pressure the others are feeling. But I would like to find a job, and soon, irrespective of my husband's position. I am afraid I am not the housewife type. And I do want to thank you for writing those letters of recommendation for me."

"I am sorry that so far they haven't helped that much," he said. "By the way, would you be interested in part-time work in the summer?"

Indeed, she had been thinking of part-time work—now that the prospect of landing a full time job seemed slim—even that of a university computer laboratory consultant had entered her mind. "Yes, definitely," she said.

"A consulting firm in Redwood City needs help on some computer work—on a part-time basis. If you are interested, you may call them. Actually call this person, a senior engineer and section chief, I think." He wrote down a name on a slip of paper and gave it to her. "In fact, he used to be a student of mine. Here is his telephone number. Or, if you like, I can call for you."

She made the call herself. Having ascertained that she was a graduate student and advisee of Williams, Todd Jensen, Williams' former student, now Chief of the Stress Analysis Section, Mechanical Engineering Division, John J. Clyde and Associates, suggested that she come over for an interview.

The firm, which specialized in design of industrial plants, was about a 20 minute drive from TUC. It occupied the 3rd, 4th and 5th floor of a 10-story building. At the interview, she met Jensen and an assistant section chief by the name of Charlie Hua. Jensen told her that they were trying to meet a project deadline for which, because of some design changes, much of the piping analysis had to be re-run on the computer, and they were short-handed. On account of a tight budget, he could only hire temporary help. Hua explained that the work involved essentially preparing standardized input from blue prints and obtaining outputs using a program, PAP IV. She told them of her experience with PAP II. Subsequently she accepted Jensen's offer of $10 an hour, working from 8 to 12 in the morning, five days a week, and she was to report to Charlie Hua.

During the summer term, she would get up early and drive to Redwood City to work until noon, and then have the rest of the day for her degree work, which she soon found to be not that demanding. In those days Panzhe usually worked late into the night. When he got up in the morning, she would have already left the house. She would be in bed when he returned home. His weekend schedule varied little from that of the weekdays. Hers was more relaxed by comparison, except when she had to travel out-of-town for job interviews. She would visit Liu Rong sometimes on Saturday and go to church on Sunday. She also found time to do some side reading—such as Greer's "The Female Eunuch," that Liu Rong had recommended to her some time ago.

She didn't see Panzhe that often. When she did, they'd exchange but a few throaty phrases. Weeks passed thus. Then without any explicit reconciliation, they began to talk and hold civil conversations, if for nothing else but to take care of household matters.

August soon arrived and her graduation was to be on a Saturday afternoon. He offered to take graduation pictures for her. She accepted appreciatively. He added that he would also like to invite some of their friends to dinner that evening to celebrate. She accepted that too.

The ceremony in the Assembly Hall of TUC on that festive afternoon was an abbreviated version of the June commencement. Nevertheless, the colors of the procession of the university officers, the faculty and of course the students, all in academic regalia, were no less impressive. In Elgar's *Pomp and Circumstance* Panzhe watched Saiyue marching slowly with fellow graduates, straight back, radiant, relaxed, with a hint of a hiatus each time she rose on the ball of her foot. "Quite a woman," he thought with pride. Yet there was also a soreness inside, akin to that he felt when he watched Sharon at her graduation on the U.C. Berkeley campus, just a couple of years ago. The graduate, like a fledgling, would be flying away. This time the soreness, which, after all, was basically of a different kind, went deeper. Then he thought his intuition could be wrong.

He and their friends applauded as she walked up onto the platform and received from the President of the University a token diploma, which would be exchanged for a real one later, after the records had been verified. In cap and gown, she had pictures taken with Mrs. McNamara, then Liu Rong, etc. When Rong offered to take one for her and her husband together, there was a slight hesitation on her part. However, they did have two snaps together, a black tassel dangling beside her beaming face under the mortarboard.

They had at a round table in the BCD Seafood Restaurant a proper Chinese dinner with six cold plates, that went zestfully with Qingdao beer, and a soup, followed by eight hot dishes. At the dinner, Saiyue announced that she had accepted an offer from John J. Clyde & Associates of a regular full-time position that was commensurate with her graduate degree and experience. They toasted her on the "arrival of double 'xi'—happiness—at the door," namely her degree and the new job. Liu Rong asked her when would she announce the third *xi*,[41] Saiyue smiled at her hollowly, not even bothering to parry for herself.

All day in front of their friends, they had talked to each other amicably when the circumstances called for it. When they got back in the car, the air grew tense again. They said only a few words about the traffic and traffic lights. After they came in the house, both went in the kitchen. Leaving the mortarboard on the dinette table, where she did much of her studies for the degree, she picked up the kettle to boil some water. "Would you like some instant coffee?" she asked.

"No. Thanks."

"I am going to make some anyway."

"I think I'll just have some water." He proceeded to fill a glass.

"On second thought, I'd prefer water too. They must have put a lot of MSG in the food. My mouth has this strong astringent feel." After she had her glass about three quarters full, she went to the refrigerator and added a few cubes of ice. "Do you want some ice?" she asked.

"No. Thanks."

She walked over to the alcove, took a chair facing the kitchen and Panzhe, and set the glass on the table, the ice cubes clinking against the glass wall. She fastened her gaze on the floating ice, glinting in the lamplight. He came over and sat across from her.

---

41. The character *xi* (happiness) may also signify pregnancy.

"Panzhe, I do appreciate all you have done for me."

"That was not much. I just made a few phone calls," he replied.

"No, not only for this afternoon. I mean everything that led to my degree. You practically gave me this degree," she cast a glance at the mortarboard on the table.

He now understood she was bringing up the "big picture," and sensed that there was more to come. "No. That is not true at all. I know you well enough that if you set your mind to achieve some goal, you'll do it with or without me, or anybody else, for that matter."

"You are overestimating me. The fact remains that without your help I would not have the degree, at least not as soon as I did. And, I just want you to know, I am grateful." She paused. Before he could think of anything to say, she continued, "On the other hand, I suppose we should start admitting that we can't continue to live together like this. It is not fair to either of us."

"You mean you are young and I am old?"

"Come on! You said you know me. I know you too. You are a gentleman, a man of culture and dignity. It is unbecoming of you to talk like a cad."

He felt abashed. "Frankly, Saiyue, I don't want to lose you in spite of everything that has happened." Her gaze remained fixed on the ice cubes. He resumed, "I know perhaps I should have worked on our relationship more. But I need to survive first. Which means I must regain my confidence and self-respect."

"I don't understand why you think you've lost them in the first place. I appreciate your qualities. Anyhow, you already have a career—one well established. I have yet to find one myself. As I told you before, age was never a factor with me in our relationship, but perhaps we did rush a bit into our marriage. In spite of your putting the age chip on your shoulder, you are not old in the sense of having a limited future. You are energetic and have much ahead of you. I know it. We both need to go forward—in our separate ways."

Panzhe felt a sudden chill and a shrinkage of his lower organ. He did not reply for a while. Then the wry thought came to him that her proposal might result in giving him true peace of mind. Furthermore, he was realistic enough to know that there was no point fighting her or trying to avoid the inevitable. "Is this what you really want? Have you thought about it seriously?" he asked lightly.

"Yes. Definitely," her lips sucking in an ice chip and clamping up in a contorted configuration, her eyes, gazing at the last fading light over the hilltop across the ravine.

He gave his face a sweep of his hand and said, "All right, Saiyue. If a divorce is what you want, you'll have it."

A few days later she retained Oliver French and filed a divorce deposition on grounds of incompatibility. Panzhe did not contest it. For the property settlement, she proclaimed that she did not want anything from him—she would not make any claim on the house, nor his pension accumulations with TIAA (Teachers Insurance and Annuity Association) and CREF (College Retirement Equities Fund). She said that with her degree she should be able to stand on her own. He offered her $40,000 cash—which he suggested she would need in order to get settled. She declined the money. She would, however, keep the Toyota that was in her name. Mr. French told them that theirs was one of the easiest divorce cases he had ever handled or witnessed. They parted civilly, with a fair measure of amicability that seemed oddly to have resurrected since the divorce proceedings began.

22

Saiyue rented a run-of-the-mill one-bedroom apartment in Redwood City close to her work place. Now as a Grade 9 Engineer in John J. Clyde & Associates, she had to herself a cubicle—about 50 square feet, slightly larger than her old domain in the Aeronautical Engineering Building in TUC—with a desk, a hutch, a PC and a book case. She was assigned to a newly formed "Computer Aided Design Group" headed by Todd Jensen. Her initial main assignment was to look into the use of a software, AUTODES, for the work of the division. She attended in San Francisco a weeklong seminar with practice sessions, presented by the company that developed the software. Many hours for going over the sample problems, notes, and the four volumes of user's manual were logged on her time sheets as her firm's investment on computer utilization. In the meantime, she would also be asked to perform certain well-defined ad hoc jobs for project work, which would be charged directly to the clients. She had been making the transition from part-time to full-time work rather smoothly and getting along well with her colleagues, except for one case. It had to do with her former supervisor Charlie Hua. Since her becoming full-time , she sensed a change in his attitude toward her.

While a temporary employee, she had found Hua knowledgeable and generous, although a bit loquacious at times. An ethnic Chinese, he would sometimes act the role of an "old big brother." Noting her industriousness and efficiency, he had once commented solicitously, "You don't have to work so hard. They won't pay you any more, or less, if you pace yourself a little."

She learned that he was born in Hunan province, went to Hong Kong as a teenager with his parents, got his BS from National Taiwan University after being admitted under the then favored terms for overseas Chinese students. He came to the United States and obtained his MS from the Illinois Institute of Technology in Chicago. A few years older than Todd Jensen, he had joined the firm before the latter did. But through the years he seemed to be stuck at Grade 16 in the firm. (The next level would make him part of the management, eligible for year-end bonus.) Two of his "contemporaries" had risen to be section chiefs, and some had become project engineers. "To be a project engineer, you have to be big and tall, preferably blond, and know how to play golf," he had told Saiyue.

She had felt that he had a rather limited view of the computer, regarding it just as a tool to handle compartmentalized, well-defined problems, such as the stress analysis of a generator mounting. The Chief Engineer, also a vice president of the firm, once issued a memo warning the engineering staff to not take computer results on faith and to always use *engineering judgment* to review them. The memo exhilarated Charlie, as if a decrement of the computer's power or name meant an increment of his. He brought it up several times with Saiyue: "Gobage in, gobage out." He spoke English with a Hunan accent, the thick lips turning over his slightly protruding upper incisors.

On another occasion, when she was still part-time, they were discussing the thermal displacement of a piping system and he showed her a method for a quick estimate of an upper bound of the displacement. She thought it was sort of ingenious and useful, although not of real major importance. Nevertheless, she thanked him. "This is neat. I appreciate your teaching me this. It'll come in handy as a quick check on computer output." Pleased by her praise, he said, "To tell you the truth, I don't normally teach these special techniques to people around me. After you get your degree and work as a regular employee somewhere, you'll learn that, in this business, you have to keep a few stratagems in your sleeves. Remember, in Chinese kung fu tradition, the master would normally withhold a couple of moves from his pupils. In industry, there is no need to show people everything you know. Hold back a little to protect your worth," he told her as if she were his favorite protege. She wondered if his attitude represented a version of the so-called oriental inscrutability.

While still in the midst of looking for a full-time job, thinking that he could be in a position to help, she had asked Hua informally about her prospect of getting one at John J. Clyde. He responded, "Things are slow. As you see, we are really not that busy. No new projects coming in." Then he added confidentially, "I know of a couple that are still being negotiated: one with the Pacific Light and Power and another with Indonesia. Until there is a new account, they are not going to hire any new people, not in our department anyway....But I can give you the names of a few other places that you can contact." Then he proceeded to give her the names of several well-known engineering firms, to all of which she had actually already sent inquiries. Later on, she had interviews with the Maryland office of Bechtel Power Corporation, and Sargent Lundy Engineers in Chicago. Both made an offer to her as a staff engineer. She asked Hua about the two firms. He spoke favorably of both—"very big" organizations with good reputations. She did not tell him that she had some reservations about the nature of the jobs offered. It sounded like routine engineering design production, while she preferred more innovative, computer-oriented developmental work.

Before she made a decision on her job choice, in spite of Hua's earlier assessment, she went to see Jensen, as a novice to an established member of the profession, to ask for his advice. She told him of the offers she had, and her reservations about them because of her interest in computer developmental work. Jensen responded with enthusiasm. They had a prolonged discussion. A couple more short meetings followed over the next few days, including one with the Chief Mechanical Engineer. And that led to her current full time position at the firm.

At first Hua seemed desirous of claiming some credit for her new position, but later he would appear somewhat sheepish that he couldn't square his earlier prediction that the firm wouldn't hire any new staff in her field. Subsequently, she found his attitude a bit confusing. Frequently he'd appear distant, even trying to ignore or avoid her. Yet at times, he would behave toward her in a rather intimate fashion, generally in front of other people—almost embarrassingly so. She disliked the situation. However, she tried to do and did her job in a businesslike manner, paying no undue attention to personal feelings.

While school dress was convenient and acceptable for a temporary worker on an hourly basis, now a full-time professional, she felt she should dress like one. She had augmented her modest wardrobe with several suits of the Jacquelyn Smith line from K-Mart. This morning, wearing a two-piece one: a black jacket with white trim (cutaway hem and frog closing) and knee high skirt, she came to work. In the elevator, sensing men sneaking glances at her, she felt pretty good about herself.

For the last two days, she had been checking the stresses in a piping system for a plant project at a preliminary stage. She had noted the day before, that the stresses in a couple of segments appeared suspiciously high. Examining the design drawing further, she thought that there might be a mistake either in the spacing, or the type designation, of certain supports. She rechecked her own work and found it to be correct. So she went to talk to Todd Jensen, who, in turn, asked her to contact the engineer in charge of the plant layout, named Amir Rahimi. She called the person, and was invited to discuss the matter in his office, which was one floor below hers.

She found him at his desk in a room with partitioned walls that did not quite reach the ceiling, but went up a lot higher than that around her cubicle. She knocked lightly on the translucent plastic panel above the wainscot. He lifted his head and stood up: "Ms. Zhang?"

"Yes. Mr. Rahimi?"

"Yes. Please come in."

Rahimi, apparently from the Middle East, was hirsute with black curly hair, thick eyebrows and mustaches—like raven's plumes—over the entire upper lip. Six feet tall and wide shoulders, the rugged features were, however, softened by the smartly pressed two-tone shirt and a paisley tie. A distinct scent of perfume came from his direction as she shook his hand and took a chair across the desk. What a princely man! I didn't think he was an engineer, she thought. The fact was that she had seen him before in the elevator and was impressed by his handsomeness and sartorial attention, which was rare among male engineers she had met.

"It's about the Tunisia project. Isn't it?" He smiled courteously, the raven's plumes lifting over the white teeth.

"Yes, you may like to look at the drawing," she handed him the blue print she had brought with her.

"Thanks," he spread it on the desk, bent and glanced over it quickly, and turned to its lower right box, where the names of the persons associated with the work were recorded.

"Oh, Albert King worked on this one. We'll need to talk with him. Please excuse me. I'll get him over here."

As he walked past by her to leave the room, she smiled her compliance, insouciantly casting her eyes about, not at any particular thing, but she could not help catching a glance of the convexities of his rear. In a few minutes he returned with King, another Asian face.

The upshot of their meeting was that there indeed was a mistake in the drawing—one of the "rigid" supports should be a "flexible" one. The corrections were noted. Throughout the discussion, she was impressed by King's perfect English, without a trace of accent, and the fact that he didn't seem to be embarrassed by the mistake or attempt to defend it in any way. He simply admitted it and jokingly said, "I did this in the afternoon of my bowling night....Sorry, I'll have to be more careful." Like a good leader, Rahimi commented that there was no great harm done as the project was only in the initial stage. Indeed, such preliminary designs were not much more than hasty modifications from some existing ones for similar plants that had been engineered and constructed already.

She thanked both and walked out of the room with a hint of a swagger in her black imitation snakeskin pumps with crimson tip and heel, fairly certain that the men's eyes would follow a ways. A couple of days later, she met King in the elevator at quitting time. Walking out together, she learned that his great-great-grandfather had come from Taishan, Guangdong province, in the mid 1800s and had worked on the Trans-America railroad. His Chinese surname was Jin ("Gold"), that had been anglicized as "King."

When she started working full time at Clyde, she used to bring her own lunch. After a time, some colleagues asked her to join them for lunch in the cafeteria down on the first floor of the building. Since then she pretty much gave up bringing her own and would usually go with the group at noon. She enjoyed the change from her small cubicle milieu, as well as the sociability and the office scuttlebutt.

A couple of weeks after she had finished the Tunisia job assignment, a computer run had kept her from joining the lunch group earlier, and now she was eating by herself alone in the cafeteria. Rahimi came in, holding a cellophane wrapped sandwich, a red-white can of Campbell soup, a Styrofoam bowl and a plastic spoon half wrapped in a couple of paper napkins. Espying her, he walked over. Smiling and nodding lightly to engage her recognition, he asked: "May I join you?"

"Of course," she said.

"Thanks. So you are late for lunch too."

"I needed to finish an item on time," she said.

"I know. Everything here is due yesterday....You eat here often?" he asked.

"Almost every working day. Haven't seen you here before."

"I don't particularly enjoy cafeteria food. Sometimes, like today, I have no choice. Just picking up something for the stomach. By the way, I trust you have no more problems with that Tunisia project item." He opened the can and slowly poured the soup into the bowl.

"No. It's done as far as I'm concerned. Thank you for your help."

"No problem. The project should thank you for catching the error at an early stage. I wouldn't be surprised if they'd ask you to help again later on....I believe you haven't been here too long. Right?"

"Yes, since about three months ago."

"That recent! I thought I'd seen you before that."

"I was temporary and part-time then. I became full-time after I got my master's."

"From where?"

"TUC."

"Oh. My alma mater's competitor."

"You went to...?"

"Stanford."

"The famous Stanford. I understand it is a top school of the country."

"Yes, it is. But not all its graduates are good though," he smiled and then chewed evenly with his mouth closed. "Did you do your undergraduate work in the United States also?" he asked, clear-mouthed. She thought he could have the food go down from the mouth without swallowing.

"No."

"Where? China, Korea or Japan?"

"China."

"How interesting!"

"How long have you been with the firm?"

"Quite a while now. Let me see....Almost 10 years. I believe Todd Jensen and I joined the firm about the same time."

"Oh," she said, "you have much seniority. Over me, at least."

"That's not important," he smiled. After pressing each corner of his mouth lightly with a paper napkin, he pursued, "Ms. Zhang....I hope you won't mind my asking. Are you married?"

"I am separated. You married?"

"I am not. I know we'll have to go back to work soon. Would you mind if we continue our conversation sometime later? May I invite you to a dinner?" He looked at her ingenuously. His eyes reminded her of those of a little Mayan boy she saw near Chichen Itza—big, shining and mild.

She hemmed for a few seconds and said, "All right."

"How about this Friday evening?"

"All right." They agreed on a time and exchanged addresses and phone numbers.

Later on she reflected: He must be around…what? Say, 35? Having worked here for 10 years already, at this age and with such good looks and still unmarried, must be a womanizer, a playboy. No doubt, a wild one, in spite of his mannerly appearance. You better watch out. But a wild engineer? Oh, it should be all right—a Stanford graduate and 10 years with the firm.

The image of the dark eyes, the raven plumes, the callipygian rear all seemed to corroborate the saying she had heard in college that Mideasterners are the best lovers. She tried to suppress her thoughts along these lines. In one moment she wished Friday to come soon; in another she dreaded its arrival—she had never gone out with a "foreigner" before. (She had not considered Panzhe a "foreigner.") The exoticism of dating one from a different ethnic background aroused both apprehension and sensuality, like two diametrical satellites orbiting her mind.

The buzz of her apartment sounded. "Who is this?"

"This is Amir, Amir Rahimi."

"O yes. Please come in." She released the front door lock of the building. In a moment a knock on the door. She opened it to a bundle of red roses and two dark eyes above them.

"Hi! Mr. Rahimi!"

"Call me Amir, please. This is for you." He offered the flowers. Not wanting him to come in the apartment, she took over the bundle, saying, "Thank you very much. I'll take care of this first and be right back."

She let him wait by the door. Unable to get the flowers into the refrigerator without risking damaging them, she lay them in the kitchen sink and went to join her new friend. He escorted her out—his navy blazer and gray gabardine trousers matching pleasingly with her burgundy jacket dress and black crepe skirt—and opened for her the door of a black Mercedes. In the car, he asked:

"Do you like Italian food?"

"I do."

"Good. I thought you might like something other than Chinese. Actually, I have made reservations at an Italian restaurant. Of course, we could change, if you like."

"That's fine."

Seated at a corner table in the Florentine's Restaurant in Palo Alto, they ordered Minestrone soup and stuffed mushroom. Then she chose fettuccine chicken Florentine; he asked for primavera, and Chardonnay wine also. Over the drinks and food he told her that he had received both his bachelor's and master's from Stanford in Mechanical Engineering. His father had been a general in the Iranian army of the Shah. His family had been living in Paris since 1979. She told him about her marriage to Lu Panzhe and that they were now getting a divorce.

"Did you come to know him here?" he asked.

"No. Actually I met him in China while he was giving a short course at the Xi'an Petroleum Institute where I worked," she said.

"That was romantic. Wasn't it?" he smiled at her.

"Well....Yes. Actually it started with respect," she said.

"Respect is a good start and needs to be kept for romance."

He sounds like a nice man, she thought. "You said you are not married. Were you ever?"

"Yes. Once."

"Yes?"

"I was married for two years. My ex-wife and I were divorced... oh...almost four years ago."

"Any children?" she asked.

"No."

She felt he was about to reciprocate the question, but he didn't. Instead, he asked, "What do you do after work, for recreation and relaxation?"

"Not much. I usually go to church on Sundays."

"You are a Christian?"

"Not really. But I enjoy the atmosphere of the church. Do you believe in any religion?"

"I am a Muslim—only nominally though. I have not been in a mosque in ages." The chuckles suggested that he did not take his religion all that seriously. "What else do you do for recreation?" he asked.

"I told you—not much. I have been busy and don't have much spare time. I have been in this country for only about two years, part-time jobs, graduate studies, marriage, and divorce....I didn't need much diversion."

"Yes, I understand," he did not smile now, and said that softly.

"What do *you* do besides work?" she asked.

"Well, I like to do a lot of things. The problem is also time. I like to play tennis, and—"

"Tennis. Everybody likes tennis," she commented.

"How is that?"

"Never mind. What else do you like?"

"I like dancing, hiking, biking, concerts....There is so much you can do around here. Perhaps, one of these days, we can do something together."

"Like what?"

"Whatever you like."

"I don't know how to play tennis. I tried a little some time ago. It was difficult."

"No, not really. But you have to pay the dues though—spend the money for lessons and time to practice."

"I don't have the money, or the time, or the patience. But I suspect that the biggest problem is my lack of talent for the sport."

"What modesty! We can always try something else, like an outing somewhere."

"Perhaps."

They chatted easily and pleasantly. It was a little past eight when they finished. Rahimi first proposed they go dancing. She didn't feel up to that. Yet it seemed too early to ask him to take her home. She was glad when he suggested they take in a movie.

They saw "Secret Admirer," a comedy, at the Bijou Theater. Returning to her apartment building, he watched her open the front door and moved no closer than to reach her with his outstretched hand. "Thank you for a beautiful evening, Ms. Zhang."

"Call me Saiyue. We need not be this formal." They held hands ready to shake them.

"What? Tsai-yeh?"

"No. Sai-YUE."

"Yes, Saiyue. Thank you for a beautiful evening."

"Thank *you*. I enjoyed it too." She shook his hand and turned.

Back stepping, he said, "Good night."

She quickly turned her head, "Good night." Closing the door behind her, she hurried to her apartment. She had a vague feeling of disappointment that the evening was not as much an adventure as she had anticipated and feared. On the other hand, she was glad that Rahimi had behaved properly, and she had faced no "crisis."

Afterwards, they went out together almost every week. They tried tennis. He was too advanced for her, and she didn't want him to take the time to teach her. Dropping that, they tried hiking. Neither seemed enthused by it. Cycling proved to be the recreational sport both enjoyed. With her experience in China, she was more than his equal. He would pick her up, lash her new Schwinn on his car and drive to Palo Alto.

Their favorite route was essentially a loop behind Stanford University. They'd start from the bike lane just west of El Camino Real along Arastradero Road. Going west with the hills in sight ahead of them, they'd turn into Miranda Avenue, crossing Campus Drive and the Stanford Golf Course, get on Alpine Road. There sometimes they'd stop to look at the horses in a riding corral. Once, after she had shooed away a big crow going after a fledgling sparrow under the fence, he bought a rose for her from a roadside flower cart—on behalf of the little bird, he said.

Skirting Portola Valley, they'd sometimes stop in Rossottis, a country style inn, to have a coke and share a hamburger. Now entering Santa Clara County, joining the southern leg of Arastradero Road and pedaling hard upgrade past the dangling eucalyptuses, they'd pick up speed on the downgrade; thus complete a healthy loop of some 16 miles.

They also had other kinds of activities together. Once they went on a boat ride at Half Moon Bay. The boat leaving the dock, the wavelets quivered rapidly and glanced bright and dark as if the water were filled with writhing silvery sardines. In the open sea, white and gray gulls hovered above the spreading wake. Behind, the land flattened; ahead, the blue waters fused with the translucent sky in an arc. By the gunwale railing she lay her head at his shoulder, immersed in the hypnotizing lapping on the hull. Having grown accustomed to his perfume, she also liked the prickly feel of his mustache as he lowered his head to sniff at her fluttering bangs. She turned her face to him. He gave her a Clark Gable-like roguish smile and a squeeze of her shoulder with his big hand. And that was all.

Another afternoon, he brought her to an Iranian friend's wedding. It took place in a hotel parlor. The bride and groom sat in the front of the room with several clergymen, who, wearing short black vests, read scriptures from a large worn-looking book. The chanting droned on and on, seemingly for hours, while dozens of guests just sat there. Her patience challenged, she felt out of place. However, they did enjoy a fine dinner afterwards. He told her that his friend and the bride were Zoroastrians, which she assumed (mistakenly) was a denomination of the Moslem religion.

A couple of months had passed since their first date, and they hadn't even kissed. She wondered about the veracity of Mideasterners' amorous reputation. It couldn't be her, because he obviously enjoyed her company. They would hug. When she lifted her face, he would turn his a little and rub his cheek against hers to show his affection. Perhaps he was a very, or overly, cautious person, perhaps his religion had something to do with it. Anyhow, he was a gentleman, a good companion to relax with after work. Certainly she wasn't going to overstep the bounds of propriety, and would wait and see.

On a Saturday evening she went to his apartment for a dinner that he said he would cook for the two of them. The living room was made to appear larger by a mirror covering the entire front end-wall above the wainscot. An entertainment center was fitted below the window facing a large tan sofa, in front of which a glass-topped cocktail table sat on a Persian rug, and behind, hung a modern psychedelic oil painting of whirling blue and white. A floor lamp stood between an easy chair and an end table. The air was scented with Chopin waltz.

They drank beer before dinner. He went on to serve her rice cooked with chicken broth and minced chicken meat, green beans, shish kebab—lamb, beef, tomatoes, onions and yellow and green peppers. They had red wine with the food. As dessert, he served her a pudding with dates that to her tasted too sweet and oily. She complimented him on his culinary skills, withholding her reservations about the dessert. Apparently pleased, he offered her coffee brandy. She declined in favor of just coffee; he filled a snifter with the liqueur for himself.

In a while, he asked her whether she would like to dance. In high spirits herself, she said yes, although she wondered whether there was enough space for dancing in the fully furnished room. He put in a tape and they slow danced to the tune of Mancini's *Moon River*, holding each other, more gentle body swaying than feet displacing. The bodies were pressing progressively tighter together.

"What's this perfume you have on?" he asked.
"Just some I picked up last week."
"You don't normally use perfume."
"That is right."
"Why tonight?"
"I don't know. I bought it. Might as well try it. You like it?" She had thought her perfume might stimulate more zest in him.
"You smell good....And I am drunk," he said. His mustache prickled her ear lobe.
"The coffee brandy got you, umm?"
"No. You!"
"You mean the perfume made the difference, not me, umm?"
"No. It is you." He stopped moving; bending his head, he kissed her on the mouth. The raven's plume brushing her cheek, she responded hotly. He ran his hand under her skirt and kneaded her buttocks. She pressed her pubes forward, and even in that suddenly highly charged and heated state, she had a vague odd feeling.

After fumbling unsuccessfully to unhook her bra, and failing also to insert his large hand inside it, he unzipped his pants and guided her hand inside. She anticipated a robust cantilever beam. Instead, she got hold of a cylinder, sizable enough, warm but limp. Suddenly he stopped—frozen like an African wildebeest anchored by wild dogs—while she squeezed it. It was tumescent but remained flaccid. She repeated a couple of times, but the results were the same.

He withdrew from her. "It's no use. I can't do it. I am sorry." He zipped up and sat down crestfallen on the sofa, his head in his hands.

Befuddled, she squirmed, righted her bra and straightened herself up. It took her a little while to realize the overall situation. From the easy chair, she said softly: "It's all right. I understand." Actually she didn't, not entirely. She had heard about his kind of condition before, but never would have expected it for his age and virile appearance.

He raised his big weary eyes and said again, "I am sorry."

"Don't say that. Are you always like this? Pardon my question—I am not prying, just a little curious."

"No. Of course not."

"You need just to wait?"

"I have waited for several years now. Darn it."

"Years!" she said. "Pardon me. If you want me to shut up, I will. Did your divorce have anything to do with this?"

"Yes and no....Yes and no. I don't want to talk about it." He got up to turn off the music and sat down again.

Neither spoke. She wondered what should or could she do or say. As the awkwardness was getting to be quite uncomfortable, he said,

"If you really want to know, I'll tell you."

"Yes?" she prompted.

"I was normal—nothing great, but...normal, when I got married. After our marriage, I discovered that my wife was sleeping around. Practically with anybody. Once she even said that she'd like to try them all if she could. She said it was a joke. But I wondered. You know, she reminded me of a bumper sticker once I saw on a coed's car: 'So many men; so little time!' But it seemed that my ex-wife meant it. It's like some kind of a disease, you know.

"One time I even caught her myself in our own apartment with another man. She said it didn't mean anything and she loved and needed me. You know what? I sort of believed it. Apart from that sickening behavior, basically, she is not a bad person. Warm but rather naïve. Anyway, I couldn't help thinking that her body was dirty with all those deposits and could not arouse myself with her even when I had an urge."

"So you couldn't, or wouldn't, sleep with her," she said.

"Not only that. How could I accept the situation? We were divorced. After that, I seem to have developed this brake or valve that I have no control over. Whenever I feel aroused, it would by itself shut off the flow before I got fully pumped up....I want you but I am sorry. I can't do it."

"Don't mind me," Saiyue said, thinking he is a mechanical engineer all right. "Have you gone to see a doctor?"

"Yes. I saw a specialist. Two, in fact. They tested me for this and that. You know, testosterone, diabetes, etc. They can find nothing physically wrong with me."

"So it is psychological."

"I don't know."

"Have you seen a psychologist or psychiatrist?"

"No."

"Perhaps you should."

"I don't know. I don't want people to think I am nuts."

"Hum." She went over, held his hand, kissed it and put it on her thigh. There was no response from him. "Perhaps, I should go back."

"I am sorry I have spoiled the evening for you."

"Don't say that. You take care."

The next day she waited for him to call. He didn't. So she called him the following week. He said that he was busy and would not have time to go out with her. She gave up on him as a boyfriend. Afterwards, when they came to proximity of each other in the elevator or in the cafeteria, she sensed that he would first try to avoid her. Failing that, he would then still greet her in a very gentlemanlike and cordial manner.

In mulling over the experience, she felt a sense of loss, but also one of relief. After that Iranian wedding that he had taken her to, she had wondered how could she ever adjust herself to a culture so different from her own background and experience.

She missed her family more keenly now, especially Baobao. Apart from the boy, who were her family? Sure, her family in Shanghai. Then, Haosheng and Panzhe? Neither, of course. She wanted to see her son. According to her own grandfather, who had been acting as an intermediary between herself and Xu Haosheng, the boy was getting on quite well in Nanjing with his paternal grandparents. She would like to bring him over to the United States. But it would involve serious negotiations with Xu and that could lead to some unpredictable situation, even legal wrangles that she was not prepared to get into just now.

Perhaps she could ask or invite her own parents to come. But she felt more inclined to invite her grandpa. Considering their different background, the trip probably would mean more to her grandpa than to her parents. Besides, he was older—her parents would have ample opportunity to visit later—and, financially, if he came, only one person needed to be supported for the trip.

She composed a letter to her family in Shanghai. She said she missed them badly, and that her job wouldn't allow her to go and visit them, but she would like to have either her parents or grandpa to come for a visit, and she would pay the expenses for the trip. Outwardly she left it to them to decide, but she was pretty sure that it would be grandpa who would come. More than likely they would consider the choices in the same way as she did. Besides, it would not be easy for her parents, still working, to have an extended leave to travel abroad.

23

After her first visit accompanying Mrs. McNamara to Hillsdale United Church, Saiyue had been going back there on Sundays more or less regularly, except during such periods as when her MS degree work was specially pressing, or, more recently, when the romance with her fellow engineer took precedence.

This Sunday, two months after she had parted with Rahimi, she was pleased to note from the "order for worship" that, for special music, in addition to an anthem by the choir, there would be a tenor solo by Raymond Dalton. She remembered clearly the name, but even more clearly the lyric voice and emotive rendition of *Comfort Ye, My People* by Handel on one occasion, and *The Holy City* by Adams on another. This morning he was going to sing Gounod's *Ave Maria*.

The music came after a reading from Paul's letter to the Philippians, exalting them to dwell on things that are true, honest, just, pure, lovely, or of good report. She thought of the similarity of these qualities with the three pursuits of life: "truth, goodness and beauty," which, as her grandfather had told her, were advocated by certain Chinese intellectuals during the New Cultural Movement (also known as the May 4th movement) in the years around 1919.

Everyone else in the sanctuary was seated except the soloist, who stood of medium height. Above the blue vestment and white surplice, the fair face had an almost angelic aspect except for the Roman nose, which imparted an impression of authority and manly dignity. The organ started tranquilly, like a purling stream, with Bach's *First Prelude*. Tilting up his head upward slightly and looking toward the stained glass window with a child-like gaze, he began softly: "*A—ve Mari-a Gra-tia Ple-na Do-minus te-cum....*" ("Hail, Mary! Thou highly favored, God is with thee....") Then the voice gradually rose—praised, pleaded, with humility, purity and reverence. A crescendo came in the invocation: "*San-cta Mari-a, San-cta Mari-a, Mari—a,*" ("Blessed Maria....") followed by the gentle supplication "*O-ra pro no-bis....*" (Pray, oh, pray for us....") And like a wave rolling in from the distance, another surge, *cri de couer*, "*no-bis peccato-ribus, nunc et in hora, in hora mortis nos trae.*" ("Pray, oh, pray for us, for us wretched sinners, now and when the hour of our death, our death o'ertakes us.") It ended with a supplicating "*Amen....Amen....*" lingering, fading—like a wisp of heavenward incense.

The worshippers in the sanctuary felt there had been a consecration. Not a sound was heard until the Reverend Norton's maroon vestment rustled, as he rose to deliver his sermon. Before commencing his homily, he commented, "After hearing music like this, how could anyone have a bad or base thought....And would you just like to go out and do a really good, Christian deed?"

After the service, she met Mrs. McNamara. They went to have a cup of coffee at the church's Social Hall and chatted relaxedly. Mrs. McNamara, seeing Michael Bellini coming into the room, said, "I would like to compliment him on the music today." The old lady beckoned him to come over.

"Good morning, ladies." Bellini was cheerful.

"Mike, good job again this morning," the venerable lady said.

"Thanks. We did not do that much today. Ray alone carried half the special music. We know he is good. But today, he was fantastic! By the way, isn't his aunt a friend of yours, Ann?"

"Yes, she used to live in this area before she moved back to Seattle. We still write to each other occasionally."

"Perhaps you can get her to urge him to join us on a regular basis," Bellini said half in jest.

"Indeed, the congregation would all like that," Saiyue joined in.

"I could mention it in my next Christmas card," Mrs. McNamara sounded earnest.

"Well," Bellini said, "I certainly wish he were one of our regulars.... But when he agrees to sing for us, he always does a great job. No doubt about it—he is good, almost professional.

"Come to think of it. He is coming to our fellowship group gathering tonight at my house. Saiyue, would you join us? You need to bring a dish though. It is a potluck affair. Ann, you are welcome too if you would like to come." The old lady was aware that the fellowship groups in the church were formed essentially along age lines. "I think I'd like to stay home tonight," she declined gracefully. Saiyue accepted. Bellini gave her his address together with a few directions and telephone number and told her to simply bring some fruit or an apple pie for dessert, at six o'clock.

Saiyue had learned from Mrs. McNamara that Bellini taught sociology at Santa Clara Community College. Music was apparently his avocation. Having inherited some hundreds of acres of land (mostly orange groves) in the southern part of San Mateo County, he seemed contented with the bachelor life of an aficionado of the arts.

His house was in the northern part of Woodside, just west of I-280. The long driveway was unpaved but well compacted with gravel, strewn with brownish cones and patches of dried needles from tall pines on both sides. Judging from the group of cars parked in the clearing by the house, Saiyue presumed that the party was well underway.

Bellini met her at the door. In his early forties, bearded, husky but soft-eyed, he looked like a somewhat smaller version of Luciano Pavarotti. She handed him two boxes, an apple pie and a pecan pie, and followed him through the foyer and a passage—forming one side of a spacious living room—to the kitchen. The ranch house, dark from the woods outside, smelled faintly damp and musty. "The guys are all out there," he said.

She could see the people out the window. The kitchen door with a diagonal spring banged behind her as she stepped onto a good-sized concrete patio. Wine bottles, packs of soft drinks, an ice bucket and stacks of Styrofoam cups stood at one end of a rugged wood picnic table. At the other end, a foursome sat on opposite benches. Strips of grassplots, tousled and chartreuse for lack of water, bordered the paved area. Unkempt clusters of orange-crested bird of paradise lined the edge of the grass behind the picnic table. By the far edge of an anemic lawn, two knots gathered, each about a small masonry table with matching stools, some seated, some standing, cups in hand, chatting easily. Further off, it was all darkish green conifer groves under a blue sky with white clouds like a flock of fleecy sheep.

Bellini introduced her to the four at the picnic table. She recognized three of them as from the church. After getting her a Coca-Cola as her choice of drink, he led her to the first masonry table.

"This is Rita...Janet...Bob—Big Bob—and...you heard him, our soloist today, Ray....And this is Saiyue Zhang. She is a friend of the church. Some of you may have seen her before. I need to talk to Elaine. Saiyue, make yourself at home. We will eat shortly," the conductor tipped his head and left.

"Join us, please. Have a seat," Ray Dalton said. He was standing across the small table from Saiyue; Big Bob, who had a seat close to Ray, moved back and pointed his old seat to her.

Smiling a thank-you, she sat down, thinking Ray's speech voice was quite ordinary, no hint of that lyric tenor quality of this morning. "A wonderful day for a picnic," she said.

"Yes." Janet, a thin blonde with a bony face, responded. She was standing on the other side of Ray, now nudging a little closer to him. "I have seen you in the congregation a number of times. How long have you been coming to the church?"

"Almost two years now. I know you sing in the choir." Saiyue answered her and turned to Big Bob, a hulk of a man with a ponytail and an earring. "I saw you in church some days but don't recall seeing you in the choir."

"No. I am afraid I can't sing." Bob said in a soft voice, rather incompatible with his husky appearance.

"He is just being modest. He is quite a musician. He wouldn't join because they wouldn't pay him," Ray said.

"Speak for yourself, Ray. Honestly, your *Ave Maria* this morning I'd be willing to pay to listen to," Bob said, nodding in the tenor's direction.

"He is paid," Rita said, smiling, "by somebody upstairs." She was tall and on the heavy side. Saiyue thought of Big Rita.

"You guys are too much," Ray shook his head.

"Mr. Dalton," Saiyue began.

"Ray, please," he interrupted.

"Okay…Ray," she smiled, "Everybody agrees that you sang so superbly this morning. Should I say, inspiringly?"

"What's this? You all gang up on me? Let's change the subject and find out more about our newcomer here. How new are you? Were you born in the Bay area? In the City of Angels? Or—"

"No. I was born in China. Came here about two years ago."

"You speak English quite well," Janet said.

"Quite well?" Rita said. "I'll say *very* well."

"I started to learn the language long before I got on the plane."

"But still, I know some Chinese who were born here, and I must say that they don't speak the language nearly as well as you do," Rita said.

"I came from Seattle," Ray remarked. "My family and I every so often went to the Chinatown there. Some Chinese, particularly the older ones, still had such a strong accent. Besides, their sentences were all so jumbled."

"Those were probably raised in a ghetto-like environment. They never had much contact with main stream America," Big Bob commented.

"True. Hopefully, that will soon be a phenomenon of the past," Ray said.

The reference to those Chinese Americans, though born in the United States, still as Chinese cast a shadow over Saiyue's mind. She felt that somehow the flow of conversation required her to say something. But what? She ended up lamely with, "I have much to learn yet about this country. But I am getting there." She chuckled to cover her self-consciousness.

"Do you go to one of the universities here, or work some place?"

Before she could answer, Bellini was calling from the kitchen door that it was time to eat. After each got their plate of food from the kitchen, they reassembled at the picnic table extended now by a bridge table. The original foursome with Saiyue remained seated nearby, Janet next and close to Ray. Prompted to answer the earlier question, Saiyue told them that she was an engineer with John J. Clyde and Associates.

Someone asked: "Is your family here?"

She answered it was in Shanghai.

"How do you like it here?" another asked.

"I like it a lot. This is a great country," she said sincerely.

"It may not be as great as you think though," Big Bob commented nonchalantly.

"Why do you say that?" Saiyue asked.

"Well, not to mention our long range problems of race, and inner city poverty, what do you think of the Contra-Iran affair?"

"I haven't followed it that closely. But, greatness doesn't mean that there are no problems. The fact that the word of the leader, President Reagan, can be openly challenged, and issues of the country can be openly debated according to the Constitution shows that this is a great country," she remarked.

"Sure, the Presidency represents only one branch of our government," Bellini said.

"I remember now. I was told that when people in China first heard about the Watergate affair years ago, we did not quite understand how President Nixon, as America's leader, could be challenged and eventually deposed, conspicuously peacefully, because of—what we thought to be—

a minor issue. Since then, I have learned that it's the separation of power that insures the health of the system," she said.

"Would you then like China to have our system of government?" Rita asked.

Saiyue had encountered questions of this kind before; thus, she was not unprepared. "I am just an engineer, no student of politics, and not particularly interested in that, except insofar as it affects my day-to-day life.... That being said, of course, I prefer democracy. And I am convinced that China will one day become a democracy. However, I had read that a true democracy requires the common people to have a certain level of education and of economical means. And I think I see the point of that too—so that they can make informed and responsible judgments. Perhaps the Chinese people on the whole are not quite there yet. The question is not *whether* but *when*, not about *the end*, but about *the means*. The current policy of economical development, I think, is a positive step toward that end." This time she felt that she had put it together reasonably well.

Bellini said, "You know, a dictator or oligarch can use the criteria for democracy you just mentioned as an excuse to avoid it. I wonder, during our Revolutionary War with England, how well educated and well-to-do the American populace were."

"It would be interesting to make a comparative study, if it has not already been made," someone commented.

Another one in the group asked, "You told us you were originally from Shanghai. I recently read a book: *Life and Death in Shanghai*, by a writer named Zheng, about her own experience during the Cultural Revolution. Do you think what's in there is all true?"

"I have heard about the book but have not read it. However, I have read and heard other accounts of that period. Even witnessed some when I was quite young," Saiyue said.

"The Chinese Cultural Revolution was just one of the major upheavals in history," Bellini commented. "During those upheavals, large enough numbers of people could and did behave hysterically and irrationally. For example, during the French Revolution, Russian Revolution, or the Second World War—particularly regarding what the Nazis did to the Jewish people in Europe. And what our own government did to the Japanese Americans then of course shouldn't be spoken of in the same breath with that. Nevertheless, it was also a hysterical and irrational act. The question for us is how to prevent that kind of behavior from ever manifesting again."

There was a hiatus. Bellini, noticing a few vacant eyes in the group, said, "By the way....What about the Yosemite outing idea we started to talk about last time."

Saiyue liked the change of subject.

After finishing eating, people remained at the table, chatting or rising every now and then to go to the kitchen for more coffee or tea. Later, they all went in the living room. The furniture appeared worn, almost shabby, except for a lustrous piano. People sat down, some on the beat-up rug. Bellini played a Mozart sonata on the piano. Big Bob fingered a Bach partita on his guitar. Next, another woman sang a couple of folk songs, accompanying herself on the guitar. Saiyue particularly liked the second one that began with: "If you miss the train I am on, you'll know that I'm gone...." Then they wanted Ray to sing.

"I did my part this morning," he said.

"I have an idea," Bellini followed. "How about asking Saiyue. Would you grace us with a song?"

"No. I can't sing," she demurred.

"Yes, you can. Ann, Ann McNamara, told me that you sang for her a couple of times," Bellini refuted.

"Oh no!...My level is too low for the ears of you professionals. I have never had any formal training in music."

"But Ann said you sang very well. We would especially appreciate a Chinese song."

"Yes, Saiyue. Let's hear it," Ray began to clap. The others followed to encourage her. Discomforted and excited at the same time, she began to squirm a little in her chair.

"Had I known this would be the price for the picnic, I'd think thrice before I came here."

"It's too late now!" someone interjected. Laughter from the group. "All right! I'll sing a song—very simple, nothing like the ones you guys do, but that's the only kind I know....It is called: 'To Pursue.'...I'll first read the translation of the lyrics for you and then sing it in Chinese. Please don't judge me too harshly. Better, just not judge at all." She got a piece of paper, wrote down the lyrics, once translated for her by Panzhe while on their honeymoon, and recited slowly:

You are the scudding cloud of the sky.
You are the racing meteor of midnight.
My heart is wrapped in a band of love.
A ray of light shines on my heart bright.
How can I bear it any longer!
How can I wait any longer!
I want, I want to pursue;
I want, I want to pursue.
To pursue that endless love abiding;
To pursue that light everlasting.

Some nodded their heads along with her cadence. She began to sing it. There was not a stir, all eyes on her—some looked serious, some curious, some amused. She started in a plaintive tone, slowly—raising her head a bit each time to inhale—and delivered the words in precise and true notes, gradually building to a crescendo at the end. The song sung in Chinese was an uncommon experience for many there. She sat down amid a round of applause.

"It's a very nice song. And the rendition is exquisite. The choir would surely welcome your participation," Bellini said. Others voiced their support.

Relieved but still not totally at ease, she murmured, "Thank you. I'll think about it."

The impromptu concert came to a natural break as several people got up for drinks, or to release part of what they had drunk before. Ray brought her a can of Coca-Cola and said to her in an undertone: "You have a beautiful voice. It has a delightful light metallic timber, like a silver flute."

"But I never had any formal voice training," she said.

"I sometimes prefer a natural untrained voice to a sophisticated one, particularly for folk songs," he said. She showed her pleasure with a sweet caltrop smile and was about to speak when Janet came over.

"Excuse me. Ray, about Yosemite, if you..."

"Excuse me, I have to talk to Mike," Saiyue left them. She thanked Bellini and apologized for having to leave then because of work the next day.

On her way back home that night, she ruminated on that part of the earlier talk, in which U.S. citizens of Chinese descent were still referred to as Chinese. Those older people in Chinatown, she thought, probably have lived, worked, and paid taxes in this country longer than anyone there around the picnic table. Would they ever integrate? What should they be referred to as anyway? Chinese? American Chinese? Chinese Americans? Americans? It probably all depends on the context. Was there an exclusion or nonacceptance element in the context of that conversation at the party? If the *Chinatown* people would speak English without an 'accent,' would there be an 'issue'? Who—the European Americans, or the Chinese Americans themselves, or the Chinese in China—would first refer to them as Chinese Americans or simply Americans?

Then she recalled that while still in graduate school, one of her design project partners, a Caucasian, referred to the proprietress of a local delicatessen as "that old Italian woman." That Italian woman had been in California long before he was born, but still spoke broken English. So is command of the language the issue?

Then Saiyue wondered why would she—herself not even a U.S. citizen yet—be so sensitive or concerned about the matter at all; she let it go.

However, she was pleased with the happenings of the day. She enjoyed the party and the music, and was glad of the broadening of her circle of contact, and of getting to meet that tenor with a silken voice and Romanesque nose.

24

"Saiyue Zhang," she announced, after picking up the phone.
"Saiyue. Ray Dalton here. Do you remember me?"
"Hi! Of course, Ray. What a surprise!" Her voice warmed.
"How are you?"
"I am fine. How do you know my telephone number?"
"You told us that you work for John J. Clyde & Associates."
"Oh, yes. How are you?"
"Fine. Thank you.... The reason I am calling... Well, I am wondering whether you would like to have dinner with me sometime." The call and the dinner invitation were a surprise, but not a very big one.

On Saturday she joined him in his crimson Volvo driving through the redwood-fringed Skyline Boulevard to the Belle Vista Restaurant of Woodside. They had a table with an excellent view of the Bay. He seemed to have very discriminating taste as he changed his mind a number of times when ordering the drinks and food. It was done only after the waitress' training—patience included—was rather thoroughly tested.

In between sips and nibbles he told her that he grew up in Seattle, Washington, where his parents still lived. He had graduated from U.C. Berkeley and had been working for the California Department of Education and Welfare. Asked how he came to sing so well, he said that he had taken voice lessons for a number of years in high school and had even considered pursuing a career in music. His aunt used to come to Hillsdale United Church when she lived in Belmont. However, it was through Big Bob, whom he had known since college, that he occasionally had come to sing in the choir.

She figured that he was a couple of years, perhaps more, younger than herself. From their tete-a-tete, she had the impression that he thought she was appreciably younger than she actually was. She wasn't about to correct him. She did tell him of her brief marriage to Lu Panzhe. Ray didn't seem to be curious about it. Perhaps he had already known—through Mrs. McNamara or some other church member. He told her that he was single and never married.

They shook hands in front of her apartment building when parting after their first date. The following week he called again, this time asking her to go dancing. When she realized that he was talking about disco, her interest was piqued, even though at the time she felt it a bit odd that the *choirboy* would take to disco dancing. She told him she had never done that before. He said he'd teach her. He took her to the D.V.9 Club in the city. The majority of its mixed ethnic clientele seemed to be of Asian extraction.

They had a drink and he started to teach her that style of dancing. Watching others also, she tried gingerly at first, but caught on rather quickly. The heavy metal dulled some senses and sharpened others. She discovered that the dance wasn't as difficult as it seemed, once she learned to follow the beat. Indeed, with the thumping drum, it was hard not to; it was simple, elementary eurhythmics.

After a couple of drinks and dances, she had her jacket off, as well as self-consciousness. In a short sleeve maroon dress, swaying her shoulders, throwing her bare arms, turning and jerking with the drumbeat, her black hair disappearing and glinting in the rotating strobe light, she was surprised that she could dance like that. It was the music and the ambience, she thought, and was elated.

Whatever effects the sights and sounds and the drinks had on her, they seemed even greater on Ray. Bumping his head, gyrating his hips, shaking his raised hands in the air, shoulders whirling, his shirt wet at the arm pits, and eyelids tremulously closing and opening at increasingly longer intervals—at times like being in a trance—he appeared to her a totally different person.

In the car leaving the club, he invited her to his apartment. She politely but firmly declined. After parking the car near her apartment, he walked her towards the building. Suddenly he turned and grasped both her arms. Saiyue, a little surprised, looked at him, saying, "What? Ray...." He pulled her close and kissed her hard on the mouth. He held her in that position, nearly choking her, until she pushed him off. Although momentarily she got a kick out of the theatric thrill of it, it alarmed her. She gasped and said with widened eyes, "What's the matter, Ray?"

"You are so beautiful," he said, staring at her. "Let's go inside."

"Ray, it's late. You should go home." Her voice was cold and clear. He looked at her dully, lowered his head, mumbled a yes, and left slinkingly. What an impulsive person, she thought.

Early in the week, he called to apologize for his behavior that night. Making light of it, she said, "It's all right, Ray. But, yes, you need to do a better job at protecting your choirboy image."

"What would you like to do this coming weekend?" he asked.

"How about we try something different, like biking. It's more healthful, you know."

After a pause, he said, "I haven't done that in ages, I warn you. I may be out of condition. You'll have to carry me home if I collapse."

She chuckled at the jest.

Saturday morning, they drove to Palo Alto, with the bikes lashed to his car, and parked it in a residential area on Charleston Road. She started to lead him along the route she used to ride with Amir Rahimi.

Ray seemed lethargic at the very start, his face too pale and eyes too dull for a young man on the young day. By the time they crossed Page Mill

Road, he began to complain of tightness in his calf. They rested a while by a roadside horse corral. Noticing the dark circles around his eyes, she asked if he was all right. He said he hadn't slept too well the night before. She told him that then he shouldn't have come and suggested that he go home to rest. Listlessly they retraced the three miles or so back to the car.

In the middle of the week, he called, sounding like his old self again—suave and confident—and invited her to a Sunday concert at Half Moon Bay. It was a solo Flamenco Guitar affair. She found that not only the music was quaintly beautiful and alluring, but the ambience unusual and pleasant. Inside a beach house, the seating was informal. They enjoyed wine and cheese as they listened to man-made music sharing the airwaves with the periodic crashing of the surf and piercing cries of seagulls. In front of her apartment building, he kissed her goodnight gently and left a perfect gentleman.

The following Saturday they went on an evening Bay cruise. The navy blue mantle of the night was trimmed with flickering lights, on the shore and about the ship, in quivering dots, pools, and strips. The music, wine and middle-class gentility aroused in her a mix of excitement and an uncertainty about the night's potential. But watching Ray quaffing the red wine in gulps, Saiyue somehow felt the element of uncertainty was greater than what it should be, and perhaps of a different kind. First she explained to herself that perhaps this unease was due to his foreignness; then she wondered why she hadn't felt it with Amir Rahimi at a similar stage of familiarity.

As they danced in the dim light to a slow fox trot, Ray held her so tightly that she felt it affecting her breathing. She told him to take it easy. He apologized. A moment later, out of the blue he said to her, "I want you."

"What do you mean?"

"You know what I mean," he pressed the small of her back toward him. She simply chuckled:

"Are you drunk or what?"

"No. I want you."

"Don't be silly!" She said in sham rebuke. He dropped that line of talk, and excused himself to go to the men's room. When he returned, they resumed joining the crowd's conviviality. An absent-minded air about him appeared that she had sometimes noticed before. That not-all-there look had given her pause when she had at times thought of "going all the way" with him, for he was a handsome and, most of the time, attractive man. She knew that the IUCD that she had in place after the birth of Baobao could be a backup system for the pill that she had procured recently.

At the end of the cruise, as they were entering the gangway, she saw a familiar figure, a man, apparently just off the boat, walking in the direction of the parking lot with a woman, who appeared to be a Caucasian and had her arm in his. It was Lu Panzhe. A moment later, she felt it strange that it should bother her, like a pebble inside the shoe, only the pebble would shortly move to the chest. With time it began to grate inside.

Approaching her apartment building, she had a notion of feigning headache, or something, to keep Ray from coming in. But she let him in, thinking it might assuage the gnawing pebble.

They dropped their jackets on a chair in the living room and kissed. It turned passionate. She let his hand get inside her blouse, fighting herself and wondering would this be the night? Pushing him off, she said, "Wait, wait! Ray. I am not ready.…I am a little hungry. I'll fix something to eat first."

He asked for a beer. She admonished him that he had already had much wine earlier. Then she added contradictorily, "If you really want to, help yourself from the fridge. But I am going to make some *lotus root powder*. Would you like some?" she asked.

"What's that?"

"Lotus root powder. You add hot water, stir and it turns jelly like. Only it's hot."

"OK. I'll try some. Could I use the bathroom?"

"Of course, go ahead. I'll need to boil some hot water first." She went to the kitchen and he the bathroom. After turning on the gas stove for the filled kettle, she went into her bedroom to change her street shoes for slippers, still wondering—and vexed by the idea—whether or not she would do it tonight.

Familiar with her own bedroom, she did not bother to turn on the light. The door between the bedroom and the bathroom was half-open. In the mirror, she was surprised to see him bending over the washbasin counter and seemingly to be snuffing at something. Her first reaction was that he was taking some medication. Then—isn't it the way some people take drugs? A little frightened, she did not make a sound. Without changing her shoes, she quietly moved out of the bedroom, thinking tonight is definitely not the night.

She returned to the kitchen and poured the lotus root powder into a bowl. The "powder" which she had bought from an oriental food store was not quite fine enough; a good part of it was like pellets. Regretting she had not tried something simpler, like oat meal or even just toast, she was now, with her head bending down, using a spoon as a pestle to pulverize the small lumps with unnecessary force, as though to vent her trouble with her discovery. Suddenly, she smelt alcohol and felt something thrusting from behind her and between her legs, her crotch grabbed, and an arm around her chest. She jerked herself free and hopped aside.

"Let's do it," Ray said.

Alarmed, she looked into his eyes. They appeared glassy. "Ray! Stop this!" she said sternly.

"Come on now. You want this as much as I do. I got it for you." He moved to unzip his pants.

"Stop it! This instant!" she commanded. "You are drunk." She scurried out of the kitchen into the living room. "You better leave."

He rushed after her and pushed her down on the sofa. All over her, he pulled at her dress.

She struggled but couldn't get out from under him. "Look, Ray. I am not clean. My period is not yet over."

"That doesn't matter. My doll! Come on. Don't fight me." He was now jerking her underpants.

"Ray. Don't do this for your own good. I must warn you I have got AIDS."

"What!" He froze.

"I have AIDS," she repeated quietly. "I wanted to tell you some time ago but I was afraid you might leave me."

He paused for a couple of seconds. "You are trying to fool me. A nice girl, AIDS? I don't believe it."

"It's your life. Ray. Think about it."

"All right, doll. I got here.…Wait.…I'll get a rubber. My wallet! My jacket! Where is my jacket?"

A whistle was heard that turned into a constant scream. "The water is boiling! Let me up!"

"I'll go, doll."

As he reeled to the kitchen to turn off the stove, she tried to decide whether to break for the door. The chances are too small, she thought, unless he falls down.

"My wallet! Where is my jacket?" Lurching to the chair, he reached inside his jacket. "Johnny, johnny.…Here you are!"

"Ray. Would you put it on in the bathroom, please?" she said earnestly. "I am not used to the sight of that sort of thing."

He looked at her with incredulity and grinned like a cretin. "OK, doll." With the small foiled pack pinched between his fingers, he walked unsteadily into the bathroom.

She quickly snatched her keys, ran and opened the apartment door. He stumbled out of the bathroom, the lower half completely naked except for a rubberized miniature lance in front of him—like a straggling soldier of a Roman phalanx. She commanded from outside the door, "Out! Out! Get your stuff and get out!"

The next few days he tried to call her. She hung up on him. Finally, she did talk to him. He apologized; she advised him to seek medical help.

For several weeks she hadn't heard from or seen him. One Sunday after church, Mrs. McNamara asked her to join her for coffee. After a few pleasantries, Mrs. McNamara asked, "What happened between you and Ray?"

"I guess we are no longer going out together."

"I received a letter from his aunt, saying that Ray had gone back to Seattle, sort of depressed, and was under the care of a psychiatrist."

"Well, if you must know…" Saiyue went on to tell her old landlady the essential facts of that night's incident, without the lurid details.

"Oh my! Oh my!" Mrs. McNamara mumbled. She was quiet for a while, her normally serene face looking troubled. "I am sorry, Saiyue! When he asked me about you, I thought you two would enjoy each other's company. I didn't realize that sort of thing could happen. I am so sorry."

"It's not your fault. How is he?"

"Mike Bellini told me that one of the choir members, Janet Lockhart, I believe, had been up there to visit him. According to her, he is living with his parents. Seems to be much better now."

"I am glad to hear that. I hope he'll get over his problem or problems, whatever they are. I wish him well," Saiyue said.

"Me too. Now I wonder whether his aunt ought to know the episode you told me."

"It is entirely up to you," Saiyue said.

"Anyway, I am glad you told me." Mrs. McNamara paused and said, "He looked so clean cut." The old lady thought of her elder grandson in San Diego. He too looks so clean cut.

25

"You look a lot better," John Wu said.

"I feel a lot better. Finally sent out the proposal last week," Lu Panzhe said. They were having lunch at the Union Cafeteria. For over a decade, they would have lunch together every so often, occasionally joined by Larry Chi. (The latter, an epicure, did not care for cafeteria food.) The practice, which had largely discontinued after Lu's marriage to Saiyue, resumed after the divorce.

"So you'll be keeping vigil for some time."

"Not really. It's off my hands. As Doris Day sang, '*Que Será, Será,*'" Panzhe said in a lilt. "In the meantime, I might as well do something else."

"Do something else!" John echoed. "Don't be overly ambitious. In the past months you had not been living right, putting everything on the proposal. You have lost weight."

"I am not ambitious. Just trying to survive," Panzhe said.

"I understand. In a sense we in mathematics are fortunate, because there simply aren't that many funding sources for research, and the pressure for money is likewise less. Still need to get papers published though."

"That's certainly true in engineering also," Panzhe said.

"You guys are lucky in that respect. I heard that in engineering one can often split the reporting of a research into several publications, *a la strip tease*, one piece at a time," the mathematician said with a chuckle.

"To be fair, often it's justified. The study may contain a number of phases, or there is just too much material for one publication with a limit on the number of words. But it does happen that the reporting is arranged so as to increase the count of publications. Counting is what administrators often do. The strip tease mode may be understandable for younger people. For full professors, it is wasteful of energy," Panzhe said.

"We seldom have that kind of situation—like a paper for theory, another for model studies, another for full scale laboratory tests, and yet another for field tests, etc. For us, a statement of the theorem, maybe a couple of lemmas, then the proof, that's it....Anyhow, what is this 'something else' you were talking about just now? Another proposal? Huh?"

"I don't like nor believe in the blunderbuss approach. You know, thinking that the more pellets you have in the shot the greater is your chance of hitting something. I try to concentrate on one 'silver bullet.' In order to make a convincing presentation, you've got to have the conviction that it is most worthy of support and will gain it. In short, be positive. So I am done with proposals for a while....I am now working on a book, the one that the representative of Prentice Hall has urged me to do for some years."

"I tell you it's a time consuming, and very low paying job," John said.

"I know you speak from experience."

"For the hours I spent, I figured I was paid about half of the minimum wage for my Boundary Value Problems book."

"I don't care about the money. Timewise, it wouldn't be that bad in my case. My notes are reasonably complete. I figure all I need to do is to polish them up and make out some additional exercises and problems. And for such chores as writing to publishers and authors for permission to quote, I think I could get some able secretarial help," Panzhe said.

"That'll be work enough. You still wouldn't have much of a social life, huh?"

"I don't mind," Panzhe said.

They were silent for a while.

"Pretty much got over it now, huh?" John looked at his friend softly.

Panzhe returned the gaze for a few seconds, and said, "I know what you mean.... You know I had some psychological preparation before I wedded her, way before that polite little warning you gave me in my office.... I suppose you might want to tell me now, 'I told you!'" Panzhe said.

"No, no," pursing his lips and shaking his head, John said, "I must say I was surprised that she didn't ask more from you."

"That has probably disappointed a good many of our local guardians of morality also.... Virtually she didn't ask for anything but her freedom," Panzhe said. "I had to give her that for what she had given me."

"What has she given you?"

"A great deal. The experience of feeling really alive! Her ultimate intimacy," Panzhe said.

"You mean sex, huh? I would admit that she has good looks, and...a certain style. But you know if sex is what you want you can get it cheaper and with a whole lot less rigamarole," John said.

"You are talking about animal sex. There is a difference between animal sex and soulful sex," Panzhe said.

"If these words had come from another, I would take them to be high-flown sour grapes. But I'd grant you some credibility, or at least sincerity.... I suppose you are a moral person."

"Not particularly in the conventional sense. I am no saint. But I like to think that I am a reasonably conscientious person," Panzhe said.

"You are a hopeless, wimpy romantic! That's what you are!" John chuckled.

"It's all a matter of taste," Panzhe said, wiping his face with his hand. He didn't like *hopeless*, but it was "*wimpy*" that hurt him.

"Anyway, Lao Lu! I am glad that through it all you are none the worse for wear. Am I right? Huh?"

"I hope so," Panzhe said. But the word *wimpy* still troubled him.

In the College of Engineering, for research proposals, reports and book writing, the secretarial work was normally done through a secretary/typist pool run by a General Services Office (which also administered a machine shop, an electronics shop and a printing shop) rather than through the individual departments. A secretary from the pool named Nora Gallagher, who had already helped Panzhe several months ago to prepare his research proposal, was also assigned to assist him for the book project, since she was familiar with the idiosyncrasies of his handwriting and his work habits.

Over a period of about five months, they had regularly talked over the phone as well as met a number of times either in his office or in her cubicle in the Electrical Engineering Building, in which the General Services Office was housed. She was five feet three or four, in her thirties, redheaded, sparkling hazel eyes over a narrow, straight and pointed nose. Still curvaceous, but five, maybe ten, pounds more would bring her to plumpness. A smoker, she was trying to cut down by gum chewing. She was an excellent typist, uncommonly adept at transcribing handwritten Greek letters and scientific symbols and expressions.

One Thursday afternoon, Lu had in his office a session with a thesis student whose earlier floundering research on the use of Fourier Transform method for base motion problems was reinvigorated by a change of input from displacements to accelerations. After the student left, Lu was about to return to his work when he heard a knock on the door. He answered, and entered Nora in a white blouse and cranberry skirt, with a big smile on her rouged freckled face.

"Hi! Nora, how are you? Got a question for me?" he asked.

"I am fine. No, Dr. Lu, no question for you. It'll take me a couple more days to have that chapter for you. I need first to finish a proposal that has a deadline on it. It's for that new professor in your department. I just left his office down the hall. Thought I'd stop by to offer my congratulations." She chewed her gum rhythmically, smiling and looking unblinkingly at him.

"Congratulations? On what?"

"On your grant. Haven't you heard?"

"I don't know what you're talking about."

"I think it's for that proposal I typed for you some months ago."

His ears began to ring. But calmly he said, "I haven't heard anything about that. Are you sure?"

Indeed, except for the initial acknowledgment of receipt, he hadn't heard a thing about it. However, that fact had kept his hopes up. It was known among university research circles that, for a proposal submitted to such government agencies as the National Technical Council, usually an early response would come as a declination. For the first two or three months, "No news is good news."

His was submitted some four months ago. So it could be! Anyway, if her news was true, it would spare him the moment of tension when he came to open the agency's official letter of response. (A colleague once confided in him that one time such a letter had lain on his desk unopened for a whole weekend. He would not want to face the possibility of rejection without the weekday work to divert the hurt from the loss of months of labor and concern for job security. That kind of nervousness is like a *coward's death* an average funding-competing research faculty would *die* a number of times in a university career.)

"Would I kid you about a matter like this?" Nora said. "Mary asked me to open for her the boss' mail. I found a copy of the grant notice to the University that the Controller's office had sent to the College." Mary, Nora's supervisor, was also secretary of the College's Director of Research.

This appeared to further confirm for him the veracity of the news, since experience indicated that the grant agency's letter would normally go to the University top administration first. "Well, what do you know!"

"I say, Dr. Lu, 165 grand calls for a celeBRAtion." Nodding sweetly at him, she accentuated the penult.

He remembered that the dollar amount was what the budget had requested. So there is no reduction of the budget either, it does look real, he thought.

He had generally a favorable impression of Nora, especially professionally. Unlike some secretaries—who sometimes would make one feel imposing or indecisive, or even stupid—Nora was always patient, understanding and cheerful, no matter how many times he wanted or changed his mind about corrections. There were times, when they were sitting close, he'd feel a flux of magnetism inducing in him a run of electricity; the current would be intensified by the bouquet coming in waves from her perfume. But the electricity was well insulated; so far it didn't seem to have any therapeutic effect on him. There were other times he felt the warmth in her friendly gaze. Although he was leery of romance, he had mentioned to her about taking her out on Secretary Day. But he had to be out of town then. She kidded him that he owed her a meal.

"Well, I guess now is the time I pay you back the meal I owe you," he said expansively.

"Just a meal? Don't I deserve a dinner?"

"A dinner, of course. Good! Nora, I'd like to invite your husband too." He had heard that she was single, and throughout their contacts, that notion was never contradicted; but he wanted to be safe.

"I am not married."

"Oh..."

"You name the date."

"How about Saturday?"

"This Saturday, day after tomorrow?"

"Yeah."

"No. I am sorry I have a date. But, then, I'll cancel it and go with you," she said coquettishly, tilting her head to let her hand run smoothly over her luxuriant hair.

"I don't want you do that. That's too much responsibility."

"No. I am just kidding. I don't have a date. Saturday is fine with me."

"Where would you like to go?"

"You are the host."

"How about I give you a call tomorrow?"

"OK. You owe me a dinner," she waltzed out of the room, the back of her skirt stretching one way and then the other.

That evening he had a hard time trying to concentrate on the book project. He took the proposal out, reviewed it and gave it some further desultory thought, such as recruiting graduate assistants.

The next morning, he called the University Controller's office. It confirmed the grant by giving him the account number for the project. Before lunch, he called Nora, "About that dinner I owe you, do you like seafood?"

"Yeah. I love seafood."

"How about some place on Fishermen's Wharf?"

"It's fine....But I have been there so many times....A friend of mine told me the other day that a Bay cruise has good seafood."

"What's the name of the cruise?"

"The Green and White Fleet, I believe."

"Yes. I have heard of it. We can try that. I'll call for reservations and let you know."

In the evening he forwent his regular work session. For hours, lying there on the couch at home, he listened to the Jupiter, the Titan, etc., feeling the blood running warm throughout the body.

The cruise ship slowly pulled away from West Marina. Standing by the netted railing, in silence Panzhe and Nora watched the glowing disk gradually sinking below the deck of the Golden Gate Bridge and disappearing into the headland under a bank of fiery clouds. Even the sun needs rest, he thought. The ship sailed on stately in a light breeze. Shortly the clouds yonder turned into deep purple streamers hung in the lavender sky lambent with a pinkish hue. Over the waters, patches of sheen in dull blue, silver and gold faded as they merged into the shade. The hills brooded in the distance. The darkness of night dropped like a diaphanous veil.

Above the waterfront, tall buildings in silhouette formed a giant histogram quickened by banks of dotted lights. The city skyline coruscated in a bluish glow. The ship now glided in shadowy waters penetrated here and there by tremulous shafts of harbor and ship lights.

They returned to the cabin, her arm in his. The food was buffet style. They had wine, salad, crab and salmon, amidst DJ music, a subdued hum of the guests and sudden bursts of laughter. The sound at times came distorted in the breeze, a bit damp and salty as the darkness deepened.

Nora wore a plum-colored dress, a pearl necklace phosphorescing over her bosom, her auburn hair combed up in a "cascade" style. "You look beautiful tonight," Panzhe, in a light brown sports coat, said in a tone more appreciative than romantic.

"Just tonight?" Her hazel eyes gleamed playfully above two pendulous pearl earrings.

"Well, all right, especially tonight. You know you are an attractive woman," he said matter-of-factly.

"I heard that line before. Thanks anyway. By the way, how is your ex-wife?" she asked.

"You know I am divorced?"

"We gossiped a little about your romance, marriage and divorce with that graduate student from China."

"I didn't know that I was that notorious."

"No, not notorious. Just that there have been a fair amount of—shall we say—nonacademic goings-on among the faculty. After all, behind the pretensions of some of you guys, you are human too. The secretaries update university romances at lunchtime as housewives watch soaps on TV. Your romance drew a bit special interest, or curiosity, perhaps, because both of you were in the College, and are Orientals…Chinese, well, of Chinese ancestry anyway.…Yet people say Chinese are old-fashioned, a little stiff, and frankly, not that romantic."

"Well!" with mock hurt and a snort, he improvised a deep-chested base voice, "You think so?"

"I am not sure; don't have any experience. Some do appear a bit nerdy though. Hope you don't mind," she chuckled.

"Why should I? In fact, I agree with you, particularly when you said, *appear*. But appearance could be deceiving. I am sure you know that China happens to be the most populous country in the world."

"Yes, that I know. One in every four or five people in the world is a Chinese. Right?"

"Yes. Every four or five, whatever. Anyway, their citizens don't grow on trees, or in rice paddies, you know?" he looked at her with a professorial face of virtuous patience toward a presumed slow-witted student. She seemed frozen for an instant, and then sort of exploded, exclaiming:

"There you go! Dr. Lu! Honestly! Look at you, and listen to you! Appearance *is* deceiving." Reaching across the table, she slapped him on the hand, the shaking earrings twinkling in the cabin light. Her laughter was almost too loud. She lowered her head to collect herself and raised her eyes to him again, "Back to my original question. Where is your pretty little ex-wife?"

"She is still in the Bay area, working for some engineering company."

"You still see her?"

"No. Were you ever married?" he asked, like a counterattack.

"Yes, once. I am divorced also."

"Oh. Where is your ex-husband?"

"He too works for some engineering company in the Bay area...John Clyde Associates or something," she said.

"What a coincidence! That's where she works. What's his name?"

"Amir Rahimi."

"Sounds Arabic."

"Originally he had come from Iran. He went to Stanford though....Wow! I can't get over the coincidence that both our ex's work for the same outfit."

"You have a boyfriend?"

"Lots."

"I mean a steady boyfriend."

"All my boyfriends are steady."

"You are not answering my question."

"OK. If you mean whether I've made a sort of commitment to any particular man, the answer is no....Do you suppose I'd be here if I have?"

"You are right," he was slightly discomposed.

"Now I can ask you the same question you asked me," she said.

"The answer is the same. I am too busy." He recovered.

"I suppose you are, cranking out all those weird equations." She paused. "Frankly, I was surprised that you asked me out."

"Why?"

"Well, I didn't figure you are the type."

"What type?"

"Know how to have fun."

"Tonight's dinner is mainly one of expressing appreciation for your professional help."

"I understand. And that's what I figured."

"But what's wrong with having fun after work," he said. She looked at him with a quizzical smile. They both chuckled.

A while after dinner, dancing began. During the slow dance, Nora held him tightly and whispered in his ear, "You are so sure-footed." For his part, it was his head he was concerned about—unsure whether that slight giddiness, even with a steady supply of fresh air from the bay, was caused by the wine, her perfume, the spongy pressure upon his chest or the soft stroking of her hand on his back. At times when she was stepping forward, he could feel her slight bumping into him. He felt sort of like in a jacuzzi. The electricity was challenging the insulation. In time he was surprised to sense pressure within his underpants.

The evening wore on as they enjoyed themselves at their end of the cabin. Nearing the completion of the cruise, among the dancing crowd, suddenly he saw in the low light a familiar face at the other end of the cabin. It was Saiyue, dancing cheek to cheek with a man—who appeared Caucasian and young. Panzhe did not tell Nora about it, but kept himself and his partner in the vicinity of their table, and later persuaded her to go to the upper deck to watch the city and harbor lights.

Driving back from the city, he was still a bit fazed inside. However, the perfume and the soft pressure of Nora's upper arm on his, felt with every animated laughter of hers or a sway of the vehicle, did help to keep him largely absorbed with the immediacy. As Panzhe approached Nora's apartment, she invited him to go in for a nightcap. He hesitated. But he had more than a hunch he wouldn't embarrass himself. Anyway, he could play it by, well, ear.

Inside the apartment, she went to the refrigerator and gave him a can of Coors and excused herself to go into the bedroom. She came out shortly—sans her shoes, and earrings. She took a Coors herself also and sat beside him on the sofa, one leg tucked under the other thigh. They sipped the beer and made small talk. In a while, she moved to lean her head on his shoulder. He turned it and kissed her. She responded by pressing her lips and rubbing them lightly against his. She squeezed and massaged the top of his thigh and eventually reached between his legs. By now the physical basis for his fear of embarrassment had totally vanished.

In spite of the alcohol, perfume and the voltage across the lips, he saw a red light. "You trust me this much?" he asked tactfully.

"How do you mean? Emotionally, morally, or what?...Healthwise?" she suspended all actions but did not withdraw.

"All of the above," he chuckled, as though it were in jest.

"I think the question is whether you trust me. Let me tell you what I think. This is just a weekend date—no more. No strings attached. Nobody besides you and me has to know about it....I'll give you a condom."

"Could I take a shower first?"

"Me too, after you," she said and went over to a bureau drawer and got out a condom from a pack and handed it to him. "Before you go in, would you unzip me?" She turned around to present her back to him. He surprised himself with an urge to bite on the freckled shoulder but forbore. The first part of his shower was in cold water.

After her shower she joined him in bed. She clutched his head as he suckled her and fondled her hair, now loose and pouring like some animal mane. All of a sudden, she slid aside and rose above him. In one swoop of her hand—he did not know then, nor afterwards, exactly how it happened—she had him in. He felt humiliated—no one had ever sat on him, astride as now or otherwise, since class bully Gorilla Jin had once in a fight in the sixth grade. But that feeling passed almost instantly. She swirled a bit to fine-tune the engagement. A few rotary cycles, like a Wankel engine, before she bobbed like a jockey on horseback, first on a trot, smooth, sweet like a cello, soon she leaned forward—shifting from the renowned rhythm of Ravel's Bolero to the steady beat of J.S. Bach. The bed groaned and grumbled. He ceased stroking her thigh and moved his hands clear from her body and made fists. Amid her grunting, he tried to recall the definitions of the stress invariants and the various strength theories. Hardly had he finished stating the Von Mises Theory, came her 1812 finale. A short sequence of stiffening, stretching and frissons, she collapsed upon him, venting beside his ear rapidly diminishing sighs and hisses, like an arrived train.

In a while, she said, "You not done?!" The configuration was reversed. As he threw away his equations and theorems and concentrated on her constricted condition, it didn't take him long.

All was quiet for a while. "You are pretty good," she said languishingly. He was going to say, "You did most of the work," but refrained. She continued, "I sometimes wondered what a skinny smart professor can do besides playing with those Greek letters, alpha…lambda, umm-ba, umm-ba…" she ended with a gushing sound, like a mixture of sigh and chuckle.

He managed to mutter a "Thank you." After they had gone to the bathroom, she gave him a hug and a peck on the lips, turned around, and shortly he heard snoring in a gentle purr, like that of a fed cat.

He couldn't sleep, wondering how did he ever get into this. The image of Saiyue with that young man? No, what a cop-out! But no matter what, this had been a most unexpected experience. He felt a primal sense of satisfaction, a manhood reclaimed and ever honorable!

Before this night he had had sex with only two women. After the Caesarian birth of their daughter, Kimoon clearly didn't enjoy the act, nor the kind of physical intimacy that she seemed to fear would lead to it. However, she would tolerate it, occasionally, seemingly more as a duty than intimacy. He would often feel responsible for that situation, troubled by a sense of incompetence, blaming himself for being unable to bring her out of a congealed state like a half-used ketchup bottle.

With Saiyue, before their estrangement, he enjoyed the intimacy as much as, if not more than, the act. In any case, her liberated attitude on such matters made him more relaxed and confident. And the results made him feel at least adequate. Later, the onset of the dysfunction was a severe, painful blow. It would be worse if there was no pressure of his work to help him forget it. But tonight—all losses were restored!

Then he thought what would happen, in spite of her assurance, if she told, and the College came to hear about this. Growing anxious, he lay awake until 3 a.m., when he whispered to the ear beside him:

"Nora...Nora."

"Umm...."

"Do you mind I go home now?"

"Now? Are you OK?"

"I am fine. I am sorry to wake you up."

"No problem. Sure you are sober enough to drive?"

"Yes." He got up and dressed quickly.

Half asleep and a red cloud over her head, now without the mascara, the liner, the powder, and the rouge, and the lipstick, the eyes seemed flat and dull, and the lips indistinct on the pale face, and she looked to him under the hallway light kind of asexual. She unlocked the door and kissed him lightly on the lips, "Remember, just a date—no strings attached. Drive carefully."

He stood outside the door for a few seconds, heard the door chain nub being slid into the metal chase, and left. He couldn't sleep at home either. Finally, near dawn, utterly tired, he dozed off, intermittently feeling Nora's body and seeing her face suddenly changed to that of Saiyue.

Monday he sent a bouquet of flowers to Nora's apartment anonymously. Nevertheless, she called to thank him.

The next weekend at a basement apartment in the city, Nora introduced Panzhe to the host, called Danny. Danny sported a pigtail and all kinds of rings on his fingers and about his head. He and Nora seemed to be old friends. Later the somewhat effeminate host told Panzhe that he was a hairdresser. Clearly Panzhe was out of his element in the room filled with reggae music, the smell of marijuana and, to him, babel among the guests.

Panzhe left the party early, accompanied by Nora. In the car she said, "I suppose you didn't enjoy it. I don't blame you. Sorry I got carried away to take you there."

"Well, I guess I'm just not hip enough. I am comfortable with men wearing earrings. But the nose rings were a bit beyond me."

"To tell you the truth, I don't really enjoy it that much myself either. It's just that I have nothing to do after work," she said, looking blankly through the windshield.

"How did you come to know Danny?"

"At a beauty salon where I used to work."

"O yeah?"

She went on to tell him some more about herself. She came from a small town in the state of Washington. Her father, a logger once and a drunkard, was abusive to her mother and siblings. He died when she was still young. Her mother, working as a waitress to support the family, went through a couple of remarriages and a number of lovers. After high school, Nora had worked as a salesgirl and on several odd jobs before she came to Belmont to assist her aunt, who ran a beauty and hair salon. "In fact, I met my ex there. He encouraged me to go to college. I attended Santa Clara Community College for a couple of terms. Then we were married. It just didn't worked out. It was not all his fault though....And...if he had not been that insulting and abusive, I wouldn't mind—" She paused.

"Did he try to see you?" Panzhe asked.

"Yes. I couldn't forgive him for his insulting and barbarous language at the times we fought....But then, thinking back these days, I would say, actually, he had a good heart and was gentleman-like most of the time."

"Then why don't you see him? And see whether he would let his good heart prevail and change his habit of insulting language."

"He did not have a *habit* of insulting language."

"Well, Nora, only you can take care of yourself."

Panzhe did not date Nora again. He managed to conduct their professional business in strict propriety via the phone and campus mail. Nora seemed to understand and respect his wishes. But it was not without considerable internal struggle and strenuous exercise of will power that he held off urges to renew their "companionship." In the meantime, however, he was glad that he hadn't sensed a whiff that anybody else in the College had a notion of their liaison that night.

26

"I'll now present, as an example, the stress check on the reinforcement around a cutout in a pressure vessel. First, the program will generate a finite element net. Next, it will perform the stress analysis, and then show the contours of such strength parameters as the maximum shear stress and the octahedral shear stress. Finally, any violation of the ASME[42] Code will be highlighted." Saiyue addresses the group, consisting of the Chief Mechanical Engineer and the Chief Civil/Structural Engineer of the firm, plus several project engineers and supervisors.

She types in the commands. The computer hums and makes an intermittent light scraping sound—like dragging a chair on a wooden floor. The screen flashes bright and dark. Instead of an expected neat net for the reinforcement around the shell cutout, a snarl of irregular lines appears on the screen. Her ears begin to burn. Todd Jensen, who is sitting nearby, asks, "What's wrong, Saiyue?" The screen stays the same—an unintelligible mess. She turns to look at Jensen, sensing also behind him the blurred images of the Chiefs and the rest. She says, "Wait, please wait.…Let me try again." She retypes in the commands. The computer hums and scrapes. A series of figures flit over the screen that ends with another chaos

---

42. American Society of Mechanical Engineers.

of unintelligible lines. Someone says, "Jensen, is this what you people have been working on? And you are proposing a new section?"

She feels sorrier for Todd Jensen than for herself. Frantically, she pushes more keys on the huge, blurry keyboard. The screen turns totally blank. Instead of the usual humming and scraping, the computer suddenly sounds a loud constant buzz, like the alarm during the building fire drill.

Saiyue opened her eyes. Her heart still beating rapidly, she shut off the alarm clock. She had set it last night to wake her up an hour early so that she could recheck her presentation for this afternoon's meeting.

It was almost dark when she returned to her apartment this Friday. She had a long day. Overall the presentation went well, despite the slings and arrows of a couple of doubters and foot-draggers. The two Chiefs appeared to receive it favorably; that probably counted the most. She threw her keys on the coffee table. Grabbed herself a Coke and sat on the sofa chair. The mind went as blank as the ceiling she was staring at. She rolled her eyes around and thought, now I know what Yan Yifeng was writing about when I was still in Xi'an. "…It's brutal in the weekend. The four walls of the apartment make me feel like a lone white mouse in a cage…."

So quiet. Saiyue turned on the radio. The mournful tune of Erik Satie only increased the negative charge of loneliness. She didn't want to cook, too tired; she didn't want to go out, too tired. She went to the kitchen, dumped some leftover rice in a pan, opened a can of Campbell mushroom soup, added water, heated it and ate it while watching the news on TV. Afterwards, she went to bed. Twenty minutes later, she felt much better. She decided to return *The Rise of Modern China*, by Emmanuel Hsu, to the library and look for another book. The telephone rang.

"Xiao Zhang."

"Yes."

"Liu Rong here. Some time ago you said you were interested in buying a house. Are you still?"

"Yes, I think so. Mainly as an investment. But you know I don't have much money."

"I understand. I have something that you might find suitable." Liu Rong—who had been working for some months now as a real estate agent—told her about a small house in Redwood City. It used to be owned by an old widower, who was an immigrant from Poland and recently deceased. The new owner, his only daughter and an aspiring singer/actress in Los Angeles, was in town and anxious to get rid of the property. Rong told Saiyue that she could get a really good deal for her.

The next afternoon, Liu Rong took her to look at the house. It was small but the price was within her range. Furthermore, the sale would cover practically all essential furniture and appliances, including a washer and drier set—Kenmore, Sears & Roebuck, two years old, like new, since the old man hadn't had that much wash to do.

Saiyue concluded the deal at $70,000, with $17,500 in cash and the rest by a mortgage. After the closing, Rong took Saiyue to lunch.

"As I told you, you have gotten an exceptionally good deal on this house," Rong said.

"You are the professional. I kind of think so too."

"Sure. If Seymour and I haven't bought that house, I would have taken this one. Or, if I have the money, I'd invest in this too."

"How is Professor Smith?"

"Well, finally the arrangement has been completed that she will have half of his retirement accumulations with TIAA and CREF. That satisfies her."

"Will you two be married pretty soon then?"

"I think so."

"When will be the big day?"

"It won't be even a small day. We'll just get it done in Las Vegas. No need to bother people. I can see the appearance of things—I would be a fox fairy, and he, either an addlebrained buffoon or a heartless wolf," Rong said.

"You are being too defensive. Not everyone is philistine and superficial, you know."

"You know Seymour and I were more like two lost souls meeting at the world's edge," Rong said, continuing on her own thought.

"Did he say that too?"

"Not exactly in those words. Basically, he said that after the youngest child was born, she not only utterly lost interest in him as a person, but also showed her tiredness and contempt of him....He was quite puzzled over her attitude. He felt that she wasn't superior to him in any way, except for her presumptuousness and readiness to fight over anything, big or small," Rong said.

Saiyue thought, that sounds like a conceited man to me. But she said, "Then why she's given him such a hard time when he wants out?"

"She does care for his paycheck. That's why he felt like a used stud, and a meal ticket or what we would call, a 'shake money tree,'"[43] Rong said.

Saiyue thought the German American wife could feel like a used mare or something. She'd like to hear her side of the story. Instead, she said, "You two have lived together for some time now. Must be getting on rather nicely."

"It has been pretty good. He concentrates on his book, doesn't bother me, and I leave him alone. We each go our own way and do our work, allowing each other a lot of space. Like…if I don't feel like going to his sister's birthday party, I don't go to his sister's birthday party," Rong said with a rise and fall inflection. "Nevertheless, we enjoy our spare time together."

"Sounds like an almost ideal relationship," Saiyue said.

"I don't know if it's ideal or not. I am old enough not to look for anything ideal in life. But I can tell you this much. It's a heck of a lot more relaxed than the one I had in Chengdo. Big-man-ism would stir up a small hassle every three days, a medium fight each week, and a big blowup perhaps every

---

43. A legendary tree from which coins would fall when shaken—often a reference to a prostitute in relation to her pimp or madam.

month or two. It was that time he struck me that I decided that one day I'd leave him. Anyway, all that's behind me now. Here, as long as I have financial independence, I have autonomy and peace," Rong said.

"Theoretically, it shouldn't be like that," Saiyue said. "In practice…"

Saiyue had another reason for acquiring the property at that particular time. Her grandfather would be coming soon to visit. She thought it would please him uncommonly to stay in his granddaughter's house, rather than in some rented place.

A month after she moved into the house, she came to the International Terminal of San Francisco Airport to meet her grandpa. She watched him coming toward her from behind the partition that marked the completion of the U.S. Government processing of international arrivals. She was always happy to see him under any circumstances. But this meeting was special, mainly because it was taking place in the *Beautiful Country* that he had often told her about in her high school years as some distant enchanting place. Furthermore, after so much had happened to her in recent years, she looked forward to talking about life with her childhood nurturer, her trusted and wise grandpa.

He looked younger than his seventy plus years of age. For one thing, he had gotten rid of his goatee. Bald at the top, his head had an encircling gray band. His face was smooth with that ruddy sheen of a healthy older person—undoubtedly his regular exercise with tai chi chuan had helped. The sclerae and pupils were still clear and distinct. The gray suit, rumpled and too small around the midriff, and the white shirt, puckered and too large around the neck, with a loose brown tie were all spotlessly clean. In spite of the bumpkin-like clothing, the white hair at the temples, the lustrous eyes and a deliberate demeanor lent a dignified air about him.

He gazed at her with a wooden smile. As she hugged him, his face contracted with emotion, eyes blinking reddish. However, it didn't take him long to recover his composure. He put his arms around her too and patted her. Shortly, he was chatting with her about the plane ride, baggage, weather back in Shanghai and other externals.

In the car out of the airport, he told her that he had finally reclaimed his old room on the second floor after her brother and sister-in-law—who had taken over the room following the Songs' move to the suburb—got their own apartment from his work unit.

"That's nice....Have you seen Baobao lately?" she asked.

"No, not since about a year ago, I wrote to you about it," he said.

"Yes....How did he look to you?"

"He looked healthy...well behaved. I sent you that picture."

"Yes."

"You know I always forward any news about the boy as soon as I have it."

"I know....From Ma's and Pa's letters, I gather their lives are much more relaxed nowadays."

"True, quite a pleasant change from those days of unending learning sessions and neighborhood meetings. Now they have more leisure. They visit the Hong Kou Park regularly. Your Ma has joined an aerobics club. She has even talked about retiring."

"How about Pa?"

"I think it's too early for him. He has taken up chess lately. Goes to the park on Sunday mornings to play with his friends."

"How are Xiao Long and Xiao Zhu?"

"Both your brother and sister are doing quite well. Since Xiao Long and his wife moved out of the house, I did not get to see them much. Well, before they moved out, I had not seen much of them either. He has his beliefs and interests. I used to think that he had greater faith in socialism than even his wife—"

"Sister-in-law still works for the Labor Union of Shanghai?"

"Yes. As you know, your brother and I don't always see eye to eye on some things. But as he matures, we have kept a sort of mutual respect. From my perspective, nowadays he seems to be more open to us....Xiao

Zhu is doing well at the newspaper, *Shen Bao*. At times, however, she complains about the pay," he said.

"I am impressed by her letters. She seemed like a schoolgirl when I saw her last. How mature she sounds now! She's got a good head on her shoulder," Saiyue said.

"So has her husband."

"A biologist. Right?"

"Yes, a molecular biologist. A very studious one, and rather quiet. I suppose scientists are like that," he said, and began to crane his head in order to keep his sight on an elevated multi-level interchange with overpasses of curved bridges. "These constructions are like structures in heaven," he said. She knew he was trying to take in as much as he could about this land, which he thought he knew well and yet was seeing now only for the first time.

After coming out of the zooming traffic on Bayshore Freeway and before reaching the house, he observed that in stages the roads became narrower, cars fewer, and speed lower. "There are so few people walking," he said. The car pulled in a short driveway of a Spanish style house, the tan stucco wall glimmering in the setting sun, while the small yard to the right was already in shade. They entered the house through the front porch with an arch doorway above a terrazzo floor. The right half of the house comprised of a living room, with a picture window facing the front yard and the street, a dining room, or eating area, then the kitchen. The left half had two bedrooms separated by a bathroom. The backyard was proportionately small, a couple of oranges still hung on a short spidery tree.

In line with traditional Chinese "modesty," even with her own grandpa, she kept apologizing that the house was too small. The old gentleman merely nodded his head and repeated monosyllabically, "Hao (Fine), hao...hao," which was also called for by "modesty," to keep in check his pride over his granddaughter.

She asked whether he would like to rest—in the front bedroom, which she had prepared for him. He said that he had slept much on the plane and wasn't tired at all. She realized that he was probably too excited to rest anyway.

They sat down at the table in the eating area, each with a cup of tea and chatted about the ordinary concerns of living. How much was the monthly mortgage, the electricity bill, etc. He shook his head at the payments after converting them into RMB$. "How much is a kilo of rice?" he asked.

"I usually pick up a package of rice when needed. I don't even pay attention to the weight or price. It's not a significant expense," she said.

"Do you remember those days when you used to bring back the bag of our monthly ration that we two would load into the rice bin?"

"I sure do. I remember hauling it up the stairs to our floor. The exercise probably helped me later to adjust to the labor at the village farm," she said. She also recalled after getting the bag up to the third floor, he would be there to meet her, having already unlocked the wooden rice bin by the door of the floor's main room in which her parents and sister slept. Saiyue and her grandpa would each hold a corner of the bag, jerk up the end of it with a certain rhythm, and watch the matte-gray rice cascading down into the bin under small puffs of powder swirling in the light from the window over the stairs landing. He would smooth the heap of rice with his palm, and in the process pick up a couple of nodules of grains lumped by rice-worm silk, crumble them, remove the sticky gossamers and return the several disentangled grains back into the storage.

She noticed that he was staring blankly at her, seemingly in a reverie also. "What's the matter, Grandpa?"

"Xiao Yue," he said, "you know that the more you grow up, the more you look like your Grandma," he said.

"I'd be very happy if I have only half of her features," Saiyue smiled that caltrop smile that the senior Zhang loved of his wife and later of his granddaughter.

"You've more than that," he said.

It was already dark outside. Saiyue said that she would take him to a restaurant to celebrate his arrival.

27

They sat in a booth at a local restaurant. Saiyue ordered wine and suggested that her grandfather try steak or trout. But he wanted a "real American hamburger" that he had heard so much about. She added a soup and salad for him. After the wine came, she raised the glass, "Welcome to America, Grandpa!"

"Xiao Yue, thank you for making this trip possible for me," the old man said lovingly and quaffed. "As you know, until now, all my life I have lived in China. Ever since I entered St. John's as a teenager, America had exerted a special attraction on me." The initial shaking in his voice was now gone. "My American professors and my friends, who had been here, told me about this country. I read books and magazines, and saw shows and documentaries on television. It was like 'scratching one's itching foot over the shoe.' Now I am able to see the place with my own eyes. Thanks to you." He lifted the glass again and took another drink.

"Don't talk like this, Grandpa, as though I am one of your friends. I am Xiao Yue, your granddaughter. I wouldn't be here but for your nurture," she said earnestly, recalling the sessions of patient tutoring he had given her in the cramped pavilion room that she had shared with him and her brother.

"I see America hasn't changed you as a person. Still you seem to have acclimated well enough here. 'Americanized' may be the right word. You look so...what's the word?" then he said in English, "chic." He pointed smilingly at her arc of pearl necklace over a white blouse framed by a green plaid blazer, and emptied his glass of wine.

She remembered that she used to have fun in discovering with him the meaning of such "new" English words or phrases as "palimony," "Voodoo economics," and "Teflon politician." She had come across them from issues of *Newsweek* that a friend of his in Los Angeles sent him regularly, and he would let her read also.

When the waitress brought the food, Saiyue, enjoying watching her grandpa's hearty mood, told her to bring more wine.

"Not for me," he said. "My capacity for alcohol is quite limited. I usually don't drink much."

"But it's just wine, and this is such a special occasion."

"That I can't deny," he acquiesced.

After the food and wine, they relaxed in the soft lighting of the booth before cups of decaf coffee. (He did want coffee instead of tea.)

"We—your parents, brother, sister and of course, me too—are all so proud of you...with your accomplishments, your graduate degree, a good job in modern technology, all in so short a time," the senior Zhang said expansively and burped.

"That's not special, Grandpa. Most of us who came over here did at least that much. Some did considerably better. They got doctoral degrees and became professors." She had not yet become so Americanized as to discard the old-fashioned Chinese idea that "Scholarship is the loftiest of all pursuits."

"Yes. You had told me that you admired the professorial life. You still can have one, if you really want it. You are young."

"Perhaps, but here, unlike in China, you need a doctoral degree just to be considered. I did give it some thought. I decided that I needed to work first in order to save some money."

"You think you might go back to school later?"

"I don't know. I may not have the drive. People say that once you've left school, it's hard to go back to the rigors of a student's life."

"I know you have gone through a lot—marriage, divorce, marriage and divorce again. I know also I am out-of-date....But we, your parents and I, don't quite see why all those drastic actions were needed. We found it..."

She suddenly felt a chill followed by a surge of fever, and braced herself for the next word. "Disgraceful?"—too much! Perhaps "embarrassing."

The old man regretted that he had drifted into a trap of his uncharacteristic loose tongue. Yet, as if under a spell, he continued, "...hard to talk about with relatives and neighbors."

She had anticipated that the topic would come up sometime, but not so soon. If it had been anybody else, even her parents, she would probably have retorted with something like, "Then don't talk about it!" But not to her grandpa. She fell silent.

Lamely he said, "I suppose you have your reasons. How would we know, ten thousand miles away," as if wishing to withdraw the previous disapproval, however mild.

"I did what I had to do—for a better life, Grandpa."

"A better life, eh? Yes? But going through all that?...In my generation you'd never get away with that." He belched a winey burp.

"I didn't *get away with* anything, Grandpa!...In your youth, concubines were legal, and women in villages were bought and sold. Times have changed, Grandpa. I just did what I had to do that was within my rights....Frankly, I sometimes marvel at the degree of commitment a young person entering into marriage is supposed to make. Commitment for a lifetime! What logic! A person hardly knows how she or he will grow and change, say, three years from now, how could one's spouse predict and be prepared to live with the other *for a lifetime*?"

"Xiao Yue!" her grandpa's face already flushed by alcohol suddenly turned grave. "You are saying careless and dangerous things. The institution of marriage affects not just the married couple. Have you thought about the children?—"

"Of course I have," she interrupted.

"The institution is fundamental to society. Social stability requires it to be taken seriously. You put your name and happiness in jeopardy when making statements or thinking like that. Do you understand?"

She had never seen him more serious before. She was struck dumb momentarily, but quickly recovered. "Oh, yes. I think I do. In jeopardy, my name? perhaps in China. But not my happiness here," she refrained from raising her voice. "I believe I have a natural right to pursue happiness as long as I don't really hurt other people. I don't act against my conscience—"

"Conscience is subjective—you need be careful there," he interrupted.

"True. We are all individuals. But I am also willing and ready, of course, to subject myself to restrictions of the law, but not necessarily to somebody else's notion of propriety. Now I don't think my actions have really hurt anybody. They may, in the long run, even enrich the lives of those closely connected." Grandpa felt a slight tingle—a possible inclusion of his? Saiyue continued, "So far as social stability is concerned, you know better than I that people in power often use the slogan *social stability* to resist change, to keep the status quo to preserve their advantage."

The senior Zhang was surprised at the vigor of his granddaughter's defense. He would like to vent off the tension in the air. But the topic was too serious to let it slide by. "Everything you said has a point. But only to a point," he said. "You need to look at the bigger picture. Do you agree that an individual can't have total, unrestricted freedom; that is, in exchange for the protection and nurture society provides, one must give up some freedom?"

"Yes."

"Overall, the system that has family—which follows from the institution of marriage—function as the basic unit of society affords social stability with the least loss of individual freedom. Otherwise, anarchy, totalitarianism or foreign conquest waits in the wings.…You can't question the institution of marriage just for your convenience. Do you question your parents' marriage?

Mine? These things follow natural laws! Of course, there are aberrations, exceptions. But overall the basic reason holds—for the proper, orderly existence and continuance of a civilized society, to minimize sadness and maximize happiness."

"I wasn't questioning the institution of marriage, Grandpa, certainly not for my convenience. I just mean that the associated rules of marriage may need modification from time to time—for example, as women join men in the labor for material production—in order for the institution to fulfill its purpose of minimizing sadness and maximizing happiness," Saiyue said.

"There have been modifications in recent decades, like the permission of divorce when there exists unresolvable conflict," he said.

"Yes. The definition of 'unresolvable conflict' changes with changes in culture and circumstances," Saiyue said.

"Well," her grandpa now felt it unprofitable to continue the topic. "As the old saying goes, 'Even an upright judge can't settle family conflicts.' Xiao Yue, as far as I am concerned, all I am interested in is your happiness, long or short range. But I do believe that the firmest foundation of it all is love."

"I can't argue with that. If it had been somebody else saying this to me, I'd think it's cliché, but you have earned your right to say it because of your devotion to Grandma through all these years, and there has been no piece of legal paper or social mores to bind you," she said.

"I am contented with her memory," the old man said lightly.

"You are blessed. Grandpa, sorry if I have been overly outspoken. I don't mean to be disrespectful. I spoke my mind to you because I trust and revere you."

"I understand. If you didn't speak frankly, it would be disrespectful," he said.

The atmosphere calmed. Without looking at her, he said, "Now that you are divorced from that Professor Lu, would you be willing to reunite with Xu Haosheng?"

"What? Why the question?"

"I just wonder. Because he still seems to care a lot about you."

"How do you know?" she asked.

"As I wrote you, he had visited us a couple of times, bringing Xiao Ming with him. From the way he conducted himself and asked about you, and also from the letters he sent me, I just have that feeling...."

"Oh yeah?" she said blandly. "It was decent of him to take Baobao to see his mother's family....Basically I want to know the boy's progress. I appreciate your acting as an intermediary," she said. "I wouldn't have troubled you if there was a better way—"

"Don't talk to your grandpa this politely," he said with a smile.

"Sorry. Truly I thank you. I hope Xu Haosheng would tell the boy about my life here too."

"I presume that he did. I've clearly asked him to do that."

"Is he still with that trading company in Hong Kong?"

"Yes." After a pause, "Your separation from Professor Lu....It's been a year now, more or less, right? Have you met any new prospects?" he asked.

"Grandpa, you are prying!" Chuckling, she felt quite relaxed now. "But I don't mind it, from you....I went out with a couple of male friends. Nothing significant came off."

"Colleagues at work?" he asked, pinching his chin—a substitute for his old habit of twisting his goatee.

"One of them is."

"Chinese, or Chinese American?"

"No, neither is."

"Oh...common background is important in relationships," he said platitudinously.

"Yes. Yet one of the things I have learned in my years here is how people from different parts of the world are alike—they have the same kinds of desires and fears, and they are in general reasonable and decent people. I have had no problem getting along with my colleagues of different nationalities, or earlier, with fellow graduate students—Americans, British, Filipino, Indians, Iranians, etc.

"But when it comes to man-woman relationships, you are probably right, a common background should make things easier. It's complex enough even with that. However, my two specific experiences were unusual....Perhaps I was unconsciously seeking the unusual," she stopped abruptly.

"Yes?" he waited.

She was amused by the passing thought how her grandpa would react if he would come to know about the details of those experiences. She continued meditatively. "I don't know...I don't know. In spite of the preparations I thought I had for life in this country, somehow I feel my roots here are still quite shallow. Unlike in Shanghai, or even Xi'an, I felt I knew exactly what was going on around me, and what kind of people I was dealing with."

"You are much better off than, say, an American-born trying to grow roots in China."

"That's probably true," she gave him a wan smile.

"So you are still searching?" he said.

"Not really, if it's all up to me. But society seems to expect me to do that. An unmarried woman is considered, as it were, incomplete, like a drifting specter looking for a body in order to anchor herself....However, if I am searching, it would be easier if I know what type of person I am searching for."

"Again, I suppose I am too out-of-date on these things to give you any help," he said.

After a moment of silence between them, she resumed, musingly, "You see, as regards Haosheng, I knew him, quite well, I think....Or at least I thought so. Except for one incident, generally he was pretty nice to me. Quite presentable—"

"What incident?"

The question was ignored. "He was actually quite smart too, but, rather lazy.... Did you know that he did not buy or read a single book in all the time I was with him? His reading was limited to newspapers, and magazines."

"Well, like you, he has good looks, which, by the way, is not always a blessing," he continued. "Also like you, he hasn't really been spoiled by that. He seems to me basically a levelheaded young man, guileless and not really pretentious. I like that quality in a person. Furthermore, judging from his recent activities, I won't say he is lazy. He may not be the same unambitious person you just spoke of."

"Maybe, from what you told me in the letters—willing to go to Shenzhen and Hong Kong to take his chances and all, maybe he's changed," she eyed him for a second, as if to allow him to give her a further confirmation. "Anyhow," she continued, "now Lu Panzhe.... Incidentally, I think you'll like him. I had sometimes called him a bookworm. But he is no bookworm. He thinks. I didn't always know what he thought."

"You mean you couldn't control him," he smiled.

"Grandpa! Don't tease me! I can't and don't want to control anybody. But I don't want to be controlled either....Back to Panzhe, he was really too old for me. Imagine when he reaches 60, I'd be just 40!"

"Well, in defense of old age, you may also figure that when you reach 50, he'd be just 70, or you at 60, he 80. That wouldn't sound so bad. Would it? But you are right. The age difference is a major factor. We can't have everything we like in life. That is a cliche....On the other hand, I'd also think that, if the professor was only ordinarily worldly-wise, it would take some kind of courage too for him to marry you."

"I never thought of it that way...."

"Maybe some special kind of love," he added.

"O yeah?" She said abstractedly, watching her own forefinger slowly orbiting the inside of the coffee cup handle. "I suppose so, even though he seemed to put his scholarship over everything else. Actually that is a kind of pride or vanity too. But then, at times it sounded just like a livelihood. As for me, I just wonder whether my life could be better...." She straightened herself in her seat, "Grandpa, did people gossip about my divorce from Haosheng?"

"We did not talk to neighbors and relatives about your marital status. Just your graduate degree and job. But some did ask whether Haosheng and Xiao Ming would be joining you soon. We just dodged such questions."

"It's funny. More recently, I sometimes think of the simplicity of life in Xi'an. Everything was set. There was no need to think or strive."

"Didn't you strive in Xi'an?"

"Not for anything in Xi'an itself."

"Simplicity, no strife! Not anymore! Opportunities and challenges seem to pop up all over China, for the young, that is. It's such a pity and misfortune for, say, your parents' generation, that they matured in that gray time slot of China's history. It did not allow them any initiative to build their own lives and to enjoy a reasonable measure of peace and prosperity. Well, it could be said that they had a measure of peace, yet so little prosperity."

"I know, for a time back in the village, I was about to give up too."

"But you didn't," he said.

"Thanks to your encouragement," she said. "I remember your saying, when I returned on home leaves, 'In the name of our ancestors, such nonsense and madness must end sooner or later.'"

"I did believe that."

"And I also recall, 'In books there are houses of gold; in books, there are beauties like emeralds,'" she smiled.

"That's what my father used to tell me. It was kind of moldy…but practical. The deciding factor was, after all, your own will. As I said before, the situation has now changed. Opportunities abound. The new generation has a chance to exert themselves, and define their own lives. That is, to develop one's potential; it should be the essence of life. Sorry for all this old man's prattle."

"No. Grandpa, this is interesting. But aren't you tired after the long flight?"

"As I told you, I had plenty of sleep on the plane. I'm fine."

"OK. We haven't had much chance to talk in years. Please go on."

"All right," he emptied his cup. "You know I have regretted I didn't do enough with my life. At the time I graduated from St. John's, some of my schoolmates went to work for foreign firms, on the career path of compradores. Some became quite wealthy and are now living well in Hong Kong, Canada or the United States.

"However, much as I admired Western culture, I couldn't suffer the bad manners of those foreign businessmen then, behaving like colonial rulers. I took what I thought was a good job—teaching high school. I sold my inherited farmland in Changshu and used most of the money to buy the alley house. I lived a life of ease—listening to music, reading poetry, philosophy and history, and making judgments on philosophers and heroes of the past and present, all in the comforts of my chair, the fragrance of a smoldering incense and the intermittent songs of a golden finch in my room....I suppose I cared too much about *yin* and not enough about *yang*."

The waitress came and refilled the coffee. After a sip and a couple of finger rubs over his chin, he continued, "I tried to live the 'A gentleman makes good himself only' philosophy. At the end of World War II, I celebrated China's victory over Japan. After the founding of the People's Republic, I celebrated China's status as a truly independent nation cleansed of all the humiliations and disgrace of the past. Yet deep in my heart, I knew that I had contributed little to those accomplishments. Then reality set in.

"What was left of my financial resources at the end of World War II was eaten away by the horrendous inflation afterwards. When the Revolution came, we had the house only. Subsequently, we surrendered the first two floors of the house. As you know, that left our family with the two rooms on the third. It was a good thing we had done that, judging from what happened later to others in the neighborhood who hadn't offered to share their houses. As a high school history and English teacher, I felt as helpless as a silkworm on a glass plate. I had to retire on a paltry pension....You wrote that now you go to church pretty much regularly. Right?"

"Yes."

"I suppose you know the Bible well by now."

"Not really. But I listen to the gospel readings at church services. After I got my degree, I did attend Bible class a few times and read it occasionally," she said.

"You may remember in your senior year in high school, we studied part of *The Gospel According to St. Matthew* as English lessons."

"Yes."

"Have you read since in the same gospel the parable about a master and his three servants?"

"Go ahead."

"A master, when leaving the house on a long journey, gave to his three servants five, two and one talent each, in proportion to their abilities. On his return, the two servants, who were given five and two talents, had invested them and made a profit for the master. He commended them. The one who was given one talent played safe and had left it unused; he presented the same to the master. This servant was reprimanded for his slothfulness."

"Yes, I remember that one," she said.

"I feel like that servant given the one talent, and would have qualms facing the master, my Maker, when the time comes to give an account of the talent given to me."

"Grandpa, I thought you were not a Christian nor religious!"

"I have never been baptized."

"But I think you are a Christian, or at least religious, at heart."

"Does it matter?" he asked.

"I sometimes ask myself that question. I don't know. About the parable, Grandpa, I think you are entirely too hard on yourself. First of all, I don't think that you are a 'one-talent-servant.' Secondly, I think you have done well with the talents given to you. Maybe I am being immodest, but—even not counting all the students you've taught and the rest of our family in Shanghai—isn't the person sitting in front of you part, even though a very small part, of what you've done with your talents?"

"Xiao Yue, you are a sweet granddaughter," the old man said quaveringly. "As one who doesn't do, nor need to do, much these days, I talk too much about myself....Now back to you," he paused. "From what I have read, life style in America is even freer now than ever before, especially for a woman, with the women's liberation movement and such. You are an immigrant; you can go as far as your talent will take you. And you have a lot of that."

"Don't make me out to be that talented or ambitious, Grandpa. Yes, sometimes, I think, why can't I be a chief engineer of my firm, or a full professor? Then, sometimes, I feel tired and that my options are getting fewer and fewer. I am not really *that* young anymore, Grandpa."

"Even *I* don't consider myself *that* old. Remember you are my granddaughter," he smiled.

"Thanks for the boost," she said. "Anyway, I kind of envy many of those American suburban housewives. All they need to do is to drive the kids around in a van to ballet, piano, tennis lessons, and/or soccer games. Then they have coffee, luncheons, bridge parties, or tennis with their neighbors and friends. No deadlines to meet, no reports to prepare and present before eagle-eyed project managers. The only persons they need to be accountable to are their husbands. Even there they could turn things around, and it is the husbands who'd give account to them."

"I don't know," he said. "What you said or seemed to imply can't be all true. Is there such a saying that 'there is no free lunch in America?' There must be a catch somewhere. Anyway, do you want their kind of life as you just described?"

"Well, I might consider it if Baobao were here with me," she said with a smile. "No, not really. Not now at least. I like my independence and my work....I am so glad you are here. You know that after a day's work, to come back to an empty apartment is no fun."

There was a moment's pause.

"Is remarrying Haosheng out of the question?" he asked.

"I won't say that."

"You know he intimated that when he comes to the United States on business, he would like to visit you. Would you like that?"

"Is he coming to America?"

"On a business trip, I understand."

"Oh.... Visit me? Sure, why not?...After all, he is Baobao's father." She said slowly, her mouth contorted a little.

"Do you mind if I give him your address and telephone number?"

"No. I don't mind."

"As I have told you, it's entirely possible that in his mind you are still his wife."

"Undoubtedly an errant, if not sinful, one," she smiled ironically. "That does not surprise me, although it is an utter illusion on his part. After all, he is a Chinese man. In China, it is *big man-ism*; here we call it male chauvinism. That's his inheritance from the culture; the baggage is on his back, not mine."

Grandpa smiled at her condescending tone and the use of *here* and *we*. "Don't you think, if it is really just that, wouldn't he simply drop you from his life, and get on with his, which, I would gather, can't be so bad. I hope I am not offending you."

She widened her eyes at him, and then said almost meekly, "Yes, indeed, I sometimes wonder why he wouldn't, like you said, simply drop me. Perhaps he wants to prove something....One never knows what lurks in a person's mind. I hardly know mine; how can I know his. I don't know about his life these days....That's true....No. You are not offending me. In fact, I am glad that you speak out, and make your point."

"Xiao Yue, you've matured much....How about Professor Lu?"

"What about him?"

"Remarrying him, since you seem to still think well of him."

"I think I have told you. Maybe I haven't. I respect him, and feel indebted to him. He had helped me so much not only to realize my wishes but also to broaden my horizon."

"Respect and gratitude could be a starting point for love and marriage, or remarriage. Think so?"

"Maybe. Told you a moment ago, I am no longer an innocent bright-eyed lass anymore. His age after all should be a factor. Apart from that, he does have some very good qualities."

"Of course, otherwise, he can't be a professor at a major university," he nodded appreciatively.

"I don't mean his academic and professional achievements. I mean personal qualities: honesty, and reasonableness.... The academic life has its attractions. On the other hand, as I saw him at his desk, hours upon hours, nights and weekends, I don't know.... Such a person, used to loneliness, self-sufficiency, can be cold sometimes. I am not sure that's ideal for me either."

"I suppose scholars are like that. Nobody is perfect from every angle," Grandpa said.

"I guess so.... Here we are, talking as though it's up to me to pick. Who knows whether either is available or still interested.... But I am in no hurry. I enjoy my work and professional growth. Besides—you'll be happy to hear this—I've taken to reading up a little on liberal arts subjects—history, social science and such. For example, you know that I have gained a clearer picture of Chinese history from books written in English."

"Really, I am glad. I hope you'll keep it up. You won't be wasting your time. That I can assure you."

"I know. And I don't have to tell you of your influence on my interest in reading."

"You are flattering me, Xiao Yue," the old man said affectionately. "I think my place nowadays is just to watch how much you can do."

"Now who's flattering whom?" She noticed his eyes had dimmed some and face sagged a bit. "Grandpa, we have been at this for quite a while. Would you like more coffee? Or would you like to go back to rest?"

"I think we should go back. I feel fatigue is catching up with excitement."

Back in the house, before they went to bed, he handed over the presents he had brought from Shanghai: A sweater and two silk blouses from her mother and father, a small brocaded purse from her sister, a pen from her brother, and a diary book from himself.

She told him that she would go to work the next day, and how he could care for himself with the food she had stored in the refrigerator. She also gave him her office phone number. He asked her not to mind him, since he needed the whole day to recuperate anyway. She said she would take him sightseeing the following day.

28

On Saturday, Saiyue took her grandpa to the city. They had an early lunch at a restaurant featuring Shanghai food in the New Chinatown and went northward to visit the Golden Gate Park. After beguiling a couple of hours at the Natural History Museum and the Steinhart Aquarium, where they watched the dolphins show, they headed for Coit Tower.

She parked the car at the junction of Filbert Street and Kearny Street, and they walked up the stone stairway to the tower. An elevator took them to the observation room. Starting from the west, Saiyue showed her grandfather the immense blue Pacific beyond the magnificent Golden Gate Bridge. She called his attention to Angel Island to the north, saying, "Many earlier hopeful immigrants from China were locked up and languished in a detention center there."

"I'd read about that. I think it was after the Chinese Exclusion Act passed the American government. Do you know the dates of that period?" he asked.

"Not exactly....Are you testing me?" she smiled. "Wait! Let me see. It was about a dozen years after the completion of the Transcontinental Railroad. The railroad was connected in 1869. The Exclusion Act should be around...1881? Right?"

"You are quite close. It was 1882. Those poor Chinese laborers! After so much hardship, sweat and frost in the construction of the Railroad, only to be persecuted after its completion."

"I know that the Act was repealed at the end of World War II. In recent years, attempts to bring to public attention the Chinese contribution to the Railroad have met with some limited success," she said.

"That is decent and fair for those who tried. I am impressed that you know these facts," Grandpa said, pinching his chin.

"As a new immigrant from China, I ought to know something about my predecessors."

Going around the aerie, she pointed out the other long span bridges, then the TransAmerica Building. The city dwellings, sparkling in the sun with their red roofs and white walls, underlain by angular shadows, rose and fell in relief on the hilly land.

Exhilarated, gazing here and there, he murmured the Chinese saw, "One hundred tales cannot match a single sight!"

After leaving Coit Tower, they drove downhill, waited in line and finally parked the car in a public garage on Kearny Street. They walked around Chinatown. He was particularly interested in the exhibition inside a small museum of the history of Chinese immigrants. He read under a glass pane a verse, the "Angel Island Cell Self-comforting Poem," authored in Chinese by a detainee, a Scholar Xu:[44]

A hundred plus sad poems adorn the wall;
Bemoaning the unkind delay are all.
Why should the wretched to the cruel plead?
It's from the lost to lost would pity fall.
Who could gainsay success reside in fate?

---

44. The original poem in Chinese was printed in the November 10, 1996 issue of *Overseas Central Bulletin (Hai Wai Zhong Xin Jian Xun)*, Overseas Scholars and Students Service Center, Committee on Youth Guidance, Executive Yuan, Taipeh, Taiwan.

Or fortune be set in a crystal ball.
Now don't complain about today's straits.
Since old times only test'd heroes stand tall.

"It's a fine piece," he nodded and remarked to her granddaughter. "Who says early immigrants were unlearned?"

"I understand that there are more such poems preserved in the Immigration Station on Angel Island. We should pay a visit to the place sometime."

Before returning, they had boiled noodles with barbecued pork at a Cantonese restaurant for supper.

Next morning, she took him to the church. After service, she introduced him to the Reverend Norton and Mrs. McNamara, as well as a few others they came upon. They stayed for the after-service coffee. While Saiyue was talking with some of her younger friends, she noticed that her grandfather and her former landlady were chatting with such amicability that it almost gave her ideas. (Indeed, subsequently, each spoke to her well of the other.)

In the afternoon, after he had a nap, she drove him to the Stanford Center. They ambled about, sightseeing as well as window-shopping. He commented that he did not expect to see that many Asian faces in the area. It also struck him as remarkable that they all appeared to be quite well-off and taking their ease—just like the Caucasians around the place. Then he admitted to himself that perhaps it was a vestige of his early experience, i.e., the *sub-colonial* environment in which he had grown up, that the scene would seem remarkable to him.

They sauntered in leisure. Suddenly, she said in an undertone, "Grandpa, Lu Panzhe is coming toward us!" He followed her line of sight and saw an Asian man in a beige sports jacket walking toward them.

It was the first time Saiyue and Panzhe met since their divorce. They stopped and greeted each other with the American "Hi!" in a low-keyed but familiar tone, like that between a teenage brother and sister.

"Panzhe, this is my grandfather;" she said, "this is Lu Panzhe." The surprised younger teacher, backing half a step, bowed and shook the elder's outstretched hand.

"Granduncle Zhang. Saiyue had told me a lot about you. I am very honored to meet you."

"I am very pleased to meet you, Professor Lu. Needless to say, I have heard much about you too."

"Call me Panzhe please. This is a very fortunate occasion for me. Er…Saiyue, if you don't mind, perhaps we can find a place to sit down. Er…May I buy Granduncle Zhang and you a snack and a cup of coffee?"

She turned to look at her grandpa, her expression genial.

"Whatever you say." He let her decide.

They sat at a table in a nearby coffee shop.

"When did Granduncle Zhang arrive?" Panzhe asked.

"Last Thursday."

"Have you done much sightseeing yet?"

"Yes, yes, quite a lot. It probably tired her out."

"Not at all. We haven't really been to that many places. Coit Tower, Golden Gate Park, Chinatown…The usual, you know.…What has brought you here to the Mall." She knew that Panzhe was no shopping enthusiast.

"I am going to the hobby store to get some thin strips to make a couple of models for the *Advanced Strength of Materials* course I shall be teaching. The school is now between terms."

"Oh yeah? This is one of the really nice things about being with the school. You have a long break between terms. I miss that in industry," she said, looking at him with a measuring eye.

At this juncture, Grandpa Zhang asked to be excused, saying he needed to go to the men's room. After assuring them that he would have no trouble finding the place and know how to return, he left alone.

"Busy at the office lately?" Panzhe asked conversationally.

"Busy lately? We are always busy. I am used to it by now though. How have you been?"

"I have been all right."

They reviewed the passersby outside the large glass window and surveyed the specials advertised on the wall. She took a sip of coffee and asked nonchalantly, "How is your attractive girl friend?"

"What do you mean?" he answered with similar nonchalance.

"Don't be modest now. The one on the cruise ship."

"Oh, the cruise. You saw me?"

"Yes."

"I suppose she is fine. We are just colleagues now."

"More than colleagues before?" she gave him a Cheshire cat grin.

He was unprepared for her directness. "Well, you may say that, for a very short duration though. It's past."

"Uh-huh," she was enjoying the teasing role. "You look well, a lot more relaxed."

"I feel fine. You look well too," he said. "How is your handsome boyfriend?"

Surprised by the counteroffensive, she wasn't sure to whom he was referring. "What boyfriend?" she muttered.

"Same place, on the ship," he smiled.

"Oh Yes, likewise, we are just friends now....Actually I doubt even that." He surely sounded confident today, she thought, and that smug grin is *disgusting*.

"Oh." He thought it unmannerly to continue that line of conversation. He waited until she took a drink and put the cup down. "How are things in general besides work?"

"All right. I have learned a lot since...in the past year," she said softly, and then, straightening her back a little, "Do you know I have bought a small house?"

"A house! Congratulations! Now that you are a landowner, would that get your parents in trouble in Shanghai?" he jested.

"Not landowner, just a monthly payer of a hefty mortgage."

"Need help?"

"Noo...oo," she pursed her mouth and shook her head.

"By the way, how long is your grandfather going to be here?"

"I am not sure. He is supposed to be going to LA sometime to visit an old friend."

"I am thinking. I assume you have to work tomorrow. Since school is between terms, I could show him around a little."

"Aren't you busy? You need to make those models—"

"I'll have plenty of time for that."

"How is your research?"

"I am doing all right there. In fact, I got that grant for the proposal I worked on."

"Oh, how nice! Congratulations!" she exclaimed.

"Thanks. It'll set my mind at ease for a while. By the way, I have drafted a technical note on the numerical integration procedure that we developed. If you don't mind, I'd like you to look it over before sending it out to the *International Journal of Numerical Methods for Engineering Science*."

"Why?"

"As a co-author."

"Oh," she was pleasantly surprised. "All right. I don't know what improvement I could possibly make on your draft."

"You'll find out by reading it over critically. In particular, check over the numerical example. I can mail it to you in the next few days."

"All right. I'll tell you what. Assuming it's OK with Grandpa, I'll let you show him around tomorrow, provided that you agree to come to my house for a dinner to celebrate your grant. I know how much work you had put into the proposal."

You don't know, he thought. Wiping his hand over his cheek and compressed lips, he fixed his eyes at her for a few seconds. "It's a deal!" he said.

Grandpa returned and apologized for having taken a little time to look at some of the window displays. She told him about the plan for the next day. He accepted Panzhe's offer with the cliche, "To accept your offer I am abashed; but to decline it would be disrespectful."

Next morning, at her house Panzhe gave her the manuscript. Before the men left, she warned them, "Don't you two spend all your time on high-flown philosophy and stuff and forget about enjoying the sights!" They just smiled.

They drove first to the Stanford University campus, which the guest had expressed an interest in. Panzhe was familiar with the place, having spent his first sabbatical of six months there. He told him of the reported background of the metal fence around the top of Hoover Tower: to prevent people—failed doctoral students in particular—from jumping off it. Zhang mentioned a story he had heard that at the University of Michigan, a graduate student of Chinese decent, who had failed academically, hid himself and lived for months in a church attic in the university town of Ann Arbor. He was discovered later, draping hair and all.

Panzhe then related the monstrous tragic story at the Iowa Institute of Technology, where a graduate student from China had shot and killed his major professor, the department chairman, his secretary, a fellow Chinese student, and lastly himself. The reason? He felt that a department award that the other Chinese student had won should have been his. Panzhe and his guest went on talking discursively about the pressures of "shame," twisted responses, human capacities for evil and the need for control of instruments of violence, such as guns.

They visited the library and had donuts and coffee on the terrace of a cafeteria nearby. Then they drove to the Technical University of California. Panzhe first showed Zhang the computer center, and then the students' PC rooms.

Behind large glass windows, rows of modernistic, gray, spotless electronic equipment were arrayed in front of young, keen and earnest faces, and hands manipulating the "mice"—the function of which was briefly explained by Panzhe. To Zhang, the scene was another example that the world was passing him by, impersonally and coolly—as cool as the antiseptic lights of the monitors.

After walking through the Union, they went to the Aeronautical Engineering Building. Panzhe invited his ex-grandfather-in-law into his office and offered him his chair. The latter declined and took one of the visitors' chairs.

"This is a very nice office," Zhang said.

"The school provides us with good facilities. If we don't do good work, lack of facilities can't be an excuse," Panzhe said.

"In my time, I hardly heard of any ethnic Chinese professors at American universities."

"True, they were quite rare. However, since World War II racial discrimination has been declining in America. Chinese Americans, like all minorities, have benefited much from the civil rights movement that African Americans have led."

"Yes. I understand....I suppose that's the secret of America's success—the ability to attract, absorb and motivate earnest people from other parts of the world. At first only Northern Europeans were involved. Then other Caucasians, and now non-Caucasians as well. I have heard this earlier saying about ethnic Chinese in America: 'When you meet one, he would be associated with either a restaurant or a laundry.' More recently, to those vocations have been added: '...or be a physician or a professor,'" Zhang said.

Panzhe sensed the light of appreciation in the old man's eyes. "Yes, physicians do enjoy high regard here. But as to professors, have you ever heard of this epigram: 'Those who can, do; those who can't, teach,'" Panzhe said.

"No, not of that one," Zhang smiled. "It sounds like a banter in a toast."

"I am not so sure. However, my daughter's generation go into all kinds of fields—business, finance, journalism, fine arts, even politics—and apparently are doing pretty well," Panzhe said.

"That's very nice," Zhang said. "What do you think has brought the change?"

"My generation has mostly chosen science related professions basically because their practices are largely culture-independent, and work performances are judged objectively. Non-technical professional practices are often culture-dependent and success depends on cultural acclimation. The younger generation's willingness to go into non-technical areas indicates that they are 'natives,' comfortable with the culture," Panzhe said.

"Cultural acclimation aside, isn't it also true that technical fields pay more?"

"Yes, at least, at lower levels. In any case, the younger generation seems to be keeping faith with their real interest....I don't mind telling you that I didn't stick to my initial major in liberal arts in college, mainly because I feared I couldn't make a living after graduation."

"I am sure you could. At most, it is a matter of a living at what material standard."

"I see what you mean."

"Of course you've heard the saying, 'Every field has its *zhuang-yuan*,'"[45] Zhang said.

"Yes. But I have also heard, 'Live off a trade; gripe about the trade.' Certainly, I am not complaining. In fact, I think one can do his best work only if he believes—brainwashes himself to do so, if needed—that his work is the most worthwhile thing in the world....Still, sometimes, I can't help admiring the works of those in liberal and fine arts. They seem to have such wide and deep reach," Lu said.

"Only the outstanding ones do though, just as in science and technology. However, in technology, you don't have to be outstanding—being competent is enough—to produce things that can be plainly seen to be beneficial to the public—like those multi-level overpasses I saw on highways that enable traffic to flow nonstop in every direction....In any case, it's human nature to think that 'The neighbor's grass is greener,'" Zhang said.

They began to talk about livelihood and greed, and rambled on sententiously for quite a while before they left the campus.

---

45. *Zhuang-yuan* was, in the imperial days, the title of the first pick by the emperor among the finalists of a national examination—the fastest track to high officialdom by a scholar. The saying means, "Excellence in any field will lead to a very successful life."

That night, Saiyue asked her grandpa with what was he most impressed in the touring of the campuses. He said it was the lavatories—they were clean, free of odor and well supplied with toilet paper and paper towels. But he did add, "I agree with you that Lu Panzhe is not a soulless technological man or a bookworm." He refrained from saying more, lest he might overly influence his granddaughter to the extent that it might be unfair to his other ex-grandson-in-law, Xu Haosheng.

At the weekend, as agreed upon, Panzhe returned to Saiyue's house for a dinner party at which Liu Rong and Professor Smith were also present.

The following Saturday Panzhe invited Saiyue and her grandpa for dinner. The elder Zhang claimed that he needed to rest at home and urged Saiyue to go. After a slight hesitation, she did. Thus she began to date Panzhe again. At an early opportunity, she unobtrusively revealed enough of Ray Dalton the person—rather talented but seriously flawed—and that she no longer considered him a friend. Panzhe offered her pretty much a level playing field by telling her about Nora Gallagher, and that their interests and tastes were basically incompatible and his relationship with her was now 100 percent professional. However, he thought it needless to reveal to her that Nora was once married to a colleague of hers at John J. Clyde.

At the start of their renewed relationship, Saiyue was deliberate and discreet, but soon discovered that Panzhe was similarly inclined. She sometimes felt that both regarded their previous marriage as if it were that of two close friends of theirs, rather than of themselves.

They went out together as good friends, almost new friends. Occasionally she would vent her irritations at her workplace. He was a good listener and would often help her reduce the significance of those irritations to pettiness. The renewed relationship came to a plateau that was not entirely platonic either. Though they did have goodnight kisses, passion was well kept in check as if by prior agreement. Of course, the question of remarriage was shunned.

Such was the state of their relationship before the arrival in San Francisco of Xu Haosheng. Saiyue had told Panzhe of Xu's impending visit. The professor realized that it was not one of those minor irritations in the workplace—in fact, he wasn't sure that it was an irritation to her at all. He had not offered any counsel on this, because she had not asked for any. Both acted as though their relationship would not be affected in the least by the visitor to come.

On this cool May night they were returning from San Francisco after an all Mahler program at the Davis Hall.

"I suppose you will be busy next week," Panzhe said.

"I am busy every week. What do you mean?" she said.

"I mean with Xu Ming's father arriving and all." It was only human nature for him to refer to her first husband indirectly.

"Oh, that, didn't I tell you?" she affected lightness of the matter. "It's not next week. It's this week. In fact, it's tomorrow; it has been moved up. Grandpa got his message the other night....It'd be awkward should he come a day earlier," she added thoughtlessly.

"How is that? Are you supposed to meet him at the airport or something?" he didn't sound overly enthused.

"No. I don't have that much spare time. I'd leave that all to his own devices."

He was glad to hear that remark.

"But I suppose I have to more or less play the hostess a little for San Francisco, although I didn't invite him here."

"Your grandpa did?"

"He just gave him my address and telephone number," she said. "When he called me, saying that he'd like to stop by on his way to New York for a business meeting, I couldn't very well refuse." After saying this, she was miffed at herself for appearing to be explaining her actions to Panzhe. The feeling turned to combativeness when she heard him asking,

"What would that hostess' role be?"

"I don't know. I'll just play it by ear. After all, he is the father of my son!"

That shut him up. Silent, he looked stiffly up the road, turning off El Camino. She felt sorry for her insensitiveness and laid her head on his shoulder, "I don't mean to sound cross. I guess I am tired, a little sleepy."

Appreciative of the gesture, he patted her head, "You go straight to bed after getting home," and swallowed back the clause, "and get ready for the big day tomorrow."

"Umm," she crowed. She wondered what would happen in the next few days. I haven't seen him for so long, she thought.

29

Cutting through the darkness, the headlight beam swept past a picture window, a stucco wall panel and an arched entrance to a porch, and the car turned into the driveway.

"You don't have to get out," Saiyue said.

"I'll see you to the door," Panzhe shifted to "P." The dog next door barked routinely a couple of times, growled lowly and quieted down.

She stepped out of the car and said, "There is light inside. Grandpa must still be up. No need to come to the door.... Thanks for the concert. Now I appreciate Mahler better."

"We'll do it again. I'll call you."

Under the starlit sky, they kissed briefly, almost ritualistically, like Russian dignitaries at some formal ceremony. As they drew away from each other, the house door banged open. Out rushed a figure, down the steps from the porch. Another followed, as though in pursuit. A slice of silvery gleam sailed toward Panzhe's chest as a man's voice called out, "You son of a turtle shameless chalk-talker! Now it's time for you to be taught a lesson!"

The target dodged, raising his arm to protect himself. A knife tore through the upper sleeve of the coat. The attacker's momentum carried him forward; he stumbled headlong and fell on the plot of grass beside the driveway. The figure trailing him from the house rushed up and sat on top of him. The dog barked ferociously behind the fence.

"Saiyue, protect yourself! Run quickly inside! Lock the door and call nine-one-one!" Panzhe shouted. He hastily got a tennis racquet out from the back seat of the car, ready to defend himself.

Instead of doing what she was told, she turned to the heap on the ground and screeched,

"Haosheng! It's you! Stop it! Stop it right now! Or you are going to jail! Is that what you come to America for? Spending years in jail?"

In the dim dispersion of the headlight, her grandpa held down, while simultaneously warning, the attacker, who had actually made no attempt to counter. Presently he got up sluggishly, and mutely let Grandpa half guide and half push him back into the house under the watchful eye of the concertgoers. The barking slackened.

"Are you hurt?" Saiyue asked.

"I think I am all right." Panzhe took off his coat slowly. Part of his ripped shirt had stuck to the wound by the half-congealed blood; but apparently there was little fresh blood. He let her tie her handkerchief around the arm above the wound, more as a gesture than a medical procedure.

"Should you go to a hospital emergency room?" she asked.

"I am not sure I need to, but it's probably a good idea."

"You know who attacked you. Don't you?"

"I think I do."

"I am so sorry."

"It's not your fault."

"Are you going to report it to the police?"

"I don't know."

At this point, Grandpa scurried out.

"Panzhe, you all right?" he asked.

"I think so."

"Haosheng is calm now. He realizes he is in trouble. He must be drunk. It's partly my fault, letting him drink that much. I am sorry," Grandpa said.

"No major harm done," Panzhe said.

"That's good. I was quite concerned." Grandpa hurried back into the house.

"Frankly, it's not like him, as I knew him. He was never violent," she said, "I'll take you to the hospital."

Teeth clenched, Panzhe took another look at the arm. "It's just a flesh wound. You don't have to come with me. I'll have it properly cleaned, just to be sure. If you need me for whatever reason, call me."

"I can take care of myself. Thank you. In case you need my help, just call. I am really sorry about this."

"As I said, it's not your fault. But you wouldn't think a college graduate would behave this way!" he said. She took it as a Confucian "gentlemanly" comment rather than a real belief on his part that a college education would eliminate violent behavior.

As he was about to step in the car, a bank of red and blue rotating lights moved up the street in their direction. He held up. Soon a police car stopped behind his. Out stepped two policemen amid resumed all-out barking.

"I am Officer McDowell; this is Officer Gonzalez. We are responding to a nine-one-one call, from a neighbor of yours, I believe. I understand there is a problem here," said the hulking one, like a grizzly bear. "Anybody hurt, needing medical attention?"

"No, it's just a minor wound," Panzhe pointed to the arm.

"Anybody else besides you injured?"

"No," Saiyue said.

"You all right? Ma'am?"

"I am fine."

"What happened?" the bear asked.

"A visitor to my house here," she nodded toward it, "came out and attacked this gentleman."

"Is the visitor still inside?" the officer asked her.

"Yes, he's with my grandfather. Apparently he had too much to drink. He is normal now. I am sure he didn't mean to harm anyone."

"Ma'am, we'll find out more about that. May I see your driver's license, sir?" Officer McDowell asked. After he got it, "Pantse Lu, did I pronounce it right?"

"Yes," Lu thought it was close enough. He also presented a business card to the officer. After a brief questioning, McDowell asked, "Do you wish to sign a complaint?"

Panzhe hesitated and looked at Saiyue. She appeared tense. He said, "I did smell alcohol. Since I am not really hurt, I'd as soon forget about the whole thing."

After the officer confirmed Panzhe's home address and phone number and returned his driver's license, he told his sidekick Gonzalez to back out the police car to let the professor go. Saiyue followed McDowell inside the house. He questioned each of the three separately in the kitchen. Overall the individual accounts seemed to be quite consistent. The alleged assailant—-also the first ex-husband of the woman who owned the house— had come to visit in the evening, having just arrived in San Francisco from Hong Kong 24 hours earlier than expected by his ex-wife. She had gone out with her second ex-husband for a concert in San Francisco. Her grandfather had invited the alleged assailant to wait in the house. While waiting, he had ingested much alcoholic beverage. Later, the approaching car's headlight brought him to the picture window. Seeing his ex-wife and her escort in an embrace, he ran to the kitchen for the knife....

The Zhangs had tried to explain that Haosheng was not a violent or dangerous person and never had a criminal record, and tonight's behavior was due to alcohol. Haosheng, the last one questioned, told Officer **McDowell that he couldn't recall what happened, aside from the fact that he had drunk beer, sherry and whisky.**

After returning to the living room, McDowell faced Haosheng again, "Xu Haosheng, you are under arrest for felonious assault. You may remain silent...." He proceeded to read him the Miranda statement and handcuffed him.

Although not entirely unexpected, the turn of events shook up all three Chinese. "But he was drunk and I believe Professor Lu knew that too. He had told us he won't press charges," Saiyue said. And her grandfather added feebly, "He had just arrived from Hong Kong. He was very tired."

"I have taken down your statements. This is a felony case. We have no choice. It's up to the county prosecutor to decide. He will take your statements under advisement," McDowell said.

"Can we go with him?" she asked.

"No, ma'am."

With a deep frown, Haosheng said to Saiyue, "Would you call the Chinese Consulate for me?"

"I think you'd better get a lawyer first. Do you know one in town?"

"How could I? Do I need one?"

"Believe me, you do. Want me to get one for you?"

"All right. Thank you."

After he left with the police, Saiyue called Oliver French, the lawyer whom she had retained before.

Having heard the story in pajamas, the attorney told her there wasn't anything he could do tonight. "For the alcohol part alone they will keep him overnight. I'll contact them and the prosecutor's office tomorrow. The professor won't press charges? Right?...Good...Yes. Chances are the county prosecutor won't either. I'd be more concerned with the Immigration people."

The last comment, which was repeated to Grandpa, made both even more disconcerted.

"What a night!" she said. "There is nothing we can do until tomorrow." She went in the kitchen to have a drink of water. She noticed that one of the set of knives, nestled in a wooden block under the cupboard and tilting like field ballistic missiles was absent. The police had it now.

"How did he happen to know about these knives?" she asked.

"I told him to use it to cut the barbecued pork for him to have along with the whisky that Professor Smith brought for the party that night," Grandpa said.

Before going to bed, she called Panzhe. He told her that he had been to the St. Luke Hospital Emergency Room and that he had the wound cleansed and dressed and was given a booster tetanus shot. She related the police's action after he had left, and that French was now on the case. The conversation ended with her saying that she'd keep him informed of any major development.

Next noon French told Saiyue that, as he had expected, the prosecutor's office had apprized the immigration authorities of the incident and was still waiting to hear from them. After spending a nervous afternoon and evening, she was relieved to learn that Haosheng would not be prosecuted inasmuch as Lu wasn't going to file a complaint. At the police station, French handed over to her, accompanied by Grandpa, her first ex-husband. He had spent some 24 hours in jail, where he had slept most of the time, gotten rid of much of the alcohol in the blood, and appeared generally none the worse for wear. They ate at a fast-food restaurant and returned to the house.

"Thank you for the help," Haosheng said to the Zhangs.

"We need to take care of one another, especially in a foreign country," Grandpa responded.

"I thought you were arriving today," she said.

"There must have been a mix-up somewhere. Probably due to the International Date Line," Haosheng said. "I am sorry I lost control. The endless hours on the plane, the drinks and the waiting—waiting for you—made me lose my head.... How's that chalk—er, big professor?" The "big" was meant to be ironic.

"He is all right. You could be in a lot of trouble if he pressed charges. This is a country of law. You can't go around pulling knives on people," she lectured him.

"I don't care." The listless tone was unconvincing.

"Don't talk like that. No one in this country dares to take a jail sentence lightly. French said you were lucky that in the last 24 hours you didn't have to share a cell with some rough character. In a penitentiary, even the crudest and toughest could have a hard time of it," she reproved him.

"Xiao Yue is right," Grandpa said, recalling some violent movie scenes of an American prison on television.

She could now look at her first ex-husband calmly. Sitting at the edge of the sofa, cheek in a palm, and elbow just ahead of his coat laid on the armrest, he appeared relaxed enough, considering what he had gone through in the last 24 hours. His face fuller with a bristly shadowy jowl, he looked a little heavier and older, not older really, but more mature, a handsomeness somewhat altered from before, but still he was that.

She had never seen him in such fine clothing before. The rep tie was loosened; the gray pants, probably of wrinkle free material, still appeared crisp. Aside from a few smudged patches around the sleeves, the rest of the shirt still seemed brightly white and pleasing with the fashionable maroon vest. With money how little time it takes for one to learn to dress well, she thought.

"Anyway we are glad you are out of jail and unharmed," she said.

"Me too," Haosheng smiled thinly, lifted his head and looked squarely at her like an appraiser. "I am glad to see you. You look well—everything about you. How are you?" he said softly.

"I was all right until I got home last night." Having said that, she felt a little sorry and followed with, "How is Baobao?"

"He is doing fine, except perhaps spoiled a little by his paternal grandparents."

"Do you have any more recent pictures of him?" she looked at him expectantly.

"No. I believe I mailed the last ones to Grandpa Zhang some time ago."

"I usually forwarded them to you almost immediately," Grandpa interjected quickly.

"Oh, yes," she acknowledged. After a short pause, she said, "We are glad to see you, Haosheng, but you can't stay here tonight." Her tone was soft though.

"Why not? I am your husband," he smiled.

"Don't joke!"

"But it's too late. I can't find a place to stay." His voice sounded like pleading and the look a little forlorn; particularly the eyes reminded her of Baobao when the little boy just woke up in the morning.

Although she felt it must be possible to find some lodging not too far away, she relented. "All right. Just for tonight."

"I can sleep on the sofa here."

"All right, we have had enough for a while. Let's rest and we'll talk tomorrow," she said.

From the linen closet she handed a set of bedding and a blanket to Haosheng. Then she went in the kitchen, sat down and had a glass of milk. Walking past the bathroom while on her way to her bedroom, she saw Haosheng pulling off his undershirt, and it had momentarily covered his face. His physique, though a little thicker around the waist, still had that masculine magnetism. It was bare except for the tight-fitting jockey shorts outlining the maleness between his strong thighs that she used to know.

She was the last one to wash up before going to bed. All lights were off and the house dark. She waited for herself to quiet down from all the activities in the last 24 hours. Gradually total stillness settled in like a fog, and she fell asleep. Suddenly she felt someone on top of her. Before she could cry out for her grandfather, a hand was over her mouth: "Saiyue, it's me. It's been such a long time." He moved the hand to her breast.

"Stop this. Stop or I'll call Grandpa."

"Don't! Saiyue! My heart-and-liver! My wife!"

She felt his strong thighs pressed against hers and the hot bulge. A viscous warmth began to permeate her body. Half resisting, half-engaging, she held her peace.

When it was over, she said to him, "You could be charged with rape you know."

"Raping my wife?"

"Yes, in this country you could be charged with that even if I were your wife. Now go back to the sofa." She now locked her room's door to the passageway also.

She would not let herself think she enjoyed the experience. However, she felt no real outrage either. The bit of hurt dignity was ameliorated by the thought that, after all, he is Baobao's father. But I'll not let it happen again.

— 30 —

In the morning Saiyue told Haosheng that the first order of business for him was to find a hotel room. He caught her tone, studied the Yellow Pages, called around some and took a room at the Sofital Hotel by Redwood Bay.

"I am sorry about last night," he said to her as he was tidying up the sofa. "You have to forgive me. In my mind, you are still my wife." His roguish grin was met by an frosty stare. Then he added, "It won't happen that way again."

"It will not, unless you wish the jail. Talking about that, don't you think you should apologize to Professor Lu? You know it was his bigheartedness that saved you serious trouble."

He frowned. "What kind of place is this? He stole my wife and I am supposed to apologize?"

"You are talking like a street scoundrel in a lawless country. If you had steam to blow off, you did it at the wrong person....Remember he may still change his mind," she said.

"Let him....Tell him....It was the alcohol. I had no intention to hurt him, just wanted to give him a scare. That is all....Or, whatever you like."

She did not offer to take him to the hotel. After he called for a taxi, she said, "If you like I could show you some sights of San Francisco."

"Of course, I'll appreciate that," he said. Now she'll be *my tour guide.*

After he left, she called Panzhe to let him know of Haosheng's being freed, and conveyed his *apology* to him, as well as her own appreciation of his magnanimity, intimating that she understood for whose sake was his forbearance intended. However, when he began asking after herself, she cut him short, telling him simply that she could take care of herself, and then brought the phone conversation to a quick end by saying that they would be in touch.

She picked up Haosheng at the hotel. After merging with the Bayshore traffic, she asked, "How did you get the job at…what's the name?"

"Zhong Xing Company," he helped her out.

"Oh Yes."

"Well, shortly after your long distance call that year, our team was invited to play in a national tournament in Beijing. We lost in the first round—"

"What happened? You wouldn't blame me for that, would you?" she meant to be humorous.

"No. Because we faced a better team. Actually I played quite well myself. Not just others said so. I felt it myself. For that perhaps I ought to thank you."

"You were fired up," she said.

"Something like that….Anyway, the game was played in the evening and shown on TV. The next morning, an old college chum called me, inviting me to dinner at his apartment. I went and it turned out to be his parents' apartment, at Muxidi. You know Muxidi?"

"Muxidi…is it in the west part of Beijing?" she asked.

"Yes. People know that's where many high-ranking officials live. Later on I learned that I was in what was known as the 'ministers' building.' Actually not all of them were cadres. Some were members of the People's Consultative Council. You know they are comparable to senators of the United States Congress."

"With the same power, no doubt," she said.

"You can spare that dig." He sounded slightly annoyed, but continued, "My friend told me Wang Guangmei[46] lived just a few floors below their unit. I had never seen such spacious and nicely furnished rooms before except in movies. You know houses capitalists and landlords lived in."

"OK. I am impressed," she said.

"I met my friend's father. His bearing told me he was a military man, although he didn't wear any uniform. He complimented me on my game, which he said he had watched on TV. Then he proceeded to ask me all kinds of questions about my background.

"I remember seeing his eyes light up a bit when I mentioned that I grew up in Guangzhou. In any case, I believe, whatever were the reasons for his questions, I left him a pretty fair impression of myself."

"I am sure you did," she said, knowing well how smooth he could be.

"The following morning," he pursued, "my friend and I had tea in one of the cafes in the Beijing Hotel. He told me about Zhong Xing Company, of which his father was a director. It dealt with a wide range of commodities. Machinery, personal computers, electronic instruments, etc., for import, and textiles, ceramics and minerals and such, for export. To make a long story short, they offered me a job."

"Hum....".

"I got more details about the offer, including a condition on my passing an English course at the Institute of Foreign Language. It didn't take me long to accept it," he said.

"Of course, you passed the course," she said.

"Yes. Let me tell you. I have never studied harder in my life," he said.

"I can see the result." She turned and cast a measuring glance at him. "Grandpa told me you are an assistant manager now. It didn't take you long to learn business either, um?"

---

46. Wife of Liu Shaoqi, President of the People's Republic before he was purged and died during the Cultural Revolution.

"Some of my experience at the mill helped. But accounting and commercial procedures I had to learn. They weren't that hard once you put your mind to it," he said.

Yes, she thought, *put your mind to it*, that is the key. He simply hadn't put his mind to it when he was with me in Xi'an.

"Soon I was asked to participate in meetings, negotiations for sales as well as purchases," he continued.

"It sounds like they had you brought along very quickly and well," she said, thinking there is of course more to business than the mechanics of business.

"Recalling that interview at Muxidi, I think they didn't just want a clerk or an accountant or someone who could speak Cantonese."

"I can imagine you are some kind of a natural in that business environment. Now, both your goal and that of the company are met."

"Goal? Well…my horizon has widened some since. I don't mind telling you that I am sure I can be more than an assistant manager."

"Ambitious!" she commented.

"Not overly. I have seen that it can be done. In fact, I know someone who has done it."

"Who?" she asked.

"Er, some old school chum.…So much for me. How about you? Your grandpa had filled me in some. I'd like to hear more from yourself," he said.

"Really, there isn't much to tell," she said. "Life here is actually very simple, mainly work, work and work."

"It may be that for most Chinese young people over here. But I don't think it's like that for you," he said.

She ignored the barb and gave him an outline of her academic and job experiences, much of which he had already heard from her grandfather.

At the same restaurant in the New Chinatown whereto she had taken her grandpa, she ordered a dish of pan-fried soft noodles with pork strands, a bowl of noodle soup with shrimp and an order of "small-steamer dumplings."

"You know the real purpose of my visit, don't you?" he said.

"I don't know your *real purpose*," she mocked him, "other than that you are on a business trip."

"That is true....Your grandpa told me you are now officially divorced, right?"

"Yes."

"You have your green card now, right?"

"Yes."

"Now frankly my condition has also improved in a major way. Not that it should make any fundamental difference. Anyhow, don't you think we should get married again?" he asked.

"Haosheng, I believe we both have gained much maturity in the past few years. I appreciate your stopping by here to see me as well as previously taking Baobao to visit my family in Shanghai. Also, I am flattered by your asking me to remarry you. But I am sorry that I am not planning on getting married right now," she said.

"Why not? Now you have what you wanted from our divorce; the reason for our divorce no longer exists," he said.

"It was then. Circumstances have changed. You and I have too," she said and caught a shadow passing over his face with a twitch of the eyebrow.

"I thought you enjoyed our reunion last night." His tone was tender.

"I detest your sneakiness. I'll forgive you just this once." She left his presumption unanswered.

"I have already promised you it won't happen that way again," he said.

She didn't like his phrase "that way"—that he had used in the morning also—but wouldn't take the trouble to challenge it.

After the food, for the sightseeing, she pretty much followed the route she had taken Grandpa. Along the way, Haosheng continued his line. "I am still the father of your son. I took care of him in your absence. I know you certainly love Xiao Ming, and also you still love me. You may deny this. But I know you do. You know I care for you....Life in the United States must suit you. You look wonderful. My feelings for you have not changed. After all, we are 'hair-tying husband-and-wife.'[47] Besides, that unctuous so-called professor is simply too old for you. Before long he'd need to soak his denture every night, like my father."

Although she thought his last remark was kind of a low blow, she felt considerable cogency in the rest of his argument. The term hair-tying-husband-and wife carried as much a cultural punch as the reference to himself as the father of Baobao did an emotional one. Besides, indeed, he seemed to be a changed man, rather determined to make a life in the business world, and to possess what it takes to do it. And last night...Still there was the shadow of Cao Rushi, though turning somewhat fainter in the years. All things considered, Saiyue was yet unsure—even perplexed—why would he still want, even so earnestly, to marry her again. Nevertheless, she was more than a little pleased about it. Then again, that was no reason to give up her independence so quickly.

"Only part of what you said is true," she responded. "We had married and lived under rather hard conditions. Now divorced we have each found a new career and improved our standards of living considerably....I appreciate very much your taking care of Baobao. Yes, I do love him. But that alone doesn't necessarily mean we should remarry....I simply don't know at this time. Moreover, when it comes to my choosing a new husband, age is not the deciding factor. I need more time to think things over."

"You want an *ocean zhuang-yuan*[48] husband? Is that it?"

"I am not saying that. You must know that I have worked so hard to have a chance for a better life. Now, I am a free woman in a free country. I'd like to take my time to do it right this time. Could you understand that?"

All afternoon, as they went through the sights of San Francisco, they dueled like this, with Saiyue parrying Haosheng's thrust. Finally, he gave up. He stayed on in the Bay area for three more days, spending one day joining a bus tour, to which he invited his ex-grandfather-in-law to be his

---

47. First marriage for both husband and wife.
48. A top scholar from a foreign country. (See foot-note for Zhuang-yuan in Chapter 28.)

guest. After a couple of days with some college friends in the Bay area, he had dinner with the Zhangs at a restaurant and left for New York City the next morning to join his business associates.

The following evening, she received a get-in-touch call from Panzhe. He told her the wound had been healing well. In turn, she revealed that Haosheng had left California, and also that he had asked her to remarry him.

"How did you answer?"

"How do you think I should answer?"

"Well...." he was noncommittal.

"I told him I needed time to think it over."

"Oh, for such a matter it is important to be careful," he sounded like a totally disinterested party. He added, "One should be careful not to make the same mistake twice."

"Are you talking about me or yourself?" she said.

"Well...."

"Are you sorry that you married me the first time?" she asked.

"No, Saiyue. I knew what I was doing. You know the university life. After we were married, I continued to conduct my life as though my university work, my research in particular, was the basis of my existence. That rejection of my proposal by the National Research Council was a real blow. I probably lost my bearings in our relationship.... But more recently, I have come to realize that my research isn't going to shake the world anyway, even if I put all my energies into it. There is no good reason that I should forgo everything else in life on its account. I can still do respectable work and earn an honorable living, but that need not take my whole being," he said.

"I am glad to hear that. Yes, you seem more relaxed lately. Anyway, you already have your accomplishments and security. You deserve them. You are in a position to order your life."

"Everyone is in a position to order his or her life."

"I have a long way to go," she sighed.

"Cheer up. The weekend is coming up. Would you like to go out for dinner Saturday?"

She thought for a moment. "No. Thanks, Panzhe. I don't think so. I have things to do."

"I understand. But we'll keep in touch."

She felt that if she resumed dating Panzhe after having met Haosheng again, she might appear to have made her choice. Although Panzhe had not talked about remarriage, at this time she wouldn't feel ready to answer him either, should he bring it up.

For the month during which her grandpa had gone to Los Angeles to visit his old schoolmate, Saiyue was alone by herself except in the office and, on Sundays, the church. Aside from those activities, she continued her program of reading. At times, her mind would turn to her unsettled private life. She'd imagine how the "Xu family life" of the three would change from that in the cramped and pinched conditions in Xi'an to all kinds of possibilities, in Hong Kong or the United States. The family could go on a vacation in a larger car, like an Oldsmobile Cutlass. Baobao would be strapped in a car seat between Haosheng, the driver, and herself. (She would still think of the boy as the toddler when she left him, in spite of his more recent pictures.) They'd cruise on the wide-open Interstate I-80, perhaps all the way to Chicago for its great museums. They'd switch to I-90 to Niagara Falls, which she had heard so much about, and continue onto the other side of the continent and to Boston by the Atlantic to fulfill a promise to visit her old friend Yan Yifeng.

At other times, she'd envision life with Lu Panzhe again, now that she was no longer a student. Actually it'd be pretty much the same as before, except that she'd be under no pressure of schoolwork. Panzhe probably would be at his desk most of the time. She could do her own work, or read—which she enjoyed so much lately—under the alcove lamp, and from time to time pause and let the mind wander a bit and then search among the sparse, firefly-like lights across the dark ravine. She could talk him into going to church with her on Sundays. Of course, life need not be so sedate all the time. There would be concerts, art exhibits, lectures and travel. Panzhe had told her in Cancun he would show her the other three oldest capitals of the world, and in addition, Paris and Vienna, where they'd visit such places as the Louvre and Beethoven's apartment. It isn't the money, she thought. Is it? Haosheng probably has the means now. Just that he wouldn't have such interest. But he has Baobao, at least at the present time.

She thought she had, in effect, already been offered the first scenario. As to the second, she was reasonably sure she could have it if she wanted. Yet it had not been forthcoming voluntarily. Had she hurt the professor too much? Probably not, else why had he restarted a relationship, even if only at a low key? Should she induce an offer for the second scenario—for the second time? Would it be decent to possibly hurt him twice?

Between spells of fancying and amidst reasoning and feeling, she was sure of one thing—she missed her Baobao. She considered ways to broach with Haosheng the possibility of bringing the child over to the United States and hoped that he would cooperate without getting the boy involved in the issue of their possible remarriage.

About two months after Haosheng had returned to Hong Kong, she telephoned him.

"Haosheng, I was thinking again—we had talked about this before — it'd be good for Baobao to come to America and go to school here. What do you think?"

"When? Now?"

"Yes, I'll support him."

"What would be his status?" he asked.

"As my son, of course."

"But his father is here in Hong Kong."

"Well, he still can come as my son."

"How about as son of remarried parents?" he proposed.

"Let's not mix the two questions," she said softly. "You know that in America he'd have better opportunities."

"That may be. But he needn't be there right now. He is doing fine in Nanjing, properly cared for by his grandparents. If he leaves Nanjing to join you now, he wouldn't have the same kind of care while you are working. Right? Later on, he can go there for college…or even graduate school. Who knows?"

"You talk as though you are his sole guardian."

"No, Saiyue. I won't presume that. But what I just said is for his good. Not mine or yours."

He's got a point, she thought. I have a chance to get the boy over here if I fight for it. But it could take up a lot of time, energy and probably money too. I better get myself settled first. She gave up, for the time being.

31

Ever since she had the regular job at John J. Clyde & Associates, the thought of a return visit to China had occurred to her every so often. She had not acted on it because her career had been making steady progress, riding on the wave of computer technology and her own efforts. And she would like to keep the momentum going.

After the last phone conversation with Haosheng, the thought reemerged. She decided to make the trip to see Baobao in Nanjing and her family in Shanghai. When she called to advise Haosheng about it, he eagerly encouraged her. In fact, he called her back later to tell her that he could reserve a tourist hotel room for her in Shanghai and in Nanjing, and she would only need to pay at the rate for a Chinese citizen on official business. That would be only a fraction of the rate for a foreign tourist. She accepted the offer.

All necessary arrangements were made. She called Panzhe to let him know about the planned trip and that her grandfather was returning with her. Panzhe offered to buy them a send-off dinner, which she initially declined. It was accepted only after he said that it was for her grandpa. His offer to provide transportation to the airport was, however, not taken up.

After a short layover in Tokyo, and another two hours or so in the air, the Zhangs found themselves high above the rich farmland of eastern China.

Miles of rice fields shimmered in golden green, crisscrossed by dikes and waterways in slices of shade and glare, and marked here and there by lines of windbreaks and dark patches of dwellings and dots of trees.

She thought of the time when she had to decide her "road ahead" after high school. Ma was recovering from a bad flu. I did the cooking, cabbage and tofu, I think. After supper, Grandpa and Pa sat up on the opposite ends of the big bed, and Ma and I likewise on Xiao Zhu's bed, lumpy cotton coats over our legs and feet—a rare incursion of frigid air mass from Siberia. A little light bulb dangled from the ceiling, casting thin shadows on the wall.

"Xiao Yue, really it's up to you," Pa had said. I just couldn't tell them that I'd like to stay in the city. Couldn't do that to Xiao Long and Xiao Zhu—they'd surely be sent to "production brigades," which I wouldn't have wanted for myself—a farmhand all my life.[49] When I told them my *doctrine of the mean* decision to request a suburban village assignment, Ma smiled ; I could see the relief in her face.

The first year in the field was plenty rough. To tap and pull those slimy leeches off the legs, browned within a week! Afterwards, transferred to the village chief's office, writing those doggerels—"Work, and work hard! Let our production bring glory to Chairman Mao!" and such. Teaching little kids was more enjoyable though. Overall, life was so bland and *boring*.... I didn't join them, but, pretending to be asleep, I listened for their stories and snickers about…that thing between the legs. Imagine, I had even toyed with the idea of getting to know that quiet tall vice captain better.

In her continued gaze down from the airplane window, she saw a lone motor vehicle crawling along a road.

I remember that well. Spring Festival's Eve. We didn't celebrate that much because of Premier Zhou's death. No bus was running from the village to Songjiang because of the snow the night before. It was slow trudging. A

---

49. At the time, only one child in a family was allowed to stay in the city after high school; the other children, if any, would be assigned to the countryside upon graduation.

warmth crept down on the thigh. I had to outfit myself for the monthlies behind that tree with a sheet of newspaper. I checked there was no picture of the Chairman on it. Could still see the red spots on the yellow stubble and white snow.

How we were shocked by the news of Chairman Mao's death. Can't even count the number of times we had shouted "Chairman Mao lives to 10,000 years!" Shortly, every cadre was talking about "pulverizing the Gang of Four."....As Grandpa said, "The dawn has finally come." The village chief probably would have let me take the college entrance examination even without Grandpa's gold-plated pocket watch. But...

Saiyue and Grandpa were met by the family at Hong Qiao Airport. The welcoming party greeted the returning patriarch respectfully and then quickly turned to Saiyue, who hugged each in turn. Her sister smilingly commented: "This is the *ocean style*." Saiyue couldn't answer all the questions fired at her simultaneously. All she could say, holding back her tears, was, "I feel fine....Glad you all look so well....We have got all our baggage here...."

Her mother and father, both wearing gray pants and white Hong Kong shirts,[50] looked healthy but older, particularly her father, gray hair above the ears and scratched bags under the eyes, appearing to be a younger brother of her grandpa. For the first time she saw her mother wearing eyeglasses. Her younger sister, Saizhu, in full bloom now, was as pretty as the peony design on her blouse, but more shapely. Her lively eyes flashed on Saiyue's pink dress with a wide black belt. Sailong, her brother, seemed heavier than before. Saiyue had remembered his closely spaced eyebrows accentuating a serious look, which she used to think incongruous with the rest of his tender, youthful face. He still had that look but seemed less strange now as the face had acquired a chiseled aspect of some grown men. His demeanor, as before, was respectful, but somewhat distant.

---

50. Also known as Hawaii shirts, shirts that are not tucked inside the pants.

After the initial excitement was over, her father said, "Xiao Yue, Xu Haosheng has sent me a telegram."

"Yes, what about?"

"Firstly, he has reserved a room at the Peace Hotel for you. Secondly—this has to do with Xiao Ming—his paternal grandparents are going to Guangzhou to visit relatives and friends. They are taking Xiao Ming with them to Hong Kong. The boy will be in Hong Kong with his father until the grandparents are ready to return to Nanjing. It means you'll have to go to Hong Kong to see the boy. He also gave the name and phone number of someone who could assist you with your travel to Hong Kong."

Frowning, she acknowledged the information. Her brother, taking care of the heavier baggage, would ride with her and their grandpa in a car that their father had borrowed from his work unit. Her sister and parents were to follow by bus.

Shortly out of the airport, she recognized, to her left, the front gate of the Shanghai Zoological Garden below the tall trees, faintly gilded in the lowering sun. The Shanghai-Qingpu Highway seemed to have been widened. In about half an hour, in the midst of increasingly congested traffic, she noted the Bubbling Well Temple. Beyond the International Hotel the road became almost clogged. Advertising signboards—winking, flashing and racing—were much brighter, more colorful and numerous and hung higher than she had remembered.

She had seen the massive crowd on Nanjing Road before—in fact, she had been a particle of the slow flow herself many times. The years' absence and living in the United States had changed her to view the sight as something extraordinary. On both sides of the road, which seemed much narrower than she had remembered, and spilling over from the sidewalk, people of all ages thronging noisily, and sluggishly, by fits and starts, like the jammed logs on a U.S. northwest river she once saw on TV. Finally, they arrived at the Peace Hotel at the end of Nanjing Road by the western bank of the Huangpu River.

She checked in. Grandpa told them that the building in pre-World War II days, was known as the Sassoon House, owned by a Mid-Eastern Jewish merchant, named Sassoon and holding a British passport. The architecture and furniture were old-fashioned. However, the ceiling was high, and the doors, windows, and molding materials were all substantive in proportion and impeccable in workmanship, giving off an elegance, she thought, which most modern glitzy constructions lacked. Before long her parents and sister arrived. Later Saizhu's husband, Wu Ruguan, also joined them. Bespectacled, lanky, probably a few years older than his wife, he stuck by her side and said very little at the gathering. Sailong's wife was on assignment in Beijing. The family had a noisy, chattering and joyous reunion dinner at the hotel.

After the family left, she called Haosheng and had her father's message confirmed.

"You leave me no choice," she complained.

"Saiyue, believe me. It was not my doing. My parents sprang this one on me. My father thought his health was declining. He wanted to make the trip when he still felt strong enough. Actually, I have to go to Guangzhou myself tomorrow to bring Xiao Ming here. He's on vacation. Will be here at least for two weeks."

"All right. I'll come."

"You have not been in Hong Kong before. It's an interesting place. I'll show you some of the sights."

"My interest is to see Baobao."

"I know, of course."

"By the way, would you reserve a hotel room there for me too?" she said.

"There is no need for that. My apartment is big enough."

"I prefer a hotel room. Please do that."

"All right."

"I'll let you know my date of arrival, airline…"

She reckoned that, as some compensation, at least she saved a round trip to Nanjing. Then an idea that had been lying at the back of her mind surfaced. She would pay a visit to the Xi'an Petroleum Institute.

Next morning, with considerable patience she got through to Wang Tang'yi, now Vice Director of the Institute—his secretary advised her. Pleasantly surprised by her call, he told her that he and her friends at the Institute would be very happy indeed if she could come. She said she would, if he could assure her of an airline ticket reservation from Xi'an to Hong Kong. She gave him her desired date of departure from Xi'an; the Vice Director told her he would let her know.

After she hung up the phone, she heard knocking on the door. It was Saizhu who was taking a few days off to make herself available to her sister. Saiyue took her to the dining room for breakfast.

They had a table by the window, and ordered *Shao Mai*[51] and cellophane noodle soup with fried bean curd. Saiyue told her sister about her plan to visit Xi'an. "I'll need an airline ticket for that."

"You better let Xiao Long know as early as possible. He should be able to arrange that for you," Saizhu said.

"I know that he has good connections in the transportation circle. When I first went to Xi'an that year, it was he, through his friend's father, got that booth in the train for me. You were so young then. How time flies! How's he? Before that, I ought to first ask how are *you* doing?"

"He is fine. Me?…Our life is fairly stable these days. Wu Ruguan is doing well at the Institute of Biological Sciences. He hopes to be promoted to Associate Researcher next year. Then perhaps he could strive for a visiting scholarship. If that materializes, would you lend a hand to your brother-in-law?"

"Of course, I'll do what I can."

---

51. A "Shao Mai," Shanghai style, is a steamed thin-skinned dumpling filled with sticky rice mixed with pre-cooked minced meat and diced black mushroom and light spice.

"About myself, I enjoy my reporter's job. But it doesn't pay that well. I have been thinking of getting into the Advertising Department of the paper. The regular pay is not that different, but there would be other financial opportunities not available to reporters."

"From what I heard, there are so many opportunities in China these days that it would do you good to keep your eyes and ears open. Have you considered working for some private business?"

"Yes, indeed. I have been thinking specially about opportunities involving foreign investment. The salary scale is much higher, at the expense of job security, though."

"You are young. Why not give it a try....Grandpa told me that Xiao Long has opened up to the family more in the last year or two. Is he still as *progressive* as before?"

"He is still that. But, yes, he has *mellowed* quite a bit. He used to be quite angry with those in the leadership whom he considered to be selling out socialism. Gradually, the evidences—you are one of them—seemed to persuade him to rethink. He still considers some leaders as unprincipled and corrupt. In fact, one time, he mentioned that he was considering joining some of his colleagues in the Railroad Bureau to protest something or other. That scared Ma and Pa. They talked him out of it. I suppose their philosophy is to play as safe as one can. Particularly with you in America, they still fear the government might turn around and attack those with foreign connections," Saizhu said.

"Do you think that's likely to happen?"

"I don't. You can't blame the older generation. They are like birds that have known the bow before. But I think the experience of the Cultural Revolution has probably immunized the country against those past extreme, know-nothing policies and acts. In any case, I think Xiao Long is more displeased with some factions of the leadership than with *foreign imperialists*. In spite of his socialist idealism, as you know, he is good, at least respectful, to Pa and Ma and Grandpa. Recently he seems just somewhat unsure of himself."

"I am impressed that you seem to be so levelheaded—and pretty sure of your footing?"

"Well, I think two more years of college education helped. I recall a seminar I attended not that long ago. A professor who had just returned from a stay in America talked about our generation. He deplored the lowered quality of Chinese youth of our time and of the acts of some Chinese students in America."

"What did he say?"

"He mentioned one incident. A Chinese graduate student purchased a camera just before a long holiday weekend, used it over several days and returned it for a full refund on some simple pretext, taking advantage of the merchant's generous return policy."

"Xiao Zhu, people like to criticize as well as generalize," Saiyue said. "For every instance of tacky behavior, there are a lot more honorable ones. Most of the students conduct themselves properly, and perform well, often brilliantly, in school or later at work. But considering Chinese students' earlier reputation in America, I am afraid the professor was right."

"Then the professor went on to sort of explain the phenomenon. He said that before the Revolution, although some had believed in Western ethics and even Christianity, Chinese people, on the whole, had Confucianism to follow. The Revolution obliterated all those and replaced them by *Communism or Socialism ethics*. As the contradictions became obvious between what was pronounced and what people learned later to be facts in such cases as those of Lin Biao and the Gang of Four, they began to question the credibility of the teachings of Socialism as well as its slogans. After the American President Nixon's visit and the opening up to the Western world, the contrast of the fruits of Socialism and those of the Western democratic and economic system made a lot of people lose faith.

"The traditional Chinese values having been demolished by the Cultural Revolution, our generation, never exposed to any other teaching, neither Confucianism nor Western ethics or religion, had no anchoring of their values. Therefore, they followed their lower instincts, superficial materialism of the moment. That's the professor's analysis."

"I think that overall he is probably right," Saiyue nodded.

"I can tell you a firsthand observation I had about the quality of people. Recently I covered a story of an alumni meeting of a now defunct missionary university in Shanghai. The youngest class graduated in 1951. It was an old bunch; many had come from outside the country, America, Canada, etc. They had a box luncheon in the main lobby of the Exhibition Hall. I noticed that after finishing eating, practically everyone went on, voluntarily, to put away empty bottles and wrapping papers in trash cans. The place pretty much remained as clean as before the luncheon. I knew how different the place would look before and after if a local Chinese group had a similar luncheon there," Saizhu said.

"I see what you mean. Westerners had made the point even in pre-Revolution times that Chinese lacked so-called public ethics versus private ethics. But I don't think the Cultural Revolution had really demolished traditional Chinese values. If it had, I believe you'll agree that the people have been reviving them rather rapidly. Tradition is like grass. It's like the saying: 'The wild fire can't wipe them out; the spring breeze blows, and they sprout.'

"Essentially we have suffered from a lack of material resources. As Grandpa often quoted, 'Having food and shelter, one knows shame and honor.' In this sense, I can see the point of emphasizing economics as the present leadership has been doing. I think that soon you'll notice that the *quality of people* you referred to will rise along with their standard of living. In fact, I have already noticed that myself, after just a few years away from the place," Saiyue said.

"In the recent relative prosperity, people's quality of life and standard of living have, overall, certainly improved. But the improvement is far from being uniform. There are of course those—with better connections—who are a lot better off. In the meantime, many actually feel the new pressures from the withdrawal of government subsidies. Like our rent, it has been rising. It used to be just a small fraction of our income. Now it is a significant expense. The government is encouraging us to buy our apartment. But we don't have the money," Xiao Zhu said.

"Can you see that you could afford to buy it *someday*? Saiyue asked.

"Someday? I think so. I certainly hope so. That's why I am considering changing jobs."

"Well, you have a goal to work for. I hope you succeed soon," Saiyue said.

"I will try," Saizhu said.

"That's the difference between our generation and our parents'."

After breakfast, the sisters went to their parents' house. As expected, relatives and neighbors would stop by—some of whom hadn't done that in months, and others even years. Some would compliment Saiyue fulsomely, and some would survey her boldly from head to foot. "The ancestors of you Zhang family must have done a whole lot of virtuous deeds. Look at your number one miss. Such a beauty! Such a genius! An advanced degree from America, a veritable Ocean Zhuang-yuan, working with electrical brains! This is truly a case of 'Homecoming in lustrous brocade.'"

Another said to her, "You haven't seen your parents for so long. A filial daughter like you must have brought for them many modern things from America."

For a minute and a half, vanity let her enjoy the attention and the praise. Soon good sense caught up, and she felt distaste and antipathy for her own initial enjoyment of the dross. Then she'd roll her eyes in secret and bore up for her parents' sake.

Her parents were eager to know more about her marriage plans. She sidestepped, saying that for now she had been concentrating on her job and wasn't particularly in a hurry to get married again. Then puckishly she referred them to her grandpa for "more details."

Before she moved to her parents' place after three nights in the hotel, she had heard from Xiao Long and Vice Director Wang, respectively, confirmation of her airline ticket to Xi'an and that from there to Hong Kong. Her mother put her up in the third floor pavilion room where she used to have a berth. In the next few days, except for a gather-together with some old schoolmates from high school and college, she relaxed with her family.

The night before her departure, her parents, brother and sister jointly invited her to a dinner at the Old Restaurant in the City-god Temple district. A shapely receptionist in a long yellow embroidered banner gown[52] met them. Saiyue thought she looked familiar.

"Excuse me. Are you Sister Ah Xi?" "Yes....Miss...Are you Xiao Yue?" "Yes." "Oh! Oh! How you have changed!" Ah Xi exclaimed, smiling broadly. She led them to a table and said she'd be back. The rest of the family said that since the Songs had moved out to the suburb, they hadn't seen her before either.

When they were almost done with the dinner, Ah Xi returned to chat with them, mainly with Saiyue. She was married. Her husband, a chef in another well-known restaurant, held a Second Degree in culinary arts. Having learned of Saiyue's recent state, Ah Xi confided in her that her husband and she were contemplating emigrating to the United States to open a Chinese restaurant and asked her old neighbor whether she could help. Saiyue told her to write and gave her a business card of hers.

Later on, back at the house, she gave, in traveler's checks, her parents US$500, and her grandpa, sister and brother US$200 each, asking their understanding that she didn't know exactly what gifts to bring them from the United States. She told them that the gifts, mostly clothing items that she had looked at in the stores in the United States, had the *Made in China* label, and that she would feel odd to ship them back to China. After some token resistance, they accepted the cash gifts, which, for each, was substantially more than one month's salary or pension. She also gave her sister her pink polyester-cotton dress—that tied at the waist with a

---

52. "Banner" refers to the Manchu system. (Its army was organized as under different banners.) The modern Chinese women's gown, "qi (banner) pao (gown)," has its origin in the dress Manchu women wore.

black leather belt—in which Xiao Zhu had shown much interest since her first sighting of it at the airport.

The next morning Xiao Zhu came first, followed by her brother, who arrived with a car borrowed from his work unit, Shanghai Railroad Bureau, to take their sister to the airport. The siblings were going to see her off there. Saying goodbye, she hugged her mother and then her father. They fussed over her and insisted, against her protest of having too many things to carry, that she take along a bag of apples and biscuits.

Grandpa was subdued. She hugged him, saying, "You take care of yourself!"

"You too. I had a very good time in California. Thank you for all your arrangements," he said.

"We'll do it again sometime," she said, but wondered herself when.

"Remember me to Haosheng and Panzhe!" Then he said in English, "Good luck and God bless you!"

"God bless you too! Ma and Pa! Take good care of yourselves!"

It was a gray dreary day, raining intermittently. Apparently there was some kind of weather system in the Pacific nearby. Her flight, No.5225 to Xi'an, would be delayed until 20:30. The airport lobby was hot and muggy. They spent half a day at the air-conditioned International Airport Hotel. Saiyue checked in at the airport at 5 p.m. After Sailong produced some kind of document, the guard at the door of the passengers' waiting room let him and Saizhu join their sister inside. It was not as crowded and noisy as the lobby, but not by much. Saiyue thanked her siblings not only for helping her on this trip but also for taking care of their parents and grandfather.

"Don't stand on ceremony with us, Sister," Saizhu said. "We are family."

Narrowing his eyebrows, Sailong said, "Truly, don't talk like that, Sister Xiao Yue, I am the son of the family. It's mainly my responsibility. Xiao Zhu has always been very generous with her time, ever since she was very young, as I remember. And you too, even then; and now you have shown your generosity with your gifts. But actually, I can tell that it is your efforts in America that have given Ma, Pa and Grandpa more comfort and joy than anything else. Your accomplishments are such a boast for them before friends and relatives."

Saiyue was quite surprised by this speech from her taciturn brother. "No, no," she answered. "You are trying to make your elder sister feel good. You mustn't say that. Time is much more valuable than money. You two give them your time and care. Besides, the money I give doesn't amount to that much. In my heart I know that you two contribute to their real welfare a lot more than I do."

"I think you are trying to make us feel good," Saizhu said. Her brother nodded.

It was announced that the flight was delayed further to 22:30. They located a branch of the Jin Jiang Restaurant inside the terminal. But it had just closed for the night. It was just 7:20 p.m.; Saiyue figured that the business had not yet been privatized.

Thirsty, she bought a can of Coca-Cola for each, losing a couple of RMB dollars in the process, as the busy saleswoman told her stonefacedly that there was no change. While they were having the cold drink, she struck up a conversation with an elderly couple from Brazil, who were also going to Xi'an on the same flight as hers. She asked them whether they had their supper. The husband told her that they did—in a room up the stairs at the far corner of the waiting room where one could get a Japanese style rice with beef for RMB$15.

Before she could respond, the flaps over the gate rotated rapidly. When settled, they read: "Flight 5225 for Xi'an Now Boarding." Her watch read 8:00 p.m. She quickly put away the unfinished can and said good-bye to her brother and sister.

She went out of the gate into a breezy drizzle. With almost blind faith she followed in near darkness the hurrying crowd on the wet and grimy pavement—the air smelling of nauseating petroleum exhaust—for some 100 yards toward a hulking plane. No sooner had she settled down in her seat, than she heard a telephone ring at the back of the cabin and a stewardess answered it. After a short exchange, the stewardess sashayed to the center of the aisle and announced: "All passengers! I am sorry. There will be a delay for take-off. Please return to the waiting room in the terminal."

The passengers trekked under a now steady rain back to the waiting room. She was happy to see her brother and sister still there. They told her that the new departure time was 22:00. They sat in front of a TV monitor. She was thinking perhaps they could try the Japanese style rice with beef. Suddenly the screen showed that Flight 5225 was boarding again. It was confirmed for her by the frenzied jabbering around her. Then, sure enough, a swarm was leaving the gate. With a quick nod and "Thank you and take care" to her siblings, she rushed after it, with the now wild-eyed elderly Brazilian couple on her heels.

Shortly after she got in her seat on the plane, a uniformed man strode up the aisle, stopped, and jabbed his forefinger in the air, apparently counting the passengers. In a while, he intoned: "We are all here. The plane is full. Let's G...O...!" With a wave of his hand, he strutted toward the cockpit. When the plane began cruising in the air, her watch read 8:30 or 20:30. She wondered what would happen had she and her siblings gone for the Japanese style rice with beef. She tried to dry her wet hair with her handkerchief and thought that, in spite of the pronouncements of modernization, air travel in China had a way to go yet to attain international standards.

She thought about her parents getting gray. People get gray with years. Then her siblings. Saizhu, in spite of her sprightly exterior, is intelligent and observant, and rather wise for her age. It's a pity I did not get to talk with Sailong much. His little speech at the airport waiting room was a surprise. It sounded more like a Chinese traditionalist than a progressive socialist. How fast those lectures at the meetings he had attended since a Young Pioneer were smothered by the re-growth of the grass of Chinese traditional values. Perhaps he and Grandpa would get closer now. Everyone is making some progress toward a better life. With that thought, her heart warmed and turned to the anticipations of visiting her old haunt again.

32

Because of the weather delay, Saiyue's flight arrived at Xi'an almost simultaneously with another from Shanghai. It was nearly 11 p.m. The commotion following the close arrivals subsided quickly after the passengers picked up their baggage and left. She was practically the last passenger to leave the terminal. She walked onto a paved apron adjoining the road, feebly illuminated by the yellow lights hung atop the utility poles. Close about her were stillness, dimness, and shadows. She began to feel uneasy.

"Xiao Zhang! Is that you?" She recognized the female voice. Two figures emerged from the darkness on her right.

"Sorry that I must have made you two wait so long. The plane was delayed," Saiyue apologized. Putting down her suitcase and bags, she hugged her former roommate Shi Renmei.

"We thought that all the passengers had come out and you might not be on the plane. The driver was fussing and wanted to leave. He just might have gone, if not for Vice Director Wang," Renmei said.

Saiyue let go of her and moved closer to the lanky man, who had been standing a couple of steps behind Renmei. In a Western suit now, Wang Tang'yi said officially, "Welcome! We are glad that you have come to visit," and extended his hand. Spurning the handshake offer, she stepped up and hugged him. That startled him. He managed to tap lightly on her back, and mumbled "Welcome! Welcome!" while she congratulated him on his promotion.

They put her up in the Institute's guesthouse, where she had gone to meet Lu Panzhe to take him sightseeing four years ago. She asked them to come in the room and presented each with a Seiko watch, saying that she might not have a more convenient time later on to show her special regards for them. Both accepted the token of friendship after the de rigueur you-shouldn't-have-done-this. Before she went to bed, she ate a few biscuits and two apples to alleviate her hunger—now glad that her parents had almost forced her to take the foodstuff with her.

Next morning, she paid her respect to Director Kang and thanked him for letting her resign from the Institute. He was gracious, telling her that he did have to respond to the Ministry twice to defend his decision agreeing to her release. "Your offer to reimburse the expenses incurred in the scholarship certainly helped your case," he added.

Now a top administrator, Wang was no longer involved in technical work. Saiyue thought his appearance had changed some—with the distinct white patches around the temples replacing the previous gray streaks, and a noticeable increase in the curvature and stiffness of the back. However, his dark face no longer had that erstwhile gaunt look, instead, there was a tinge of ruddiness on it, and his brow was smoother now. But, at first, she felt he was somewhat more reserved than she recalled. She wondered, because she thought he wasn't the kind of person that a higher rank would make more distant.

Wang had been observing her also. Her western dress, pearl necklace, and gold bracelet were new. Her manners also had a distinct American component. However, they seemed natural, unlike the affected airs of some overseas Chinese. This former demure subordinate was essentially the same ambitious but conscientious Xiao Zhang. He spoke freely to her now and asked after Professor Lu, and showed genuine concern when told of their divorce. He arranged a luncheon in her honor with a number of her former colleagues in attendance, including Senior Engineer Zeng, her first supervisor, who now worked in the Department of General Affairs. To Saiyue's surprise, Zeng was quite warm to her former headstrong subordinate. Saiyue was glad to reciprocate the courteousness.

Now the former staffer was treated almost like a "foreign expert." There were the usual ceremonies and a seminar-like question-and-answer session about her experiences—essentially all technical, particularly computer utilization in engineering. She did her best to respond straightforwardly to the questions—including some for which she admitted that she did not know the answer. Thinking that she had made a contribution, she felt good about the session.

After the lunch, people went back to work; Renmei, who had requested a two-day leave for her friend's visit, accompanied Saiyue to walk around the Institute compound. She tarried a moment or two at her old office, and later got up to the 4th floor of Building 8, her old dormitory. The green farm fields just beyond the compound wall were still there, but several new three-story concrete buildings had replaced the ramshackle black tile-roofed tenements.

She went with Renmei to her apartment. She and Lo Yungchen were now married. The apartment was assigned to them after their daughter was born. The unit was a little larger than the one Saiyue had lived in at the Mill compound; moreover, they didn't have to share it with any other family. The apartment door opened to the living area. Along a side wall stood a TV set (color, Renmei proudly told Saiyue). A rattan couch lay along the opposite wall. A table butted against the wall facing the door. Renmei brought tea from the kitchen just behind the refrigerator. The two young women sat down at the table to catch up. Renmei told her that their living standards had been improving. Both she and her husband received an annual bonus as much as their salary, and they could save up a good part of it. Renmei was now an assistant supervisor in the Assaying Laboratory. Lao Lo, no longer a player on the basketball team, had become its coach. They had a 2-year old daughter.

"Now, Shanghai Mademoiselle, no, American Mademoiselle, tell your old roommate all about your adventures in the Beautiful Country."

Saiyue didn't plan to get into any depth of her personal life, but then she thought, How many old friends have I got? She went on to give her a concise—with some elaborations when her friend asked for them—but more or less complete account of her life there and her current dilemma of sorts.

Renmei was enthralled. As she listened, her right eyebrow danced, mouth twitched, and the big eyes shone, watching Saiyue's expressions intently. She was pleased that Saiyue trusted her so and volunteered that she would treat her story confidentially.

Renmei observed that love life seemed a lot simpler in China. As to her friend's dilemma, from her vantage point, she opined, on the one hand, a full professor at an American university surely meant a great deal of social status, let alone the intellectual side of it. Yet, by Chinese tradition, the relationship of a "hair-tying" husband and wife was hard to renounce. She seemed oblivious of the fact that it had already been renounced, at least de jure. And, by now, probably only a very small fraction of the people in China could match Xu Haosheng's "condition," namely, financial condition. Although it might not be as good as the professor's yet, its prospect could be as good or even better. Besides, there was Baobao to consider, and the professor's age too.

"You are a big help! Everything you said I already know," Saiyue said. She thought that her friend, contented with one lover in her life, her husband, understood her dilemma only partially. Yet, to be fair, she wasn't sure she had adequately articulated her feelings to her. Of course, she could have done that only if she had known them herself. Anyhow, it seemed futile to go any deeper into her situation in the short time they would have together.

"Come on now, American mademoiselle," Renmei said laughingly, "Don't complain. I wish I were in your kind of dilemma. But, of course,

I don't have your looks and figure. How do you keep it so trim and curvy? Look at me—fat as a pig!"

Saiyue had noticed that indeed her former roommate had grown plumper. "You are not fat. Only full-bodied and sexy, like Yang Gui-fei," she said and smiled at her indulgently, enjoying the kind of intimate friendship that seems to come more easily between women than between men. "You know the saying, 'The mind at ease; the body gains.' I wish I had your kind of tranquil life—no hassle, secure in every respect."

"In graduate school did you take a course in diplomacy as well? I don't have your talent or energy. Have to be contented with this so-called tranquil life," Renmei said, with contentedness.

"No, I am not trying to be polite. If five years ago I were in your present kind of condition, I would not necessarily have tried so hard to go to America," Saiyue said equivocally.

Later, she accompanied Renmei to the Institute nursery to pick up her daughter. The little girl had a round face and big eyes, a chip off the old block. The nursery reminded Saiyue of the one at the Mill and the manner that Baobao would run toward her—with his body turned sideways.

Shortly Lao Lo returned to the apartment. Heavier and with a paunch now, he welcomed Saiyue heartily, quoting the classics, "What a pleasure to have a friend coming from afar!" Noting there were only tea cups on the table, he jokingly scolded his wife. "How come you are so stingy. Just tea? No other refreshments for an old friend who has come ten thousand miles to see you?"

"We have been so engrossed in reminiscing that I forgot. But we had a full meal before we came in. Besides, we are going to dinner shortly. Now you can play the role of a gracious host. Go and fetch the osmanthus cake in the tin can. Quick! Go now!" She slapped his wrist and pushed his shoulder.

"OK! OK!" he smiled. "In the office, my boss orders me around. At home it's the wife! Even tougher!...." He nodded to their daughter, "Come on! Let's go get the cake. You can have one slice. Daddy is going to fix your supper soon." Saiyue watched the little girl toddle after her daddy into the other room. Saiyue turned to look at her friend. Renmei's eyes gleamed; they shared a smile.

"A beautiful girl," Saiyue said. "Perhaps we can become in-laws, eh?"

"I thought you have come from America, the bastion of human rights....Sure. Only I am afraid our little daughter won't have that kind of good fortune."

In the evening the Vice Director and the Los jointly gave Saiyue a dinner party. Again Senior Engineer Zeng was there. She sat beside the Vice Director. During the dinner, she would admonish him not to eat certain foods in a way that suggested a degree of intimacy. That sort of pleased Saiyue. By the end of the party, she had promised several former colleagues that she would help their relatives to get information about graduate schools in the United States if they would write to her first.

Next morning, before Renmei came to pick her up, she spent an hour or so talking shop with Wang and the new Vice Chief of her former work place. When Renmei asked her whether she'd like to pay a visit to the Textile City, she hesitated, and then asked,

"Do you think we can manage to go to Huaqing Palace?"

"Don't be silly! Not that you are leaving later this afternoon. You know that!"

"You are right," Saiyue said resignedly.

They got off the bus at the entrance to the Textile City. Neat small shops had replaced the unkempt food stalls that used to line the path of compacted earth, which was now paved. The mill compound looked more prosperous on account of new constructions, some done and others in progress. They walked to her old apartment, looked around a bit and hurried back. Saiyue didn't particularly want to meet anyone she had known there.

After getting off the tram at downtown, they walked up the terrace of the Bell Tower and looked around the classical structure. She told Renmei, "You know these curved eaves give me such a warm feeling inside." She bought Renmei lunch at Chang-an Restaurant.

Near dusk, they said good-bye in the airport. After an embrace, Saiyue headed for the waiting room door where uniformed guards admitted passengers only. There were little activities in the twilight. The dark green fields around it appeared quiescent; far-off chimney smoke twisted languidly. Soon the plane was over the wide ranges of the Qinling Mountains, then over the basin of the serpentine Hanshui River. Winter wheat having been harvested, the fields were dammed up into rice paddies. In a few minutes she could barely make out the tenebrous, dense subtropical timber over the Daba Mountains. Then it was too dark to see. Leaving Xi'an behind, she leaned back and closed her eyes. The thought of seeing Baobao next made her conscious of her own heartbeat.

In some two hours she heard the PA announcing that they would be landing shortly in Kowloon. In the humming and intermittent groaning of the hydraulic system, looking out the window, she saw nothing but a dark void…then a few pinhead lights, slowly increasing in number. Suddenly, lo! Ahead, against a black blanket lay a spread of twinkling diamonds, rubies and emeralds, as though some god had poured them from a cornucopia over this part of the earth. The lights became denser and brighter. Sea and harbor lights, stringing land vehicles, high- and low-rise buildings, glimmering, glistening and glowing. Larger and larger Chinese characters jerked and, as it were, tried to jump off from the building walls to meet her. For an instant she thought the giant wings might tip the top of a building, as the plane swooped down toward the runway of Kai Dak Airport by the bay.

33

Entering the terminal concourse, Saiyue soon caught sight of Haosheng among a small crowd. He had a boy with him. She rushed to meet them a little distance away from the throng. After a quick smiling nod to Haosheng, who took over the baggage, she opened her arms, crouching and saying, "Baobao, Baobao, do you remember me?" She moved to embrace the boy. He shied at her action. Hurt for the boy and herself, she pulled back her arms and repeated, "Baobao, do you remember me?" her voice choking. The boy looked at her with increasing intensity. "Go to your mama," Haosheng nudged him. He hesitated for an instant and shuffled stiffly forward. She lifted him up, and saying, "Mama missed you so…much," she rocked and squeezed him. "You have grown to be so…heavy."

"Then why don't you let him down," Haosheng smiled.

She did. "Let me look at you." The boy, on the chubby side and with short hair, now looked at her with a faint smile of amusement and curiosity as if she were some kind of exotic animal in a zoo. He was light-skinned like his mother; his slightly hooked nose resembled that of his father. But the caltrop mouth definitely came from her. He wore a white shirt, gray short pants and two-tone—white and crimson—tennis shoes. A little red bow tie looked so cute on him. She ached in sweetness.

"Now, do you remember me?" she repeated, wiping her eyes with the back of her hand.

"Papa said you are my mama. You come from America?" the boy said slowly.

"Yes! And you are my Baobao! Yes, I left America…oh…ten days ago. I went to Shanghai and Xi'an. Actually I just came from Xi'an. Do you remember Xi'an? You were born there—do you know that?"

"I came from Nanjing," the boy said, louder now.

"Yes, I know," she said. "How have you been?" She was still holding on to his shoulders.

"Gong-gong and po-po[53] brought me to Guangzhou. Now Ah Yu takes care of me here, but I'll be back in Nanjing for school."

"Ah Yu is our helper at the apartment," Haosheng explained. Only now Saiyue exchanged appropriate greetings with her ex-husband. His hair stylishly long with the dry look, and in a loose Hong Kong shirt with large blue flowers and smartly pressed white pants, she thought he cut a rather striking figure.

He led them out. It was hot and humid outside the terminal. They waited till Haosheng pulled up in a glossy black car, which she recognized as a Mercedes, even shinier than Rahimi's. After they got in, he told her the car would cool soon.

"Is this yours?" she asked.

"No, I wish it were. It's the company car. The boss and the other assistant manager are both out of town; I get to use it. I could have asked the driver to come tonight. But it's Sunday and I knew you wouldn't have much baggage…."

They were passing through Kowloon heading for Hong Kong Island. Along the long straight Nathan Road, the kaleidoscopic scenes and din— of the cars, taxis, double-decked buses, bright headlights, forests of

---

53. Gong-gong means grandpa; po-po, grandma.

many-colored neon-signs, brilliantly lit shops and lots of people—absorbed both mother and son.

"Saiyue," Haosheng began.

"Yes."

"About a hotel room for you—"

"Yes."

"I looked, but I couldn't find anything suitable."

"How come?"

"My apartment is in an essentially residential area. I looked. There simply isn't any decent hotel around. There are a couple of small hostels 20 minutes or so away, by walking. But they look crummy. Why don't you just stay in the apartment."

"Well, it wouldn't be convenient. You know that," she said rather emphatically.

"It will be most convenient for everyone concerned. Certainly for Xiao Ming, if you don't mind sharing a room with him. And I can assure you that you will not regret it."

She understood the significance of the assurance. After a moment's silence, she said, "OK. We'll give it a try. I'd love to share a room with Baobao."

After they crossed the harbor into Hong Kong, Haosheng took them to a restaurant on Queen's Road for supper. He told her that it was just for the stomach, and he'd entertain her properly later. He ordered pan-fried prawns, a couple of other dishes and a soup, and Coca-Cola for everybody. She wanted milk for Baobao. Unable to speak Cantonese, she had problems in communicating with the waiter, who knew little Mandarin. Haosheng intervened and found out that they didn't have it.

"That's all right. I'll go out and get some," he said, patting the boy's head lightly. "You wait here with your mother."

"No, I want to go with you," the boy said.

Saiyue felt a hot wave and a little numb. It's not his fault, she told herself. "Baobao, we can have some Coca-Cola first. Your papa will be back soon."

"You wait here with your mama. I'll be back soon," Xu said firmly.

The food came before he returned. When he did, with a carton of milk, he noticed that she was feeding the boy with a spoon from a bowl of rice in her hand and a plate of assorted food selected from the dishes on the table.

"He can feed himself." The scene amused the father.

"That's all right. I don't mind," she said. The boy, chewing evenly, now wearing an inane smile, kicked his legs slowly. As they were partaking of the food, she noticed that Haosheng still, as he used to do, wagged his knees while eating, and let the prawn shells drop directly from his mouth onto the plate on the table. It now annoyed her.

The apartment was about the same size as her Redwood City house. However, in lieu of a dining room, a dining table was set to a side near the window of the living room. There was one more bedroom—close to the front door—for a live-in helper.

After they had settled down for a while, Saiyue said to the boy, "Shouldn't you be in bed now, Baobao?"

"I am Xiao Ming, not Baobao. I am a big boy now," the boy corrected her.

"All right. Xiao Ming," she chuckled, "let me help you wash up." In the bedroom, they talked desultorily about his life and school in Nanjing. When she was helping him to unclasp the bow tie, she asked, "Did you have this in Nanjing, or did papa buy it for you in Hong Kong?"

"No. Auntie Rose gave it to me. Don't you think it looks smart. That boy in *The Little Rascals* on TV had it too."

"Who's Auntie Rose?"

"Papa's friend, I think," he shrugged.

Later on as she brushed her teeth, she asked herself again, who's Auntie Rose? She watched herself in the mirror, giving her shoulders a shrug too, thinking I have no right to ask. Before she went to bed, she thought of locking the door of the room. Then seeing Xiao Ming sleeping on the other bed, she simply closed it.

When she woke up the next morning, she smelt a whiff of fried egg. Xiao Ming was not in his bed. It turned out that she was the last one to get up. The others were already having breakfast that Ah Yu, the live-in help, had cooked. Ah Yu, a smallish young woman about 20, swarthy and plain, could manage passable Mandarin. She also prepared a good enough breakfast of porridge with diced thousand-year eggs, served with several dishes including pickles, fried pork threads and tomato omelet, in addition to banana and tea.

Saiyue told Haosheng the first thing she needed to take care of was her return airline ticket to the United States. He said that his office could help.

She went down with him and Xiao Ming to the parking garage of the apartment complex. Among the Hondas and Fords, there were also quite a few Mercedes and Jaguars. A man in a white shirt and black trousers was waiting for them. Haosheng introduced him as Lao Jiang, the company chauffeur. The latter drove them downtown and let them off at the Bond Building in the Central District.

Zhong Xing Company was up on the 5th floor. Under the bright lights of the reception room, a young woman, dressed smartly in blue, sat at a gray modernistic desk. Haosheng led them past her, who greeted him politely, and crossed a door that opened to a large room. A dozen or so workers were at their desks or computer monitors. At the end of the unmarked corridor, another young woman at a desk behind a low railing stood up with a quick smile and said "Good morning, Mr. Xu." Saiyue noted that Cantonese seemed to be the regular dialect of the establishment.

"Good morning," he replied in Cantonese, and then switched to Mandarin, "This is…Ms. Zhang, Xiao Ming's mother. This is Ms. Zhou, my able assistant."

"Ms. Zhang. How are you? Xiao Ming, how are you this morning?" Her Mandarin carried a heavy characteristic Cantonese accent.

After exchanging pleasantries, Saiyue followed Haosheng into his office. It was a smallish room with the desk facing the door. On one side of the desk was a small table with a PC; on the other, stood a small five-star flag of the People's Republic. A picture of the cloud-girdled peaks of the Huangshan Mountains hung on one side wall, facing the willow-lined Su Embankment along Hangzhou's West Lake on the opposite wall.

Xiao Ming sat in his father's tall-back swivel chair behind the desk, oscillating himself with it. She gave Haosheng her airline ticket, saying "Thursday." He nodded and went out of the room. Through the open door, she could see him instructing Miss Zhou as he handed her the ticket.

Returning to the office, he signed a few documents and announced that he was ready to take them sightseeing. The intercom buzzed. "Mr. Xu, a Mr. Tan is here to see you."

"Mr. Tan?" he frowned.

"Yes, from Bangkok, Thailand."

"Oh yes. We are about to leave. But—" he ran his tongue over his lip and said, "Send him in."

He asked Saiyue and Xiao Ming to wait outside while he talked business with the visitor. "It won't be long," he said apologetically.

Shortly, the receptionist led in a thin man with a dark complexion, wearing a brown Hong Kong shirt and a straw hat. He carried an attaché case, nodded and smiled unctuously—showing two large gold front teeth—to Ms. Zhou as she opened her boss's door for him.

Saiyue waited, sitting in a chair by Ms. Zhou's desk, while Xiao Ming relieved his back itch against its corner.

As Ms. Zhou was rummaging for the airline's phone number, the phone rang. "Assistant Manager Xu's office," she spoke in Cantonese. Then switching to her Mandarin, "Mr. Xu has someone with him....All right. I'll check. Please wait a moment." She pushed a button to talk to her boss. "President Rose Guo is on the line." Seeing the connection was made, she returned to her own work. The name caught Saiyue's ear.

"Is this president of some firm a lady?" Saiyue asked the secretary in a tone of casual curiosity.

"Yes, she is the president of Lian Fa Company," Ms. Zhou answered. Saiyue wondered, Auntie Rose?

In a few minutes, the thin man with the unctuous smile left. Haosheng led Saiyue and their son out of the building and waited. Before long, Lao Jiang drove up and they got in the car. She was surprised to learn that the driver had never parked it. There was practically no place for parking in the area during that time of the day. He had simply been circling around to wait. Haosheng told her that, in fact, that was a major reason for having a chauffeur.

After they visited the Bank of China Tower and the new Hong Kong Bank Building, they window-shopped about the arcades of Prince's Building. Jewelry displayed on rich velvet, sparkling in recessed lighting, aroused much curiosity in her. So did the high prices, which she found as interesting, even amusing, as the articles themselves. An emerald bracelet with diamond studs was tagged at HK$160,000, or about US$27,000.

Later walking along Queen's Road, while Haosheng was studying the window display of a men's clothing store, she browsed over the precious stones in the showcase of a jewelry shop next door—so small that it was more like a stall. A ruby ring caught her eye. She asked the shopkeeper, a young woman, to show it to her. She told her it was a cat's-eye ruby. The stone was set against two smaller diamonds. The tag price was HK$12,000—less than one tenth of that emerald bracelet. As Haosheng returned to join her, the woman told her she could have it for HK$9000. She said she just wanted to look at it. When they turned around to leave, the woman said that they could have it at HK$6000. But they did not respond.

Haosheng took them to the Jade Garden Restaurant on Charter Road for lunch, where they had the well-advertised double-boiled duck with parsley and stuffed bean curd. Afterwards, he returned to the office, and Lao Jiang drove the mother and son back to the apartment to rest.

In the evening Haosheng suggested that they visit a nightclub and leave Xiao Ming in the apartment with Ah Yu. But Saiyue wouldn't have the second part of the suggestion. So all three went to the Harbor City Restaurant and Nightclub. They ordered dinner, wine for the parents and milk for the son. Before long the boy complained that the band was too loud and it bothered his ears. However, there was little they could do short of leaving. He didn't want that either, so they stayed.

The food was ordinary. That didn't bother the clients; the people came here for its entertainment program. It consisted of a series of performances by solo vocalists, including the star, Teresa Kelly, backed by a dance troupe of four well-endowed females and two males. The singers sang mostly in Cantonese. Once during the show, the star, humming and stepping with alternately thrusting, jerky shoulders, came down from the stage to greet the guests. Saiyue was most amused by the sight of her son, wincing and grimacing, tight as a knot, as the beautiful performer planted a kiss on his cheek.

At an intermission, in the bustling of servers and loitering of guests, a middle-aged portly man appeared before Xu's table, as though beamed in from outer space. He wore a silk plaid jacket buttoned over his ample paunch, which required the upper body to lean back some for balance, and over which lay his plump fingers clasping a cigarette. "Lao Xu! How are you! Nice to see you! Hey-hey-hey-hey." The Mandarin hail-fellow greeting carried a Shandong accent.

Haosheng stood up to shake his hand, which was adorned by a diamond the size of a marble, glistening in the pumping.

"I am fine. Nice to see you too," Haosheng said, and turning to the seated mother and son, "This is Yuan Lao-ban.[54] This is…Ms. Zhang. And…our son, Xu Ming."

Saiyue nodded and smiled. Yuan said, "Ms. Zhang's come from America. Right?"

"Yes. Originally from Shanghai though, now I work in the San Francisco area."

"How nice! A fine boy here!" His hand directed toward Xiao Ming and withdrew quickly to put the cigarette to his mouth for a quick but deep suck, the flabby cheek suggestive of dissipation.

"Call him 'Old Uncle Yuan'," the father ordered. The command was followed. "Where is your table?" Haosheng asked.

---

54. "Lao-ban" or "proprietor" is an honorific appellation for a businessman.

"Over there, close to the stage," Yuan motioned to the far right, "you can see my friends. Ju Lao-ban and his madam are here too." Saiyue saw, a few tables away, two men and three women sitting around a choice spot for the show. She thought one of the women seemed somewhat familiar, but because of the distance and lighting, it was just a notion.

"Yes. Perhaps I should go over and say hello?" Haosheng said.

"No, no...That's not necessary," Yuan sounded emphatic about it. "The show is resuming soon. Well, are you enjoying it so far?"

"I think Teresa sang well, as usual. I am sure you enjoyed it too—a connoisseur like you," Haosheng chuckled, nodded and swung his hand smoothly toward Yuan in a gesture as though he were introducing a star artist to an audience.

"Yes, I did. You should have heard her, or seen her, when she was younger. But, in any case, now I like the dancers equally well. Hey-hey-hey-hey!" Yuan then turned to Saiyue, "You better return here soon. Our Lao Xu has been restless. Other than that, everything is fine! Hey-hey-hey-hey!" The hollow laughter, sounding louder each time repeated and accompanied by a paroxysmal shaking of the shoulders, began to bug her. "Please excuse me. I think I'll visit the gentleman's room before the show starts again," Yuan said.

Glad to hear of his leaving, she thought she had noticed that the smile on the moon face had disappeared for an instant in which he seemed to have nodded in Haosheng's direction.

"I guess I need to go too." Haosheng followed him.

When they returned, the drum of the band began to roll. "Well, I better get back to my party," Yuan said.

"Now you just enjoy the show and don't talk business. Hear me? Give others a chance to make a living too. All right?" Haosheng, rocking his shoulders a little and chuckling relaxedly, waved goodbye to the portly man.

"Listen who is talking! Nice to see you both and Xiao Ming. Everything is fine! Be seeing you soon! Hey-hey-hey-hey!"

After watching the potbelly waddle away, Haosheng sat down and told Saiyue that Yuan owned much real estate in Hong Kong Island and Kowloon. He also ran a trading company. In fact, Zhong Xing Company had recently purchased from him a large quantity of Shandong marble tiles for exporting to the United States. She commented only that the man had an awfully loud voice.

The band had now resumed in full force. It was so loud that it evoked in Saiyue a faculty of hers—of shutting off the surrounding noise and activities—that she had often employed for her studies and work since her grade school days. The room was darkened, except for a few starlike lights up on the ceiling. For a moment, she was gazing at the glimmer across the ravine from the alcove dinette table of the Pleasant Drive house, and the serene Adagio of Beethoven's Emperor Concerto wafted up from Panzhe's study.

When the show was about to end, Saiyue noticed that at Yuan Lao-ban's table, the somewhat familiar woman and a man by her side had gotten up on their feet to leave. The man was shorter by almost a head. Suddenly Saiyue felt pretty sure who the tall woman was. Her blood pressure went up like that of an athlete just being informed of an upcoming contest. She did not say anything to Haosheng, not then.

It was past 11 when they left the car at the apartment garage, she holding Xiao Ming's hand on one side and Haosheng's the other. Once inside the apartment, the boy, very tired, quickly went to bed. She sat on her bed to change her shoes, wondering how to relieve her itching curiosity without compromising her dignity. It was more than curiosity; it tended toward anxiety—a state like that of a field commander hungering for intelligence on an enemy deployment.

He helped her out. At the door, he asked, "Would you like to have a cup of tea or something?" Haosheng was standing by the door. She went out to join him.

"Cao Rushi was there tonight. Wasn't she?" Saiyue began, after a sip.

"Yes. I was wondering whether you would recognize her."

"How long has she been in Hong Kong?"

"She was already well established here when I first came."

"Why didn't you tell me in California?"

"I saw no particular need. In any case, Zhong Xing and their company are, generally speaking, competitors. I haven't had much contact with her. Even in the same city and same line of work, we run into each other only once in a long while. In fact, she functions at my boss's level.... I did meet her recently though, at the Wing-on department store, while I was getting Xiao Ming's tennis shoes."

"Oh...Did she get him that bow-tie?" she said.

"How did you know?"

"I have my source of information," she nodded as if she was gloating.

"She's got an English name now, Rose?"

"Yes, it sounds like Rushi, when pronounced with a Cantonese accent. How did you know?"

"Interesting. Is she also President Rose Guo?" She ignored his question.

"She is president all right. But not Guo, Rose Ju. You know Ju is her husband's name. She is President Ju of the Lian Fa Company."

"Yes, I know. How come Ms. Zhou called her President Guo."

"Ms. Zhou? Guo?...Oh, I know. This morning in my office. Ju in Cantonese sounds like Guo in Mandarin. Ms. Zhou has never been out of Hong Kong, you know. Maybe she has been in Guangzhou."

"President! Impressive. From accountant to president. You said you didn't have much contact with her. Why was she calling you?"

"Not much doesn't mean none. Their company needed a quantity of electrical fans to complete an order from some client in Southeast Asia. She was trying to contact my boss for help. In his absence, the call was transferred to me."

"So she runs that company."

"Not only that, I understand that she is one of its major stockholders, although her husband does own the controlling shares. He travels a lot, getting business all over—Bangkok, Jakarta, Manila....As president, she runs the day to day business of the company."

"He doesn't go to Guangzhou, Shanghai or Beijing?"

"No, not since his father and uncle got in trouble some time ago, on corruption charges. Ju Tiger, as he is known here also, had probably foreseen that. Long before his family businesses folded, he had set up the company here in Hong Kong with his wife running it."

"Would his travelling give you two lots of chances?"

"Um?...You are as direct as your old self, aren't you?...No, I know better. I don't want to fool around with that Tiger."

"Why not? You did before." She thought it was time to let it out.

"What do you mean?"

"Did you think I was really that dumb?...About that night, some six years ago, of what you said was Cao Rushi's farewell party. Do you remember now?"

Haosheng looked at her with disbelief, speechless for a while. "I guess you knew," he said, "I must give you credit for being able to hold it in this long....I am curious. Why didn't you bring it up then?"

"I was pregnant. I didn't think our marriage could survive if I brought it out into the open." She didn't go into why she wanted it to survive at the time.

"Why not when you called from America for the divorce?"

"I didn't want to provoke you that way. Sometimes, feeling shame, people grow angry, and their actions become unpredictable. It could have been provocative—"

"You didn't bring it up even at Redwood City."

"What'd be the point? You were my guest. Why the embarrassment? It was that to me too, you know."

"Yes, I see. But much has happened to each of us since," he said seriously. "We could start with a clean slate. What I have told you tonight is the truth."

"All right. So far I think I believe you. Fair enough. So, why is it that you don't want to 'fool around with that Tiger' now?"

"First of all, six years ago it was just a one-time affair that just happened due to special circumstances and coincidence. She and I thought we'd never meet again. Now it's different. We all live here. You know, as the saying goes, 'A rabbit wouldn't eat the grass around its burrow.' Besides, the *tiger* has grown wings. I hear he now has ties with secret societies—ruthless, violent gangsters, frankly. Most importantly, I still want you, the mother of my son, as my wife."

"How sweet of you!" She felt pretty good about the conversation, not only because it answered a number of questions for her, but also this time the answers sounded straight enough. Her mood showed on her complexion, smooth, relaxed and slightly flushed.

He stood up and extended his hand, "Let's go to my room." She regarded him, tall and handsome with his slightly hooked nose, like a life-size trophy. She couldn't overly blame Rose Cao if she had designs on him. Saiyue eyed him with a mock reproach, and with a shy smile, took his hand.

34

Next morning after Haosheng left for work, she took Xiao Ming for a walk. They sauntered from the residential neighborhood to a small business area. At a department store, she bought a parasol, a baseball hat, two storybooks and a pocket size photo album. The hat and the parasol helped to shield them from the sun. Further on, they went into a Dairy Farm where she ordered chocolate milk for her son and ice coffee for herself.

"Remember the other night we met at the airport?" she asked her son.
"Yep."
"Did I ask you 'Do you remember me?'"
"Yep."
"Well, you never did answer that question for me. Now do you remember me?"
The boy stopped sipping the milk from the straw, looked at her with widened eyes and laughed. "Of course, I do. You are right here, ha, ha, ha, ha!" He pointed his chubby finger across the table.
She too was amused by his sense of humor. "No, no. Don't be naughty, Xiao Ming. I mean at the time we met at the airport did you remember me, recognize my face and know who I was?"
"Yep, Shanghai-po-po showed me your picture."
Of course, Shanghai-po-po was her mother. "Oh, when?"

"When papa took me to visit them in Shanghai."
"Oh, do you remember Xi'an?"
"No."
"Did papa show you my picture?"
"No."
"Did gong-gong or po-po show you my picture?"
"No."
After a few seconds, she asked, "Were you happy in Nanjing?"
"Yep."
"Did you miss your mama sometimes?"

The boy shrugged his shoulders, and then said without apparent emotion: "Sort of. Sometimes, er, yeah, mamas of my friends came to school and brought them things and stuff…."

She dropped her head for a moment. "Do you know that I, your mama, love you very much?"
"Yep."
"How?"
"I just know." The boy began to fidget in the chair, his feet knocking the legs of the table.

"I am going to give you a picture of me. Will you promise to keep it safely."

"Yep." She got a picture of herself from her purse, put it in the small photo album and gave it to the boy. He looked at it for a couple of seconds, held it in his hands and resumed drawing the chocolate milk, making a vacuuming sound now. Then he stood up and inserted it in a back pocket of his short pants. She made him promise always to button the pocket and not to lose the album.

"Remember, although I will have to go back to America in a couple of days, I will someday take you there. Would you like that?"
"America?…Yes."
"That may happen soon too."
"Yes."

In a little while, she asked, "You told me that Aunt Rose gave you that nice bow tie, right?"

"Yep."

"Where did she give it to you?"

"At the store."

The answer satisfied her.

Haosheng returned after lunch to take them to Stanley, a village known for fine merchandise at discount prices. On their way southward, winding up the hill, they stopped at a lookout where they could have a panoramic view of Victoria and the spread of the Central District buildings, tall, bleaching, almost glaring, like giant rectilinear crystals grown on some other planet. Haosheng shot a few pictures of the mother and son and asked a fellow sightseer to snap a couple of all three of them standing under a tree with the Bank of China Tower in the far background.

Down along Repulse Bay, clusters of high-rises drenched in sunlight. He told her that some of the firm's clients lived in there. At Stanley, they parked the car in a residential street and walked to the market. There seemed to be so much to see. They decided to do their shopping separately and meet afterwards in front of a snack shop. She was pleased that Xiao Ming now of his own volition came with her. She bought a couple of T-shirts, a sweater and a jacket for him, and two blouses for herself. At a sportswear shop in a narrow street, she browsed for a while and bought an "alligator" polo shirt and a Fila tennis shirt.

They returned via Aberdeen Tunnel and stopped for tea at Lee Garden Restaurant in Happy Valley. Back to the apartment, she gave Haosheng the polo shirt. He presented her with a Gucci handbag, made of alligator skin. It seemed to her a duplicate of the one she saw on her first visit to an American shopping center. At the time, seeing the price tag, she had thought she'd never own one like it.

He apologized that he had to go to a business dinner to which only men were invited. She was glad to have a break from the activities and an opportunity to spend a quiet evening with Xiao Ming. Ah Yu cooked dinner. Saiyue's offer to help was firmly declined.

After dinner, she started to watch television with the boy. The variety show couldn't hold his interest, and he soon became restless. She took to reading to him the Chinese version of the *Jungle Book*—one of the two storybooks she bought for him in the morning. On the sofa, the boy ensconced himself in her bosom. She would smile indulgently as from time to time he would interrupt with such questions as "Why he not run faster?" in a retrogressive lisping kind of baby talk, and then put his thumb in his mouth. For a while she enjoyed seeing him like that, then she admonished,

"Don't put your thumb in your mouth! You don't want to have buckteeth when you grow up. Do you?"

"I haven't put my thumb in my mouth!" he said, pulling it out.

After seeing him to bed, she returned to the television and, joined by Ah Yu, watched the night's segment of *The Red Chamber Dream*. The young helper was much impressed by the colorful costumes of the women, while Saiyue felt the story moved too slow, almost painfully so. After it ended, turning the TV off, she told Ah Yu to go to bed, saying that she'd wait for Haosheng herself.

Around midnight, she opened the door to let him in. She could smell the stench of tobacco.

"Sorry I am late. I wanted to come back earlier." Now alcohol scent was added to the air. He walked into the living room and slumped on the sofa. "I thought I wasn't too bad at psychology. Why do I always lose at those fist games!"[55]

---

55. A drinking party game for two players, in which simultaneously each would call out a number and show a hand, the fingers of which would configure another number, the player having called the correct sum of the two hands is the winner. The loser is to take a drink.

She pointed out to him that there were what seemed to be lipstick stains on his shirt collar. He explained that at such business parties there were always invited "wine companions," and it would be gauche to act like a prude. "Believe me I didn't even look at the girls. All evening long all I could think of was you," he grinned at her. She said she had heard enough. He invited her to go to his room. She declined, saying it had been a long day. He didn't persist.

He had to work all day the next day. Accompanied by Ah Yu, she took Xiao Ming to visit the "Hu Wenhu Gardens." The boy was fascinated by the statues of the mythological Chinese characters on display, and enjoyed the associated morality stories his mother told about them.

Ah Yu had mentioned earlier that she had often visited the Women's Street with her friends. Intrigued by the name, Saiyue asked her to take them there. It turned out to be a crowded street with stalls over a long stretch right in the middle of the road. Most of the goods were of the cheap kind or knockoffs. The air in the neighborhood smelled foul of a mixture of motor exhaust and burnt cooking oil. They left quickly.

For a change of scenery and air quality, Ah Yu led them onto a boat at the Star Ferry. The fresh harbor breeze at the upper deck reinvigorated them. After landing on Tsim Sha Tsui, they walked about the Ocean Terminal Shopping Center and had diem-sum at Maxim.

That evening, Haosheng took her and Xiao Ming to Hopwell Center. He told her if she preferred Western food, they could go to the rotating restaurant at the top. She opted for Chinese food and they went up to the Round Dragon Chinese Restaurant at the 60th floor. It was the first time that she ever rode in an elevator outside a building. The night of Hong Kong appeared like a large black curtain, studded with glistening pearls, sinking slowly. Since she was leaving the next day, he said, that they should have something special, like bird nest soup, fish stomach, giant black mushroom, etc. He also ordered wine and wished her a safe trip.

After they finished and came out, the pearl-studded curtain rose slowly in front of them. She took a look at Xiao Ming, chubby and sweet, and then at his father, erect and self-possessed. What a difference from those Xi'an days, cramped in that small room with practically everything tucked in underneath the bed—the suitcases, the wok, the cutting board, the noodle box, etc. She grasped Haosheng's hand and squeezed it as they left the elevator.

After Xiao Ming went to bed, she joined Haosheng in his room. Throwing restraint to the wind, she let herself go. In the afterglow, Haosheng sat up against the headboard, smoking.

"Saiyue," he began.

"Mm," she responded lethargically.

"You know I should thank you for pushing me," he said.

"You have naughty thoughts again?" she was jocund.

"Now who is having naughty thoughts? Seriously, I mean, when I was back in Xi'an by myself, if you hadn't asked for the divorce, I would probably have continued to idle my life away. I would never have driven myself so. You know that I went through a crisis. Either I fight back and prove to you and myself or I sink into oblivion."

"You have done well," she said.

He continued, "For the good of the boy, I say again we should get married, I mean remarried, soon." She was a little annoyed by his presumptuousness. But it was she who had just made him so confident.

"Where?" She sounded concessive.

"It doesn't matter. Here in Hong Kong, Shanghai? Not Xi'an, heavens!"

"How about America? Would you like to come to America?"

"That is a possibility. But I think a greater possibility is for you to come to Hong Kong."

"Why? Because Rose Cao is here? And you don't want to move away from this place?"

"Now you are being childish. She is living in a different world, Tiger's world, which I like to stay as far away from as possible. Are you really as jealous as you just sounded."

"I am not jealous! Just kidding," she smiled mechanically. "But I must have a job."

"With my job here, you know, you don't have to work."

"That's out of the question. With my job in America, you don't have to work either," she sounded energized.

"I get your point. You are as feisty as ever, eh?" he gave her arm a tweak. "Really, 'it's easier to alter a mountain or a river than to change one's character.'…With all the construction going on or in the works—the big one being that new airport project—your graduate degree and experience, it shouldn't be difficult for you to find suitable work here. I can start to look into it for you."

She did not answer for a while. Then said, "But you know, this place seems so crowded, hemmed in, in spite of all the glitter.…Besides, what'll happen after 1997 when it's returned to China?"

"Who knows? It's almost a decade away. Don't worry about it!" he said.

"Still, America is a most stable place. Anyway, I have to go back tomorrow to work for John J. Clyde yet. We'll have time to see how things turn out. Perhaps you could make some preliminary inquiries for me."

"I certainly could. Meanwhile, I'd like you to take this with you," he turned and opened the drawer of the nightstand, took out a small box and handed it to her.

She opened it. It was the cat's-eye ruby ring she had regarded in the little jewelry shop on Queen's Road. "What a surprise! Haosheng! Are you really rich or generous, or both?" she gave him her sweet caltrop smile.

"Both!" he said, putting it on her bare ring finger.

She looked at it admiringly, rotating it in the lamplight. Each of the two diamonds setting off the main jewel was about the size of that which Lu Panzhe had given her. (She had put it away after the divorce.)

"Well, you like it?" he asked.

"Yes, it is beautiful."

"It's yours."

She stared at it for a while. Her expression changed gradually. Her eyes darkened a bit and the caltrop smile was replaced by a slight twist of her upper lip. "I can't accept this from you right now."

"Why not? As a re-engagement ring, all right? Take it with you."

"No. I can't. Not until we are actually married…remarried."

Next morning, Haosheng left for the office early but would be back in time to take her to the airport. Xiao Ming stood around and watched his mother arrange and pack her things. Saiyue, blinking her eyes every now and then, told the boy to go on to the living room and play.

Later she asked him, "Is there a telephone at Gong-gong's place in Nanjing?"

"No, but Shang Gong-gong next door has one."

"Do you know how to use the phone?"

"No."

"Let me show you."

She took him to the phone in the living room and proceeded to teach the boy. Initially the boy was a bit bewildered but became excited when he proved to his mother and himself that he could dial to get the time. She then gave him a card with her home and office numbers—including the international access digits—and taught him how to make a collect call. She asked for the photo album, which she had given him before, and put the card and also a US$20 bill inside it, in case he had to pay for a call.

"If for any reason you want to talk to me, you can try the telephone. All right?"

"All right, Mama."

Later at the airport, she made Xiao Ming promise again not to lose the photo album and hugged him for a while. "Mama will be with you soon. Be a good boy."

"Yes, Mama. Good-bye, Mama. Come to see me again."

"I told you I will. Be a good boy," she swallowed and hugged him again. She gave the father and son each a quick kiss on the cheek and turned to join the departing passengers.

35

As the plane climbed, leaving Kowloon behind, Saiyue watched its shadow—thrown by the western sun—like that of a cruising shark, skim on the blue waters. Past a village with a scattering of boats nearby, man's handiwork became rare. An occasional ship at the tip of a vee looked like a stationary, brooding water beetle. Several heaps of white fringed green islets slowly approached and passed; there was nothing but the deep blue Pacific and the wide azure sky, meeting at the far milky rim with touches of pink.

She thought of Xiao Ming first with his cute little bow tie—and quickly she obliterated the image of the bow tie. His two-tone tennis shoes...his laugh at Dairy Farm—silly but cute...his baby talk while lying in her bosom, listening to her reading of *Jungle Book*. Come to see me again. I will have him with me....There is no question that Haosheng is a changed man. He seems to be a man of substance now, certainly there—almost as advanced as America.

She thought she could proceed to execute her decision without any real encumbrances. Specifically, she did not need to advise Lu Panzhe about it, but she also knew that it simply wasn't her style.

During the flight and the weekend after she had returned to Redwood City, she mulled over how to tell Panzhe about it. In the first two days of the week, she had to put everything aside in order to respond to urgent items awaiting her at the office. She began to think seriously about Panzhe again on Wednesday. Finally, she came to the obvious approach. Tell him in person, point-blank—no letter, not on the phone, no beating around the bush, cold turkey.

That night she wrote down what she would say, "…I think I should tell you this directly. I have decided to reunite with Xu Haosheng. I did not arrive at this lightly. This time after I saw and lived with Xiao Ming for a few days, I realized how much the boy and I missed each other, and the decision became obvious. I hope you will understand.…I hope that it won't upset you. If you like, I would be happy to spend a last weekend vacation with you, for old time's sake, at a place of your choosing."

She felt more relaxed after having drafted the speech and had a good night's sleep. Next morning, she read it again and confirmed that it was what she wanted. (She did this consciously out of a practice she learned years ago to keep the draft of any important communication overnight in order to avoid mistakes of impetuosity.) She intended to have it done and over with at a dinner to which she would invite Panzhe. From her office, she called his in mid-morning. No one answered.

After several futile tries to reach him at his home that night, and his office the next day, she called his department office.

A woman, apparently a secretary, said, "Professor Lu is in the hospital."

Surprised, she asked, "What hospital?"

"St. Luke's Hospital."

"Can you tell me what's wrong with him?"

"I am not sure. I heard that he might have suffered a stroke."

"A stroke…oh…oh…Is he in danger?"

"I don't know. I am sorry."

"Thank you," she hung up. A stroke…a stroke! Her brows knit, upper lip twisted a little, eyes locked on the telephone buttons.

Whew! My God! Luckily I haven't made the wrong choice, she thought. Too bad for him! She tried to return to her work. The computer code she had been trying to fix since the day before, all appeared to be so much mumbo jumbo. Stroke? I've heard of that. What exactly is a stroke? Brain damage! Brain death! People die from it! Is *he* going to *die*! Suddenly her heart raced and eyes hollowed. Within an hour, she made her way to the volunteers' desk of the hospital. A white haired lady told her that Lu Panzhe was in Room 503 of the Neural Care Unit on the 5th. floor.

"Are you a relative?" the volunteer asked her.

"Uh, no,...sort of, very close friend," she said.

"Well, I'll give you this tag. You go up there and ask at the nurses' station and see whether they will let you in."

Room 503 was the second door from the wing's entrance. The nurses' station was further down the hallway. On a placard taped to the door, she could see Panzhe's name. A little distance down the corridor two workers, nurse's aids or cleaning crew, were busying themselves. There was no nurse at hand.

She slipped inside the room. A curtain hung from an encircling track in the ceiling, enclosing much of the front half of the room. However, the bed therein was unoccupied. She semi-tiptoed in further. On the second bed a man lay under a gray blanket. An intravenous tube, drooping from a suspended bag terminated under a small pad taped over the back of the hand. The left eye was covered by a black patch, the other one closed. Over the nose perched a plastic oxygen mask.

She walked over to the bedside. In the pale window light, the lower lip, dry and scaly, pulled a little wryly. His hair was rumpled, even the eyebrows seemed stiff and disheveled, the skin of the face appeared loose and strangely flushed, and the pepper-and-salt stubble around the mouth reminded her of a photograph of a derelict in an art exhibition at the University museum. He didn't look like the urbane Lu Panzhe she used to know. Hung above the bed, the patient's pulse swept wavily across a cardiac monitor. She bent down and moved her hand toward his rumpled hair and withdrew it. In the monotonous purr of the oxygen supply and the chick-like beeps of the monitor, she sat in a chair like a statue, watching him.

"Hi, Saiyue!" A whisper woke her. A tall young woman with prominent cheekbones was looking down at her. Saiyue recognized she was the patient's daughter, and behind her stood a young man. "Sharon!" The women shook hands.

"How long have you been here?" Sharon asked.

"A while now. He has been sleeping. Is he like this all the time? How is he?"

"They said he has stabilized now. Yes, he sleeps most of the time. The nurse told us he has been given tranquilizers. He had talked to me before we left for lunch." Moving closer to the bed, she called lightly, "Dad...Dad!"

"Let him sleep," Saiyue said.

"It's all right. The nurse had told us it's all right to wake him up every now and then," Sharon said.

Panzhe's right eye opened and tried to focus. She sidled back a little. Saiyue stepped up, bending over and saying lightly,

"Hi! Panzhe!"

He looked at her intently with the one eye, and uttered throatily, "Hai...yeh."

"Don't you worry. You will be all right. Just relax and get well," she said, brushing back a strand of hair that lay over his forehead. The eye closed again.

Sharon, absorbed by the scene for a moment, suggested, "Perhaps we could go outside and talk."

"Is it all right to leave him alone?"

"I think so. His condition is being monitored continuously at the nurses' station," Sharon gestured toward the cardiac monitor.

Out of the room, she introduced the young man, "My friend from New York, Mike Rubinstein. This is Ms. Zhang. My ex-step-mother." (Hearing the last relational reference, Saiyue instantly felt closer to her ex-step-daughter, who seemed much warmer than when they met at the wedding.)

"I am pleased to meet you," Rubinstein said. Looking a few years older than Sharon, he had bright eyes, dark curly hair and a rather earnest aspect.

"How do you do? When did you two arrive here?"

"We came yesterday...." Then Sharon told Saiyue what she knew. Apparently Wednesday morning just getting out of bed, her father felt so dizzy that he could hardly stand up, and his right side "felt funny." He sensed it might be something serious and called his friend John Wu, who came over immediately and took him to the hospital emergency room. At the time, his speech became a bit slurred. The hospital staff suspected a "cerebral vascular accident," i.e., a stroke. A CAT scan showed no hemorrhage. He was put in the neural care unit. He asked John Wu to phone Sharon. After she got in touch with the attending physician, who confirmed the diagnosis, she immediately arranged to fly out, accompanied by Rubinstein.

"Is his condition serious?" Saiyue asked.

"The doctor said a stroke is always serious. But he doesn't think it a life threatening situation now."

"What is the prognosis?"

"The doctor said we'd have to wait and see. They are going to give him another CAT scan," Sharon said.

Saiyue went in again and came out a while later. "He is sleeping soundly. I think I'd better be getting back to my office. I'll see him tomorrow. If you need me for anything before then, please call me." She gave Sharon her office and home phone numbers and left.

Saiyue came back to see Panzhe the next day. The room was crowded. The attending physician, surrounded by his juniors—resident physicians, interns and two nurses—was starting to examine Panzhe, strapped in a wheel chair without the eye-patch and oxygen mask. Behind them stood a man whom she recognized as his brother from Los Angeles, Panbao, sans the constant smile.

The doctor, middle aged with graying sideburns, rotated Panzhe's right foot up and asked him whether his toes had moved up or down, and repeated the question after rotating the foot down. He would instruct him to grab and squeeze his hand. He asked him what he ate this morning. The patient's responses seemed to please him. Finally he asked him: "What's my name?"

"Er...nest Johnson," Panzhe replied slowly.

"Good." Dr. Johnson nodded and turned around and made a few remarks to his young proteges. A male nurse helped Panzhe get back on the bed. Dr. Johnson was about to address Panbao. The latter introduced Saiyue to the doctor as the patient's former wife. The doctor told them that the CAT scan showed the infarction was quite limited, and that the patient appeared to be in pretty good shape. Overall, Dr. Johnson was optimistic about his recovery.

He would have him moved to the rehabilitation ward the next day. He expected that, with physical and speech therapies, the recovery process should accelerate after a couple of weeks. In the meantime, the patient probably would still need moderate assistance—such as in transferring from bed to chair and vice versa, in changing clothes, even in feeding. The physician also mentioned that the family should get in touch with the hospital's social worker about possible assistance.

After he strode out with his entourage, Saiyue walked over to the bed, "How are you feeling?"

"A lit...tle weak, o...therwise I feel...all right....Thank you for...coming." He spoke slowly, but reasonably clearly. His smile was weak but the gleam in his eyes showed cheeriness of spirit.

"Don't thank me. You just get well. Did you hear Dr. Johnson? He said you should recover in short order."

"That's right. Now we are all quite relieved," his brother chimed in. At that moment, Sharon entered. After a brief exchange of greetings, she was told of the doctor's prognosis.

"That's great," she glanced at her father, whose eyes were now closed, and moved her hand under her chin in a thinker's pose. "I need to find some help to take care of Dad. Apart from that, now it seems there isn't any real need for me to stay here. Mike and I are on a special project. If an emergency comes up, I could always get here quickly."

"Dr. Johnson said that we should talk with the hospital's social worker," Panbao said.

"We can do that right now. I'll ask the nurse and try to locate the person. I'll be back," Sharon stood up and made to leave.

"I'll go with you," her uncle said.

After they left, Saiyue drew her chair closer to the bed. Noting some movement under the closed eyelids, she asked, "How do you feel now?"

"I…feel…fine. A lit…tle sleepy.…Pretty…messy situ…ation. Eh?" he opened his eyes and smiled wanly.

"Don't worry. You'll get out of this in good shape," she moved her hand to feel his forehead. He pulled his hand out from under the bedcover. The hands joined and lay on the edge of the bed. He looked at her with obvious gratitude. She gazed at him tenderly, her mouth contorted a little, when he closed his eyes, she bent down and lay her head on the clasped hands.

A few moments later, hearing footsteps, she lifted up her head, brushed back her hair and saw the return of Sharon and Panboa. "She is not here today," Sharon was referring to the social worker. Saiyue took her leave, saying simply that she'd be back.

The next morning, she went to the church slightly earlier than usual. To her friends she appeared distracted, replying only cursorily to their greetings. During the service, sitting at the end of a rear pew, she would look blankly, then close her eyes, open them again after a moment, her gaze now directed at the stained glass windows, as though searching for some specific detail in the figures and setting of the composition. After Bach's "Jesu Joy Of Man's Desiring," the words resonated in her:

"...For I was a-hungered, and ye gave me meat; I was thirsty, and ye gave me drink; I was a stranger, and ye took me in; naked, and ye clothed me; I was sick, and ye visited me; I was in prison, and ye came unto me....And the King shall answer and say unto them, 'Verily I say unto you, Inasmuch as ye have done it unto one of the least of these my brethren, ye have done it unto me.'"

"Is he less than 'one of the least of these my brethren'?" she asked herself.

After church she went to have lunch with Liu Rong who wanted to hear about her recent trip to China. Before ordering food and drink, Saiyue told her of Panzhe's illness and that she was considering taking care of him until his recovery.

The waitress came, served them coffee and left with their orders.

"That'll be very noble of you," Rong said.

"I don't mean to be that. He was good to me. Since he has no relatives here, I think I should do it. It's no big deal. The doctor said the recovery won't take long."

"Do you intend to go back to him?"

"You mean remarrying him?"

"Yes."

"It has nothing to do with that. This is just a one time thing," Saiyue said.

"Like paying off a debt?"

"Not exactly...maybe."

"Umm...Now, about your trip, what strikes you most?" Rong asked.

Straightening her back a bit, Saiyue said, "I am impressed most with the improvements in people's standard of living. For example, consider housing for my family in Shanghai or my old colleagues in Xi'an...." She started to brief Rong on her trip.

Their orders came. As they ate, Saiyue related her days in Hong Kong. She commented humorously how her son corrected her from calling him Baobao instead of Xiao Ming. Then, noticing the pensive look in Rong's eyes, she curtailed her enthusiasm, mindful of her friend's daughter being in Chengdo still.

"So you lived in his apartment all the time there?" Rong asked.

"Yes."

"You and he are going back together, getting remarried?"

"Well, I had thought so," Saiyue said.

"*Had thought?*"

"Indeed he is a changed man, much more purposeful than before," she had a swallow and began again, "He seems to have found his niche in that part of the world—where business seems to be the only business of life."

"Did he propose remarriage to you?"

"Yes."

"Then, why *had thought?*"

"Well, the night before I left Hong Kong I almost made that commitment to him. Now back here, I have had time to think and take a more objective look at the situation.... Surely, the most important reason for me to reunite with him is Xiao Ming....Actually, if it were not for the boy, I just might not want to marry anybody. Why not just live together? However, I'll admit that the boy's father has been pretty good to me, except for that one occasion I told you about."

"You mean that accountant old flame of his?"

"Yes....You know. She is also in Hong Kong, now president of some trading company. In fact, I saw her."

"How interesting! Did she have dealings, I mean business dealings with him?" Rong asked.

"Yes. But her husband, as the chairman of the board, controls the firm." Saiyue said.

"Humm...interesting....Do you still think of her as a challenge?" Rong asked.

"What?"

"You heard me. Is she still a challenge to you?"

Saiyue did not answer immediately. Then, she said, "I don't know....No, no, why should it be so?"

"How should I know?" Rong smiled. "In any case, make sure you do things for the right reason."

"Perhaps that's why I said, 'I had thought.'...Well, in any case, now any progress along that line will have to wait," Saiyue said.

"You mean because of Professor Lu's illness."

"Yes."

"What a situation!" Rong said, "Would this complicate things? How would Xu Haosheng take this?"

"He doesn't know it yet. But I'll be straight with him."

"I suppose your heart has overruled your head," Rong said.

Saiyue was relieved that her friend did not say anything more negative than that. "Whatever...I follow my conscience. I have time. I'll wait and see....How about you? What's the status of your daughter?"

"Her father is still dragging his feet, just out of spite, I think. In time he'll recover his senses and let the girl come."

"I'd think so. Hope it'll be soon. How's business?"

"It's been quite good. We finally got a pretty big deal closed—pretty big for me at least. A house for almost a million dollars. Paid in cash. Imagine! The customer is from Hong Kong. He is apprehensive about what'll happen to that place after 1997, when it will be returned to China. 'A clever rabbit's burrow has three holes,' you know. We hope he will send some of his Hong Kong friends our way," Rong said animatedly.

"So you have made a hefty commission on this."

"Not bad, even though I got only a quarter of the total after the split. This lunch is on me, Xiao Zhang. Now if you know someone from Hong Kong, or any other place for that matter, who needs the services of a real estate agent, send him or her on to me. My associates and I can work out a percentage for you," Rong said.

"I am not interested in the broker business; but I'll do that for you anyhow." Saiyue said a little absent-mindedly, her mind's eye seeing a cloud labeled 1997 over that island.

In the afternoon, she went to the hospital. Crossing the lobby to the elevator, she was surprised—there Amir Rahimi was, sitting relaxedly in a chair. He stood up, and nodding and smiling, began to walk over. She met him halfway, and they shook hands.

"How are you?" he asked, the raven's wings lifting. She thought he looked chipper.

"I am OK. I come to visit a friend. And you?" she said.

"I am waiting—for a friend who has gone upstairs to visit a colleague of hers."

Hers? "Nice to see you. You look well. I'd like to talk with you some more, but some other time. I have to go up now," she said.

"Take care. Nice to see you too," he smiled.

On the fifth floor she was told that Panzhe had already been moved to the Rehabilitation Ward on the fourth floor.

When she turned into the hallway of that floor, she saw a woman in street clothes coming out of a room down the corridor. Saiyue thought there was something familiar about her gait and straight carriage. As she passed by, Saiyue couldn't help notice her blooming red hair. Seconds later, when Saiyue realized that she had exited from Panzhe's room, she felt pretty sure who the woman was.

The room was about the same size as the old one, having two beds also. But there were none of the solemn monitors with tiny blinking lights or travelling waves. The curtains around both beds were open. The other patient, a big middle-aged man, was sitting in a chair, reading. Saiyue coughed lightly. Panzhe, lying in bed, turned his head, and finding Saiyue, his eyes brightened. Smiling, he said, "Hi!"

"How are you today?" she asked.

"I feel better. Saiyue, this is Mr. Mur…phy, Mr. Murphy. She is Ms. Zhang." He spoke slowly but it sounded clear enough except for the last word "Zhang," which was a little slurred. She and Murphy nodded to acknowledge the introduction.

"Have a seat please," Panzhe said. She pulled up a chair near him while his roommate moved to lie down and let the two alone. "He had an…open heart surgery," Panzhe began in Chinese. "Thank you…for coming again."

"Did Dr. Johnson come this morning?" she asked.

"No. But I did talk to the doctor in charge of my reha…bilitation, a Dr. Kramer."

"What did he say?"

"My therapy process will start to…morrow. All three of them, physical, occupa…tional and speech therapies."

"Oh, three kinds, eh?"

"He doesn't think I need much speech…therapy."

"How long will they last?" she asked.

"He said that it's hard to say. It may vary from three…weeks to…six…months."

"Oh." She thought he did seem appreciably more spirited and stronger than yesterday. Apparently he had shaved also. "Do you eat well?"

"All right. They are still feeding me with…soft food. I seem to have improved some on…my drinking."

She watched him for a moment. "Panzhe, did your redhead girlfriend just visit you?"

"Yes. She is not my girlfriend. She left just before you came in. You pro…bably ran into her."

"Yes, I did.…Is she going to take care of you?"

"No. Why would she? It was just a cour…tesy call. She said she had an appoint…ment in the hos…pital, and stopped by for a brief visit…as a colleague."

"Oh, sure?" Se smiled mischievously.

"Abso…lutely!"

"What appointment does she have with the hospital? Oh! Forget it! It's none of my business. Panzhe…." She paused.

"Yes?"

"Listen! I think I can take care of you until you recover from this illness," she said.

He looked surprised. "I am not your responsi…bility. You don't have to do this."

"I would like to."

"Are you sure?" he asked.

"Panzhe. Do you ever recall a case that I would offer to do something that I didn't want to?"

He regarded her for a moment, smiled knowingly and said, "No. Not really! But, still, Sharon can make arrangements for me."

"Did you hear that she is hot on an important project at work. You don't want me to?"

"Of course I appre…ciate your help. I am sure it would…indeed help Sharon out too. I just want to be sure that you know you are under no obli…gation to do this."

"I know that, Panzhe. All right then, it's settled. From what Dr. Johnson said, I don't think it'd be such a big deal. I think I can do this and still go to work in the office."

"I wouldn't have it…any other way. Say, how was your trip?" he said.

"Fine! I had a good time. I can tell you about it later, but here is something for you," she said, showing him an A&P shopping bag, "Want to see it?"

"Yes, what is it? Something to eat?" She took out from the bag a tennis shirt on which he immediately recognized the logo. "A Fila, ou!" He meant to say "wow!"

"Yes, you better get well soon in order to wear it on the court."

He looked at her for a while as though she was a stranger. Then he said, "Thanks, Saiyue! Where did you get it?"

It was not her intention to lie, but not wanting to complicate matters at the moment, she said, "Shanghai. Nowadays, you can get practically anything there."

Sharon came in. She told them that earlier she and her uncle (who was on his way back to LA) had talked with the hospital social worker and had obtained the names of several home health agencies that she would contact the next day. Her father told her about Saiyue's offer.

She looked at her ex-step-mother with her almond eyes open as wide as they could, "Are you sure you can do this?"

"I wouldn't have offered it if I couldn't," Saiyue said.

Sharon, maintaining a countenance of seriousness and sincerity, said, "I know Dad will appreciate your help. You don't know how much this means to me. Frankly, with my biggest project thus far going on, I feel so lucky to have your help. It's so very nice of you."

Saiyue wanted to say "I am doing this for your father, not you." Instead, she simply smiled agreeably.

They talked about possible scenarios that depended on the patient's progress, insurance terms, hospital rules, etc. Sharon gave her the hospital social worker's name and the names of the home health agencies and exacted a promise from her that she would let her know whenever she needed relief. Sharon returned to New York the next day with her boyfriend.

The following night after Saiyue returned home from the hospital, the telephone rang. It was from Hong Kong. Haosheng told her that Xiao Ming was already back in Nanjing. The reason for his call was that he had come to know someone who had connections with a leading local engineering consulting firm and would be glad to speak on her behalf to one of its top executives, and then he added, "…To get the ball rolling, he needs to have your resumé. Will you get it to me as soon as you can?"

For the past couple of days she had been wondering how to let Haosheng know about her decision to care for Panzhe. She hadn't expected that an opportunity would present itself so soon. She sucked in a breath and said,

"Haosheng, I appreciate your help. But I think we better put the resumé thing on hold. About my job, frankly, the more I think about it, the more I feel I should keep mine here. In my way of thinking, it deals with the frontier of my profession, and I can hardly think of another one that would better promote my professional growth."

"You are talking about working with computers," he said. "How do you know that the job here would not involve that? Don't forget Hong Kong is a very modern place."

"I know that. I am talking about not just using computers but enabling others to use computers. That aside, there is another point. I am still concerned about what life in Hong Kong will be like after 1997."

"That is a long time off," he said.

"Not that long....And there is yet another, totally different, matter," she sucked in another breath.

"Yes?"

"Recently, Lu Panzhe had a serious illness. He has no one to take care of him. I think I should look after him until he recovers. So it's best that we wait a while."

"What!" he sounded incredulous. "What's his problem?"

After listening to her summary of Panzhe's case, he said, "You don't owe him a thing, you know."

"But it's a good thing to do."

"How about us? Our family, the things we talked about before you left here....You don't owe him but you owe your son—" he jabbed.

Vexed by his mentioning Xiao Ming, she almost blurted out, "Don't use the boy—" Instead, she said, "Strictly speaking, you are right. But Lu Panzhe was a big help to my career....The doctor has said the recovery won't take long."

After a tense silence, he said, "I have always known you as an independent woman. It appears that the years in America have ever so intensified your willfulness. You are not the only woman with—"

"I know," she quickly followed up, "there is Rose. Right?"

"Rose....There you go again! There is nothing between her and me now. But you and I have plans discussed the night before you left here!"

"I can't resume that discussion until I am done with Lu Panzhe's case. I need to do that."

"All right, suit yourself."

From then on, their relationship again fell in limbo, but they kept their communication channel open mainly on the subject of their son, Xiao Ming.

In those early days of Panzhe's recovery, Saiyue would come to the hospital twice a day, from seven to eight in the morning, and from six to eight in the evening. She would help feed him when the nurse could use the relief. After a week, he no longer needed speech therapy, nor help in taking his meals.

After three weeks, he was able to put on his shirt, and his socks with a socks-aid. He still needed help to pull his pants above the waist after he had put them on himself. He could move his legs and walk slowly using a cane and a brace on his right leg. Dr. Kramer commented that his recovery was one of the fastest he had ever witnessed. At this point he was discharged from the hospital.

A Mexican attendant was hired from one of the home health service organizations, mainly to help Panzhe in transferring from bed to wheel chair and vice versa. Saiyue moved into the Pleasant Drive house and stayed in Sharon's old bedroom across the hall from his. She did the washing, cooking, driving him to medical services, etc. He continued the physical and occupational therapies as an outpatient with follow-up visits to Dr. Johnson. His strength and neurological recoveries progressed steadily and rather rapidly.

By mid-December, he had almost completely recovered. The leg brace was taken off, but he still walked with the cane that he seemed to have grown accustomed to, more psychologically than physically. At that point, Dr. Johnson permitted him to go to the office three to four hours a day.

36

Saiyue drove Panzhe to the university on his first day returning to work. She left only after watching him step into the Aeronautical Engineering Building. Secretaries in the Department office congratulated him on his return. Some colleagues stopped by his office to welcome him back. By mid-morning he had made a good start at the accumulated mail. Nora Gallagher came in.

"How are you? Glad to see you've recovered." She gave him a brief hug.

"Thank you."

"I saw your ex dropping you off. It was she, wasn't it?"

"Yes."

"You guys getting back together?"

"She has just been taking care of me. There is no talking about getting back together—if you mean back to our earlier relationship—"

"That's even more decent of her."

"Well, she's done a good job looking after me.... How are you doing? You two still going to the Clinic? Are you done with that?"

"It has been a long road," she said. "We have a couple more sessions to go yet. They have been very helpful. Thank you for your encouragement. Amir is a good-hearted man. He is trying to talk me into going to Europe with him."

"Are you?"

"I am inclined that way. I have always wanted to learn French—*parler français*, you know."

"I'll lose a capable helper in my work. But your happiness is more important, of course."

"I'll say. Well, nice to see you back. If there is more you need done for your book, or anything else, give me a buzz. Don't work too hard now. Take care. Bye."

When Saiyue and Panzhe were still married, on a couple of occasions she had asked him to go to church with her. He would decline, saying that he did not mean to be irreverent or flippant, but he thought he'd have a lot of time with God later on. He figured he'd rather use the time in this world to do the things of this world, and trusted that God would forgive him if he'd begin to concern himself with matters of the other world when he got there.

Apparently this cavalier attitude of his underwent some changes since becoming unable to do a number of this-worldly things after the stroke. He had recently accompanied her to church a few times. He now had a Bible on his bedside shelf, and the tasseled bookmark crept down through the pages of the gospels. He told her that it was mainly the peaceful atmosphere and soothing music that attracted him, thus avoiding the need to talk about any other kinds of pull or motivation for the activity. She understood because that was what she used to say.

On Christmas Eve they went to Hillsdale United Church together. The worshipful ambience was seldom more heartwarming and hallowed than the sights and sounds on this night. The sanctuary was adorned with beds of white, gold and purple chrysanthemums, yellow and red poinsettias and hanging green boughs. Panzhe tried to sing along following the hymnal—some carols sounded familiar, and some not, from the reverential "O Come, All Ye Faithful" to the tender "What Child Is This."

At the end of the service, the congregation filed out of the sanctuary, each holding a candle, singing "Silent night, holy night!..." In the hallway, the candles were blown out, and in bright lights with the air smelling faintly of fishy wax and burnt wick, everybody wished everybody else a Merry Christmas, joyously but not boisterously.

Since Panzhe returned home from the hospital, she would give him a quick good night kiss before they went to sleep in their separate rooms. That kiss had moved down from the forehead, to the cheek, and lately to the lips. But it was very brief, essentially ritualistic, and devoid of emotion. This Christmas Eve, he tried to hold on to her, and let her go only after she, like a professional nurse, smilingly told him that she was there to look after his health only.

Nearing the year's end, Dr. Johnson concurred in Panzhe's returning to full-time work, starting from the winter term in January. The department chairman agreed that he would only do research and supervise theses, i.e., no classroom teaching.

On New Year's Eve, when Saiyue returned from work, he showed her a letter from the editor of the *International Journal of Numerical Methods for Engineering Science* informing them that their manuscript had passed the review process and was scheduled to be published in its September issue.

"Panzhe! This is my first real publication you know, in an international journal, no less. Thanks!" She gave him a hug.

"You could have a lot more if you want to go that route. You could do it," he said.

She gave him a double take, and said, "I don't know about that. But this is very nice."

In the evening they went to a New Year's Eve party at the Wus' house. It was full. Some 30 guests were seated at the long table in the dining room or one of the bridge or drop-leaf tables set up in the adjoining living room and family room. As they were about to start dinner, John Wu proposed a toast congratulating Panzhe on his rapid recovery.

He responded first with thanks and a toast to the Wus for hosting the party. After the drink and applause, he declared his thanks to John for taking him to the emergency room and to those who had sent him good wishes during his illness and recovery. "But I owe my rapid recovery mostly to one person," he continued, "who has taken care of me for the past several months. Here she is—Zhang Saiyue." Amid cheers, he turned to look at her. She was sitting to his right, head tilted, smiling with wide-eyed innocence.

"I drink this in your presence to attest my gratitude to her," he drained the goblet in his hand and showed her the emptied glass. Her eyes shone in its reflected light.

Apparently pleased, Saiyue turned to Karen Chi at her right, commenting in Mandarin, "Xiao ti da zuo!" Noting her friend's blank look, she suddenly remembered her limited acquaintance with Mandarin and said in English, "Panzhe made such a mountain out of a molehill." Her friend now smiled and said, "He was fortunate to have your care."

After the brief ceremony, as people began to eat, she said to him, "You are certainly talkative tonight," and looking at him sweetly, squeezed his hand under the table before picking up her chopsticks.

After dinner, apart from a few who preferred just to chat, there were bridge and mahjong groups, as well as dancing, and karaoke singing. The latter had of late become a fad among the Bay area Chinese American "yuppies"—although many of them weren't so young anymore. They'd sing both Chinese and American songs. Caught in the spirit of the moment, Saiyue sang freely with the group. She even soloed the old Chinese popular song: "*When Would My Gentleman Come Again?*" She also enjoyed singing with the group "*The Tennessee Waltz*" and liked the haunting tune.

The Wus' imitation crystal punch bowl had been refilled twice before midnight when champagne was served. The revelers counted down the seconds with the lowering ball at Times Square on TV. With the arrival of the

New Year, couples kissed and wished each other, and then everybody, a happy 1989! Panzhe even felt a flicker of her tongue between her warm lips.

On their way home both were in high spirits, she humming "*The Tennessee Waltz.*" After their good night kiss, she let him bury his head in her bosom. "Are you in shape?" she asked lightly holding him in her embrace.

"I am in good shape. Haven't you noticed that I've even discarded the cane." He wanted to find her breast.

"Let's go to your room," she said.

Speechless, they undressed and just held each other for a while. After they were united, he said to her, "God made you, and God made me." And passion took command.

Afterwards, she patted his back, "Bookworm, you have fully recovered!"

He had always considered the appellation an endearment. He had missed it so. Hoarsely he whispered to her ear, "Saiyue, marry me again!"

After a brief silence, she said, "Finally...." She was quiet again; then let out a sigh. "Panzhe, you are very sweet, a gentleman, and you will always have my gratitude and respect." Giving his cheek a kiss, she moved out from under him, saying, "We'll talk tomorrow. Let's catch some sleep."

They got up late the next morning. All day she did not bring up the subject of remarriage. Neither did he. In the evening, they joined a small party at the Chis. Returning home late, they said a simple good night to each other and retired to their separate rooms.

The following morning it drizzled, and a mist covered the ravine. Sibelius's *Andante festivo* flowing slowly from the radio, Panzhe was browsing the latest issue of *Newsweek*. Saibing came to him.

"Panzhe, some three months ago, I promised you that I would take care of you until you recovered. Now that you have, I am moving back to my house tomorrow. I don't want this to develop into a more difficult situation than I am already in now."

He listened like a convict before a sentencing judge. After looking at her for a few seconds, he wiped his face with his hand and said, "You know what I would like you to do. You also know that I will never try to stop you from what you really want to do.... Not because I wouldn't try; but I know it's useless," he smiled artlessly, as though amused by the recognition of his own plight.

"You talk as if I have an arctic heart. I don't," she said. "The other night you honored me, asking me to marry you again. But my circumstances are difficult. I hope you'll understand."

"Is it the boy?"

"My circumstances are difficult," she repeated.

The challenges and opportunities in computer utilization kept on growing. For her contributions, she had been promoted twice—up three grades since first joining John J. Clyde & Associates full time. After work she continued to find satisfaction in reading up on such nontechnical subjects as history and sociology. Occasionally on weekends she would have lunch with Mrs. McNamara or dine with Liu Rong. Panzhe had ceased calling her after she had declined his invitation a week following her moving out of his house, saying that she needed time to sort out her feelings.

In one of her more or less regular communications with Haosheng, she had mentioned in an offhand way that Panzhe had recovered and that she was done with his care. But when asked whether she would resume their *Hong Kong plan*, she maintained her position that it remain on the back burner for the same reason as that she had given Panzhe. Haosheng did not press either.

In his next letter, he told her that he and some associates had been planning to organize a business of their own. The following month he wrote her that the prospects of that plan looked better almost each day. He and two business friends had gotten verbal commitments from a number of investors for sufficient capital to form an import/export company with its headquarters in Hong Kong, and he would station in the United States—in the Bay area. With the size of investment involved, he should have no difficulty in getting a visa, and he expected all paper work to be completed in approximately two months. Then he proposed that they start planning their wedding after his arrival.

Outwardly she received the news placidly. But she felt her days of procrastination were numbered.

A few days after the letter, she received a phone call from him.

"Have you gotten my letter?" Haosheng asked.

"Yes."

"The one about my proposal for our wedding."

"Yes."

"Good. Something else I need to let you know. My father's health has taken a turn for the worse. As I had told you before, his heart condition has deteriorated since returning from that trip to Guangzhou last year. He tires even from washing his face in the morning. My mother, getting on with age herself, told me that she couldn't take care of both him and Xiao Ming for long. I have been wondering whether to ask my aunt to care for the boy. You remember my father's sister you had met in Nanjing?"

"Yes. But a great-aunt is no parent or even grandparent. The boy's care is no real problem. I'll get him here," she said.

"That could be an alternative, but the paper work will take time. Besides, I am not that sure whether it would be to his advantage to leave China so young. We talked about that before. A few more years later, he'll be old enough not to forget his Chinese tongue. In any case we can talk about that after I come to California."

Saiyue thought Haosheng might have a point regarding having the boy remain in China long enough in order to retain the language, but that issue was not relevant to the topic at hand, i.e., to relieve her ex-mother-in-law of the boy's care. "Well, he can live with my family in Shanghai. Grandpa would be glad to help. I am sure."

"That could be a workable idea."

She thought that again he sounded as though he had forgotten the boy was supposed to be under the joint guardianship of both parents. However, she didn't want to argue the point then.

The question regarding their son not quite settled, he said, "By the way, what do you think about our getting married soon after my arrival in California?"

She wondered why the tack. Going along with him, she said, almost resignedly, "I suppose we can work that one out. You are coming here anyway. Then wouldn't it be a good idea to have Xiao Ming come here too?"

"Well...Of course," he said.

"I can have my parents and grandpa take care of him until he leaves China. I can start the paper work tomorrow," she said.

"No need for that much of a rush. Moving the boy now away from Nanjing to Shanghai, and soon afterwards from Shanghai to America, would be unnecessarily disruptive for him. I think my mother can handle the situation a while yet. Why don't we start the paper work after our wedding. Then the petition to the American Immigration authorities would be a more compelling case. It won't be long now."

Saiyue had an unpleasant taste in her mouth. Even though she herself had been leaning in that direction, she thought Haosheng had again used Xiao Ming to push their remarriage. However, at the time she didn't feel like making an issue of it.

37

He was shaving on a warm Hong Kong morning in mid-May. A breeze puffed in from the open window, and a silvery line flashed above his forehead like a miniature lightning. He froze his twisted face, moved his head closer to the mirror, hunted down a white hair and pulled it out.

You are not getting any younger, Xu Haosheng! But you have worked hard. You are making progress....I am getting there. Just a few more signatures and drafts to go. Strange how a person, once bitten by the business bug, is never satisfied. Not that long ago, I was contented to work for the Mill, almost a glorified gopher—didn't realize it at the time though. Wayward as she has been, I have to give her credit for pushing me—*humiliating me* may be closer to the truth. She spurred me to leave the dead-end basketball court to join Zhong Xing. Learning English and business, going through phases of trainee, operative, and staff to assistant manager. Now on my way to becoming my own boss! And she, with all that technical training and graduate degree, is after all an engineer, and an engineer is always for hire, an employee. Me, my own boss! Why not? Cao Rushi has managed. Well, she isn't quite there yet either. Tiger still calls the shots. Their operations are much bigger though. I'll have a long way to go before getting in their league, even after I get this thing going. And I have to get it going first.

He patted some Aqua Velva on his face and brushed his hair. Tilting his head a few degrees, he stared at himself for a few seconds, and giving the cheek a gentle slap, he took leave of the mirror. After dressing himself, he strode out of the bedroom towards the dining table in the living/dining room. No breakfast on it yet. Ah Yu hurried in with the serving tray, apologizing, "Sorry, Mr. Xu, I'm late this morning. My brother came from Guangzhou last night. He said he had something important for me from my parents. Truthfully, I thought I could get it and return in time. Sorry, I'm a little late."

"That's all right. How is your brother?" He knew Ah Yu was quite proud of her studious brother in Guangzhou.

"Very well, he hopes to go to South China University next fall."

"That's great. How is Guangzhou?" He still had a bit of a soft spot for the city where he spent his childhood.

"Nothing special. But my brother did talk about demonstrations being organized by college students. You know, like those in Beijing on television. Truthfully, he also said that there would be similar demonstrations right here in Hong Kong to support those mainland students."

"I heard about it too," Haosheng said. He wondered how long would this demonstration business in Beijing go on; it had been simmering ever since Hu Yaoban[56] died. How come every time a big shot died, there would be turmoil? And Tiananmen seems to be the spot where people would go to vent their pent-up emotions. That time after Premier Zhou's death, even I almost went there with the school group.

"By the way," Ah Yu said, "did you ask the Telephone Company to check our phone?"

"No. Why? There is nothing wrong with our phone. I used it last night."

---

56. A leading "liberal" in the Chinese Communist Party. Died April 15, 1989. Students mourned his death at a rally in Tiananmen Square. That started the Tiananmen demonstrations that were to last until June, 1989.

"I know. Yesterday, there was this man. He said he was from the Telephone Company and wanted to check out our phone, and it had to do with the people upstairs. Truthfully I didn't understand it. But since he had the Phone Company's uniform on, I thought it'd be all right. He was here five minutes, at most ten, and left. Strange! I saw him again this morning. Truthfully, I am quite sure it's him, without the phone company technician's uniform though, sort of skulking around, between here and the corner of the road."

"Well, as long as he does not come to bother us again. Leave him alone." Haosheng was anxious to finish his breakfast and get on the road for the day's work.

He had a pretty good day. Had dinner with his associates and estimated with them that within two weeks, at most four, they should be ready to apply for registration with the Hong Kong government.

He drove his Honda Civic into the dimly lit apartment garage. Before he spiraled around to park, he noticed in the outside mirror a shadowy figure flicker past. He didn't give it any more thought than taking it to be just another tenant coming home. The car parked, Haosheng released and flipped aside the seat belt buckle, turned and stepped out. Noting that the buckle lying on the floor might not clear the door when being closed, he bent down to tuck it in. A streak of light flashed across the corner of his eye followed by a mix of a hissing and a shattering metallic sound.

He fell down. Another similar sound was heard. His body lay on the concrete floor, motionless. The shadowy figure moved slowly toward the body, the hand holding an object with an elongated tube, silhouetted against the faintly florescent Hong Kong night beyond the parapet wall that bounded the garage on three sides.

As the figure came near the body, the car door suddenly swung out flat smack against the approaching person. Haosheng in one motion flipped up and jumped on the backward stumbling man. A muffled shot hit the ceiling, spraying concrete chips. The two persons struggled and grunted.

Four hands were clamped together in a chunk around the gun with a silencer. Yet another muffled shot, the struggling shapes of the night momentarily froze into a black statue. Then one started to slump. Haosheng stood watching, the gun now in his hand. The other figure slid down and curled on the floor, a patch of his pongee shirt grew dark, and the darkness slowly spread.

"I am shot! Call a doctor. Save my life!" the curved body groaned.

"I could kill you now, you son of a turtle! What did I do to you that you'd try your virulent hand on me!"

"Nothing."

"Who sent you?"

"I don't know."

"You don't, eh?" Keeping an eye on the assassin, Haosheng opened the car door, which had been knocked shut during the struggle. Crouching, he reached in and got out a recorder that sometimes he used for his brainstorms or letters. He pressed the recording button. "Now tell me who sent you."

"I don't know. Get an ambulance! Save my life! Have mercy!"

"I'll do that as soon as you tell me who sent you. Tell the truth! You lie, and I lie about getting that ambulance. I'll enjoy watching you son of a turtle drown in your own blood!"

"Oh, uh, OK. OK....My big brother sent me."

"Who is your big brother? What's his name?"

"The big brother of my society."

"What society?"

"I can't tell you."

"As I told you, I am just going to stand here and wait until you do, or you leave for hell first!"

"OK. OK....It's some Lao-ban. He wants the job done. Oh...uh...oh..." The man was obviously in pain.

"What's the Lao-ban's name?"

"They call him...Guo Tiger."

Haosheng was stunned for a moment. If he called the police, his conflict with Tiger would become irreconcilable, and chances were that he would be the loser in the end. In that case, he'd be better off leaving Hong Kong. But he had no real choice. He had shot a man who would surely die if he did not call for help.

"Now, say it clearly. Again, who sent you to kill me?" Haosheng moved the recorder closer to the man's mouth.

"A man named Guo Tiger."

He checked the playback, went inside the apartment and called the police.

Even as he was calling the police, he realized that the incident shouldn't be a total surprise to him. He recalled that night at the Harbor City Restaurant and Nightclub when Saiyue was visiting. Nearing the end of an intermission of the floorshow, Yuan Lao-bang had signaled him to follow him. Under a dim red light over the emergency exit near the gentlemen's rest room, Yuan said, "Lao Xu, this has nothing to do with business, and indeed nothing to do with me. But we are friends; I like you and don't want to see you get hurt. There is something I think you ought to know."

"Go ahead. You know I respect your opinion," Haosheng said.

"It has to do with Lian Fa Company. The word is that its owner, or the controlling shareholder anyway, won't tolerate anyone fooling around with the Company's president. He'll be severe with the offender."

"Yuan Lao-bang, you can be more direct with me than that. Rose and I *were* close friends. That was a long time ago—before our separate marriages. Now here in Hong Kong, our relationship is strictly business. In fact, I don't mind telling you that within a week after I first arrived in Hong Kong, someone phoned to warn me about the same matter. A lot more bluntly than you just did."

"Did you believe him?"

"I certainly did. Actually, as you probably know, when our firms had dealings, it was my boss she talked to, unless he was out of town. In any case, she and I have no personal relations. None," Haosheng said.

"I am glad. Mind you, all this has nothing to do with me. I am doing this for friends. Everything is fine! Hey-hey-hey-hey!" Then he continued with a mock serious face, "And now, another word of advice from a friend. If I were you, I'd watch my behavior if I want my ex-wife to be my wife again. She is quite a lady," he smiled with a confidential nod like an impressed connoisseur.

"I know what you mean, but we men have needs. As the sage said, 'Food and sex are nature.' So sometimes I had to buy a meal. Right?...But back to the original point, I know better than to finger the whiskers of a tiger."

"As I said, everything is fine! Hey-hey-hey-hey!"

Indeed I have kept my word, Haosheng thought, except perhaps on one occasion, and even that was essentially a business affair. He recalled that meeting with Rose across a small table in a cafe of the Peninsula Hotel.

"I appreciate your help. For this job, I can't trust anybody else," Rose said.

"I am glad to be of help to you. You know that. After you talked to me, I got on it as soon as I could. It took a bit of doing to find the identities of the drawers of those checks. As you suspected, both drawers were women. Here are their pictures that you wanted. The addresses are on the back."

Taking over two snapshots, Rose looked at them and sneered. "Who or what are they?" she said.

"The one with short hair is Wanda. She is a call girl, lives in Kowloon. I tracked her down myself. The one with the long hair is named Pearl. She is a tour guide in Bangkok. I had someone find her there," he said.

"Who is this someone?"

"A business acquaintance of mine. There is no risk involved here. He is an overseas Chinese, who grew up in Thailand. Living in Hong Kong now, he travels regularly to Bangkok on business."

"I see."

"Back to Wanda, I managed to talk to her quite a bit."

"Turned on your charm, no doubt," Rose said.

"I did feign an interest in her, for the mission's sake. Anyway she admitted that Tiger would visit her once, certainly no more than twice a week. Each time no more than a couple of hours."

"What else?"

"You want some of the lurid details?...OK....She said she knew his type. Complaining about his wife's frigidity and that sort of routine. Wanda even elaborated some. She would groan, tighten, gasp and scream a little."

"I didn't know he was that capable," she said ironically.

"You know that her faking gave him confidence and her a monthly check. Even that, in case you feel cheated, she actually mocked him as a baby Panda for his groping," he chuckled lightly.

"Interesting, our *tiger* is a baby panda," she smiled with disdain.

"The case in Bangkok is similar. Now what are you going to do with all this information," he asked.

"Nothing!" she said. "I'll just keep the pictures, for now. You know, I thought if he's going to spend money, he'd at least get some pretty ones. I don't mean to be immodest. I'd prefer my own face to these."

"Come now! How could you demean yourself so—compare with them! In no respect can either hold a candle to you, face or otherwise. You had told me that before you married him, Tiger, the sharp and able Vice Director of the Northwest Electrical Company, acted like a clown when he found himself alone with you. And even before that, I had told you that you have a reputation of an intimidating presence for men. My guess is that your beauty and person continued to overwhelm him after your marriage. He probably had some kind of complex when in the bedroom with you." Smiling, Haosheng seemed to enjoy his Freudian role.

"I don't know about what complex. But away from business, I find his tiger epithet almost pathetic. He probably knows that," she said.

"That is why he has been trying to recoup his confidence and manly dignity with other women," he continued with his theory.

"With money, actually....Whatever, but regarding your theory about me, you were not intimidated," she eyed him straight, challenge-like.

"That was way back in Xi'an. I am a little now," he said.

"There is no need," she looked at him softly.

He felt a couple of taps—of her heel—on his calf under the table. "But I am a lot more intimidated by Tiger and his rough friends."

There was a pause. "Well, thank you again. How much do I owe you?"

"Nothing. I did this for old time's sake."

"There must be considerable expenses. I should reimburse you."

"All are minor items. In any case, it's all right. I can handle them," he said.

"Well, I owe you one. I'll leave now. Perhaps you want to wait a few minutes before you do."

In the living room, with subdued lighting, of a small elegant house by Repulse Bay, Rose Cao Ju was watching television. She and her husband Ju Tiger had had dinner, served by a maid, during which they had hardly exchanged a word.

His restlessness annoyed her. He had been pacing around the house, in and out of the living room, the study, and the foyer.... Now he sat stiffly on a sofa, vacantly eyeing the TV screen. A telephone rang. He jumped up and ran toward the study. Before he got to the door, he stopped, realizing it was from the TV. "His mother's!" he cursed and returned to the sofa. He sat there for a few minutes before rushing into the study again. In a little while he was back to the living room, looking out the window over the shadowy beach and the dark waters of the bay.

Surely something is wrong, Rose thought. I don't like it. He has been behaving rather strangely lately. What's going on? All our businesses are doing well, at least those involving the firm. It must be some deal I don't know about. I thought I knew about all his doings, including those sluts. She turned off the TV and said,

"Ju Jun," she had always addressed her husband by his full name—a practice, which she had kept ever since he began courting her, to indicate her indifference to his power and position. "What's the matter with you lately? You seem so antsy. What's bothering you?"

"Nothing!" he said impatiently.

"Don't treat me as a child. Something is the matter. Why don't you tell me? Perhaps I can help."

"I told you nothing is the matter. I don't need your help. I've got all the help I need. You, in fact—"

"What?" she prompted.

"You!…Forget it! I'll tell you the whole story later. I am waiting for a phone call."

"Why?"

"Why? Why? You just won't quit. Will you?" he snapped at her. "*You are the problem*. I want people to know, never fool around with Tiger's wife!"

"Who fools around with your wife?"

"Interesting that you'd ask. Need I name him? I am a reasonable man. Obviously I can't blame him for the relation between you two before our marriage. I even ignored the rumors in Xi'an after our marriage. Because they were just that, rumors. I don't suppose it could amount to too much since it was such a short period. But it's different now in Hong Kong. We all live here. And I had warned him before."

"You mean Xu Haosheng?"

"Is there anyone else?"

"Well, true, before I married you, we were intimate once," Rose said, "But—"

"Don't say *intimate* in my face!" he shouted.

"You don't have to shout. It won't make your case, nor you, any stronger," she said calmly. "There has been nothing private between him and me in Hong Kong."

"Oh yes? So what were you two doing in the Peninsula Hotel…some weeks ago while I was away."

"Some weeks?"

"Say, three."

"Three weeks ago?"

"Are there other times?"

"Oh, that! We just discussed business."

"You discuss business in a hotel? Why not just by phone or in either one's office?"

"Well, if you must know, there's some private business."

"Uh huh! Now that sounds more truthful! Like what?"

"Like about you."

"Me....?"

"Yes. I had him find out to whom you were writing those monthly checks drawn on a private account of yours—hidden from me—with the Commercial Bank of Southeast Asia," Rose said.

"Of all the people in the world, why did you ask him?"

"In this particular matter, he seemed to be the person I could trust the most, for your sake and mine," she said. "Ju Jun, next time before you change your old brief case, make sure all the loose bank statements of your secret accounts have been taken out."

"You have been searching my brief case?"

"Normally no, but at the time you changed to a new one, I just checked the old one to be thrown out and found those bank statements in the secret compartment. In any case, that was a more reasonable thing to do than having me tailed."

"I didn't send anybody to tail you. It was reported to me by my associates."

"You mean those 'society brothers'?"

"They are not brothers. They are operatives."

"Whatever they are, they weren't competent, not doing a thorough enough job."

"How do you mean?"

"If they were, they would have known and reported to you that Xu Haosheng and I just had tea and talked in the hotel cafe. Nothing to get excited about."

"Are you telling me that you two went to a hotel just to have a cup of tea and to talk in the cafe?"

"Lots of people do. As I told you, I asked him to find out more about those checks that you wrote. Would you like to see pictures of your girlfriends?"

Tiger fell silent; his eyes and nose and mouth all worked. "His mother's!" He shouted and hightailed to his study. Soon she heard him talking over the phone and starting to yell, "His mother's! Call it off!... Try! His mother's! Listen to me! Try! Call it off!" He hung up. The house was suddenly quiet. Only the sound of surf was heard, getting louder.

In the wee hours of the next morning, a team of Hong Kong police knocked on the door of the Repulse Bay house. Let in, they told Tiger, "You are under arrest for conspiracy to commit murder." Before he left with them, Tiger called Huang Dawei, a well-known solicitor under retainment by Lian Fa Company.

The distinguished solicitor was unable to free Tiger on bond, because of the gravity of the case and concern that the suspect might try to flee the island. In the jail's visitor's room, the solicitor told Tiger not to worry; he would work out something to bring the Chinese government into the case. And he comforted Tiger further: he would try to convince the prosecutor that the government couldn't win the case in court on the word of a small-time gangster against that of a well-established businessman. The solicitor might have a point there. However, it was never put to a test.

The following dawn a police officer and Huang Dawei came to the Ju house. Rose received them without makeup. She was shocked as they informed her of her husband's death. They explained to her that in the night his foul mood and limited command of the Cantonese dialect got him into a scuffle with a cell-mate, who had just been put in there, drunk and perhaps also under the influence of other substances—which might explain his unusual strength. He held Ju and banged his head against a flat steel bar of the cell grille and fractured his skull; he never regained consciousness and died in the hospital.

Later on, she also read from *Xing Dao Daily* that, on the same night of Ju Tiger's demise, the accused assassin of Xu Haosheng had died under the mysterious circumstances of a heart attack. It was reported to be caused by a rare reaction to a sedative drug administered by the hospital staff intravenously.

Two weeks after Ju's funeral, in a booth of a tea house on Tai Wai Road in the outskirts of Kowloon a man and a woman were talking earnestly. The woman wore sunglasses and was so plainly dressed that she might be taken as a sales woman with a sore eye. The man's black trousers and white shirt were almost identical with those of at least half a dozen or so male customers in that lower middle class eatery.

"Are you all right?" he asked.

"I am fine," the woman with the luscious lips said. "Busy though, so many items need to be taken care of. But I think the able solicitor finally saw the light that it's in his interest to be on my side."

"I had thought he would be able to get Tiger out on bond before he became embroiled with that drunk," Haosheng said.

"He tried. It didn't work. The police said Tiger might flee. Huang said that since the fall of Tiger's relatives in Beijing, he had no pull with the Chinese government; moreover, the current demonstrations in Tiananmen had made the Hong Kong Government more wary and stringent. It was bad luck for him. The assassin had died in the hospital. Huang thought that he was poisoned by his own associates. The government would have no case on Tiger. He'd be scot-free," Rose said.

"And I'd have to flee," he rhymed.

"Well, let the dead bury the dead....How are you doing?" she said.

"Not bad. Busy with plans for setting up that business. We still need to hear from Indonesia....Getting there though." He wouldn't want to talk business so soon but for the fact that over the phone she had told him the meeting would concern business only. He had qualms about her meeting him just two weeks after her husband's funeral.

"So you are going ahead with that—moving to America."

"Yes, unless something extraordinary develops here."

"What do you mean?" she asked.

"Well, nothing in particular. You are almost the sole owner of Lian Fa Company now. Aren't you?" The thought that she might propose marriage, or something along that line, had crossed his mind before coming to the rendezvous.

"Yes, with Tiger's shares coming to me. That will be the case—no matter how many times his cousins call from Beijing, making ridiculous statements. I can handle them, or now rather Huang Dawei can. This is Hong Kong, a place of law."

"Can I help?" Haosheng asked.

"Yes, I think so."

"As I told you before, I don't intend to remain married to Zhang Saiyue for long. Just want this wayward woman to have a taste of the feeling of being dumped."

A moment of silence fell between them.

"I suppose she's the only one who hasn't tasted that. But you can dump her now if you want," she said.

"It's not the same. But, as I said—"

"Haosheng," she interrupted, "I am not saying that you were proposing a moment ago. But speaking for myself, I don't want to get married now, not only because it doesn't look right. I've my freedom, and I like it. I'll be frank with you. I like your company. I'd like you to stay in Hong Kong and forget about your smart engineer ex-wife in America." She paused for a couple of seconds and continued, "I'll offer you a Vice Presidency of Lian Fa Company provided you sign a contract, with a signing bonus of 5000 shares, to stay at least three years. In case you are interested, the latest quotation is HK$295 a share. During that time you'll work only for the firm, but at the end of it, you'll get 15,000 shares. Of course, those are in addition to the regular monthly salary and benefits comparable to the market."

"What happens at the end of three years?" he asked.

"We'll see then. By that time, I might want to move to America myself," she said. "You can't ignore 1997 forever. Anyway, we can talk about that in due time."

Haosheng did some rough calculations, at the end of three years, the shares alone would be worth almost a million US$. How come the women that matter to me are all so tough? he thought. In a way he was glad, and even proud, and then a feeling of sadness came over him,

"Where is the soft poetess Cao Rushi?"

"I never wrote a poem that's worth the name," Rose said. "But I know what you mean. Let's not dwell in the past. We are having better lives now. Aren't we?"

"How about our tender feelings for each other?"

"That's a separate matter. This is business. I told you before we got here, this would be a business meeting....I suppose we don't really have to hide or fear anything. But I think if we are to have a relationship, we should be discrete. No point in offending the sensibilities of society in its face."

He told her that he'd think about it.

38

Since Saiyue first came to the United States, she had heard some Chinese (Charlie Hua among them) say that Americans weren't really that interested in or concerned about affairs in China. These complainers can't say that this time, she thought. Americans would watch the goings-on every night on television. Even Todd Jensen—who seemed to have no other interest apart from company business than the San Francisco Giants and Forty-Niners—asked her about it this morning. *It* being the student demonstrations at Tiananmen Square in Beijing.

This evening she returned home from work late. She changed her street shoes to slippers and turned on the TV in the living room. In the kitchen she pressed down the rice cooker switch and grabbed a Coke from the refrigerator. "Now in Beijing's Tiananmen Square..." She hurried back to the living room and sat down on the sofa to watch.

Hundreds of makeshift tents, like bamboo shoots after a spring rain, pitched on the vast grounds in front of the ancient Gate of Heavenly Peace, crowned with the double-deck golden serrate roofs with upturned eaves and flanked by stout claret walls. A sea of humanity. Groups of spectators—some wearing sunglasses, some visors, a few with caps, and many with the ubiquitous black handbags. A little boy, wearing a look too heavy for his tender age, in the arms of an old man with a white goatee, but not old enough to lose the light of excitement in his eyes. All crowd together to watch the students.

These mostly hatless, black-haired students in white shirts put themselves forward for their cause, reminding her of a photograph, which she had seen in a history museum, of earlier protesters in olden style gentlemen's long gown and tunic, the grandfathers or great grandfathers of the present generation. They had gathered exactly 70 years ago on the same site before the same august edifice, demonstrating for their cause[57] —a nation free from foreign domination and dedicated to modernize herself through democracy and science.

Here come the marchers. Along the broad boulevard—it's the capital's Chang'an (Eternal Peace) Road, lined with tall posts, each with a cluster of spherical lamps like giant white pearls—dozens abreast process slowly, row after unending row. Banners and streamers—white with black characters, red with gold—raised on held staffs, announce themselves—workers, newsmen, monks, PLA soldiers, teachers, and of course students of universities, institutes, school after school.

There are bicycles, microphones, megaphones, trumpets, newspapers, magazines, food, cotton comforters, first-aid boxes, ambulances, and…flowers.

A bespectacled young man is speaking and gesturing zealously with a Caucasian man, apparently a foreign reporter, surrounded by a group of the speaker's wide-eyed colleagues. Others are resting, sitting down on the ground, hands clasped over knees drawn-in, staring with a determined, pugnacious, thoughtful, or even sagacious face, like those of the terra-cotta warriors she saw in Xi'an.

A young woman and a young man are dancing, with remarkable grace to the strumming of a guitar, in a mixed style of Iberian flamenco and

---

57. The protest was triggered by the decision of the Allies, at the Versailles Peace Conference ending World War I, to transfer Germany's rights in China's Shandong province to Japan, instead of returning them to China. (Both China and Japan had joined the Allies against Germany.)

Chinese rice-seedling choreography, or is it a blend of the classical Chinese dance and the Mexican Folklore ballet she saw in Cancun. It appears as though the whole business were a picnic.

A picnic! "A revolution is no picnic," so said the one whose portrait hangs there below the white balustrades of the terrace above the Gate. Hence, this is no revolution. But a plea? He had also said that he was "a monk with an umbrella overhead, heedless of law and heaven,"[58] leaving no doubt about his fearless spirit contending for his goal. And what a goal it was!

Like Sun Yat-sen and Chiang Kai-shek, he had striven to lead China to become a modern nation free from social injustice and foreign subjugation. He had done much. However it is reckoned, undeniably the effects are of first order. If he were alive, as he watches the scene on the Square, how would he, a scholar of history among other accomplishments, compare these students with their predecessors who had helped him to defeat Chiang Kai-shek, as their predecessors had helped Chiang to defeat the warlords earlier in the century?

These restless sons and daughters of the warriors of Emperor Qin Shihuang, and the sons and daughters of the poets of Tang, and of the beautiful women of Jiang-nan, and of the toiling masses of the ages in the valleys and basins of the Yellow and Yangzi rivers—what do they want?

See the banners flapping in the wind: "Down with Corruption!" "Freedom!" "Democracy!" A white banner covers a bus: "The Heart of the People Cannot Be Insulted!" Yet another, a huge one, proclaiming "The Soul of China!" waves broadly on top of the Museum of Chinese Revolution to the east of the Square.

The television camera returned to the reporter. He emphasized again the potential significance of the scene, followed by his concern over the

---

58. The pun, in Chinese homonyms, consists of "law" (men's law) for "hair" that a monk has none, and "heaven" (heaven's law) for "sky" that the monk is blind to because of the umbrella. Thus, the term denotes one who heeds neither men's nor heaven's law—an arrant rebel.

sanitary condition of the place and the weather forecast of rain and possible storm. Then in a brief panned scene, Saiyue thought she had a glimpse of her brother Sailong standing among a small crowd. Her heart jumped. She sharpened her focus, but the image was gone. No, it can't be; he is in Shanghai, she told herself.

The segment on Beijing was followed by a commercial of United Airlines. Saiyue sat there a while to calm herself. She got up and turned the TV off. An urge seized her as suddenly as the silence in the room. She went up to the window, gazed out into the heavens, and said, "Lift up their hearts! Grasp the moment! Help Democracy come! Protect these young men and women from sunburn, night chill and storms!"

The Sunday service at Hillsdale United Church was over. It was a lovely morning in late May. Saiyue was talking with Mrs. McNamara on the portico. A pair of blue jays flew past the terrace and over the hedges across the street. Saiyue saw Panzhe tarrying there, seemingly waiting for someone.

She recalled seeing him in the past month a couple of times after service, leaving the sanctuary ahead of her. By the time she was out of the hall with the slow stream of worshippers, he had disappeared. She surmised that he was avoiding her. Lately she had wanted to talk and thought of calling him. Then considering that Xu Haosheng was coming, she refrained. It would just complicate things.

Today after quickly taking leave of her old lady friend, she walked over, "Panzhe, are you waiting for someone?"

"Hi! Yes, I have been waiting for you."

"Is anything the matter?"

"No. Just that I haven't seen you for a while. Thought that I might buy you a dinner," and he hastened to add, "Please understand I am not proposing a date, just a dinner together as old friends."

He sounded like a high school boy fearing rejection, she thought and felt a stab of sorriness. "Of course, Panzhe. I'd like that. Anytime you say."

"Are you free tonight?"

"Yes."

"How about I meet you at seven at Charlie Brown?"

"I'll be there."

She arrived at the restaurant at seven twenty. "I am sorry I am late. I was talking to Liu Rong and lost track of time."

"It's all right," Panzhe said. "I trust she's fine. I understand she's doing rather well in the real estate business."

"Yes, that part is true. But today we talked about something else—something money can't buy."

"There are lots of things money can't buy," he smiled wryly.

"She and I were talking about health," she said. "She had a biopsy surgery on a breast four days ago. As I was about to leave, she returned my earlier call to her."

"Is she OK?"

"Yes. Fortunately, the tumor was benign. Nevertheless, it was a trying experience for her, she said, particularly in the night, wondering about the results, and she said that it put things in perspective for her."

"I can relate to that feeling," he said.

"So we went on talking and I forgot the time. That's my excuse for being late....Sorry," she said.

"No need to apologize. That was a valid excuse, if you needed one....Along the health line, I guess you didn't know that your former department chairman, Professor Duan, had been hospitalized twice recently for a bleeding ulcer."

"Former? No, I didn't. I hope he is all right," she said.

"He is back to work now. But he has resigned from the chairmanship."

The waitress came and took their orders.

"I knew Dr. Duan had an ulcer problem. I recall you told me once that he had *promised* to double the size of his department? I think it'll do him good to be relieved of that kind of pressure—after all, health is the foundation of life in this world," she said.

"As the saying goes, 'Keep the green hill, and there'll always be fagot for cooking,'" Panzhe said.

"Right. You know his case sort of lends support to a recent decision I made."

"Yes?"

"A couple of months ago, I met at a computer conference an executive of an engineering firm in St. Louis, Missouri. He called me later, asking whether I'd like to join them."

"Interesting."

"Subsequently, I learned that his firm is appreciably smaller than John J. Clyde. If I go there, I'd be responsible for organizing and leading a computer group. There would be a sizable salary increase and a *promotion* to section head or something."

"Did you accept it?"

"The title doesn't mean much. It's just some internal thing; they can call you anything they want—at no cost to them and no real benefit to me. The salary was tempting. But they are not as well established as John J. Clyde. Anyhow, I finally declined the offer," she said.

"The money didn't do it then."

"No. I had considered that, at my present job, in order to do the work properly I have been as busy as I ever want to be on a regular basis. I already have to put in more than 40 hours a week, 45…50, sometimes more. For us tagged as professionals, there is no overtime pay—company rule. I can imagine the pressure I would be subjected to if I took the St. Louis job. No free lunch, you know."

"It's nice to know that you are in demand though. Not everyone would give up a 'sizable' increase in income."

"Well, 35% or so is sizable. However, this little episode did lead to a small increase at John J. Clyde. Somehow they got wind of it and gave me the increase to *encourage* me to stay," Saiyue said, and lowering her head, added lightly, "Besides, I like California."

"I am sure you can be a good leader and administrator if you want to be," he said.

"You talk as though you want me to leave California," she sounded peevish. "I am not averse to advancement. But right now, I think I'd rather keep up with technical progress than worry about the productivity of my colleagues. In time maybe I'll give it a try. Actually my material life is good enough for me as it is. I enjoy the things I do in my spare time. If I surrender that, what kind of life will that be? You have to keep a balance.... However, I wouldn't stand on my desk and shout about it."

The waitress brought the drinks.

"You are wiser than your age," Panzhe said. "Let us drink to your health and happiness," he lifted the glass and looked softly at Saiyue.

"To yours too." She gave him her caltrop smile and they drank up. "After all, you were my teacher."

"I never taught you much about computers," he said.

"You are dissembling. You know what I mean.... How are you doing?"

He clamped his lips and moved his fingers across his forehead deliberately as though to smooth its wrinkles. "Oh, I am all right. I have been rather busy, actually. Got a lot done though. Let me see.... I returned the galley proof of the book to the printer a week ago. Before that, I had to send out the technical report of the project. Also have gone through three theses in the last month. By the way, I visited Sharon three weeks ago, just for a weekend. She sent you her regards."

"How is she?"

"Fine. In fact, she got a pretty good year-end bonus for the work she did while you were helping me during my convalescence. Like me, she is very grateful for your help."

"That's nice. I mean her bonus.... Now, report sent, book done, theses read, daughter visited. It sounds like you are preparing to die or something." She caught herself abruptly. "Sorry, Panzhe, the uncultured, raw side of my Socialist upbringing showed again."

"That's all right. The outside is not important. A crude diamond is better than a polished rhinestone."

"I am not sure what you mean, except that I am crude....Anyway, my apology."

"No need. I should apologize—I didn't mean you are crude. I meant you are natural. But, truly, there were occasions that I didn't mind the thought of dying, peacefully though. But they were rare. These days I feel I have 'miles to go before I sleep.'"

"That's a lot better. What I meant before was that it sounded like you were winding up things in preparation for some big event."

"Oh.... There is no *big event* for me," he wiped his face with his hand and shook his head lightly. "Talking about big event, by the way, what do you think about those young people in Beijing these days?"

Saiyue was momentarily unprepared for this sudden change of subject. But she was more than interested in the new topic. After a pause, "You know," she said, twisting and adjusting herself a little in the seat, "Before I got here, I had thought that that would be the first thing we'd be talking about tonight.... What can I say about them? I have seldom been more stirred in my life. I have nothing but admiration for those young hunger strikers, putting their future careers, perhaps even their lives, on the line. You have to give people their due when they put their lives on the line. Watching all those hundreds of hunger strikers and thousands more who have knowingly placed themselves in jeopardy in order to support the strikers, I would say, 'Don't you worry about China, even if these young men and women fail this time.'"

"I too was exhilarated by the scenes on TV," he said. "But after the emotion quieted down a bit, I am not as optimistic as some American reporters there who seemed to see this as a peaceful revolution. You know the American network news went over there to cover the Gorbachev visit and sort of stumbled onto this thing. Dan Rather and Charles Kuralt of CBS said the obvious—that we are witnessing history. What a bonanza for them as newsmen! But it's probably even a greater break for the demonstrators—all that free publicity!"

"Yes," Saiyue followed, "To have the whole world see that not all Chinese are selfish, small-minded, and can't see beyond the material interest of themselves and their families. Did you see on TV that young woman, who, months pregnant, left Chicago for China to join the students?"

"Yeah, it was moving," he said.

"Just between you and me, it abashes me to watch them—and I don't usually get abashed easily."

A faint smile flickered past his face.

She pursued, "I am embarrassed that I played no part in this, no more than that server over there," jerking her head in the direction of a nodding waitress at another table who was writing down orders while leaning her weight on her back foot. "You know, I thought I saw my brother there on TV."

"Really, marching in Beijing?"

"No, among a small group of bystanders. But I am not sure it was he. As I told you he lives in Shanghai. But it would be kind of nice if it was he."

"All these happenings are heartening so far," Panzhe said. "But somehow I have an uneasy feeling. I watched the scenes of the meeting between the student leaders and the government leaders. Frankly, I wish the students would be a little more mannerly—"

"Whose side are you on anyway?" Saiyue interrupted.

"Relax," he smiled. "I wish there were no sides—"

"You sound like a typical sentimental, fence-sitting, petty bourgeoisie intellectual," she said.

"That was a mouthful. But I plead guilty to all that. Seriously, I am on the side of the Chinese people. However, I question the maturity of those student leaders. After all, China is a large and complex country, and it is no simple matter to organize, keep the peace, and administer her affairs. Imagine the number of mouths that need to eat each day....I don't know how this whole drama will play out....I am concerned about the news that marshal law may be imposed."

"I am too. My brother may be there. Perhaps I ought to call Grandpa to ask."

"I thought you said it would be nice if he was there."

"I said that. Didn't I?...I'll let you in on a secret," Saiyue lowered her voice, "I said my first private prayer in my life—all by myself—on their behalf, on everybody's behalf."

"That's more than I have done....Hum, surely, people over there have a lot more at stake than you and I. What's at stake for us?...What gives us, living in American security and comforts, the right to pass judgment on either side? That being said, as a point of goodwill opinion, I think it would be wise for the student leaders to be more conciliatory than they have been thus far. If there are violent changes, the stability of the nation may be threatened; the gains, economic and of other kinds, of the last 15 years or so could be jeopardized."

"The older generation always talks about stability and uses it to suppress progress," she said.

"I know I am old."

"Come on! Don't be so sensitive! I don't mean you personally." She gave him an assuring smile.

"That's OK....Your remark is a fair one. A moment ago, you expressed a more mellow view of personal life. I believe that, regarding China's national life, in time you'd also be more patient and mellow, and see it in a longer perspective. Like you, I also think that China should have a democratic system. The trick is how to accomplish that by nonviolent means, introducing changes gradually, but persistently."

"How do you propose to do that?"

"I am an applied mechanist—not a politician or statesman," he smiled.

"I know. Your mechanist's response is certainly less emotional than most. But it sounds rather idealistic to me. As you know, it's unlikely that people in authority—in a non-democratic system—would yield power willingly. They yield only to pressure," she said.

"I agree. That pressure will increase naturally with the enlightening of the populace at large—not just the students—through education and freedom of information. With advances in electronic communications, we are entering the so-called information age, you know."

The waitress came and served the food.

They went on to talk about the problems of China's political system. Nearing the end of that topic, they had finished the food and were drinking coffee. Panzhe said, "Often at a dinner party, John Wu, others and I, like a lot of other new Chinese Americans, would indulge ourselves in chatting about the history and politics of China. I suppose our discussion tonight is little different from those kinds—neither of us would know any more about the subject after the session than before....But tonight I have the feeling that you are not the same person as when you completed your MS degree....Have those readings on history and sociology had something to do with it?"

"It's all very elementary and superficial for the initiated, I suppose. But for me, it has been broadening, yes," she said.

"Don't be modest. I know your mind is like an eagle with the talons to grasp and maw to digest."

"Am I that fierce to you?" She frowned.

"Sorry, no invidious comparison is intended. I mean only that your aptitude is not limited to technical subjects. You hadn't spent the time to think about non-technical subjects before. Now, you seem to be putting part of your mind on them, and I can notice the difference," he said.

"You are greatly over-estimating me," she was smiling now. "I am just trying to imitate you—*trying to grow*. Didn't I tell you only a while ago, that you were my teacher? Didn't you tell us that 'If you don't progress, you regress.'"

"You mean that 'Learning is like rowing upstream' metaphor. I told the class mainly with reference to modern technology, the need to keep up—all within the framework of making an honorable living," he said.

"Panzhe, that's a one-dimensional growth!" she said protestingly.

"What can I say? You are right."

They fell into silence, for a moment.

"Remember the time I asked for your help after the tour in Xi'an?" she said. "It seems such a long time ago. Practically all my goals then have been reached. My degree, my job—"

"You had those at the time of our divorce," he commented.

"Yes, yes..." she sounded flustered. "I mean, you know what I mean....one-dimensional..."

"I think I do. And the world isn't one-dimensional."

"What do you mean?" she said defensively.

"I know you did miss Xiao Ming dearly, and of course still do," he said.

She was relieved that Rahimi or Dalton did not enter into the conversation. "If you mean my breaking up the Xu family that time, it wasn't I who started it." As she had on a number of occasions before, she had a notion of telling Panzhe about Cao Rushi, but thought it irrelevant. Her head lowered, eyes on the spoon being thoughtfully turned, she said slowly, "I want you to know that what followed was not just of passing interest to me. It is a beautiful part of my life. I will always cherish that."

He did not respond.

She continued. "By the way, Xu Haosheng is coming to the Bay area to set up a business office." She felt that that moment was as good as any to let him know.

"Oh yeah?...I understand." Expressionless, he didn't seem particularly surprised or discomfited either.

"Before he comes, I would like to repay you tonight's dinner," she said.

"Er....That's not necessary."

Saiyue studied the coffee cup and hoped for more from him. None came.

"How is Nora?" She broke the silence as she lifted her face to look at him.

"What?…Nora? At the school?" He was surprised and wondered at the absence of a teasing or mocking tone.

"Yes."

"I heard that she had gone to Paris with her ex-husband."

"Oh."

She took a closer look at him. He has his hair grown longer than before, now running behind his ears and touching the open collar. Streaks of gray at the temples. Getting older some. A somewhat ruddy complexion, quite unlike that of someone who has had a serious illness not that long ago. A few etched lines here and there, but the countenance is as serene as she had ever seen it since Xi'an. Those book knowledge, titles—Dr., Professor—papers and awards are not all that big a deal. Scores of universities each have hundreds of them, and turn out hundreds more every year. But here this person, at bottom, is a good man, good to me at least.

She suppressed a sigh. "Panzhe!" her eyes lambent with tenderness and her mouth contorted a little.

"Yes."

"I wish I could split myself into two halves."

They looked at each other deeply. Nothing added.

Out of the restaurant, they walked to the parking lot's edge overlooking the bay. It was a full moon tonight. Gauzy clouds like Chang-E's[59] sash floated over the jade ball, and below, silken streaks glimmered on the dark waters. On land the automobiles moved on the lit roads like blood corpuscles flowing in its veins. Across the bay quivering dots of light spread sparse and far, joining the stars.

She turned, gazed into the distant deeps, as though trying to reach, across the moonlit hills and ocean, that ancient country now in the throes of being reborn, Nanjing, Shanghai, Xi'an…and whispered, "So near and so far."

---

59. "Moon goddess" in Chinese mythology.

She put her arm in his and leaned her head against his shoulder. He turned, hugged her, pressed her back toward him, and lodged his head between her neck and shoulder, while she clasped her arms around him.

"I'll call you about the dinner," she said lightly.

"Don't worry about repaying tonight's dinner. Take care of yourself."

When they let go of each other, their eyes glistened in the moonlight over San Francisco Bay.

39

The following Wednesday afternoon, Saiyue returned home and went through her routine of changing shoes, getting the pop, etc. She turned on the TV, took a drink, sat on the sofa and began to go through the day's mail. After the monthly electricity bill and bank statement, an envelope addressed by handwriting appeared, its upper left corner indicating Lu Panzhe. She straightened herself to read it.

"Dear Saiyue:

Almost nine months ago, although my body was partially paralyzed, my mind was clear. In fact, I think, it was clearer than usual. Lying on the gurney and surrounded by that stark whiteness of the emergency room, I thought I was going to die. But I was not afraid; I felt strangely peaceful. In that moment I remembered you and the sweetness of our life together, our sharing of tenderness as well as passion of the night. And in the fresh air of some early mornings, we had our breakfast on the patio, listening to the cardinals' call and watching the sun slowly gild the hill across the ravine. And the gliding blue jays reminded me of the magpies we saw together at the Longevity Hall site. I shudder to think how lonesome and sad would I be then, if there were no memories of you and your radiant face.

When you resumed dating me, after our divorce, I thought I had a chance of regaining your love. Subsequently, I realized that I had a formidable competitor, and with Xiao Ming, my ultimate defeat was almost assured. (How I wish we had a child of our own that would make it a more even match.) In spite of that, I still hoped against hope.

Three months ago, I found in my mail a photograph of a threesome: you, Xiao Ming, and his father, with the Bank of China Building in Hong Kong in the background. It did not take me much thought to realize with whom your future and happiness lie.

By the time you read this letter, I should be on my way to China. I have accepted a visiting professorship at Northwestern Institute of Technology in Xi'an.

As we talked about it the other night, the happenings on Tiananmen Square are exhilarating. The old country is renewing herself. People have different ideas regarding what she most needs at this time—political reform or economic reform. I have little to offer to either. But no matter which, she needs an educated populace. There I think I can make a contribution, however small. Through that I wish I might not only promote her welfare but, in a broader sense, also that of my adopted country. From her soil, I have grown much, and from layers of gratitude, my love for her has also.

Finally, I'd like to present you with a poem in remembrance of our shared life:

The magpies calling and wheeling above,
You come lithely like the Weavess[60]
Down the celestial bridge arching across

---

60. Chinese mythology has it that, Weavess, who had lived east of the Milky Way, became derelict in her weaving after she married Cowherd and lived in his place, west of the Milky Way. The angered Heavenly Emperor ordered her back to the east, and allowed the couple to meet only once a year, on a bridge across the Milky Way, accompanied by magpies, on the 7th day of the 7th month.

The Pacific waves ten thousand miles wide
And two decades of a plodding life.

Jiang-nan's scents are fresh and her voices gay.
Together we tame the flood of numbers stream.
Together we search the old country's days,
Past, passing and to come, for roots and dreams.
No more is my mute lamp my only mate.

Dazed by the dazed eyes, I wander and wonder
In the musky valley and on saline peaks,
And lose myself in the spiraling deeps.
Long fingers crocheting a net upon my back—
As though I'd flee, my tongue tip is branded black.

O scintillations! O tenderness and passion!
How you lead me into the Fifth Dimension!
A vibrant existence, ineffable sensations,
Unexperienced in the workaday domain
Wherein the unexamined life would have remained.

I'll seal them in these lines as deposition,
When summoned to sessions of silent thought.
And pray for your care and benediction.
I'll go do my share—nothing else need be sought.
For I have known the Fifth Dimension.

Panzhe.

    Saiyue put her hands down, the letter in her lap. She sat there motionless, her lips screwed and her eyes glazed over. After a while, she said, "You Bookworm! So, you think you have arranged my life for me?"

After another moment, "Teaching?...I always wanted to be a teacher. I can teach too."

The phone rang. She gave her head a shake, wiped her half-dried tears off her face, and went to the dinette to pick it up.
"Hello!"
"Wey, Saiyue! Haosheng here."
"Yes."
"How are you?"
"I'm OK."
"Your voice sounds kind of strange. You all right?"
"I'm OK."
"Sorry I haven't been in touch with you for a while...."
He went on to give her a brief account of the attempt on his life and the end of his nemeses.
"That's terrible. You OK?"
"I am fine." He paused. "Something else has come up also. Actually it follows from the incident."
"What is it?"
"You may say it is of the once-in-a-lifetime category."
"What is it?"
"I have been offered an opportunity right now that would take me years of work to get, even with luck." He told her of the offer made to him by Rose Cao.
Saiyue kept silent.
"Are you still there?" he asked.
"Yes....Do you find it embarrassing to have a woman boss?" she asked.
"Saiyue, it's all business, I assure you."
"It is a lot of money."
"Well, the bonus monies are substantial, but they are not the most important item. It is the experience and connections at that level of actions that are invaluable," he said.

"You mean bigger business and more money, of course."

"Certainly potential for that. After three years, I'd have all the contacts I need. Then I can really be on my own, operating at a much higher level than what I have been planning to reach in the past months."

"So?"

"I am asking you to wait for me."

"What?"

"I am asking you to wait three years for me, while I work in Hong Kong. Then we'll have a firm financial foundation."

"I like to believe that right now I already have a firm financial foundation. At least, as firm as I think it needs to be," she said.

"Well…it's funny. Back in Xi'an it was you who wanted more, which boils down to money. But you may not know that money has a different meaning in Hong Kong."

"I guess I don't. What's the difference?"

"Here, money is not just materialistic. You don't think of making it only to buy or do things. It's an end in itself. The process of making it is exciting, uplifting, knowing people are watching, admiring your doing it, like shooting the ball into the basket."

"I guess that's right—for you," she paused. "Tell you what. Go ahead and sign that contract."

"So you'll wait for me?"

"No. I don't think so. I do wish you good luck though."

"It is a truly rare opportunity for me."

"I know. Sign the contract.…Now let's talk about Xiao Ming. I'd like to do my share of caring for him," she said.

"We talked about it before. It's better for him to stay there until he is old enough to retain the language.…Regarding my parents, I could ask my aunt to relieve them, or I could get him here to Hong Kong," he said.

"I told you before, a great aunt is no parent. Who cares for him in Hong Kong? Your new boss? since you'll be busy building your new career."

"He'd still be essentially in China," he said.

"In China or not, it's my turn to care for him. I trust you haven't forgotten the guardianship is joint? I am ready to go to Nanjing to claim my right."

Haosheng fell silent momentarily. "You don't have to get so excited about it. Let me see....Tell me, who—your father, mother or your grandpa—would go to Nanjing to get the boy? So I can tell my parents."

"Well, please tell them it could be any of us....Chances are good that I'll go myself."

"Really? Anyway, I'll let them know. We'll be in touch."

"Of course."

She hung up the phone.

The blue jays were heard cackling in the yard. She saw the magpies wheeling over the site of the Longevity Hall.

—THE END—

9 780595 094622